Confessions from the Think Tank

Vol 1

Confessions from the Think Tank

A Kids' Space Camp Charity Anthology

Edited by Rob Tannahill

Dark Moon Rising Publications | Virginia

70 Foxwood Drive
Rocky Mount, Virginia   24151
Tel: (540) 257-2861

Printed in the United States of America

Introduction

What's a "thinktank" or Think Tank? In effect, they are places to consider hypothetical situations, places where great minds get hyperbolic under the auspices that they might avoid chaos, the crumbling of the empire, or the economy, that sort of thing. Think Tanks were, at their inception, particular to scientists and public relations people, but now, anyone can be a part of one. We do it all the time. Your meme group just might be a Think Tank. If it isn't, I guarantee there's one watching you all cavort in text. Why? Anthropology. What's that? The study of human behavior. Why? For uses. Like what? Knowing the best way to sell goods to you, the good little consumer. Knowing what you like to wear on your body. Knowing what music you like. Your sense of humor. That sort of thing. To control your movements. Keep you all punching the time clock. Getting laid. Sniffing things that are *supposed* to be illegal, but does anyone (aside from the cops) really give a flying fuck about that?

This is cynical, but it's also true. And now you know what a Think Tank is.

I was always intrigued by these Think Tanks. These days, I wonder if it might be cool to work for one. Not in any "let's manipulate the population into choosing anger at every turn so they'll never learn their own creativity and rise above the slaves' mire we've made for them" kind of way, but in a much more etheric, light-working kind of way, if you dig that sort of thing—not that the powers that be would ever approve one of such an unprofitable species. From what I've read (books such as Annie Jacobsen's *The Pentagon's Brain)* Think Tanks first existed to troubleshoot the workings of a nuclear bomb. For those of you who are old enough to remember the whole WASP/Yuppie movement—in the Reagan years, they were used, just to give one fairly saccharine example, to figure out the best way to promote and grow the Moral Majority and turn the young people away from the Hippie culture. So it goes. If you just look at the world, you can see how they might be used to come up with the best scheme to set the public's teeth on edge for things like for-profit war and globalization—the acceptance of a Dogecoin society, selling smart cities, and the list goes on.

If I just *say* that title to you, Think Tank, the first thing your brain is likely to throw at you is the fact that they're hiding the truth about aliens from us…this is my guess, carny that I am—and that's what I've tried to bring to the table here with my crew of constituents, fellow authors who are also interested in things like the truth about aliens and how the government (and we ourselves) screw with our behavior.

David L Tamarin gives you a POV peek at a great and terrible behavioral experiment.. Experience the tale yourself and be chilled to the bone. Hop through the various dimensions with Megan Guilliams. Dine with Rocky Colavito at a greasy spoon just like any other…only not. Join Neil Sanzari in the cosmic consciousness of acid dreams. Take a misty mountain hop with Kasey Hill…only watch out for anything that looks like you. Be privy to the last testament of Dr. Garret J. McColl, complicit in the alien apocalypse…these and more mind-warping tales await. Alien Tricksters. Talking heads. Mandela Effect madness. Dystopian Drug Worlds. 22 tales of horror and one admittedly controversial yet compelling essay await. Welcome to the Think Tank. These are our Confessions.

We hope you love them.

Contents

I am a Slave to the State and I Love It

David L Tamarin

I The Subversive

My name is Philip K, and I am an enemy of the state. I am a writer, an intellectual, and a student of the psychedelic. I am a transgressor in every aspect of my life. I was a soldier, and the strategies and weapons I learned to use, I turned around and used against the state. I have seen the war machine from the inside, my mind enhanced with phencyclidine. I have learned the ways of war and will use my techniques to conquer your children's minds and hearts. I am on a mission to destroy. Subvert. I am a degenerate human being, at home in my filth, a feral animal on the inside behind this skin mask. I am a machine gun, a time bomb, an explosive device filled with nails and shards of glass covered in bat feces about to explode in the center of a hospital before a nuclear meltdown. I am the Ebola Virus. I am Schizophrenia Personified. My track marks have tiny mouths that scream in silent pain. I assassinate presidents. I sabotage nations. I am Lee Harvey Oswald. I am Osama Bin Laden. I am George Bush. I am Adolf Hitler. I am Typhoid Mary. I am Albert Hoffman, Pied Piper of Innocent Youth. I am Charles Manson. I am the Zodiac. I am Son of Sam. I am Edgar Allen Poe. I am the Night Stalker. I am H.P. Lovecraft. I am Ted Bundy. I am the Marquis de Sade. I am John Wayne Gacy. I am Jeffrey Dahmer. I am the Boogieman. I make snuff movies out in the desert. Movies where we kill and rape the whole fucking family and then sell it to some right-wing senator with a hard-on for nuclear power. I am God, the Devil, and Everything in Between. I bisected the Black Dahlia when I was loaded on heroin and posed her body in the grass by the sidewalk. I fucked her while she was alive and when she was dying, and when she was dead. I am Armageddon, and I Hate The Fuck Out of You. I am a syringe with AIDS and heroin, inviting you to disease and addiction, and misery. I am a shotgun pointed at the head of Uncle Sam. Your dope-sick kids worship me, and I'm taking them to Hell. I am a threat to others. I am a threat to civilization. I am the illness of pollution and corruption made stinking flesh. Fuck You All. I'll fuck women, men, and everything in between. If it has holes, I will fuck them. If it does not, I will make my own fuck holes. I'll carve up a baby and serve it for Christmas breakfast to JonBenet and her piece of pineapple. If you threw acid on my face,

1

I would look on the outside like I do on the inside—incredibly deformed and hideous.

So sayeth the writer.

The children all listened and followed; the sounds of their marching black boots drowning out their parents' screams and prayers.

The son of the President of the United States of America took two hits of Orange Sunshine lysergic acid and then, four hours later, fired a shotgun into his head, completely obliterating it. It was streaming on the internet, and most of the free world saw it. It became the most viral video of all time, except for a video of a large cat attacking a small, terrified dog.

II A Meeting of Puppet Masters

Professor Frank served up a cup of coffee to the two military officials, the one intelligence official, and himself. The coffee was laced with high concentrations of dextroamphetamine, as was the custom in these strategy sessions.

"The problem is this fucking writer, this degenerate piece of corn-holed shit. He is an ex-soldier himself, so he's popular among the men. Talks with their lingo. He talks to them in a language they relate to. And his message is an unmitigated fucking disaster," stated Colonial Hayes (a descendent of the same Hayes family responsible for Hollywood censorship starting during the Depression).

"Subversion, anti-authoritarianism, and permissive sex and drug use!" blurted out Sergeant Headray. "And it's making its way through the military like a fucking poisoned worm crawling around in that apple you polished to give to your teacher. His writing is not protected under free speech laws. It is viral and thus a disease, albeit a mental one, which must be combatted without regard for bullshit rights. It's not enough to just burn these fucking books. And it's not enough just to burn those who read them. We have an outbreak. An epidemic worse than Ebola."

Professor Frank suppressed a smile. Sergeant Headray tried using new vocabulary to impress others, but he invariably pronounced the words wrong. He had mispronounced the words viral, albeit, and epidemic (which he pronounced "aca-DEEM-ic").

"What are you saying?" asked the Professor, unsure what the unstable military man had said. The guy did have a great big steel plate in his head. He looked like the offspring of MechaGodzilla and G.I. Joe.

"You need to get him to write shit that's more patriotic. Moral. We did, to flip this guy. Get him working for us. All his subvert fans will follow along. We need to kill this revolution using mind control tactics. That's why we need your help, Professor. As you know, the Center for Ethical Medicine is one of our front groups, and they will give you everything you need to figure out a scientific way to give an attitude adjustment to this guy."

The Professor started drooling like a Pavlovian dog as he massaged his erection, trying to do it inconspicuously but accidentally letting out little grunts of pleasure. He came in his pants, fantasizing about abusing his power.

For days, he fantasized about the plan and over his ability to exert mind control and make men puppets. He would cum up a woman's ass while fantasizing about shock treatment and inhumane conditions and control and power. Sometimes, he would snap their necks when he was done with them.

III The Z Wing

People were literally afraid to speak its name. Murderers and Molesters, the nation's toughest of the tough, the baddest of the bad. And they were all afraid even to whisper its name. But the Professor loved to shout its name when he was fucking one of his dope-whores, which was pretty regularly as he was taking high-powered testosterone and erection enhancement pills as well as the street drug Ecstasy. His semen was the color of scrambled eggs, and he had a penis deformity that required regular surgical intervention. He hated dissidents, and the Z Wing was a Heavy Interrogation/ Mind Control center. Patients never walked out as the same person as when they went in. The Z Wing killed souls.

IV Men Without Faces Make History

"Here's the plan. Mr. Big-Shot Subversive Writer sees a therapist three times a week. We got a hold of the therapist, and he'll do whatever we say. We had our best agents use photo-manipulation elements, or pho-mas, as they are known, to create a very realistic sadistic child porn snuff film. We feed him a combination of Thorazine and psychedelic drugs and make him watch the eight-minute video on a loop for seventy hours, and by the time we are done with the interrogation, he'll be able to convince us all he had done it. He will be so convinced and convincing that you won't believe he was guilty, even though you'll see them manufacture the evidence. Anyway, we will have the therapist state that the writer is a danger to himself and others due to psychotic reactions to PTSD symptoms and place him in the Richard K. Nix-Phillips Hospital, which is a private corporation under our control. Once there, he will murder a fellow psychiatric patient and be transferred to the Methadox Clinic for the Mentally Incompetent, Drug Addicted, and Subversive Personality Types, where Professor Frank has free reign and Agency funds for Project Lone Wolf. There, we break the writer and then create a model citizen from scratch.

"Any moral objections?"
Their laughter echoed through the room.
"I guess MKULTRA is still alive."
"Alive and well, yes."

V 1000 Hours of Isolation, Repetition, Deprivation and Epic Drug Use

Philip K tried to move, and the effort caused him intense pain. There were feeding tubes filling him with protein and nutrients to keep him alive, and there were tubes inserted into his bladder and kidneys for waste removal purposes. Surgical glue kept his lips together. Surgical glue kept his eyes sealed shut. Another tube went into the big vein in his right arm and pumped him full of methadone, diazepam, Thorazine, Seroquel, tranquilizers, muscle relaxers, sleeping agents, and even some deadly nightshade—belladonna to put him into a twilight trance. His ears remained untouched, and beneath his pillow, a tape played the writer stating, "I am a slave to the state. I am here to do the work of the state. I denounce my former writing as criminal, and from now on, I will uphold the values of the Intelligence Community and will change the focus of my writing so that it encourages young men to join the military to fight the war on narcotics. I will encourage narcotics users to overdose so that our community can be drug-free. I will murder free thinkers to stop subversion. I will testify against myself so that I might go to prison for a proper re-education…I confess. I am a criminal and an enemy of the state. I confess and am a guilty man.

The loop was four minutes long, and the writer's voice is tense from the loaded pistol that was covered in cocaine and jammed up his anus when he was forced to make the confession tape. The loop played endlessly for days at a time. He could soon recite it by rote and found himself chanting the words. When he disobeyed, they played a loop of his family members screaming at him, calling him useless.

His world was dark, and all that existed was the voice, his voice, confessing his crimes.

And every eight hours, without ever missing a session, they brought him to the Z Wing and subjected him to extreme bilateral frontal lobe shock electroconvulsive therapy, with wires attached to his testicles delivering high voltage burning pain to bring home the message. After a time, he came to look forward to this treatment as it was a break from the isolation and the repetition of his confession tape.

After an indeterminate time, it was all a blur, and his mind was scrambled eggs.

Phase II was initiated. Along with his confession, they blasted the industrial noise of Einsterzende Neubaueten, along with sounds at a precise pitch that causes nausea, dizziness, blurred vision, extreme confusion, and delusions of Deities. All results were from CIA psyops.

Risperidone and Paralytics were added to the drug regimen. As was LSD, mescaline, psilocybin, liquid THC, and DMT.

During the Electro-Shock Therapy, he was sodomized by the largest inmates who had been drugged up on Viagra, Testosterone and Cocaine.

Professor Frank recorded footage of the deprogramming and reprogramming, and he watched it in slow motion as crack whores sucked him off. He ejaculated down their throats as he stared at the insane eyes of the former human being who was still trapped in this world in his flesh-and-bone prison.

Sometimes, they blasted a TV recording of a Christian preacher screaming about sin.

Sometimes, they blasted recordings in foreign languages. There is a heavy, static-distorted sound underlying the North Korean news. This terrifies and isolates the subject.

"Schizophrenic Junky."

"Are you ready for an attitude adjustment?"

"We know you."

We know everything about you."

"Every moment of your life has been recorded."

"We have technology to read your thoughts, which we have been monitoring and transcribing since your birth."

"We know you better than you know yourself."

"Better than you think you know yourself."

"When we tell you how to feel, you will feel that way."

"Right now, you will feel regret and shame for your unpatriotic and obsessive transgressions."

You will seek the approval and forgiveness of society."

"You will come to acknowledge the superiority of Nazi philosophy and your betrayal of your race."

"We know you want to commit suicide—that's why you've been giving paralytics, Shakespeare."

"You can't move, yet you can feel pain. Bet that sucks, huh Shakespeare?"

A loud sound goes off in the room. A siren so loud that blood begins dripping from his ears.

They inject him with a non-lethal dose of arsenic, and he gets so, so sick. The paralytics wear off, and his body goes into convulsions as he begins vomiting and spraying the room with painful diarrhea. His methadone and diazepam have been cut off, and he is deeply dope-sick and in the middle of withdrawal hell. The marrow in his bones freezes. Dead birds fall from the sky.

"Until you hate yourself like we hate you, we can't make the pain stop."

"Until you hate yourself like we hate you, we can't do a thing."

VI ENHANCED INTERROGATION TECHNIQUES

"We know exactly what you did."

"We have forensic evidence."

"We have surveillance tapes."

"We have multiple witnesses."

"You have failed the Lie Detector machine, which is infallible."

"We found trace DNA evidence matching you to multiple victims."

"You had Motive."

"You had Opportunity."

"You knew all the victims."

"When the murders started happening, multiple reliable people came forward telling us it was you."

"You are the only viable suspect."

"You have choices."

"You can admit what you did."

"People will understand."

"Your family and friends will understand."

"The Judge and the Probation Officer and the Courts will understand."

"But if you don't confess, they'll be looking for blood, and we can't help. Fuck, man, we wouldn't want to help you, not if you don't confess. I know there's a rational reason for what you did, and I need to hear it from you. Everyone will go easier on you when you confess. If you don't, they will think you are a liar. Which will taint everything you say and do. If you don't confess, even tying your fucking shoes becomes sinister. Your attorney will probably throw the case due to the public pressure. All those problems can be eradicated, but this is time-sensitive. Confess, and confess right the fuck now, and everything will be easier for you. If you have to do time, we'll make sure it's a nice, comfortable prison. One of them...country club-type prisons. You'll be surrounded by other white people. If you prefer, you can go to maximum security for life. You can take solitary confinement to protect yourself, but you'll go crazy. And if you're in Gen Pop, you are a walking target, a potential rape victim. The guards? They won't give a fuck about you, and they won't do anything to help."

"We have new technology. Crazy shit. We know when you're lying. Our machine said that when you said you had nothing to confess, you were a fucking liar, and we all saw it. But first, let's give you an incentive to be a participant in this."

"See this ball here? Watch this. I press a button, and it starts expanding. It starts heating up—see it turn orange. Blades start sticking out. Pretty cool to watch, right?"

"But when we have one in your asshole and two in your mouth, you'll find that they are as far from cool as possible."

"See this picture? This is what you'll look like when this ball is done with you."

"You look like you're about to vomit."

"Tell me the first thing in your entire life that you remember. Don't lie. Confess. Confess. You will feel a weight fall off your chest."

VII The Nature of Tragedy and the Projected Lifespan of the Doomed
   Transgressor.

Fuck them. Let them hurt you. Let them mutilate you. Let them destroy you. Let them make you insane. Just don't fucking do what they say. Don't confess to anything. That's how you win. A shallow victory for sure. Because they'll just torture you until you die of shock…but you can't let them win. You are deep into the next phase of interrogation. You are spread-eagled, naked, lying on your stomach, your limbs cuffed to the bedposts. There is no mattress. You lie on a rusty, scratchy, bloody spring that has heard thousands of hours of screaming and suffering. They insert a tube into your rectum. It is freezing, and your body convulses in pain. They shove it in further and further. Ice-cold water fills your body, and you feel your heart and brain freeze.

The doctor shows you a syringe. "This will take away all the pain," he says as he injects it into his arm. "This, on the other hand, Mr. Subversive Artist Fuck, will enhance and multiply the pain," he says as he shoots you up. Your blood boils, and you feel your eyes bulging out of their sockets. Every little muscle in your body, every particle, every DNA cell, is a writhing, twisting, icy agony that is like nothing you have ever even contemplated. You are humiliated and defeated. You would have confessed right then if you could just function. But your head isn't working. Thoughts weren't forming, and you could not express the confused feelings in your head, feelings of fear and confusion and repulsion and self-negation.

"You'll be getting a shot like that every four hours for the duration of your life…which won't be long. It will only seem that way."

Sounds of laughter pierce their way into your head. You don't find it funny. You realize you cannot breathe.

The questions begin again.

"Ever cheated on your partner?"

"Ever looked at a little kid and get a hard-on?"

"Ever look for child porn on the Internet?"

"How old were you when you first stole something?"

"Stop lying, or we take a torture break, get you to start cooperating. Want to be hung from the ceiling with fishhooks attached to your balls, holding you up? If you weigh too much, they rip, and you fall, followed by a rainfall of blood from your balls. Do you like the sound of that? Do you want to confess?"

"Maybe you're covering up for your family. Maybe we should get them down here and question them. If it's not you, it's them—that's what you're telling us, right? And you're saying you didn't kill anyone. So you must mean that your mother and father, your wife and children, committed the crime. Tell us what you know about what they did. Or what you did. We know it was one or the other. Who is going to fry, you or Mother? Who is going to burn until the air stinks with the haze of burnt flesh chewed up and turned to smoke? Someone is going to burn, and you're going to fucking tell us who it was. Confess."

"You know what I can do to you? Do you know what I'm thinking of doing? These officers will hold you down while I remove your belt and make it into a noose, then hang you until you're dead. Shit, I just did that very same thing a few months ago. No one got in trouble. Shit, I almost got a promotion. Guy was a pedophile. Is that your deal, you fucking deviant? Confess your sins and deviations so that you may be saved from an eternity of burning fire! Confess or die hanging. You know how long that takes? I do. I have it on tape, and it is 43 minutes. I have watched it dozens of times. We all have. It makes my dick hard to watch that shit. 43 minutes hanging in the air, choking. We'll have to break your arms so you can't break free. Do you want 43 more minutes to live? 43 minutes of pure agony. Gagging, choking. It's like drowning. It's horrible. Confess and save yourself that pain. And don't leave behind a legacy like that. Confess."

Fourteen hours of interrogation, always by new men, then two hours naked in a freezing cold bathtub, your head underwater, breathing through a straw. Then they tell you: if you beg, you can have a nap. And you beg. They let you nap. Not long. Then it's another fourteen-hour session, followed by a two-hour cold water immersion session. Then maybe a nap, maybe another session.

The bastards are always accompanied by angry barking dogs whose fire they can barely contain, dogs beaten and angry and hungry, so fucking hungry. Sometimes…they feed on you.

Four weeks of this.

Then back to your bed. An IV line lets a paralytic flow through your veins, and you cease all movement but blinking. You watch films of your family being tortured. Sometimes the films are computer stims but not always. You watch the films on a loop. Amphetamines mixed with the paralytic keep you awake and paranoid. You can't scratch the invisible bugs you feel beneath your skin and in your eyes, which feel like they are screaming obscenities at you and spitting venom. A week of no sleep, and the hallucinations begin. After two weeks, they take over. You are given anti-psychotics, and you wake up naked in a glass cage. You can't move. You are immersed in water. There's not much air, and there are piranhas in the water.

You are force-fed the vomit of the insane, the feces of the perverted, the piss of the depraved cold heart, the blood of the weak, and the toxic vomit of the sick.

With a gun to your head, you stab a goat in the neck and drink its blood in front of children who are tied up and so thirsty for a little splash of blood, and they all have their tongues out. You imagine their teeth biting through you as you are eaten and converted into shit and voided into a cesspool.

They fill your room up with schizophrenic, violent sex offenders and force them with cattle prods to scream at you.

VIII Re-Education of the Subversive

The following section has been redacted in its entirety.

IX Discharge

I confess.

I am guilty.

I have sinned.

I have transgressed.

I am the enemy of the State and the People.

My number is irrelevant, as am I. I am only as good as my service to the state, which has been dismal, and which is why I am taking my life and urging my followers to do the same. If you slit your wrists, go vertical, otherwise; you will live. Give yourself to the state. Embrace the nothingness that is your "self" as a dependent entity, not even real, without someone spying on you. Give up your sentient status and join your mind with the state. The time for war is now.

The time for population control is now. This is your government speaking. You must listen; you must obey. Otherwise, you serve no purpose and will be disposed of like foul-smelling garbage. Be the state. Be no one. The time to surrender was yesterday. Your only future is the state. Burn. Like kerosene. Like books. Like flesh.

Burn.

The Lights

Megan Guilliams

There they were again…those damned lights, and every time Walton closed his eyes, they were all he could see. Flashing blues and reds, with a hint of green in there for variety. The lights had not always been apparent, but Walton was starting to forget a time without them. They rolled and moved around inside him like a parasite itching to escape, but he didn't know what it wanted to escape from. He'd long ago learned that Earth was nothing more than a spinning prison. There was no escape…not really, anyway.

On one of those rare nights he had managed to fall asleep despite the glorious, blinding flashes, he was stirred from his bed by the ringing of a telephone. Rolling over with a groan, he looked at the digital clock on the table and said a few signature curse words before picking up the landline. Walton was among the few people he thought still had a phone connected to the wall. Most people had them connected to their hips now, scrolling through social media like mindless drones. Not Walton. No, he preferred the old way of doing things, and he wasn't going to leash himself with a phone or any other electronic device that let the government track his every move.

"This better be good." Walton moaned into the receiver as he rubbed the sleep from his eyes with his free hand. "You woke me up, ya bastards." The last statement was more for himself than for the person on the other line. It didn't really matter if he'd been woken up or not. Walton was an old bitter coot who'd kick your dog if you weren't looking. Biting his bottom lip, he waited for someone to talk on the other end, but all that was there to meet him was static and then a busy signal. Grumbling a few more times, he slammed the phone into the cradle and fell back into his bed. Walton's head almost missed the pillow completely, clipping the corner of the bedside table. Again, the man sat up in a tizzy.

"Fucking good for nothing wooden table." Touching the back of his head, he pulled back a little blood and knew he needed to clean the point of impact. Shit like that was always happening to Walton. It'd been going on longer than the flashing lights; that much he knew for sure.

Walton could remember the day he and his now-dead wife Margo had purchased that damned table. He had thought it was hideous, but his wife thought it was 'to die for!' When she passed in December of 2012, it had been covered in her medications. Over a dozen pill bottles and abandoned glasses of half-drunk water littered its top. Walton hadn't considered himself a sentimentalist, yet he couldn't bear to part with the table after her funeral. The water rings and stains left behind by his sweet Margo were how he remembered her. He guessed everyone grieved in their own way.

Swinging his feet from the bed, Walton padded across the wooden floor to the open bathroom door. He didn't think about turning on a light. Why should he? He hadn't moved the furniture around his house in almost three decades. Walton could have been blind and not tripped over anything. He stopped in front of the mirror, looking at his reflection as his eyes adjusted to the darkness. The only good thing about being awake at this hour was that the lights weren't bothering him anymore. You see, that's what baffled the doctors. Walton could only see the lights when his eyes were closed.

A slight glimmer of light shone through the window over the shower. The crest of the moon had set up shop there for the time being, making the area in which he stood a cascading fever dream of odd blue. Opening the medicine cabinet behind the mirror he was staring into, Walton looked over his array of medicine bottles. The doctors he had gone to see had put him on everything they could think of to stop the weird hallucinations, to no avail. Nothing worked, and soon after, he stopped taking any of the small white and yellow pills he had been given.

"So, when did these lights start appearing?" The doctor had asked.

"Around the time my wife died...no, a week or so after."

"And they just keep happening every night?"

"Like clockwork."

That was the beginning of the end for Walton. After that, everyone he had gone to see suggested it was a side effect of losing his wife. A 'Broken Heart Symptom,' but Walton didn't feel brokenhearted...at this stage in his life, he wasn't sure what he felt.

Grabbing a white first aid kit wedged between the Clozapine and the Ziprasidone, Walton put it on the counter beside the sink and opened it carefully. Everything had changed after Margo passed. Even his memory of how things used to be began to twist. They were initially small things, like his neighbor's hair color. Janet's hair had always been blonde, so when she walked out of her house on New Year's 2012 with brown hair, Walton had to comment. It was odd that her husband wrinkled his nose and laughed, stating that he could never have dated a blonde, let alone marry one, and Janet nodded in agreement. Maybe they were trying to make the transition easier, or Janet had always been a brunette, and Walton was losing his mind. It had gotten worse and worse as the years passed...and for some reason, he blamed it all on the lights.

In 2013, the Mass General Store had changed its name to General Mass, and no one seemed to notice but Walton. In 2014, his brother's son Klark changed majors in college from Math to engineering, which, to Walton, was almost the same thing, but no one would admit to the old switcheroo. These little things began to add up over the years, and with every little tweak of the timeline, the lights…those DAMNED lights got brighter and brighter. Nothing he did could get it out of his head, and he thought this was just the way things were supposed to be now.

Turning his head as best he could, Walton splashed some water on the gash and added some antiseptic ointment. Finally, he slapped a bandage on the whole thing and called it a night. He didn't care if the sticky bits got caught in his hair. He had been losing his lush brown locks for a while now, and a few strands less wouldn't matter much. Laughing to himself, he padded across the bedroom floor and slipped back into bed as if nothing had happened. As he closed his eyes and the lights began to dance just under his lids, he couldn't help but think back to this morning when he had had enough of the subtle changes and let everyone on the block know.

First thing, after his coffee, Walton had stepped outside for his morning walk. His car was usually parked out on the side of the road, but today, someone had moved it, and the color had changed subtly.

"No, this can't be right!" Walton had exclaimed as he reached down and grabbed his old-fashioned paper from the ground. *"I'm the only one with the keys to my car! I didn't park it there. I know what I did! I know what I DID!"* Looking down at the front page of the now Times Mass he read the headline. His cheeks began to burn with anger as he barged back through the front door without another thought about his walk. The president had changed. Had he missed an election? How could this have been? The date on the calendar was correct, but new holidays had popped up, ones he had never heard of before. What was happening? Why did no one else remember it the way it was? If Margo were here, she would have seen it too. She always saw things for what they were.

Allowing himself to drift off to sleep with unease, Walton thought that would be the end of it. Maybe when he woke in the morning, everything would right itself. Maybe the weird lights would fade, and Janet's hair would be blonde again…maybe he wouldn't be so upset with the world. He didn't know how long he had been in bed before the phone rang again, but when it did, the man sat up with a start. Something was different about the ring this time. It sounded rushed and urgent, giving him the distinct impression that the person on the other side of the line had something unrelenting to tell him. Shaking his head, Walton knew that couldn't be right. Phones don't ring 'differently.' They just rang. Reaching across the bed with an unsteady hand, the old man picked up the receiver and put it to his ear. This time, his words didn't sound so angry. This time, they sounded timid and weak.

"Hello?" Again, there was nothing but static. Walt was going to hang up but stopped himself when he finally heard the person on the other side of the line.

"You need to stop!" The voice began. It sounded a million miles away. It didn't matter how far it was; Walton knew that voice. He had lived with that voice for thirty years. It was the only voice he had ever cared to listen to, and now it was back, pleading for him to stop...stop what exactly?

"Margo?" Walton asked. He knew it was absurd. She had been dead and gone for a dozen years now...but it was her voice just the same. "What is it? Who is this? It can't be you...whoever this is, I'll kill you for pretending to be her!"

"You have to stop!" The voice continued. "You have to stop. They're coming. They see you, and they're coming." The woman's request had slowly turned into a demand as the reception on the phone line grew worse. Walton didn't know if it was his imagination or if the room had begun to get darker, heavier...colder.

"Who is this?" Walton demanded as he tightened the grip on his phone. His knuckles began to whiten as his anger bubbled to the surface. Finally, he pulled the phone away from his ear, jerking the cord from the wall. He threw it across the room and fell back into bed, careful he didn't hit the corner of the table again. It was too late for tricks and games. He was old, and it was time for sleep.

The moon set as the sun began its appearance. Walton rolled over in his Queen-sized bed and reached across the mattress. He had no clue why he did this, but it had been his routine for the last forty years or so. The sun was flooding into the bedroom as the birds outside chirped loudly. Walton's head was throbbing, and he could only assume it was from the lump he had taken on the nightstand a few hours before.

"Nothing a little aspirin can't take care of." He mumbled to himself. It hadn't occurred to him that someone else was in the house. Someone had opened the bedroom window and laid out his clothes...and now that same someone was in the kitchen making him breakfast. No, it hadn't occurred to him until the smell of fresh bacon wafted into his nostrils. Blinking a few times, Walton looked around the room, taking in the bright yellow wallpaper. His wallpaper wasn't yellow. It had always been eggshell white. His wife wanted yellow wallpaper, but he wouldn't give in...and yet here it is, in all its glory. Ugly, yellow paper.

"Walt, dear, would you be a doll and go to the store for me and pick up some milk after breakfast? I know it's your day off, but you would be doing me such a huge favor."

14

"Day off?" Walton muttered. "I've been retired for years now." The man gingerly touched the back of his head, but there was no lump, no bandage, just a thick brown mane that almost touched his shoulders. What was going on? Gulping in the air, Walton coaxed himself out of bed, blinking heavily. The lights were gone. They had vanished completely, and in their place, he got yellow wallpaper and bacon. As much as the man wanted to rejoice, he couldn't find the emotions. Something wasn't right. It started there, out in the world, but now it was at his doorstep, oozing in through the cracks of his unfamiliar house and invading his life. None of this was right. No matter how much he wanted it to be, it just wasn't.

Walking towards the bedroom door, Walton made his way down the short hall, looking at the framed photos on the wall. They were all professional shots of Margo and him. Some of them were taken right here in the house, but others were action shots while they were at the beach or hiking in the mountains. This wasn't Walt.

Stopping in the doorway, he watched the back of his wife's head as it bobbed up and down in front of the stove. She wore a little white dress with a pattern of red roses on it. It was a sundress. The kind that fit from the waist up and ballooned out from hips to knees, hiding any imperfections time may have blessed her with. Margo's cinnamon-colored hair was up in tight curls that barely bounced when she moved about the kitchen. He knew if she turned around, he would see a set of ethereal green eyes set wide in her heavenly heart-shaped face.

"The bacon's almost done, sleepyhead. How do you want your eggs?"

"Over easy." Walton hadn't realized he had said anything until the woman laughed and turned around. Her eyes twinkled against the natural light of the sun…they were gray.

"Over easy it is then." She sang as she walked over to the refrigerator. It was a round, bulbous-looking thing that Walton had never laid eyes on before. It was almost as if the things around him were shifting and moving without being prompted. He couldn't focus, and when he did, he forgot what he was looking at almost immediately…and it all started after he looked into Margo's hideous gray eyes.

She was bent in front of the fridge, looking through the shelves for a carton of eggs. There was beer on the first shelf, and six of them had been evicted. Touching the back of his head again, he could feel the dull pain returning. He used to be a drinker in his twenties, and if today was his day off, he more than likely tied one on hard the night before. Had his life up until now been nothing more than a bad dream? Had he dreamed it all? He couldn't have. No, he DIDN'T!

Sliding across the floor in his bare feet, he stopped at the countertop, just in front of where Margo had laid out the bacon strips. Margo had put them on a few pieces of paper towel to sop up the grease. He wasn't worried about the bacon; he was more interested in what was in the drawer underneath. Sliding it open, he pulled a knife from its slot and inched ever closer to Margo. Her back was still to him.

"Do you remember our honeymoon to the Grand Canyon?" Walton asked as he took another slow step towards her. Laughing, the woman turned, holding a carton of eggs that she'd presumably cut in half.

"Oh dear, how many beers did you drink last night? We've never been to the Grand Canyon. We went to New Mexico. Don't you remember?"

No. This wasn't his wife, his house, his life! Wrapping one arm around Margo's shoulders, Walton willed his other hand to slip the hefty blade between two of his wife's ribs. He couldn't see it, but he imagined her giant, gray eyes were wide with shock and dismay. Dropping the eggs, Margo let out a blood-curdling scream that echoed out onto the street through the open windows. Pulling the knife away, blood began to spurt out all over the floor, warm, thick, and salty. It smelled like copper, old pennies in a can, but that didn't stop Walton from coming in for more.

Snatching the woman up by her throat, Walton slammed her against the open fridge door. The light from the interior began to flash green as the thermometer dinged. It was there to remind whoever was cooking to shut the door. The contents of the giant round tub had become far too warm.

"Why?" Margo mouthed as she clawed at his hand. Sneering, the man pressed the tip of the blade against Margo's chest, playing with the buttons on her dress. Sirens were coming from down the street. He knew he didn't have a lot of time.

"You aren't my wife!" Walton spat, "You never were, and I told you I would kill you for pretending to BE HER!" Slicing Margo from sternum to groin, Walton watched as the life left her body. Margo's intestines slipped out from the opening, falling onto the floor with a splat. He had to have cut a little too deep because seconds later, the smell of putrid shit wafted through the blood and gore. There was only one more thing left to do.

Dropping the knife, Walton padded back to the bedroom. His feet left smeared prints along the wood, but he didn't care. At some point, the bird that had roused him had flown away, leaving nothing but a few branches between him and the police cars that surrounded his house. "Nosey fucking neighbors," Walton muttered as he stopped by the end of the bed. Kneeling, he opened the chest. He never kept it locked...why would he?

"Walton Jones, come out with your hands up!" Some newbie police officer had gotten to play with the megaphone. How nice. The gun felt heavy in his hand. The blood had begun to dry, so his grip was true. Approaching the window, Walton stared blankly at his freshly cut lawn. Had he done that, too, and not remembered? Nothing made sense.

"My name is Walton Jones, and I know what I did. I know what I DID!" Lifting the gun, Walton pointed it at the kid with the megaphone.

"He's got a gun!" Another officer shouted. Seconds later, a shot rang out. It wasn't from Walton; no, he never kept his gun loaded. It was from an older cop, and his aim was true. One single bullet was all it took. Square—right between the eyes. Walton stumbled a little and reached back, touching the exit wound; looking at the fresh blood on his fingertips, he laughed a little and fell onto the ground face up. As his eyes fluttered shut, the last thing he saw was the flashing red and blue police lights swirling and dancing, trying to escape.

The Portal

Mawr Gorshin

I found my way back to our apartment, panting and staggering from dizziness and headaches. Our friends, neighbours, and roommates were shocked to see me emerge all of a sudden in front of the door, ringing the doorbell because I didn't have my key. One of them let me in. In exhaustion, I collapsed just outside where the others were sitting in a circle in the living room.

"Stella!" said Connie, who was sitting right by where I'd fallen. "What happened to you? Where's Lee?"

"She's dead," I gasped.

"What?" everyone shouted almost at once.

Connie helped me up and had me sit beside her on the sofa. I was trembling all over, my face soaked in tears, wincing from another headache, everything around me swirling. Connie put her arms around me, put my head on her shoulder, and slowly rocked me back and forth.

"Shh, shh, shh," she said. "It's OK, it's OK, sweetie. You're safe now. Whatever happened out there, it's all over now."

"No, it isn't," I said in a shaky voice. "If anything…it's only beginning." I began sobbing.

"What do you mean, 'only beginning'?" a man sitting beside Connie asked. "And what happened to Lee?"

"Hole…in some bushes by a tree in the park," I began in sobs. "Portal to outer space…spaceship, or other planet…I don't know. Aliens…dog-like robots, I think. DARPA. MKUltra. Milton Friedman. Ronald Reagan…I'm more right than I thought I was…a conspiracy…Earth is an alien colony!" I was speaking faster and faster with each phrase, my voice going up in a crescendo of hysteria. "They put drugs in me…*mind control*…Lee, she's hacked up into a million bloody pieces…they chased me out…barely escaped alive…ran here!"

"Honey, calm down," Connie said, stroking my hair and still rocking me. "Slow down. You're not making any sense. Just take a few deep breaths, try to relax, and when you're calm, tell us everything, one step at a time, in order, OK? You're safe now."

"OK," I said, then took a few deep, long breaths, and I felt my heartbeat slow down. I was shaking less and less now. My head was still pounding with pain, and still swimming.

Connie gave me a tissue from the coffee table to blow my nose with and wipe away my tears. "OK, Stella," she said. "Tell us everything—right from the beginning."

I took another deep breath. "OK," I said, "you remember how Lee and I walked off from the party after we all did that hit of LSD—I guess, four or five hours ago…"

"Actually, that was last night," the man next to Connie said. "And I think we all know what really happened to you, Stella. It was just a bad trip." He rolled his eyes.

"Shut up, Doug," Connie said. "I don't care if that's what really happened…" I heard her whisper to him, "which it probably was…" and she continued at her normal volume, "Stella needs to talk about what she experienced, to get it off her chest, and she needs us to listen, be empathetic, and validate her. Sorry, Stella, go on."

"No acid trip would have made me hallucinate something this intense," I said. "I *was* drugged with some kind of hallucinogen by the aliens out there, but it was something so powerful, it would make LSD seem like…I dunno…*coffee* in comparison."

"Oh, come on," Doug said, laughing. "*Alien* dope?"

"Shut up!" Connie said. "Let her talk. Stella, let's come back a bit. You were with Lee in the park, and where did you go? What happened to her?"

"We came to this really dark area, a lot of bushes clumped together, and a really dark spot, a recess, in the middle," I said. "We'd been walking for quite a while, and we were tired. It was stupid that we left you all, but we were too stoned to think straight. Anyway, we sure regretted having walked off. We went to the dark area just to sit down and rest 'cause the LSD trip was really starting to overwhelm us. As we walked into the dark, it started to look more like a tunnel of infinite blackness. We got curious, and instead of sitting down as we'd planned, we went in further and further. It felt as if…someone was beckoning us to come closer. It kind of…sucked us in."

"*What* sucked you in?" Connie asked.

"The…portal," I said, looking down at my feet, embarrassed that no one would believe me.

"The portal?" Connie asked with a sneer. Doug was snickering.

"It's how Lee and I were transported from Earth to the aliens' spaceship, or planet, or wherever we ended up," I said, then winced again from my headache. "It felt as though our bodies were transformed into…electrical waves, or something, for the purposes of space travel…something like that. I don't know. Then we got there, and we transformed back into our flesh forms. And then, the nightmare really began."

"OK," Connie said. "So what happened?"

"As soon as we rematerialized, we didn't even have time to process what had just happened," I said. "We found ourselves in an empty white hall. I felt a prick in my left arm, just under the shoulder. Some kind of injection. I looked to my left and saw Lee getting an injection of some kind, too…only it didn't look like a needle stuck in her arm. It looked like the sharp end of a tentacle or a long porcupine's quill or something like that. I looked behind her and saw this…ugly…monster."

"What?" Doug said. "You were high." He laughed.

"Shut up, Doug!" Connie said. "Continue, Stella. What did this…monster…look like?"

"As ridiculous as this sounds, it looked like a huge pile of shit, about our height, with these long prickly things sticking out of it," I said. "At the end of one of the pricks was some green slime dripping off of it. I imagine that must have been what was put inside us…some fluid from their bodies? I don't know. Anyway, I didn't really have time to take in all of what was happening—it all happened so fast. I didn't even have time to scream at the thing because of what the injection did to Lee."

"Oh, this'll be good," Doug said, sneering.

Connie looked back at him and scowled to shut him up. I almost fell to the floor from my dizziness and the pain in my head. Connie helped me back up. I sighed, then continued my story.

"Something…was cutting its way out of her head," I said in sobs. "Like an expanding ball of spikes, or knives, or something. She was screaming and shaking in pain. Her blood was flying out in all directions. Her eyeballs popped out. Her teeth flew out. Her head cracked open. Her brain, melting, was *oozing* out. Then her head just exploded. The same thing started happening in her torso. Her ribcage busted out of her skin again, with blood spraying everywhere, including on me. A spike poked out of her heart; her stomach and intestines were all hanging out. These balls of spikes now had a vertical pole going from the floor straight up to and above where her head had once been, so her dead body didn't fall to the floor; it just hung there, impaled." I sobbed some more and grunted from my headache.

"Oh, my God!" Connie said, seeing drops of blood on my clothes. Doug was laughing.

"Whatever had been injected into me was totally different, of course, more like an intense drug," I said. "As I said before, it was far too wild to have been a continuation of the LSD trip. Everything was getting darker, wavelike. I ran down the hall, barely able to keep from falling. I was beginning to get the feeling that an alien intelligence was being born inside me, an extension of the consciousness of that alien turd with those porcupine quills that had pricked me—it would soon take control of me, it seemed. I turned a corner and came to a room filled with a combination of those tentacled and quilled alien turd people, along with humans—scientists, judging by their long white jackets—all sitting around a large table, as if at a meeting...oh, and there were robots, of some kind."

"What kind of robots?" Connie asked.

"Oh, some looked dog-like, others almost like...I dunno, elephants or something; it was all so weird," I said. "All eyes turned to me; not that the aliens had eyes, but I guess they were looking at me, too. On the walls, I saw a picture of—oh, wow, this is so weird! Ronald Reagan. Also, photos of Milton Friedman, Leon Trotsky, Nikita Khrushchev, Mikhail Gorbachev, Augusto Pinochet, Adolph Heusinger, Theodor Herzl, and Margaret Thatcher. Mixed with these portraits were also ones of those turd-aliens. There was also the DARPA logo. On a whiteboard was written, among other things, in what looked like an alien language, MKUltra, all in black magic marker. One of the humans there, a middle-aged man, said, 'There she is. Our newest operative.'"

"Operative?" Connie asked. Doug was laughing even louder. I felt another dizzy spell hit me.

"Yeah," I said, wincing from my headache. "He said I was to go back to Earth and talk about all my progressive causes as much as I liked. I could even tell them about my alien abductors—that was fine. Nobody would believe me, so I could rant on and on about them as much as I pleased. They were that confident I'd do nothing to harm their cause, which—they said in all frankness—is to colonize the Earth and sap it of its resources, then once it's totally desolate, the aliens and their human collaborators will go find another planet to exploit, deplete it of its resources, and move on again. No one on Earth will ever be able to stop them because they've cleverly figured out ways to keep us all divided against each other, too busy fighting each other to fight them. Even many of those who claim to help us and our causes on Earth are actually secretly working for the aliens, traitors to humanity, as I deduced by a number of those human portraits on the walls of that think tank room. The aliens have every confidence that no one will believe they even exist, let alone plan to take everything away from us."

"You're right about no one believing you," Doug said with a chuckle.

I glared at him, sighed, and continued. "I often speak about the corrupt government and its dominance over the world through the CIA and things like DARPA and MKUltra. Well, I realize now that it's much, much worse than that. You know how some countries, like South Korea, are just vassals of the American empire? Well, I'm telling you—what I saw up there, in outer space, in that…zone, whatever it was, that was part of an alien empire, with human collaborators in DARPA, the CIA, and all that. The Earth is a vassal state for an alien, intergalactic empire! We are *their* Third World! And they want me to take you…to…" My headache was killing me.

Doug laughed out loud. "Jesus Christ, Stella!" he said. "You and your goddamned conspiracy theories!"

"Doug, will you shut up!" Connie shouted.

"Connie, she just had a bad trip," he said, still laughing. "Everything she said she saw was just a figment of her imagination, all products of thoughts she'd had long before the acid trip, only it's much more intense now."

"Doug, you are not helping! Go on, Stella."

Another dizzy spell was stopping me from continuing for the moment.

"Stella," Doug said with a sneer, "if aliens are colonizing the Earth, why don't we see any of these turd-people with whips and chains enslaving us?"

"Because obviously, they don't want to be recognized as such, you moron!" I replied, my patience with him thinning. "I have the alien presence in my body right now. I'm trying to fight it off and stop it from controlling me, the struggle against it giving me dizziness and headaches. There are scores and scores of operatives walking the Earth right now…with this alien presence in their bodies. They're aliens in human guise! There have been such operatives— judging by the photos I saw on the walls of that think tank, they've worked here for at least a century now, if not longer. Some of them were people whom I know pretended to advance the cause of socialism but really helped reinforce capitalism and imperialism. As I understand now, it's an *alien* imperialism."

Doug laughed out loud.

Connie sighed, then said, "Go on, Stella. You were talking about them making you an *operative*."

"Yes, as soon as I heard the word 'operative,' I could really begin to feel that alien presence asserting itself inside my body, trying to take control of my mind. My body was moving in ways I hadn't intended. It felt like demon possession. I stepped toward all of those in the room, even though that was the *last* thing I wanted to do. I involuntarily asked, 'What is my mission?' A man told me to go back to Earth and…get more people…into Zone S, which is where I was, I guess. The people were either to be experimented on or to be killed if they were deemed useless or dangerous, as I guess Lee was deemed to be. After all, we all know how much she wanted us all to get organized against the governments of the world. Anyway, it was then that I realized that the scope of my suspicions about the power structures of the world was much too narrow—what's going on up there in space means things are much, much worse. The aliens are colonizing the Earth!"

Doug was chuckling again. The others tried to ignore him.

"I knew I wouldn't have control over my body for much longer, so I just bolted out of the room," I said. "My body's been in agonizing pain ever since, what with me trying to stop the alien intelligence from controlling me. I ran back down the hall I'd just traveled. On my tail, I could hear the metallic rattling and clanking of robot legs on the floor. As I continued running, I looked back in all reluctance and dread: those demonic robots, mechanical hounds of hell, as well as a couple of those huge…elephant-like things, were chasing me."

The others were scowling at Doug, who cupped his hand over his mouth and tried to make his laughter inaudible.

"I could see a black hole in the wall far off by Lee's bloody, mutilated corpse on that pole," I said.
"That had to be the portal back to the Earth. I looked behind me again and saw those things getting closer to me. The dogs' metallic teeth were snapping just behind my ass with clangs that hurt my ears. The stomping feet of the elephant-like things were big enough to crush me, and they were getting dangerously close, too. I began running extra fast, with large strides, and managed to distance myself from them a bit. But that hole in the wall seemed farther away from me than it had originally been, and I could feel my control of my body slipping away, bit by bit."

"Like your control over your mind," Doug said.

"SHUT UP!!!" everyone shouted, including me.

"My legs started wobbling, and the drugs injected into my body were trying to make me stop running," I went on. "I made every effort to get my legs moving, but I could only budge a bit, and I just didn't have the strength anymore to overrule the mind control of the drugs inside me. I collapsed on the floor, and my chasers caught up to me. They had now encircled me, with only a bit of space between me and the portal unblocked, though I couldn't move. It was as if my tormentors were tantalizing me with the frustrated hope of escaping."

"If this *drug* had total control of your body, how come you're free of it now?" Doug asked with another sneer.

"You think I'm free of it now?" I asked, looking up at him with a sneer of my own. "I've been fighting this drug with all of my conscious effort this whole time, and I'll probably be fighting it for the rest of my life—in *perpetual agonizing pain!* I'm telling you: there are people on our side who aren't really on our side. There are always people supposedly working for progressive causes who are actually compromised. As I'm speaking, Doug: READ BETWEEN THE LINES!!!"

"Stella, give me a break," he snorted.

"Doug, for the last time, shut up," Connie said.

"Anyway, those dog robot-things were all staring at me with hateful, flaming red eyes and bared, hungry, saw-like, sharp steel fangs," I said. "I was sure I was as dead as Lee. One of the elephant-things walked up to me. I was sure it was going to step on me: it had its front right leg raised. I closed my eyes, ready to accept my fate. But instead of being crushed, I was kicked hard in the ass in the direction of the hole. In fact, I flew right into it, sucked right inside. I felt my body turn back into those electrical waves...then, when I came out of the portal and back into the dark recesses of the park, I got my body back. I scrambled to my feet and came here."

"Wow," Connie said. "That was a...wild story."

"I'm glad you don't believe it any more than I do, Connie," Doug said with a smirk.

"The point is, Doug, I, unlike you, can listen with compassion," she said, glaring at him.

"Look, you don't believe me, and I don't expect you to," I said, standing up straight and breathing calmly. "But it can all be proven if you'd just come with me to the park." Almost mechanically, I walked away from the living room toward the door, motioning to them to follow me. They did, Connie first.

"Come on, all of you," she said. "Maybe we can find out what actually happened to Lee. I have a bad feeling, from seeing that blood on Stella, that somebody with a knife murdered her."

We left the apartment and reached the park, heading off the path and over the grass near that group of trees you can see over there. Feet stepped on twigs and leaves, cracking and crunching them. A streetlight or two from just outside the park helped us see. Then we reached the recess.

"Here it is," I told them. "If you go in far enough, you'll get sucked into the portal. Your body will turn into electrical waves for the journey to where the aliens, their human collaborators in DARPA, and the dog robots are. Whether they kill you, inject you with mind-controlling drugs, or otherwise experiment on you is anyone's guess. Enter at your own risk. I don't think I care anymore. There's nothing I can do to save the Earth from the alien takeover, anyway."

"Stella, no offense—but you're crazy," Doug said.

"Don't believe me?" I said. "Go in then. Prove me wrong."

"In a heartbeat," he said, then ran inside.

We heard a faint sucking sound ten seconds later.

Silence for another minute.

"Doug?" Connie called out. "Stop screwing around in there and come back."

Silence.

24

"He's such an asshole," she said, then went in.

A faint sucking sound.

"What, is she in on the prank, too?" a male neighbour of mine asked.

"Wanna go in after them?" his female roommate asked, looking at me.

"I…am never going in there again," I said in a shaky voice, my body all rigid.

"I'm sick of all this suspense, and I don't believe in aliens," the man said. "Let's all go in *together*, in case it feels scary for any of you."

They all went in.

A faint sucking sound.

And that's the end of my story.

So, do you believe me?

No?

Well, let's go to where the dark recess is. Follow me…

Here it is. Go on in…

What? Me? Go in with you? I told you, I don't dare reenter. Go in yourself.

What's the matter, scared? You should be…

Well, if you don't believe my story, just go in and prove me wrong…

Go on…

Oh, finally, you have the guts to go in and look…

[*suck*]

[*Using my cellphone*] Zone S? This is Stella. I just sent another one in. [*laughing*]

God Complex

Alison Armstrong

Some people have been noticing that reality seems to be slipping these days. At any given moment, they discover they have accidentally wandered into a slightly mutated clone of it. Most things look the same, but one little detail is off, in an almost comic way, as if God or the Almighty Intelligence, the prankster in charge of the universe, is trying to keep them guessing.

Sometimes, I even forget that I am the prankster, the creator of everything. I watch as these tulpas innocently go about their daily business, never suspecting they aren't real and that nothing they do even matters. I watch them celebrating their ridiculously trivial accomplishments or mourning loved ones that never existed until I imagined them into being. A blink of my eye, and they are gone, poof!

Sometimes, I laugh at these characters of mine. Sometimes, they even move me to tears, and I flood the earth with my salty deluge, seas rising, ships sinking, cities and whole nations washing away. Then I dry my eyes, the sun comes out, and everything is as it was before.

I marvel at my ingenuity—all the books, movies, music, and artworks my imaginary beings have produced. From time to time, I slip in little self-referential jokes, hoping the smarter of my people will catch on to my ruse. For example, Mark Twain's short story "The Mysterious Stranger". In that one, I nearly divulged everything—but since all my imaginary beings believe the story was fiction, they don't take it as seriously as they should.

Another example—the TV series "The Prisoner". Here, I reveal that no one can escape the reality I created for them. Observing their efforts to escape, I almost admire their determination, but then I remember they are only doing what I scripted for them anyway.

I even have another layer of absurdity in some cases where one of my created beings even pretends to be me in a story that he/she/they write.

I marvel at my singular humor, at the ways I use my created beings, such as David Lynch and Philip K. Dick, to hint at my secrets but then disguise those revelations as works of surrealism or some other type of fiction.

My newest idea may be my most ingenious interactive project yet. To make things even more interesting for this project, I have decided to take a temporary human form and let other humans make a study of me in their laboratory. I chose a form that I, like many of my creations, find pleasing: a youthful adult male with lush dark hair, large hazel eyes, and a slender, agile physique. In this form, I will pretend to surrender to their scientific and psychological research. Although I, of course, already know what the outcome of their research will be, I will make myself forget it for the time being so that their research techniques can entertain me.

Case Study Research Notes

The patient, a young male aged 25, presents with symptoms of schizophrenia disorder, taking the form of a "god complex." Except for his psychological symptoms, he appears to be in good physical health.

He was admitted to our study this morning after he was transferred from the university's psychiatric clinic as a result of his intractable delusions that he is God and that no one else exists. He has willingly agreed to take part in our study, consenting to ECT and/or psychotropic medications, to help understand the etiology of his psychosis and perhaps assist in the treatment of similar cases in patients. To further our research, we and the patient have agreed that no anesthesia will be used during the procedure so that after each session, the patient can write down his thoughts and sensations.

Day 1

Searing current jolts through my body, making it spasm like a worm wriggling on blistering cement. A coven of voices cackles in the static. I never knew what physical pain and fear felt like from the inside out. Sensations resonate through my flesh to my very soul, the soul of everything I created.

Whatever certainties have shaken away, convulsion by convulsion. I keep reminding myself that this was my choice and that I can stop this any time I want. However, the intensity of the pain and the horror of the thoughts rushing through my mind overwhelm my ability to focus. Maybe it's just this human form that makes me doubt what I know is the truth. This weak, physical shell of blood, muscle, bone, and organs. All those messy organs that shit and piss and vomit. I now know what it is like to feel ashamed, vulnerable, disgusted, and afraid.

What am I afraid of, though? After all, I set up this scenario, subjected myself to it, and will prevail, no matter what. I control these beings and am just letting them control me. I can stop at any time.

Oh, God, the pain! Why do I address myself in these moments? Am I a puppet repeating what I have instructed my own creations to say when pleading for something?

I command you to stop! I try to scream, but the bite block prevents me from doing so.

What have I consented to? Why? These questions swirl through my mind like a tidal current. The more they swirl, the more confused and unsure I become.

"Relax," one of the masked assistants murmurs. "It will all be over soon."

Memories (my own or some of my creations?) replay themselves.

I am in a church of some sort, and the person claiming to represent me is addressing his audience (a group of children dressed in identical uniforms). "You must repent your disobedient ways," he preaches. "As the Good Book says, 'Though your sins are like scarlet, I will make them as white as snow.' Surrender to God, faith, and true, sincere repentance can cleanse those stubborn stains within your soul."

Why would anyone tell a child such a thing? I wonder. I am angry at this minister for the foul words he attributes to me.

One of those students, a young boy with dark hair, looks afraid. I suddenly remember what it was like to be a child, even though I could not possibly have ever been one. After all, nobody came before me because I created everything.

Of all the people in that church, that boy is the only one whose mind I seem to enter now. I watch him as he leaves the church following the sermon.

He is heading home. Throwing his books upon the table, he opens up a notebook and begins to scrawl words on the blue-lined paper.

He writes, scowls, then erases his words. The cycle continues until he has veritably shredded the paper with his repeated pencil scrawling and erasures.

Whatever he wanted to create has been destroyed, cast out of temporary existence. He stalks off like a disgruntled creator, dissatisfied with himself and his creations, ashamed of something they revealed about himself and the sins he hides.

Although his parents are in the room, they don't seem to notice what he is doing or sense his anger. And I, for some reason, can't access their minds or get them to care about this child I so strongly identify with for some reason.

What is happening to me? Why can't I escape this situation, this entrapment inside that little boy's thoughts?

Day 2

Another memory surfaces, and again, it features this boy and his thoughts.

An adolescent now, he is riding his bike at dusk. The sun's setting rays shimmer against the red and golden leaves like stained glass windows in a cathedral. Holiness abides within the prisms, secrets of death and rebirth, darkness and light. A beam of light penetrates his heart, filling him with a frightening yet arousing sensation that radiates from his chest downward to the throbbing bulge inside his pants. He yearns for something that he knows can never be attained. Even when the throbbing ceases and his pants are damp, the longing simmers inside him, a desire tinged with shame.

He realizes then that he has been touched, tested, and anointed by God. Soon, he will become God.

But how can God suddenly become God?

Day 3

The boy is at church again, and he is holding the chalice that is supposed to represent my blood (or is it my son's blood?) These humans' interpretations of my ways are confusing and contradictory. Sometimes, they even start wars over details such as this, with each side claiming to be supported by me.

After the people in the church are finished sipping the blood and chewing on a wafer that is supposed to be my body or my son's body, they sing a few whimpering songs, asking for forgiveness as well as songs promising their devotion.

When the sermon has concluded, and everyone except the minister and the boy has departed, the minister whispers to the boy, then leads him into an office.

I can't see what takes place there. I feel as if a white shroud has been placed over my eyes. My body feels numb…helpless as whatever happens there to that boy in that room takes place.

Afterward, I hear what the minister says to the boy, his voice echoing as if he is speaking in an underground cave.

"You have sinned, boy," the minister says. "And you must pay your penance. Only then will God forgive you. I will show you the way to absolution. But first, you must be obedient. Do as I say, just as I do what God says. He has commanded me to be your guide, your teacher. Now, close your eyes and repeat after me: 'I am sinful; I need saving. I surrender my body and soul to the Reverend, the faithful servant of Your word."

There is a pause, and I wait for something dreadful to happen, something I can't see. The waiting is terrifying, like the moments of apprehension in a horror movie when the unseen monster, heard growling and stomping through the fields, approaches the cabin where the innocent victim futilely cowers.

"Just keep your eyes closed, son, and open your mouth. All will be over soon," the monstrous voice murmurs.

The moment of dread has arrived. There is no escape.

Day 4 (before session)

Last night I had a strange, troubling dream that I was on an island.. As in that TV series, "The Prisoner," everyone else on the island seemed content, gossiping as they sipped their cocktails and watched the waves playfully tumble against the shore.

I was sitting on a white wicker chair, mesmerized by the motion of the waves, that eternal exit and return. If I were a wave, I would leave and never return. I don't like going back. I don't like seeing these images of the boy and the church. (Somehow, in this dream, I forget that I am God and can leave any time I want.)

Throughout this dream, people dressed in white, carrying white and red parasols, stroll along the boardwalk. Back and forth, up and down, like carousel horses riveted in place, repeating the same motions until the merry-go-round eventually pauses.

When I wake up, I feel as if I am spinning, white-coated people whirling around me, poking me with needles.

When the dizziness recedes, I notice a new person has joined the doctors and assistants for my treatment.

The new person, a middle-aged man with a bald head, looks vaguely familiar. In some other context, I may have seen him, maybe ages ago. The bright white light beams down upon his shiny head, making it glow like a crystal ball. If I look into the scrying orb, what will I see, past or future, joy or sadness? For some reason, I am afraid to look too intently upon it or even at the man himself.

Around his neck, the man wears a large cross with a red stone in the middle where Christ's heart is said to beat its last earthly pulsations.

As the relaxation drug is injected into my arm, I hear a conversation between the man and the other staff.

"This time, we should achieve victory," the man murmurs. "He's beginning to have doubts. He's remembering things. Once he remembers everything— realizes the error of his ways, then we can wipe clean that slate of blasphemous sin and fill his newborn soul with the truth we have pledged to preach."

The voices echo as if they are leading downward into a cave.

"Follow," they say." Follow and let it all be revealed."

I do as they ask, for there is nowhere else for me to go. All other exits are blocked.

As I walk along the narrow, rocky path, the chasm below reminds me of a sinister, crooked-toothed mouth.

"Open wide," a voice commands. "Open your mind and heart."

Ahead of me on the path, I see the boy, older now, a young adult. He is standing beside the minister.

The minister is also older, and his hairless head glows like a candle, lighting the darkness.

"I am the light, the only light," he says, turning to the boy. "Come to me, and you will be safe from the darkness of your troubled, muddled mind. Try as you might to flee, you cannot escape your torment by denying the truth. You cannot know God except through me."

Illumined by the light of his gleaming head, I see other people in the distance. They're wearing white coats. Stethoscopes and scalpel-bladed crosses dangle from their necks.

In unison, they begin chanting. "Oh, lost lamb, face the truth, flee and then return home to us."

I stare at the boy in front of me and walk towards him. I grasp his arm, feeling a tingle surge through me, a jolt of terror and recognition.

I am touching my other hand. I am seeing through his eyes, my own eyes.

The white-coated, crucifix-bearing bald man beside us is the minister who said he wanted to save us/me if we let him.

But I am God, I tell myself. I am all-powerful. How could this man have ever had control over me?

I close my eyes, envisioning escape. Part of me breaks free, becoming God. It drifts away like a bubble, floating high. It nears the roof of the cave, brushes against it, soft as a caress, then bursts.

Inside me, something also bursts, pain flowing through me, all the pain I tried to hide. Tears sting my eyes, streaming down my face, each droplet a descent into shame and horror at my powerless humanity.

I feel the minister's arms around me, and I hear a chorus of voices.

"Come to us, our long-lost lamb," they chant. "Only we can banish your confusion. Only we can heal you, mind and soul."

I struggle to free myself from the minister's grip, but his hands are too strong, too tight, and the voices of the chorus too disorienting. Crucifix scalpels glistening, voices still chanting, the doctors hover over me.

Unable to escape, I surrender, their lamb, their sacrifice. They lay their hands upon me, and I am saved.

My final words, written here, are testimony to the truth that finally set me free.

Jumping Skins

Neil Sanzari

Neil Armstrong had just walked on the moon when I jumped skins for the very first time. After school, I used to stop by the swamps in the park across the street from where I lived. I was totally obsessed with catching salamanders, and we had newts in great quantities if you knew where to look. Newts didn't bite you, and as far as I could tell, they didn't give you warts either.

I once lifted a rock to find a serpent coiled up underneath, lying perfectly flat to match the contour of the stone's underbelly. He must have been dreaming, and alas, I had awakened him from his slumbers. And then he was gone in the blink of an eye, and I hadn't even seen where he'd run off to…he was so fast. He was like greased lightning. I was left there holding the rock, dumbfounded. Crouching over the spot, wondering if he had ever really been there or not.

He had this beautiful color to him, like a thing out of a dream. He was completely white with a blue cast to him—it was as if his presence had changed the day's lighting all around me. Surrounding me with its atmosphere. Maybe the world had been awakened from his dream. And maybe it was his dream and not my own that I was growing up in.

Felt like the sun had dipped behind some clouds at that precise moment. Just like only a few years later, when I was just a tad bit older, growing up too fast. My well-upholstered adopted cousin from Seoul, Korea, beckoned me from behind one of those ornate folding walls bejeweled with pictures of dragons and samurai. Giving me a wink and a nod, she did, while she shimmied out of her shimmering strapless.

And I didn't even think to look up at the sky. The sight of that supernatural snake so enamored me. Surely, he looked like a dragon from myth and legend. The snapshot taken long years ago, with these eyes now full of cataracts, still lingers like the smoke of a freshly snuffed cigarette.

And so, the day went from being sunny to overcast with the lifting of that rock. Perhaps I had stumbled upon a switch to dim the outdoor lighting with.

And now the only thing wrong with catching newts was those haunting expressions of theirs, which told of how terrified they were. And still, I just wasn't getting it, until suddenly, one day, I was made to look up at myself through their eyes. And I saw this giant, vaguely familiar from the disadvantage of being trapped within the clutches of his hand, and I wondered if he was going to eat me raw or not. Was he going to put out one of my eyes and throw in a batwing to cook me up within a pot of boiling water like some witch's recipe straight out of a fairy tale?

*

I had stolen only one other thing in my life, and that was a toy skeleton from a five-and-dime up in Secaucus around Halloween time. I remember being five years old because we had only lived there for a year or so when my father, who had grown up during the Great Depression and been raised by immigrant workers, was trying to catch up with the Joneses.

Yes, I am old, but I was younger back then, and the world has never stopped being wonderfully fascinating with all of its horrors so tantalizing.

It's this thing you see all around you, and it just never stops happening.

*

Casey Scapula had dared me to steal another kid's bicycle as part of my initiation into the Walton Street Gang, where my grandparents had bought a haunted landmark building. One of the few left standing after the British had burned the city down to the ground back in the 1770s—not even 200 hundred years beforehand.

My jet-set father had left us for another family. A *Cosmopolitan* model he'd met on a commercial shoot for *Smirnoff,* who had wooed him away from us. She left him breathless, as per the brand's dated tagline. In a monsoon, my sister and I were unceremoniously dropped off at our mother's parents' house down in Toms River after she had been put into an institution. After we stopped for some Carvel ice cream on the way down the shore from up in Secaucus, my sister got carsick in our grandfather's '65 Chevy. Marguerite was blowing chunks on the dashboard, and our Irish Grandfather had lost his mind cleaning up the upholstery in the downpour. All because of his daughter, our poor dear mother, who had been caught fighting it out with our German shepherd over the last lick of toilet water, thanks to our father, who had stopped paying the bills, leaving us virtually destitute.

The ten-speed was too tall for me to ride at the time, so I ran uphill with it alongside me at shoulder height up the winding streets, trying to outrun the kid I had stolen it from. Oh yes, I was afraid of getting caught. I knew I was doing something very, very bad. Very bad, indeed. It made me a nervous wreck; you see, my mother had made me give that toy skeleton back to the old lady behind the counter at the five-and-dime, up in Secaucus around Halloween time just a few years beforehand. My mother had taught me right from wrong, but here I was doing it all over again; it was even worse now than before because I knew. I already knew how to live my life because of the good information given to me by my mother. The kid from whom I had stolen had to be at least five or six years older. He was on the high school track team, and I was in the fourth grade, for Christ's sake. I knew he was dogging my trail. I heard his track shoes on the pavement just a few steps behind me. Was it because he was black and I was white that he had given up his pursuit, worried that my word might be taken over his if any adults had gotten involved? I only assume I can only imagine because he was quite capable of catching up to me, but he had given up on the chase as I mounted the hill, turning around to see where he'd gone off to. And believe me when I tell you that I wanted so badly to give the ten-speed back to him. But it was far too late for that.

*

When I'd finally handed off the bicycle to Casey in his father's garage, along with all the other hot goods they had stored away in there, it was with a heavy heart...I had fallen from my mother's grace, who suffered in the nuthouse because of us.

I told Casey I didn't want to be in his gang anymore. And he said that I had better watch my back because they would be coming for me now that I was on my own. They didn't take kindly to folks snubbing their invitations. They were going to make me squeeze lemons. I remember Tommy Pete throwing a bottle of beer at me like Casey up at bat, and me ducking just in time, and the bottle shattering against a tree right next to my face. And a shard scratching my temple just enough to make me bleed. I remember catching a praying mantis at the Food & Fuel, and Casey taking a claw hammer to it. Dashing it to pieces. I remember watching the other gang members stone a flock of passenger pigeons, who were fostering their nurslings beneath an overpass, killing fourscore or more in the process. I remember Tracy Boyle sucker-punching me in the gut while he was belly-laughing. The pain wouldn't go away until the very next day, leaving me to cry through the night because it hurt so bad. I remember my grandmother slapping me around in a furious outcry. Backhanding me at full force because I had peed on the toilet seat, and she had sat in it by mistake. I never did that again. And so, she had civilized me to some extent.

I was terrified, but I knew they would be coming for me even if I hadn't joined their gang, what with Jersey being a microcosm of the whole nation, whose north and south sides hated each other. And here I was, being from the north and a Bluebelly to the core, stuck in the Deep South of New Jersey.

After our folks had reconciled, Father had come to his senses, but only for a moment. You see, did I hear through my sister, Marguerite, about

Casey Scapula having dropped a cinder block on his knee and how he had refused to go to the doctor because he was afraid, and so his leg went untreated. He had to get it cut off because of the gangrene that had quickly spread, making him taste of the grave.

*

I remember being that praying mantis the day Casey had taken a hammer to it and dashed my brain to pieces. I saw the blunt instrument of my doom coming down upon me while I grappled with the dilapidated aluminum siding of his parents' house. At first, it was just my hind leg that got blasted into Kingdom Come, and then I took a hit full-on in the shoulder that didn't stop there until I'd lost my head completely in the process. My head popped off in a geyser of bug juice and bounced until it landed on the broken patio bricks, where his drunken dad would often barbeque the chicken and the shish-kabob and that mouth-watering corn on the cob bathed in melted butter during summertime.

I remember being one of those nurslings still wearing a fragment of my eggshell atop my head as if it were a baby's bonnet the day the Walton Street Gang stoned our entire flock to death. They committed genocide against my race. Passenger pigeon blood dripped from the underpinnings of the overpass. A ghostly cloud of speckled turtledove feathers with intermittent hues of iridescent turquoise lay suspended in the air, frozen in time, refusing to comply with the will of gravity.

*

After returning from our time at our grandparents' house down the shore, my sister and I got back into the swing of things up in Secaucus. She went bananas for Barbie. And my new obsession was boxer turtles, so I built a pen for a mating pair that my dad had bought me at the local pet shop. My dream was to own a pet store someday when I was older.

I stacked bricks and natural rock formations together into an unprecedented series of earthworks to create an underground shelter for Mr. and Mrs. Turtle. I fashioned the miniature complex after the megalithic phase ruins called Angkor Wat, found in the jungles of Cambodia. I drew all the gods and their supplicants on the stones I had assembled, using a black magic marker from detailed photographs and illustrations that depicted the major and minor arcana of the deities worshipped. I had UFOs zapping monkey men like the combat depicted in the superhero comics of the day. All this I did for Mr. and Mrs. Turtle.

Mrs. Turtle had a distinctive look to her anatomy that clearly marked her as female in comparison to Mr. Turtle, who exhibited a demeanor purportedly masculine in nature. But who knew? I never got to see them *do the Do.*

Meanwhile, Mrs. Turtle's shell stood taller and squarer than her husband's. She reminded me of the way cars appeared back in the early fifties. She looked like a highboy. A 1953 Cadillac, while her husband could easily pass for a Bullet Nose Studebaker-Hearse of the same year. With orange polka-dots. That said, they both needed bodywork, and quite frankly, the cheddar for that kind of maintenance just wasn't in the kitty.

But at night, I kept having bad dreams of the two of them being harassed by giant predators who had come to wreak havoc upon their happy home. The one I'd built for them just outside in the backyard without taking into consideration that summer was almost over, and I'd have to make accommodations for them indoors until the weather returned back to normal after the long winter that was on its way.

One dream had this evil weasel breaking and entering, trying to get at the Turtle couple, but they had shut themselves up in the bedroom. They were good citizens. They didn't want to hurt anyone. They just wanted to be left alone. Left to their own devices.

One morning, when I came out to see if they had made it through the night after some particularly hairy dreams, I found Mrs. Turtle out in the front yard of the Turtle Temple lying on top of her eggs. They were blue like robin's eggs, and she kindly let me hold them for inspection. But Mr. Turtle was nowhere to be found. I asked myself—did he run off like my father?

*

My sister and I were getting back into the swing of things up in Teaneck, which was right next door to Hackensack, because our folks had sold the house in Secaucus. And we were just in time for Halloween that year, our favorite holiday, second only to Christmas. But our mother wasn't having it because she'd just been alerted by the 6 O'clock News to the fact that there were certain imbalanced individuals out there with a penchant for pure evil, individuals who were bent upon poisoning the candy and boobytrapping candy apples with razor blades for to slice up poor unsuspecting children with.

The reports were floating in on the airwaves at an incredible rate on that fateful evening about such victims having fallen due to the schemes of these shadowy figures pretending to be "nice people," opening up their front doors for us, giving us their candy full of peril, and therefore, ruining the holiday spirit forever and ever.

Although my sister and I couldn't fathom why an adult would go to such lengths to hurt poor children, we threw our feet down in a synchronized tantrum that brought our poor, dear mother to tears. She was so scared for us. And so, she bargained with us, ordering us not to eat any of the candy that we might acquire in our travels—until she had inspected each and every little piece when we got home that night.

Although it was the hardest thing I'd ever done in my life up until that point, I listened to our poor, dear mother, whom I was so glad to be home with after the ordeal of my parents' separation. But my sister, who was younger than I was, hadn't fully grasped why our mother had sent us to live with our grandparents in the first place. And even though our folks had reconciled, my sister secretly held onto a grudge like no other and blamed our poor dear mother for our father leaving us from the get-go. There was no changing her mind on the subject. Where I trusted our mother wholeheartedly, Marguerite held onto a different perspective and snickered at our mother's orders with contempt. Believing that our mother didn't love her because she had been seemingly cast aside like that.

*

Marguerite was wearing a blue, shiny suit with a black bowler hat that our father had given her for the occasion. It was more prop than anything else. He helped her to make a clay prosthetic for her nose to look like an old man's schnozzle, and she stuffed a big pillow under her blue coat. She was a sight to behold. A true enigma in the offing. And so, I asked her what she was going to be for Halloween, and she said in a flat, low voice, "a fat man." Both of us laughed so hard our faces hurt. And the glue holding her prosthetic nose in place suffered from the tears we shed, so it had to be reattached.

The suit was a trophy from one of our father's surreal shoots for a *Smirnoff* ad before he had lost his job on Madison Avenue, only to land another high-salaried position with a prestigious ad agency in the Chrysler Building.

*

Oh, my poor dear sister, I will never forget having jumped skins once again, as was my talent up until adolescence. I remember being that loathsome little apple maggot you never saw coming, trying to warn you. That detestable larva of a codling moth, who tunneled his way out of the bruised crab apple on that fateful evening when you bit into the caramel coating without hesitation; you had trusted these strangers, who had given you the homemade candy apple with a smile, despite our mother's explicit instructions.

Close Encounters of the Cold Kind

J. Rocky Colavito

UFO sightings bring out the woodwork's weirdest. They all pass through my place to either grab a burger or drown their sorrows over the fact that the only evidence of the visitation is in the addled recesses of the minds of witnesses or alleged contactees. Here's the thing—I've seen the cavorting lights myself, always in formation doing aerobatic maneuvers that even the craziest blue angel pilot wouldn't attempt. They're always at a distance over the mountain ranges that surround our little corner of the Southwestern United States. Yes, there's a proximate airbase that's so defined by rumors that no one really knows what's going on there. The airmen and women who venture from it, airmen and women who seek what my place offers, are the epitome of the strong-silent type. Whether in or out of uniform, they don't say much, and they don't tip well when they do. I've taken to jacking up the prices of their orders to make sure that the staff gets what they deserve.

But they do speak volumes in other ways; their faces bear the same unsettled expressions as if they've been party to some sort of unnatural or immoral experience, either as observers or, God forbid, participants. I can usually tell the difference by the jitteriness of the latter sort. I even had one grab up a steak knife and swing it at one of the servers when she brushed against his back while delivering another table's order. The others at his table brought him into line; he apologized, and the server got twenty dollars as compensation for being half scared out of her wits.

If you look closely at their eyes, it will appear as though they're looking either through you or over your shoulder at something behind you that only they can see. I think that's probably why most of them wear sunglasses whenever they're here, day or night. On the rare occasions when one of them has removed his or her sunglasses (yes, there are women stationed out there; they're just as rattled), the eyes are haunted, refusing to focus on anything other than whatever floats in the background.

Among the rumors about the base are whispers that there are a bunch of scientists out there, as well as the air personnel. What they are doing is open to wide speculation. Some say that they're the ones behind the UFOs and that a brand-new shock and awe weapon is in the works in some sort of subterranean laboratory. Others posit something more sinister…something involving the airmen and women who are allowed to visit our little town.

I keep my opinions to myself; I've been down this road a time or two already. I was hoping that Fireforge, Arizona, was gonna be the last stop on my quest to get away from West Virginia, New Mexico, Mississippi, Illinois, and all kinds of places in between. It's ironic that I should end up in a place that's a hotbed for UFOs; I deliberately avoided Phoenix because of the disappearances, but the sightings and occasional contacts always manage to follow me.

It sucks to be me, if I may be honest. But it is my lot, so I've learned to live with it.

And I'm reminded of this by a day like today. The bar is having a slow lunch hour so far. All I'm serving are four regulars who are huddled up against the bar, except for one who is having a liquid lunch. Civilian jobs at the air base have undergone a new round of cuts—blame the federal government or the shadow doors for closing the checkbook—and the local pickings are slim until they finish building that huge ass truck stop out by the interstate. You know the one I mean—has a ball cap-wearing beaver as a mascot.

Hank, Phil, Sam, and Lewis are the four locals; the latter three are unemployed, hoping their applications to the truck stop bear fruit. Hank owns the local convenience store and has job security; also, he has no life since the only people he can hire are not what you'd call reliable or available. Down to the last person, none of them seems to understand why they get fired for just not showing up for work or calling off at the last minute. Hank is here having his breakfast, just having worked off a graveyard shift and eight to twelve before he could arm-twist someone to come in and take over. He's not drinking because he's gotten too used to getting calls at home about something going wrong at the store or an irate patron complaining that someone hasn't shown up.

"If it weren't a corporate mandate, I would close the fucking place at midnight and just leave the pumps on regulators. Card only, fifty-dollar limit." Hank moans as he carves off a piece of his breakfast steak, layers it with an egg and some hash browns, walks it through the steak sauce on his plate, and shoves it in his mouth.

"Anyone see the lights last night?" Phil asks. He's one of the last group of government layoffs. He's a mechanic and a damn good one. But he doesn't have the means to take on much work at the trailer he calls home. He can still change your fluids and spark plugs, rotate your tires, and put in any part you bring him, but that's not enough to balance out his unemployment, which he is still waiting on.

"Yeah, they was kinda pretty this time, lots of pinks and yellows." Sam is the saddest case of the three; a great hope of the town for fame and fortune, whose shot was undone by getting high-lowed by a linebacker and defensive back in the rivalry game a few years ago. He hung on to the ball but had both knees blown out and, on top of that, suffered a concussion so severe it still plagues him six years later. His disability helps. As did the insurance payout from the school, but he was too addled to finish his education. He does odd jobs around the town and is a regular presence whenever there's a need for volunteers or unofficial cheerleaders.

"I saw gold and really light oranges," Lewis adds. He's another Air Force base job casualty. He minded the fences surrounding the base, walking perimeter patrol in an open jeep, stopping to fix any defects. Eight to ten hours a day under that sun, even with a hat, special sunglasses, and SPF 100 sunscreen, he looks like six feet of beef jerky with eyes whose pupils look singed. He's got obvious skin cancers on every exposed part of his body…but has decided to self-medicate rather than go to the doctor for treatment.

"I wish I could've seen them," Hank moans through a mouthful of food. "Had to clean up a mess some punks made. Kid puked and shit all over the floor in front of the cooler."

"That's why we don't serve drunks here." I refill his decaf, holding back my suggestion that he should maybe switch to decaf iced tea; it's fresh-brewed.

"How about you, Cold? What colors did you see?"

I think through my answer carefully.

My place is called Cold's Shots, and, yeah, Cold is my last name. No, I'm not the one that's part of the mythology, the one who kept popping in and out of some poor sap's life in seventy-five in West Virginia. I've done the genealogy; my people are aptly named because we originate in the Northern reaches of England, and we either fought against the Normans or ran south, just ahead of them. I won't bore you with the other details. The only thing I'll add is that my first name does indeed begin with an I (like the other guy's name). It's Ignatius, but no one, and I mean no one, has ever called me anything but Cold. It was made easy by the fact that I was an only child, and I was quick with my fists if anyone ever made fun of my first name.

People just got used to using my last name; it's cool.

"Just bright white. I didn't spend any time watching them. I close up shop by midnight, you know. I saw three of them hovering in a diagonal formation over the western mountain range when I left to drive home. They'd disappeared by the time I got home."

"Isn't it strange that we all saw the same thing differently? I saw three lights." Lewis said.

"So did I." Sam's contribution takes longer to get out, taking extremely long pauses between each word.

"And that makes four who saw three." Phil notes. Hank got left out because he was too busy to observe.

I'll let them chew on the mystery. Just to keep it that way.

What they don't know keeps them and the rest of the primitives safe.

I don't have a direct report per se; I have an arrangement with some folks who work better in the shadows or at the tightest edge of your peripheral vision. Count yourself lucky that you haven't gotten a good look. Remember what happened to people who looked upon the gods in your mythology? Yeah, a bit like that, only what happened to those poor saps in the stories is a day at the spa compared to what happens to someone who sees the things I have an arrangement with.

The pain of having every single atom of your being explode in a slow sequence like a string of firecrackers is exquisite and incredibly painful to observe. What's left looks like liquid multicolored shit. Sometimes, an eye somehow survives.

I'm an emissary, my formless self—stuffed into a fleshbag I obtained when one of the pregnant females had a fourth-kind encounter. Actually, it was the whole family. I was placed within a gestating infant and then abandoned on this planet to be raised by a kindly older couple. Yeah, a bit like that superhero everyone liked to watch. I was a good child, but when my foster parents outlived their usefulness, I gave them a peek at what I really looked like. Luckily, they went quickly, dissolving into dust instantaneously as they held each other. That tugged a bit at my heartstrings, but it was all part of the plan. I took their name and genealogy (which was actually fun research—learning the primitives' history is enlightening.). That was the start of my assignment; working my way around the country trying to tamp down rumors about and discoveries of the deal my race cut with the United States military. Technology for a beachhead, a deal that pops up time and again in the recorded history of your species.

There are those among the species who are paranoid about our motives; world conquest and subjugation are common fears. We aren't interested; we're hunter-gatherers. We want knowledge of other worlds and species. I'm wired to accumulate history. Others of my kind who live around the world doing similar work, study art, culture, media, fashion, you name it. We are the collectors of the sum of a species' existence. If you can believe it, the process sustains our species. We feed off the accumulated knowledge of others. Our barter with this species is a means of furthering that knowledge.

I'm told by one of my colleagues that there used to be a science fiction-themed television series about a group of space explorers or soldiers (the lines blurred) who were guided by some sort of rule that prohibited them from interfering in a culture's development in any way. We found that humorous given our need for knowledge, and the easiest way to get that knowledge is to offer something to reverse engineer and develop. It's mutually beneficial because the knowledge machine gets new fuel, and we get more food.

In case you're wondering, we aren't stealing the knowledge, leaving the primitives with empty heads and erased history. We collect, process, parcel out, and share with others of our kind. Nobody realizes that we're learning…from you primitives.

It's my job to make sure that a condition of blissful unawareness is maintained. And I'm getting a sense that maybe things might be starting to go sideways within this group of four.

I'm zeroing in on Sam; he seems to be the least able to process complex ideas, but within your history, poets have often written about how children had the clearest sense of vision and went blinder as they aged because experience and its attendant cynicism clouded that vision. Sam, as noted, was severely concussed, and it appears that his condition has reverted his vision to child-like clarity. He was the one who saw the uncamouflaged light colors. The others saw the colors your defense agency wanted them to. Not so with Sam."

And that is a problem.

I ask Sam to hang back as the others leave. I tell him I have some chores around the bar that I need help with and that I'll not only comp him his dinner and give him a ride home but also pay him. He's eager to help and would be even if I didn't offer any compensation.

"Gee, thanks, Mr. Cold, gives me something to do and keeps me out of the bars, oops, just kidding there!"

I laugh right along with him at his joke and set him to work. I flip the "closed" sign on the front door and walk with him back to the room off the small delivery dock. I lugged in some cases of liquor this morning, and I'll have Sam put them up for me and bring out bottles that need restocking.

I explain what I want him to do and set him to work. He's strong as an ox and, sadly, about as smart in the eyes of the people who see him. I do more than see, and I know there's more to him. I've come to realize that there are all kinds of intelligence and that the most dunderheaded of individuals might have brilliance enough to rival that of, well, draw a great thinker's name from a receptacle.

"Wild night you all had there, eh?" I ask as he muscles the case of bourbon onto its side on the shelf, taking care to get it all the way on and secure the bottles.

"Nothing special, really, Mr. Cold, just the lights playing tag near the mountains. They sure was pretty, though."

"Yeah, oranges and purples."

Sam stops and waves a finger at me like a metronome. "Uh, uh, they was pink and yellow; I know what I saw." He goes back to wrestling the next case onto the shelves.

"Yeah, that's right, mixed you up with someone else, sorry about that. Gets confusing around here sometimes."

"I'll tell you what's confusing, Mr. Cold," Sam grunts as he raises the second case, this one of vodka, onto the shelf above the bourbon, "that everyone else sees different colors whenever they see the lights. Last week, old Lewis said he saw blue and red. This week, he saw gold and orange. Me, I see the pinks and yellows every time."

My heart lags, and what you call sadness washes over me. I may have to let Sam in on my little secret. He'll be missed, and the visitation may have to wait, but he's already seen too much.

Trouble is, I really like the guy. And I feel as sorry as my kind can for someone dealt the hand fate gave him.

"I'll tell you another thing that's funny, Mr. Cold, how it is that no one believes me when I says I've seen one on the ground. With guys in full-body suits and helmets, like one of them old-timey ass-ter-nots working on it. Tell you true it was an honest-to-goodness flying saucer, right out of the old movies. Danged me that I ain't have my phone with me—I'd a gotten me a picture otherwise."

"When did you see this?" I ask casually.

"You gonna laugh at me?" he asks accusingly.

"No, why would I? People tell me they've seen all kinds of weird stuff. Before I came here, I had a whole bunch of folks tell me about something with a ten-foot wing spread and red eyes like brake lights that flew over a car going a hundred miles an hour like it was standing still."

"Really? Gosh, that would have been something." Sam looks envious.

"See, I'm not gonna laugh. When did this happen?"

"Couple-three weeks ago, it was way out in the desert near the mountains. I was out looking for my mama's dog…them coyotes out there've been known to take down pets. Didn't find old Fred until I heard him whining under the back porch. Poor dog was blind—like his eyes had been cooked white."

"Where did you see it? How close were you?"

"Like I said, out in the desert, near the mountains. It was on the desert floor. Had some kind of light they were using to do the work. Like a shop light only on something like a tripod."

Sam definitely saw something that he shouldn't have.

"Like I said, they was working on something, had a piece of the outside of the thing opened up like the hood of a car. One of them seemed to be supervising the two others."

"Did you hear anything? Did they see you?"

"Nope, I was pretty far away. Had my night binoculars with me 'cuz I was looking for Fred. I hid behind some boulders and watched."

"They finished whatever they was doing, shut the hood, and reboarded. Thing started glowing yellow and turned to pink when it flew off. Joined the other two that was hovering in the air while the crew fixed it."

Sam grabs the last box; it's filled with whiskey, and he puts it on the shelf next to the bourbon.

"Which do you need to me to bring out, Mr. Cold?"

"One of each, Sam. Then I'll get you started on picking up the parking lot."

Sam happily goes about filling a roll-along garbage bin with the debris that found its way into my place's parking lot and uses his great strength to raise and dump the bin into the dumpster. He makes three trips, then offers to sweep the lot.

"Just get the broken glass." I hand him a broom and a long-handled dustpan. He gets back to work.

I watch as he does this; he's really careful in his work. When he set up the cases of liquor, I noticed that he lined everything up perfectly; when he replaced the old bottles with the new ones, he made sure that the labels were centered perfectly. He goes over each place where there is broken glass several times. He takes his time, runs his hand along the ground, and verifies there are no shards. He makes five trips with the dustpan to the dumpster and lopes back to me like a puppy looking for a treat.

"Need to check my work, Mr. Cold?"

"No, Sam, I think it'll be fine. Want to help me set the tables for dinner? Suzie is gonna be a little late today, cheerleading tryouts and all."

"Sure thing, Mr. Cold. Always happy to help out."

We go through the ritual of wiping down the tables, condiment bottles, salt, and pepper shakers. I proudly notice that Sam even takes the time to wipe down the seats in the banquettes, booths, and chairs. He's nothing if not thorough.

We survey what we've done, and Sam looks at me as if he wants more.

"Have a seat at the bar, Sam, I'll draw ya a draft."

"Where's your crayons and paper if you're gonna do that, Mr. Cold?"

I do a double-take and burst out laughing. Sam looks crestfallen.

"Why are you laughing at me? You promised that you wouldn't." His face screws up like he's about to cry.

I put a hand on his shoulder; "I'm sorry, Sam, it's just that what you said was really funny. It was like you thought I was gonna draw you a picture of a draft beer."

"Well, what else would you put it in but a pitcher?"

I laugh again in spite of myself. Sam looks sadder.

"Why are you laughing at me? I'm not telling jokes. You're like everybody else, always making fun of me because I got hurt and don't think, so smart as everyone else."

I sense that I have wounded him, and I apologize again.

"Sam, you may not realize it, but the things that you said were really funny. It's something called word-play—you took the words that I used, or their soundalikes, to make something funny out of them. Bartenders use the word "draw" to mean the same thing as pour, and picture and pitcher sound very much the same. You made jokes because you took what I said literally, and they were funny. What you said was funny, not you. Big difference there."

Sam looks like he's settled down, though he seems a touch different. "If you say so, Mr. Cold. You've always treated me fine, it just feels funny that you'd suddenly make fun of me."

He sits back down at the bar, and I get him his beer. I slide it across to him with a hundred dollars in fifties underneath it. He picks up the bills and pockets them.

"Beer's on the house. Got something in mind for dinner? I can get it started for you."

"How about one of them pizzas, with all the stuff?"

"A super deluxe, coming right up. Watch the bar for me. If Suzie shows up, can you let her in?"

"Sure thing, Mr. Cold."

I quickly put the pizza together. I slide it into the oven. I'll check it in fifteen minutes. Sam is halfway through his beer and looking at his phone when I return.

"What's up?" I pick up his glass and refill it.

"Nothing much, just a text."

"Anyone I know?" I ask jovially.

"You might," he says in a much different voice, and I realize the con is up.

I initiate shifting into my true form; he's already a step ahead. By the time I've shifted, he's become something that will kill me.

His face has become a mirror, and my kind, well, while we can look at each other with no problems, we cannot survive a glimpse of our reflections. It has the same effect on us as it does on a human.

46

Sam looms over me as I sink to the floor and start to dissolve. He clues me in on the situation.

"You're out, we're in. These fleshbags are always looking for a bigger and better deal. All we had to do was say that we'd help them conquer each other and they were all over it like the starving primitives that they are. Let the games begin."

Boy, these primitives are fifty shades of fucked, I think as I dissolve into nothingness.

Mission: Lucia

J.C. Maçek III

It's a little-known (or at least little-admitted) fact that one of the most effective forms of torture is boredom. Another of the most effective forms of torture is irritation.

Think about it. Physical pain is excruciating and exhilarating. It is undeniably a terrible thing and not at all enjoyable, but the excitement of such torture gives the victim a thrill and an adrenaline rush. They would more likely prefer to be without such agony, but real torture comes in the annoying healing process and inability to function properly long after the endorphins subside.

Similarly, being locked in a small room with nothing to do is ultimately a more horrible torture than waterboarding. Neither is pleasant, but waterboarding ends after long stretches.

Why do you think torturers loudly play terrible songs on repeat? Annoyance and boredom are incredibly effective forms of torture.

Enough extreme renditions of *Three Blind Mice,* and you will tell your torturer anything she wants to know.

I know these things. I know them because I pay attention.

I pay attention to everything. It helps that I don't have any kind of day job getting in my way. I hate work. My parents always demanded that I get a job. I insist I'm better off playing video games, surfing the web, and hacking. They finally gave in, just like I knew they would. I've got a pretty decent mancave down in their basement now. They're still relatively young and healthy, but when they die, the house will be all mine.

Like I said, it's easy to keep up with the really important things in life because I devote my time to it. I know the truth about chemtrails, black helicopters, Abu Ghraib, Gitmo, the *Deepwater Horizon,* Roswell, the JFK assassination, 9/11, even the Illuminati and the New World Order.

It's all out there, in one place or another, if you know where to look and where to hack. I do. Either in message boards, Imageboards, Wikileaks, the dark web, or in databases we hack into, if people like me want the information, we can find it.

Some might call me a conspiracy theorist, but I totally reject that term. I don't believe in Q-Anon or Pizzagate…or that the moon landing was faked or any bullshit like that. I know better because I pay attention, and I do my own research, far beyond fuckin' Wikipedia.

I'm not a conspiracy theorist. I'm a realist. I get my information from the real world, unlike all the sheeple out there. I could tell you things that would blow your mind.

In fact, sit back and relax. I'll tell you something now—your mind will be blown higher than any mushroom cloud or flying saucer.

Ever heard of Nellis Air Force Base? Yeah, you probably have. It's a big and remote military installation in the Great Basin Desert, that vast desert in the United States.

Conspiracy theorists are going to tell you that they're hiding something on that base. Guess what, cousin; they're hiding things on every single military base around the world. That's what military bases do. If bases weren't hiding things, they'd all be open to the public.

Nellis, of course, has its secrets, and any conspiracy theorist you've talked to is wrong about what those secrets are. Most will claim Nellis is hiding something about aliens and top-secret aircraft based on alien technology there. Some even claim that's where the fabled Area 51 and Hangar 18 are. They're all wrong.

I know the truth because I spent the time weeding through the bullshit and finding out the truth. It took months, and I even had to sacrifice a lot of my video gaming time to uncover everything, but I got it. Hell, for a week or so there, I didn't even shower.

My mom got so mad at me when she came to collect my laundry. I told her that I was onto something vital there, and if I had time to throw away my pizza boxes and take showers, I would do it. Damn, that lady is a nag. I feel sorry for Dad sometimes.

Anyway, the truth about Nellis isn't aliens or experimental vehicles or weird experiments, really. The truth is both much more mundane and much more spectacular than any of that.

The truth about Nellis is that what they're hiding is a prison. That's the mundane part. You're probably feeling a bit let down by that revelation, right? Well, don't be, because the spectacular part is just who and what is being *kept* in that prison.

Oh, how rude of me. I didn't introduce myself, did I?

Many of you know me as Lord_Bludd_6969. That's the old gaming handle that I've kept as a username ever since. I know…I've told most of you that before. We've probably played some games together by now, even.

My real name is Eli Woslov…and if I ever have kids, I'll forgive them for changing the name.

Then again, I'd have to meet a woman in real life to have actual kids, so...ladies?

Oh, okay, I kind of left you hanging there, didn't I? There I go, building up this whole secret prison in Nellis AFB, and then I start bitchin' about not getting laid.

Okay, back to reality.

Yeah, Nellis is hiding a prison within its confines. It's in the very middle, the most remote part of the Great Basin Desert, in a natural rock structure that the government had secretly hollowed out.

Here's the biggest kicker. There's only one prisoner being held there.

Not one *type* of prisoner. Not one *cellblock* of prisoners. One *single solitary* inmate. The entire prison, all the hollowing-out, and secret construction and misdirection were all done for one *individual* subject.

Why? That's got to be your big question, right? Why? What or who is so damn dangerous that a whole prison had to be built in the middle of the wasteland just to contain that single inmate?

That's when things start falling into place in your mind, huh?

What or who would the government want to keep in a prison in the very middle of the largest desert in the United States?

Why, someone or something deathly allergic to sunlight, of course.

And it would have to be a very powerful someone to warrant such an effort, right?

Are the wheels turning yet?

Yeah, you feel me.

Either Nellis Air Force Base is hiding the world's most evil Xeroderma Pigmentosa patient, or they've imprisoned a vampire there.

Spoiler warning: It's the latter.

What's even more fascinating is that the prisoner is a *lady* vampire. Yeah, and from what I can tell, she's hot, too.

The government calls her "Lucia". I'm not sure if that's her real name, a pseudonym she's adopted over the years, or if it's just a government codename.

I haven't been able to uncover *everything* just yet. But I will.

What I do know is that she's been there for decades. They built the prison back in the 1950s after they arrested Lucia somewhere around the outskirts of Berlin.

Since then, they've fed her enough blood to keep her healthy, and they've had some top scientists working on the possibility of turning her unique case of vampirism into a weapon for the military. So far, it hasn't happened, at least not that I've found.

They don't want to kill her, but they're sure as hell not going to let her go.

During the day, she's kept in a heavy stone and steel sarcophagus at the center of the prison. Each passageway is lined with mirrors that redirect the sunlight at all hours directly onto her tomb. If she tries getting out, she dies. Period.

She's given three hours, not all together, to get out and stretch her legs during each day when she is fed, her vitals are taken, and any needed tests are run while the mirrors face away from her. If she tries to escape, Lucia burns in the light.

During the night, she is completely quarantined. Artificial sunlight made from UV lamps and every other radiation simulation floods the chamber around her coffin, making sure she never tries escaping.

And they've covered all the bases, too. Every bit of math has been done to ensure that even if all redundant systems failed, Lucia still wouldn't be able to get away.

For example, let's review Scenario C3344-A from the containment document I hacked. In this scenario, Lucia manages to break out of her coffin just as all the power goes out for the ultraviolet projectors. Let's say she breaks past the guards around the exits and their lasers, crucifixes, garlic, and holy water all fail to keep her contained.

Even then, Lucia's power levels, based on the amount of sustenance she's been given, would not be enough to get her across the desert and into shelter before sunrise. She would beg to be let back into her dark casket. That is, *if* she survived the hundreds of thousands of land mines in the sand. Whew!

And that's just one of hundreds of contingency scenarios they've outlined for her containment.

She ain't going shitwhere, man!

That leads me back to my original point about boredom being the most severe form of torture.

Have you ever been sick to the point that you couldn't get out of bed? You try entertaining yourself with television, games, the internet and books, but eventually, everything bores you, and you just get irritated. You know how your legs and back stiffen up and crack when you move? Right, and this only makes you more annoyed, and the boredom never ends?

Imagine that feeling lasting not for a couple of days or a week, but every single day for seventy-five years. You're alone in the dark, fed enough to survive based on health and energy calculations, you're surrounded by men whose job it is to keep you locked down, and you don't even have a book, magazine, game, TV show, or website to entertain you.

That's Lucia's life, or un-life as it may be.

And for what? Just because of what she is. She can't exactly stop being a vampire, can she?

Needless to say, I sympathize with the poor girl.

So that's why I'm on this quest to get her out of there. Yeah, good old three-hundred-twenty-five-pound Eli Woslov: Lord_Bludd_6969 himself. I'm gonna rescue a fair maiden. Me.

I defy you to tell me what "conspiracy theorist" could do something like that!

Don't worry. I'm not getting caught. I've got some help. And all this I'm writing now, well, it won't be seen unless I disappear. If I drop a semaphore file once every week, my SFTP procedures won't post all this to the internet. If I disappear, the world will know.

Yeah, this is one secret that won't stay on the Dark Web forever, boys and girls.

Stay tuned.

*

Well, it's been a fascinating few weeks.

First, I've made new connections, and I've secured a way onto the base. Second, I've knocked off a bit of weight. I begged my dad for a treadmill, and he said something sarcastic about how much my big ol' butt needed it (asshole), and he bought me one. It's a great deal of work, but I want to be in fighting form for my, you know, mission.

I've also gotten more information for my quest. I had to use the ARPANET remnants that are still connected to the military networks for the hack. It's all text, but it's enough to break into the areas I need. And there are some juicy tidbits up there.

More than that, I found out that Lucia isn't German. She was arrested in Germany, sure, but she's actually Wallachian, which makes her Romanian. Sexy, right?

But it gets better.

When she was arrested, they found paraphernalia on her that hinted at her origins. She carried a five-hundred-year-old sigil of the *Societas Draconistarum*, the Order of the Dragon.

Do you know what that means? Based on the dates and region, it means Lucia is most likely part of the House of Drăculești. That means this vampire babe might just be the bride of Count Dracula himself.

I'm so excited I can't even believe it!

I wonder how grateful she's going to be when I rescue her. I bet she'll fall in love with me right on the spot. Nobody's been nice to her in three-quarters of a century. She's sure to love me, right?

Right.

Don't worry. I'm still dropping the semaphore files. The government hasn't caught onto me yet, and they're not going to.

In two weeks, I'm taking a bus to Nevada, and the real adventure's gonna begin. I'm gonna blow the lid off Nellis' super-secret prison and their super-secret prisoner, too.

The Bride of Dracula will be the Bride of Eli "Lord_Bludd_6969" Woslov. Word is bond.

*

I've been too busy to update this document, so let me do it now.

Lots going on…I'm nervous. I feel like it's the week before my wedding night. Yeah, I realize it's probably still too soon to count on losing my virginity to a goddess like Lucia. But come on. How could she resist?

And I'm down to a svelte 294 pounds now. Yeah, nervousness has caused me to miss some meals. I'm still using the treadmill, so I look good. Lucia will also think so, I'm sure.

Just her and me in that sandy chamber at night. UV projectors off. Moonlight. I can't wait.

I can't wait!

Our story is so romantic that we'll be telling this to our great-grandchildren. That is, if vampires can have babies. I'll ask her later. Or maybe we'll just "keep trying" till we're sure.

That's the fun part, right?

Oh, you'll like this. Turns out I've pinpointed the exact right spot where Lucia's prison is. I plugged the loose coordinates into Google Earth, and what did I find? A big NOTHING!

Yep. All the paths, roads, sand waves, telephone poles, cacti and rocks; they all just stop for about a square mile. The government really didn't think we'd notice that, eh? Ha!

So even if I can't rely on my new contacts, I'll know where she is.

I'll find her. I'll save her. She's gonna love me.

Time to drop another semaphore file, and then I'm packing for my trip.

*

I'm here. The bus ride was boring as hell, but nothing compared to what my darling Lucia has been going through for longer than I've been alive. I've got to remember that. With all that torture and the boredom and irritation, she's had it worse than me, or anybody.

That's one reason why I love her.

I kind of need a shower, but I haven't had time. I sweat a lot. Plus, my hemorrhoids hurt. Luckily, the bus stopped at a lot of fast-food joints, so I got to try some delicacies in various states I've never been to. Taco John's is my favorite.

But speaking of food, that was my way onto the base.

See, when you come to the checkpoint, you just need to say you're going to The Pub, which is a restaurant here on the base. They let you in, totally. It's not even that uncommon. Other bases also do it, I've found.

So here I am, having a beer and waiting for my contact.

In the chat rooms that my online friends and I started, I got lots of help. Hackers and truthers like me tend to give each other assistance when we need it. It's a super cool community, especially for a bunch of guys you've never met. One of my mission allies, a dude I used to roleplay with online, hacked a guy's cloud and found all these gay romance and sex pictures between him and a military man of certain distinction on this base.

Who cares, right? Gays in the military aren't even frowned upon anymore. Well, his wife would sure care. His three kids would surely care. And the military does care if you commit adultery, which that military man surely did. So right now, I'm waiting for him. He's going to get me into the restricted area. I've already printed and laminated my phony IDs, so from there, it's a straight shot.

The next several hours are going to be the most dangerous of my life, but Lord_Bludd_6969 didn't spend all that time playing Dungeons & Dragons without learning a little *something* about courage, am I right?

*

Where to begin?

The plan went well. Actually, the plan went *too* well, up to a point.

For all my bravado, I really thought the United States Military and one of its most secret black ops locations would have been harder to get into.

I guess they figured that military bases are impenetrable anyway, nobody knows about this desert prison, and nobody would have the cojones to go there if they did.

But cojones, I got.

That's not to say it was easy. The Air Force thought of just about everything. A single tram is allowed in and out of the prison, and it's open air, like the kind they use for the Universal Studios Tour. That way, if Lucia managed to get to it, she wouldn't have any shelter from the sun.

Even the biohazard gear and the clean suits are made especially to degrade under UV light, in case Lucia got smart and stole a full-body covering to crawl across the desert in.

Yeah, they thought of everything except Eli Woslov.

The military guy with the lover boy on the side came through and got me into a restricted area. Using my phony ID (it checked out hitch-free after my buddy hacked into the database and plugged in my Kanban scan), he got me onto the tram with the science team. Then, it was just a case of staying behind. Lucky for me, the real scientists were, for the most part, fat dudes with beards, too. Okay, yeah, so I guess I've gained a few pounds back. Sue me.

All I really had to do was hide until nightfall, which I did.

Lucia's cell is on the top level for maximum sunlight flooding. Although there are guards on standby below, only two guards at each of only two entries keep her secure after sunset. As it turned out, they weren't even wearing gas masks.

Know who was wearing a gas mask? Eli Woslov, that's who.

I crept up the steps and dropped a canister of knockout gas, putting out the first two guards. Then I used their console, first to disable the alarms. Second, I used it to lock the portals to the top level. Third, to open the cell and fourth, to turn off the UV projectors…fifth and finally, to open the other side of the cell. I rolled a second can of knockout gas to the second set of guards, and they were out before they could call anything in.

I felt smart, at least for that moment.

I took a minute to catch my breath. After all, this was the biggest moment of my entire life. No, I don't mean that I had broken into a secure military installation and incapacitated the guards. I meant because I was about to meet the love of my life.

Slowly and deliberately, I shut down all the locks to Lucia's sarcophagus, and I heard the magnetic seals shut down.

I pushed the stone slab atop her coffin to the side and then lifted the steel door to, at long last, see her.

Immediately, I felt pity for her. It was worse than I realized.

She was lying on the cold, hard metal and had only a couple of thin blankets to lie on and to cover herself. Yes, they kept her nude. She was treated worse than a lab animal, which I guess is what she was to them.

She looked up at me with the darkest black eyes I had ever seen, showing her beauty and her fear. I reached out to her.

"I'm Eli," I told her. "But you can call me… Lord Bludd."

Her look of fear slowly faded, and in what's possibly the happiest moment of my life, Lucia took my hand.

I helped her out of the box and stood her up, getting my first real look at her.

And let me tell you, I wasn't disappointed.

She had the most perfect body I have ever seen. Hard in all the right places, soft in all the right places, and firm in every place.

Her skin, though, didn't look like any human skin I had ever seen. Her skin was slate gray. She almost looked like a living black-and-white photograph.

Her hair was as black as her eyes. She looked through her straight strands at me with her beautiful, dark eyes, still unsure of me.

So, I touched her arm, biding my time before I touched the rest of her, and I told her, "I'm here to rescue you."

I had always wanted to use that line. Luke Skywalker, right?

She reached over to touch my hand, and I saw her long nails and glanced down at her black bush. Damn, she was the most beautiful woman, the most beautiful anything, I had ever seen.

"Oh, how foolish of me," I then said, reaching into my clean suit. "You must be starved."

I produced a pouch of blood I had stolen from a blood drive, and she immediately started sipping from the tube like it was a kid's drink box.

I could see the gratitude in her eyes as she sucked and looked up into mine. My heart fluttered in excitement, lust, love, and anticipation.

I could only imagine what was coming next. With her renewed strength, I hoped and even counted on the idea that she would offer herself to me then and there. It would be our first time of many. Then we'd escape together. Then...who knew?

She finished drinking, and I said, "I'm going to get you out of here, love. You and me." I dared to put my hands on her bare hips and went on. "If you need more blood, there are four airmen to drink from right here. Just tell me, and I'll drag them to you till you're strong enough."

Then I dared to rub my hands up and down her cool, soft, smooth, firm hips with the utmost affection. I was going to show her the love she had been missing for so many torturous years. Then it would be our time.

And again, I was not disappointed.

Lucia did lean in to kiss me, first on the cheek, then on the jaw, then, romantically, on the neck, where her warming tongue separated her lips and gently, playfully touched my skin.

I gasped. No woman had ever kissed me like that. It felt so sensual and romantic and perfect.

I slowly raised my hands from her hips to her ribs, readying myself to caress and massage her firm, naked breasts with their barely discernible nipples, nearly as gray as her skin.

I pulled her back slightly, ready to look into her eyes and kiss her lips for the first time before letting my hands explore her perfect, bare body.

56

But Lucia did not follow my lead. Her lips stayed where they were, only parting slightly. And then I realized just why she wasn't moving. Her fangs replaced her tongue, and she bit down hard into my jugular vein.

"No, Lucia, no," I screamed, fighting her back. "Not me, not me! I'm here to save you! I'm your man!"

But all I heard back from her was the hungry *glug, glug, glug* as she swallowed, draining me of my blood.

"I've got food for you," I croaked in shocked betrayal. "Airmen! The guards! I'm here to *help* you."

Lucia was too strong for me to fight. She had me in her grasp. I soon realized what an idiot I was. How stupid was I?

The government was treating her like an animal because, in essence, that is what she is. Lucia isn't human. She's no different than a wild wolf. She could strike at any time. It was just her nature. Here, I had been planning to make love to her; instead...I was her midnight snack.

Stupid fucking Eli.

When I was at my weakest, Lucia's movements changed. Instead of sucking, I heard some clicking sounds in her throat, and she regurgitated something back into my veins. Some kind of bile or maybe just blood, refined by her body into something else. I'll never know.

All I know is that any thoughts I once had of her being my bride died then. Instead, I was Lucia's servant. She had sired me. I wasn't exactly a vampire. I was something like Renfield, halfway there, still able to face sunlight.

Still able to serve her as her familiar.

Her *virgin* familiar, goddammit.

Without speaking, she started to give me instructions. She said she left me alive to serve her and fulfill my promise to get her out of there. She was only making sure I did so.

She would next feed on the fallen guards while I implemented my plan.

But I still had a tiny bit of free will left.

So, I walked out into the night, thinking about how all this started. I was just some dumb hacker and, yeah, I'll admit it, Conspiracy Theorist. I had stumbled upon this theory; for once in my life, I was right.

I'm writing this now because I want the world to know what happened. Maybe they can prepare for her before she reaches populated areas. I won't be stopping the upload anymore. No.

I won't be with her either. I won't even be alive.

I don't mean that I'll be undead. No. Here I am typing this onto my satellite phone, standing on the ledge high above the minefield. I'm going to drop myself into the mines. Surely, a big enough blast will kill even a half-vampire.

Then Lucia would be fucked.

Just not in the way I had hoped.

Yeah, I can see the mines, just like in the charts I illegally downloaded. I know just where to jump to blow myself up. This document will be posted for all to read, and the secret will be out, and Lucia will have no help at all.

That'll slow her down for a while.

I'm sorry, world. I am such a stupid loser. But it's all about to be over. All I must do is save this document, then jump.

And I'll do that in just a minute.

Lucia, my beautiful Lucia, is in my mind again. She's calling me. She needs me.

I'll go see what she wants, and *then* I'll blow myself up.

The document can go out *after* I help Lucia and *after* I blow myself up.

And it will.

I promise.

Scott Should've Lived

Walter Wiseman

Fuck.

FuckfuckfuckFUUUUUCK!

Goddammit. Scott is dead!

His skin and flesh melted down into a puddle of human soup as one of those things climbed out of his carcass. A week ago, everything was normal; the world was chugging along at its usual mind-numbing pace, and I was cool with that.

That's a bitch ass lie. I hated my life. I was twenty-five, working at the same UPS store that I got a job at straight out of high school, and I was bored out of my mind every bitch ass day. Making sure there's enough packing tape stocked on the shelves and printing endless runs of shipping labels over the course of an entire eight-hour shift eats away at your soul.

But compared to this? Pure nirvana. These days, everything is chaos. Surviving even the next minute envelopes my whole life. I never had to do anything like this before. I was always comfortable and didn't want anything that I didn't have. I lived simply, and I had a relatively easy life.

Then six days ago, the whole world went batshit. Out of nowhere, these alien bastards started popping up and spreading like locusts across the continents, devouring everyone in their wake. City street gutters were clogged with the soupy remains of tens of thousands of people. The stench that began to rise was...*pleasant.*

See, these creatures exuded very good smells. Green smells like freshly cut grass. Heady scents of roses, honeysuckle, and even pine emanated from their flesh. I have no idea if they're plant-based or whatever...I just know they smell goddamn yummy.

But they're deadly as shit.

My roommate, Scott, was the first one to hear about what was happening. His social media pages were flooded with the news. He hollered for my ass to show me. I thought it was a load of bullshit until we heard screaming outside—there was our neighbor across the street, Jeannie, turning into goo as one of the creatures crawled out of her. I'd never seen anything as remotely disturbing as watching one of those monsters hatching out of poor Jeannie. Remembering how what became of her skin and muscle had slowly oozed across the pavement like a giant, bloody-snot colored slug gave me chills.

The Incredible Melting Jeannie was day one. I'll be honest. We were a little twisted up about it. I even got a ball cramp that day. But by day two, Scott and I knew we were in real danger. These fuckin' monsters from space, you can never really tell if what you're looking at is a face or some whole other shit. Their eyes and mouths seemed to coalesce out of nowhere on what I guess is their...head? The shape is certainly head-ish. Hard to explain because their heads and bodies seemed to all be part of the same shape, a somewhat globular, jet-black mass. That's another thing; the sound these things made was like the music wooden wind chimes make when the hollow wooden tubes clunk and clank together. And these fuckers are fast! They have four spindly spider-type legs that click-click-click when they move, so they're on top of you before you can say, "Holy shit! That's not a plant!"

When we went out on our foraging expeditions, we noticed that a few stray hunters, almost like sentries, would roam around during the day to get a random human who wasn't paying close enough attention to their surroundings. But at night, they scoured the streets and buildings, their jet-black skin helping them disappear into the shadows. We knew we had to get out of the city, like *now*. We packed only a few things, hopped in his Range Rover, and headed for the country, not even once looking back.

We drove as fast as we could further away from the city. We were hellbent on making it into the mountains and just figuring out a game plan after we felt we were a safe distance away from the genocide. We were 23 miles from the only dirt road leading up the mountains when we decided to stop in this shitty little town for some last-minute supplies. Just 23 more fuckin miles! We came across a gas station with the lights still on, so we pulled in to refuel.

"You think these pumps work or what?" Scott asked.

"Maybe. Lights do."

We parked in front of the general store and surveyed the area from the safety of the car, only getting out when we felt everything was okay. There was no movement, no loud alien wood chime chatter, just the placid breath of the earth on our skin. But it was quiet, a little too quiet.

We stretched out in what began to feel like oppressive silence. I told Scott that we should hurry up, get what we needed, and get the hell up that mountain. He readily agreed. We slowly crept up to the store's front doors and peeked through the glass. Not a creature was stirring, not even a mouse...because he or she was lying dead at the front of aisle 3.

I pulled the door open as silently as possible and made my way inside. The electricity was still on, but some of the perishables had definitely gone bad. The stink of rotting fruits and vegetables wafted through the air. The sickly sweet scent teased the nose. We split up to get our supplies, light pop rock playing

60

over the store speakers. Nothing like listening to Sheryl Crow sing about Santa Monica Boulevard during an apocalypse seemed far too fitting. Lyrics could use a little jimmying. All I wanna do-oo-o…is not be plant muck. I got a feelin'…you get the idea.

Pulling my old backpack off my back, I made my way to the liquor section. With all this madness going on, I planned on getting fucked up with a bottle of expensive whiskey after we made it out to the middle of nowhere. I searched until I found the most expensive bottle and grabbed it, thrusting it into my bag. For good measure, I grabbed two more. After gathering my emergency (or just whenever) supplies, I went in search of more life-sustaining ones. I made my way down the soup aisle and dumped a whole case of ramen into my bag. Next, I got chips, cookies, and two bottles of water. Proud of my survivalist snack acumen, I wandered somewhat casually around the store until I found Scott.

"I got some first aid stuff, some matches, some packs of lighters, lighter fluid and some other stuff we'll need. Did you get the food?" Scott asked, his voice a whisper.

"Yeah, I got us enough to last quite a while," I said.

"Okay, good. Let's find out which building might have camping supplies. We'll need a tent or two and weapons of some kind, and hopefully some guns," he rasped. Scott definitely sounded like he'd done this before. "If I have to, I'll settle for loose rebar."

"Scott, you definitely sound like you've done this before," I said.

"Shhh! Keep your voice down!" He said intensely. "There could still be one of those things lurking around out here. And yeah, kinda. I was an Eagle Scout, weren't you?"

I sheepishly looked down at my feet, ashamed at being so careless, ashamed that my childhood was more of a 'TV as a babysitter' childhood. It never mattered until now. I like video games.

"Okay, let's go." He cocked his head toward the exit.

It wasn't too hard to find a camping supplies outlet. There were maybe five buildings in the whole town. One had a sign that read: Calvin's Camping Supplies. I was lulled into a false sense of security because it seemed like everything was really going to go our way; we would survive this debacle. I was horribly wrong.

We decided that sharing a tent would be the safest plan of action, so we found a nice, roomy-as-hell six-person motherfucker. We also spared no expense where comfort was concerned, loading up a half dozen sleeping bags, two large air mattresses, and a couple of fluffy pillows each. With everything stowed in the Rover, we were ready to make our final escape from the last vestiges of what was once civilized humanity.

"I'm going to take a piss before we go. You need to?" Scott asked. I shook my head *no*. He went to take his leak on the side of the general store.

The surrealism of my whole situation hit me like an iron right cross from Mike Tyson as I slid into the passenger seat of the car and closed the door. This whole ordeal was totally fuckin' nuts! Fleeing to the mountains from deadly aliens that turned people into flesh slop! I mean, what the actual fuck?!? It was like a bad dream that never ended.

I thought, if this is a dream, what happens if I die?

Scott was returning from his piss, a comical look of exasperation on his face.

He stopped and took a big sniff of the air.

"Do you smell flowers?" he asked. Then it hit him.

He was only a few steps from the car door when one of the blobby plant aliens knocked him to the ground with a flying tackle. I popped that door handle and leaped out of the car, booking straight back into the store. Scott is (well, *was*) a good roommate, but my cowardly sense of self-preservation propelled me to leave him alone to his demise. Like I said, video games—not hero crap. I booked to the back of the store and jumped, mostly, over the meat counter. A meat scale caught my foot, and I tumbled loudly to the ground, racking a rib. Silently screaming, I dragged myself into a corner next to the meat case and breathed my pain and anxiety away. I prayed the beast hadn't seen or heard me and would leave after infecting Scott with its foul seed.

The alien began to make its wooden tube chatter. The dirge got louder and louder until Scott let out a blood-curdling shriek. Then…silence. All was quiet and still again.

I'd never seen it, but I heard stories about what the aliens did to their victims. According to conspiracy theorists, the aliens used a barbed appendage that poked up somewhere from underneath their bodies, and they used it to pierce through a person's belly button to plant a seed. Seed? Egg or larvae? Whatever they did, I knew that Scott would be soup in less than an hour.

And this is where you met me. Remember up there when I was all like, "Scott's dead!" and shit. Frozen in fear. Stalked by the newest edition of pure nightmare fuel. Good buddy outside prepping to be a flesh glob in the parking lot.

Not fun.

One of the store doors opened, and I could hear a soft shuffling. The ugly alien asshole was searching for me. No one knew how they hunted. Whether they used sight, sound, smell, whatever—are they like the animals we have here—if this was like a video game, they would be. And they could be, dammit. Right now, looking at the monstrosities made me feel like we really *do* all live in an alien-made matrix of some kind. I curled up into a tight ball, my breath shallow, undetectable in every sense. I hoped.

And Phil Collins was singing, *Something Happened on the Way to Heaven*. Jesus. This playlist for Armageddon would have been comical if not for the all-pervasive sense of terror. I listened as bottles clinked, bags crinkled, and cans fell over and rolled off the shelves. The sounds would come closer, then go further away, come closer, then ebb. Then flo-oo-ow. Swish up one aisle. Swish down another. Closing in. Christ! This determined predator was doing a thorough sweep of the store!

The only door in the meat department led to the inside of a walk-in freezer. The bitter irony of only dead ends was not lost on me. A bottle hit the ground and shattered at the front of the store, and the irritated thing grumbled to itself. The electricity finally failed, and the beast shut up, which made me tense up into a tighter ball. The stillness dragged on for ten seconds, two minutes, ten minutes. I started to relax. I felt the beast must have moved around.

Nice. I let out a long, slow sigh—

SPLAT!!

A Not-So-Mighty Mouse's little dead body landed in front of me a few seconds later, dead eyes staring straight at me with what seemed like a glazed-over, mocking gaze.

I screamed until my voice was nothing more than a harsh whisper.

As if waiting for this final break in my sanity, the creature made its appearance from over the top of the counter, the sweet scent of lilac permeating the air around it. With a slight jump, it plopped down at my feet and stood staring blindly into my eyes. No longer screaming, I sat shaking from naked fear, knowing this was it. Doo-wop. This was the end. Fin. Done-zo.

The material that it was made from crept over my feet, up my shins, past my knees, and I just sat there. Frozen from fright. Its face before mine, the alien opened two of the most beautiful, golden eyes I had ever seen. The urge to weep at their beauty was almost overwhelming, and a few stray tears did trickle down my cheeks. A smiling mouth materialized, the type of smile your grandma would give you as she snuck you a freshly baked cookie behind your mom's disapproving back. I returned with a joyous grin and almost didn't feel the pain of its impregnating hook-arm stabbing through my belly button into my liver.

We almost made it. Scott and I were this fuckin' close to making it. Oh, well, it could've ended a whole lot worse for me.

Reflecting on my wasted life, consciousness fading, all I could think to myself was, 'the fuckin UPS store, man…'

Them Hills Have Magic

Kasey Hill

I have always said, "Them hills have magic." Most people don't fully comprehend what I mean when I say that. The Appalachians are the oldest mountain range in the world. Running from Canada down to Alabama, its footholds dig deep into the earth, and there is an energy that thumps and hums so loud you can feel it in your bones. It was the home of many Native tribes before the white man took over the land. But even as they destroyed the homes and bodies of the Natives, they couldn't destroy their souls that remained tethered to the land. The Natives understood the power the mountains had in them.

Tribes were left alone in the mountains for the most part. Some lived side by side with the pale faces who had arrived by boat, initially landing in Jamestown and spreading outward. The pale faces didn't have much luck with starvation and the harsh winter cold. The first colony to arrive in what we now call North America was one of the unlucky ones who disappeared without a trace, leaving behind a single word carved into a tree: *Croatoan.* Throughout the years, scholars have tried to come up with answers as to what happened to the people. No bodies or skeletal remains were ever found. Some believed they walked out into the sea to drown. Others believe a Native tribe hunted them down and killed them.

As time went on, Irishmen settled the land as well in what would be known as the Appalachian region. They lived side by side with the Natives and often intermarried with them. The Irish brought their own magic practices from the hills of Ireland, and together, they wove a new style of living. Once the slaves had been freed and moved northward from the bayous of Louisiana, a triune of power was formed. The old magic of the hills of the Appalachians mixed with the magic of Ireland and the conjuring of the Haitian Vodou and hoodoo forming in the Creole parts of the colonies started what would be known as Appalachian folk magic. A Magic that has been passed down through generations and crafted within each family with a subtle difference to distinguish lineage learning.

What many forget is that it wasn't just magic. Folk tales were also born in the hills. Monsters, legends, and myths ran rampant, and those tales spread far and wide. When I say, "Them hills have magic," I'm not just talking about the folk magic they practice. I am talking about the ethereal energy the mountains have that predates the arrival of man in the New World. Those monsters, myths, and legends came from something older and darker than the boogeyman tales of monsters under your bed or in your closet. The Irish mingled easily with the Natives because they had one thing in common that goes unlooked in modern storytelling. The Fae not only lived in the hills of the UK, but they also lived in the hills of the Appalachians.

The Cherokee, in particular, have their tale of the Nûñnë'hï, who were an immortal race of supernatural beings. They weren't ghosts. They weren't nature spirits, and they weren't gods. They were the little people, and the little people took the Cherokee tribe into the mountains to save them from the Trail of Tears…never to be seen again. But this is just one tale that they had in common with the Irish. The other tale? In Irish mythology, they have what is called a pooka. It's a type of fairy that could shapeshift into anything, including human form. Many of the common translations for this fairy in the old world called it an evil devil. In Native mythology—and I say Native mythology because this myth isn't particular to just one tribe—they called it a Skinwalker.

You will know when a Skinwalker is around. You will smell their abject reek. They stink of decay and rotting meat, like an opossum that's been dead on the side of the road for two weeks baking in the hundred-degree rays of the sun. The smell isn't the worst part. Skinwalkers are believed to be shapeshifting witches. And I don't mean witches like the mountain folk. I mean the witches that the medieval stories are about. The evil ones that could turn into anything and even unlock your door by doing so. In the old world, the mountain magic folk were called things like Cunning Folk or, in the case of the Irish, Bean Feasa, the seeress. Many people believe the church corrupted the origins of witchcraft and tells the tales of innocent, outspoken women who were burned at the stake. However, the magic folk knew that there were "evil witches" who shapeshifted and took the lives of people. The infamous story by the Grimm Brothers, Hansel and Gretel, was just one of the stories the mountain folk in the old world spoke about. Those witches were the Skinwalkers of the Native legends.

Skinwalkers could mimic the voices of the people from whom they took form, as well as worm their way into the heads of people to cajole them out into the open. My Mawmaw Cricket warned me several times about being out at night. Living in the hills of West Virginia, we were surrounded by the Appalachian Mountains. We lived on the other side of Spruce Mountain in Sycamore Holler. I heard all the warnings growing up. Beware the Wendigo because it will eat your heart from your carcass. Beware the Raven Mocker because it will steal your heart without leaving a scratch on your body. Beware Aint Peachey because she's looking for her kidnapped baby and will happily take you in its place. But most importantly, don't go outside after dark. Don't whistle after dark. And if you hear someone in the dark, you do not answer them. You do not pay attention to anything that you see after dark, and you get home as fast as you can.

Like most kids, I believed all to be poppy cock. They were just stories to keep inside, so we aren't running around like hoodlums in the neighborhood after dark and getting into mischief. I was a good kid. I wasn't going out at night to drink and smoke meth. Quite honestly, the times I did go out were on the Sabbat days, and I don't mean church either. We went to church on Sundays, but on the Sabbat days, we normally had a big shindig. The older folk would bring their banjos and guitars, and we would jig and flatfoot even past sundown while they drank their shine. They never did anything magical, though. Magic was what I craved in my life. I wanted a traditional sabbat celebration where we called forth the Lady of the Mountains and paid homage to her. I mean, of course, we left offerings at the bonfire, but you just couldn't feel her there. I wanted to feel her. The actual Sabbat celebrations wasn't for the kids. I knew grownups did their own thing after the barbecue. I wanted to know what those things were.

My oldest brother was left in charge to babysit us that night while our parents went out like they usually did. What they didn't know was that Timmy always had his girlfriend come over after they left. He'd leave the TV on for us in the living room with a plate of dessert and sneak off to his room to do whatever he was doing with her. The younger of us was always put to bed, leaving me, my older brother Jeff, and my sister Brittney, who was the oldest, sitting in front of the TV. After I finished eating the dump cake Timmy had given me, I fake-yawned and stretched my arms out.

"I think I am going to head to bed," I told Britney and Jeff as I stood from my seat.

I walked my empty plate to the kitchen sink, rinsed it off, and put it in the dishwasher.

"Don't do it," Jeff said, not breaking his gaze from the TV.

"Do what?" I asked innocently.

"You know what. Don't do it," he replied. "Aint Peachey will get ya."

"I am going to bed," I said, walking in the direction of my room. "I have no idea what you're talking about."

"Even worse, the Skinwalker will get ya," Britney chimed in, also not breaking her focus on the TV.

"You two need a hobby," I replied, opening and closing my door behind me.

"Mothman!" Jeff shouted just as my door shut. "Don't forget the Mountain Dew and Slim Jims offering!"

I rolled my eyes. "Assholes."

I walked over to my window and popped it open, climbing out. It was hardly a drop to the ground since we lived in a mobile home. I quietly slid my window back closed so no critters would get in while I was gone. Couldn't have Mom and Dad questioning how they got into my room since I wasn't supposed to be out. I peeked around the corner of the house to see that the adults had all finally gathered together near the trail that heads up the side of the mountain. They were all dressed in crimson robes and held torches. I smiled. This was it.

The trail they took was the same trail Old Man Thompson used to go 'senging during its peak season. I kept my distance as they made their way upward to the top. I walked in darkness and had to find my footing in the right place so I wouldn't break a twig and signal them all to my location. I straggled further and further behind until I could barely see their torches. I reached the top and looked in both directions for any sign of where they had gone. I saw the faint light disappearing into the thicket to the right and took off running, hoping a stray quartz boulder wouldn't take me down on the way. As I grew closer to where they had disappeared, a faint smell of dead animals infiltrated my nostrils. I hoped to God I didn't step into its rotting body, but the smell didn't get closer, so it must have been on the further edge of the clearing.

Pine trees ripped at my face, and briar bushes clawed at my legs as I trudged through the woods following their light. I should have jumped into a pair of pants before leaving. I didn't think about the briar bushes or the possible swarms of mosquitoes that could eat me alive out here. The light began to grow brighter within a grove of trees. I got as close to the edge of their circle as I could without being seen. All of the adults stood around a stone altar filled with candles, incense, and jars of moonshine. Their torches had been placed in metal holders so the circle would be lit up with light. Their heads were covered with their robe hoods, so I couldn't tell who was who, but when the person in the middle spoke to everyone, I immediately recognized the voice of Old Man Thompson.

"Tonight, we gather here under the Thunder Moon to not only offer up to the moon Goddess but also to acknowledge the union of the Sabbat God with his consort. We celebrated day, and we celebrated night, and now, we pay our respects."

The circle moved as each person laid something on the altar as an offering.

"These offerings to the Old Gods come with a petition and shall protect us and our loved ones from the evil that walks these hills."

More and more of those in the circle laid things on the altar. I could hardly make out what anything was, but I did see some sort of symbol fashioned from what could only have been grape vines, and possibly pine slabs.

"The Old Gods of our heritage—Haitian, Irish, and Native—have always answered our call for protection. Our valley stays safe from the Wendigo. Our properties stay safe from Aunt Peachey. And our children stay safe from the Skinwalker."

What the fuck?

"Every person who has joined here tonight has left their offering as we have done for the last 200 years. In doing so, we complete the circle of trust and love. Join me as I call upon the Lady of the Hills and the Devil himself to aid us in our petition."

The fucking Devil? Are we Satanic?

"Cailleach, hear our plea! Protect us from the evil shapeshifters who followed our people to this place."

He raised the jar of moonshine he held up to the sky and then took a drink of it. The jar was passed around the circle, and everyone took a drink. When it came back to him, he set the jar on the altar.

"Papa Legba, hear our plea! Protect us from the evil presence which has followed our people to this place!"

He pulled something from within his robe. He struck a lighter and placed a strange cigarette between his lips and lit it. He inhaled the smoke and then passed it around the circle for each of them to do as well. Once it reached him, he ducked it out and placed it on the altar.

Oh, the Devil himself. Gotcha.

"Nûñnë'hï, hear our plea! Protect us from the evil that existed long before man walked these hills!"

He removed a knife from his robe and very carefully cut the palm of his hand. He passed the knife around the circle and took a spot within the circle. Once the knife came back to him, he put it away in his robe, and they all held their hands out in front of them, making fists so they could squeeze blood out to form a circle of blood.

"These are our offerings!" he said and raised his hands in the air.

Everyone in the circle did the same. "So mote it be!" they all said in unison.

Is this it? That's all?

"This circle is closed," Old Man Thompson announced. "You all get back to your homes now."

The circle turned into a line. They each took their torch from the respective holder and walked out on the trail I could now see. I didn't dare make a move to give away my position, so I waited once more for the light of their fires to disappear before I walked into the circle they had left. I pulled my phone from my pocket and turned the flashlight on to look at everything they had left on the altar. Most everything was handcrafted offerings with symbols on them.

They all had the same symbol, but a different mark was left, I guess to indicate which family it belonged to, like a family crest. As I was nosing around, I smelled the dead animal smell again. This time, it was stronger.

"How did they even get through all of that without gagging?" I mumbled to myself.

A twig snapped off to my right in the thicket of the trees, and I quickly shone my light over there. Bears were notorious in these parts, and I wasn't going to get eaten. I quickly scanned the area but didn't see anything.

"Must've been a coon," I told myself reassuringly.

"Leeanna!" a voice called out.

Shit, Mom.

"Leeanna, come here now!" she said again.

I was busted. I began walking to the sound of the voice that had called my name.

"Leeanna!" it shouted louder, but this time, there was a warble to the voice, and I stopped.

"Mom?" I asked, shining my light down the trail.

I didn't see anybody.

"Mom," I called again.

Twigs began to snap like popcorn, popping on the stove as something ran around the outside of the trees. My flashlight couldn't keep up with the creature's path. It was so fast that I could barely discern what streaks I saw pass before my eyes. I began to run down the trail the adults had taken—all the while, branches broke behind me as something large ran through them. I entered the clearing, and the rotting stench of meat once again hit my face. I heaved and once more passed my light around the area. A low growl sounded behind me at the edge of the woods, and I turned around to see if it was a bear. As soon as my light hit the creature, a sound very similar to the sound of dinosaurs in Jurassic Park erupted from the mouth of the thing. I backed up and stumbled over one of the quartz rocks that jutted from the ground, landing on my ass as it began to walk toward me slowly.

It stood upright on its back legs like a human, but it was nothing but a skeleton with fleshy strings of meat and tendons covering it. As it walked toward me, skin and blood vessels began to grow all over it. I scrambled to my feet, and by the time it was just ten feet away, I stared back at a spitting image of myself.

"No," I whispered to myself. "No, Skinwalkers aren't real."

"Skinwalkers aren't real," the thing mimicked.

It sounded just like me. It looked just like me. It licked its lips, and an insidious grin flashed across its face, showing razor-sharp incisors for every tooth.

"You smell so good," the thing said as it closed its eyes and sniffed the air. "I can smell your tiny little pituitary gland all the way from here."

I backed away slowly so as not to cause the creature to leap at me.

"You're going to taste like magic," it warbled. "Mountain folk always taste like magic."

I turned on my heels and sprinted for the trail that led down the mountain with the Skinwalker running full stop behind me. The light from my phone bounced around the trees, and I saw red eyes all around me. Growls escaped the lips of whatever monsters lurked in the shadows. More of those deafening roars the Skinwalker had made as a beast filled the night air on both sides of me.

"We are everywhere, Leeanna," the mimic howled. "And when we eat you, we will feast on everyone in that hollow. They won't know any better than to believe we are you."

"They will know!" I screamed as I continued running.

"We will have your body, your pretty face, your voice, and all your memories," it said as it grew closer and closer.

The thicket crashed around me as more of them joined to chase me. I could see the beams of the streetlights cutting through the treetops. I was almost there.

"We will start with your little sister Carrie first," it continued. "And then, little Bobby."

"No!" I screamed.

"And then Britney next. Then Jeff and Timmy. Finally, your mom and dad," it went on. "My family will be your family, and there's nothing that Cailleach or Papa Legba or any of the people you pray to can do to stop us."

I reached the end of the trail and saw my house. All of the lights had been turned off, but I knew they would hear me banging on the door. My lungs were burning, and my body stung from all of the branches and briars that had ripped at my body. My legs ached. A muscle cramp was beginning to form in my side, but I pushed harder, running straight for my front door. I jumped the steps two at a time and twisted the doorknob. It was locked. I began to bang on the door.

"Let me in!" I screamed. "Let me in!"

A light came on in the living room, and I saw my mom and dad open the curtain.

"Mom! Dad! Let me in!" I screamed. "They're coming for me!"

70

They stared at me through the window.

"It's me! I am not a Skinwalker!" I cried. "Let me in before they eat me!"

The door unbolted and opened, and I fell through the door, kicking it shut. I got up and ran to the window to peer out. All around the house, the Skinwalkers stood. Mom and Dad stood beside me, looking out the window.

"They're real," I whispered, panting heavily.

"What have you done?" Mom asked me as she peered around the house.

"I followed y'all tonight," I began.

Dad spun me around and shook me by my shoulders. "You weren't supposed to be there!"

"I'm sorry," I cried.

Mom ran for the phone and dialed a number. "They're here," she said as soon as someone answered.

They replied, and Mom said, "Okay."

She hung the phone up and walked into the kitchen. She returned with a knife, walking straight over to me.

"No, no," I pleaded. "I am sorry. Please don't kill me and feed me to them!"

Dad held me fast while Mom pried one of my arms up. She sliced through my hand with the knife, and I let out a yelp. Dad quickly covered my mouth so I wouldn't wake anyone up. They walked me to the door.

"No!" I cried as tears streamed down my face. "Please," I sobbed.

They opened the door, took my hand they had cut, and pressed my hand against the door to leave a bloody handprint. They quickly shut the door as the Skinwalkers ran up the porch. When they hit the door, they howled.

I stepped through the crowd of Skinwalkers and stared at myself in the safety of the house. I spoke directly to me, "You are safe for now. But you will mess up again. Or another one of you will be curious, and when that happens, we won't hesitate with the cat and mouse game."

They vanished into thin air, and the putrid smell followed.

Mom wrapped my hand in a dish towel as she and Dad began telling me all about what they do after sundown on the Sabbats and why the kids are never invited.

"I used to have a sister," Mom began. "Her name was Debbie. She was just like you. Always wanting to be in with the grownups. Pretty. You look just like her."

"What happened to her?" I asked as she began to clean my hand and wrap it in a bandage.

"She got curious like you one night and snuck out," Mom replied.

"And?" I asked.

"She never came home," Mom replied. "A few weeks later, late at night, we heard her calling from outside."

"How come she didn't come inside?" I asked.

"Because you have to invite a Skinwalker in," Mom replied. "It wasn't Debbie. It was just her skin."

"Invite them in?" I asked.

"An open door. An unlocked window. That's how they get in," she replied.

"My blood on the door?" I asked.

"Marked this house safe," Dad replied. "Your blood is now tied to the ceremony. It only works if everyone there leaves a blood sacrifice."

"Is that why Debbie was taken?" I asked.

Mom nodded. "They hunted it down and trapped it," she replied.

"What happened to it?" I asked.

"I don't know. They never told us," she replied.

"Did they ever find your sister's body?" I asked as she taped the last bit of tape to the gauze.

"No," she replied. "And that's enough story time. It's time for you to go to bed."

"Are the woods ever safe?" I asked. "Not after dark," she replied as she walked me to my room. "That was just one of the creatures that live in these parts."

"So, everything is true," I asked as I took my shoes and socks off.

"Everything is true," she replied.

"Even Aint Peachey?" I asked as I climbed into bed.

"Especially Aint Peachey," she replied as she tucked me in.

"It had your voice," I told her as she was walking out of the room.

"What?" she asked as she spun around.

"It called to me with your voice," I reiterated. "It said my name with your voice."

The color drained from her face. "Goodnight, Leeanna."

"What does that mean, though?" I asked as she was closing my door.

She stopped. "It means she's back."

"Who?" I asked.

"The one that took Debbie and spared me," she replied. "Debbie didn't go alone."

I lay in bed trying to go to sleep, but I just couldn't. I was still completely terrified by what had happened. I looked over at my window, and my heart skipped a beat. I jumped out of bed and ran over to it, throwing the lock back into place. I climbed back in bed and stared up at the ceiling, trying to think of fuzzy panda bears, cute kittens, and unicorns. As my brain slowly unwound, I felt the exhaustion from the depleted adrenaline that coursed through my body finally take hold. My eyes grew heavy, and I was close to falling asleep. I rolled over on my side to get comfortable when the sound of a creaking door jostled me from my doze. I turned my head toward my closet door as it slowly began to creep open.

"Leanna…"

How I Got My Second Brain

John Reti

Don't ask me why I was in the desert. There are times when things need to be moved from one place to another. That's all you need to know. It was my birthday, my party. I drove for twelve hours, that's half a day's driving—normal enough for a suburban dad, but needless to say, that ain't me. I was cruising, picking out a spot where I could handle my gravedigger's task. Sand, water, can you smell the air? I could. My mind floated. I first thought it was a rock, but there the sucker was, just a' starin' at me, and last I knew, rocks ain't got eyes. I would have thought it was a mirage when I first witnessed it, but why would I mirage myself up a birthday present? Aside from the eyes, the whole thing was wrapped like any gift. I guess my benefactor (so to speak) left the eyes out to catch mine. If I left it for myself and forgot, I surely picked the right spot to do it. When I got out of the car, I felt like the only man on the planet.

I stepped in the sand, thinking, *what ya got for me there, fella?* Wrapped. A bow tied around it, and some chiffon puffing out around where its ears ought to be. In a box with oversized eye holes cut into it. With a *big* red bow. Just a' sittin' in the sand.

Lastly, there was a gift tag taped to it.

Blank eyes glared up at me through the holes. I got the idea that its eyes were on stalks. Whodunit? Who was the stuffer who'd stuffed you in here for me? My brain is playing tricks on me. It does that a lot. I didn't think the cactuses and vultures were having a birthday party. They could've been, though. There are stranger things in Heaven and Earth, oddities…you'd never guess.

For you, the gift tag proclaimed.

What a coincidence! *I* was me, and I had been all my life. I squatted down next to it and worked at the wrap with my hands. Large, wide, calloused, my hands. Good at undoing, these hands, undoing as they were undoing right now. I thought of the work I still had ahead. It was a lot…I hurt momentarily and then got the lid off the box and tossed it aside.

The googly eyes of a mannequin head stared back up at me. I laughed long and loud. A fucking plastic person and not even the good parts—as I was about to kick the present down the road, and the eyes opened—my own followed suit. I felt the lids stretch my temples.

"Hellooo!" the plastic head blurted, its voice awkward and robotic as if it hadn't finished learning how to speak.

I couldn't understand how it talked in the first place and asked, "What the fuck, man?" I danced upon my shadow, I jumped the fucken me, the fucken me thing sang the answer in pixelated joy as it rang up from the ground. I picked the thing up and started to look for a pole string or a wind-up contraption, not to mention any kind of microphone device. I gripped all four sides of the mannequin's head more vigorously than the time I got kicked out of the mall. I grabbed the thing by its little plastic lips—who the fuck is doing this—eye-to-eye with the block of wood with a human face expecting to get the uncanny sense of cold plastic like a tingle in tooth and belly and though I enjoyed that weirdness in the stare and yes, a certain cold…it was not empty like I expected, there was something there. Animation…like life.

I lifted the head, threatening to cast it down towards the sand or maybe slam dunk the bastard into the ocean. What the hell…if I had any sense, I'd have smashed that thing onto the hot sandy ground without a second thought—luckily for that thing, I got no sense…more lost than a legless man yearning for fresh kicks at a shoe store.

It says to me:

Here to assimilate, here to assimilate.

I dropped it on the ground too late. The mouth puked tentacles. Slithering things wrapped around my waist—I pulled my handy-dandy pocketknife as its thrashing tentacle got hold of my arm. I slashed, the cut hissed—a purple ooze splashed, mucking up my flesh. The tentacles fell to the ground, *ahhhhhhhhh* one for mankind, I cried. I dropped the thing and gave it a kick, and the head cracked and rolled along the sand.

Done, I collapsed into the sand and caught my breath. I said no to assimilation today.

Me fucken me—it's me I am you ya fucken fuck-augh!

I felt sorry for it. Poor thing, poor like me. I looked over at the gray-scaled pile of tentacles—four of them to be exact—some had found a new way out through the neck and looked like gigantic vocal cords thrashing upon the ground, doing the whole terminal waltz.

Moan. And Roll. Moan. And roll. Groaning of a mannequin head.

Fucken me, fucken me, it whispered.

"Shit. You're dying, ain'tcha buddy?"

"Fucken me," it said, its baritone hollow, fuck. I might not have had a brain, but I had a heart. I went into my car and grabbed the only thing I knew of that fixed all problems—a big ol' bottle of North American booze, the great etheric panacea.

"Fucken meeeee! Fucken meeeeee!" It whimpered.

"Oh now hush, Fucken Me. I got what you need."

I grabbed the mannequin's head. I placed the bottle to a hole in the lips and

I poured it in. The tentacles slithered out of the way so I could get the bottle into its middle.

Ooohhhhhhh ahhhhhh!

"I told ya," I said. "What else is there?"

The head was happy now.

The hour grew late. It was time to leave. I got up. The thing cooed on the ground, sure that I was leaving. It asked, *can I go too?* I looked down and exhaled a little bit of suspicious air; what are you, mind without body, mind without body, mind without body…*ohhhhhh*. That's why you were fucking with me, yup yup yup take with you, take *me* with you, no fucking around? Noo noo noo, no more assimilation? No more assimilation—that is why I now carry a present filled nicely with bubble wrap everywhere I go. That wasn't my only present that day. When I got back to the car and popped the trunk, I saw that the other mannequin I had, this one perhaps a bit softer than the one I'd found now, was gone.

"Drink," Fucken Me said. I gave him one.

Well, why not? I laid the box on the upholstery over the back seat. Sat myself down in the driver's seat, started the car, and drove away from the beach. Now you know how I got my second brain.

Chip on my Shoulder

J.L. Lane

I could hear it, the tick, tick, ticking of it. I couldn't pinpoint where it was coming from, but I knew it was inside of me somewhere. It was lodged into my body, and I could hear the static ticking, almost like it was coming from my brain itself.

I knew what it was, yet I couldn't recall a time when it could have been implanted. A ticking chip monitoring my every move was stuck inside of me. I don't know if I am supposed to be able to hear it. I doubt it. Chips aren't supposed to be detectable like this. Mine must have been malfunctioning. What would happen to me if it completely broke? Would it harm me? Kill me? It was a chance I wasn't willing to take.

When it first started, it was a small discomfort in my collarbone and the occasional click here and there, something I barely noticed. I figured I had just slept wrong on that side of my body, and the clicks were similar enough to cracking joints from my aging bones for me to dismiss them.

I could not have been further from the truth.

During the days that followed, the pain increased, and the cursed ticking kept getting louder and louder. By day five, it was all I could focus on. The gradual transition from a natural crack to a more electronic click would have been easy to miss for many, but I found myself hyper-fixating on it. It didn't take long for it to affect my sleep. If not for that intolerable sound, the pain was enough to keep me up at night.

It has been 34 days now, and I can still hear it ticking away, sounding closer to my brain than ever.

I have tried to locate it many times. I placed two fingers on my collarbone and pressed down, allowing my hand to travel from one side to the other, but no matter how much I investigated, I could not pinpoint it. So, I got a magnet off my fridge. I was worried at first that if the magnet scrambled it, then it could paralyze me or even kill me, but I couldn't allow myself to think about that for too long. I just had to get it out of my body at any cost. I could not cope any longer.

I placed the magnet against my collarbone and moved it around. It didn't take long for a soaring pain to shoot up my neck and into my ears. A deafening ringing overwhelmed me, and I felt like I would lose my hearing if I continued. I threw the magnet across the room and screamed out in pain and frustration. It was a scream I could not hear, as the ringing didn't go away. Not at first anyway. It took days of sounding like I was underwater before my hearing returned completely.

I have not been to work in weeks; I haven't been out of the house at all. I just lay here in my bed listening to the ticking on repeat. I have food delivered to my house and request that it be left on the doorstep, but recently, I've not been able to bring myself to eat. It went from me having three meals a day to occasional snacking, then just drinking soup, and now, not even a sip of water passes my lips. There are ten tins of soup and a loaf of bread out there still, forsaken on my doorstep. I am sure the bread is nothing but green mould by now, as it has been left in the summer sun for a week. I just remain here in my pit, unable to focus on anything but the ticking from within. I no longer get up to use the bathroom, I do not have the mental or physical energy to.

I would end it all now if I were strong enough, just to get it over with quickly, but I can barely lift my head anymore. I will just lie here until I waste away to nothing. Even with my broken psyche, I cannot help but wonder how long it will be before I am found. How long before my absence becomes a concern? Or the stench of my corpse gets someone's attention? Will I be so decomposed that the chip is visible to the poor soul unfortunate enough to discover me lying here in my own waste? Will I be missed by anyone?

I don't have many people in my life. I am an only child, and with both my parents already gone, I have no immediate family left. I have always been a loner. Other than saying good morning to my neighbours and engaging in light conversation by the water cooler at work, my social life is non-existent. I don't really have anyone I would call a friend. Maybe that is why I was chosen— because I will not be missed when I am gone. Whilst I understand why I was chosen, I guess I will never know what the chip was supposed to do. What was its purpose?

I can feel my lifeforce draining from my body, and there is no time left to wonder why, to ponder my underwhelming life anymore. No time left to fix my mistakes or find true peace. Not everyone gets the closure they long for, and I'll just have to be okay with the fact that I am one of those unlucky people. I'll just have to be okay with my fate now. Maybe that is my closure: being okay with not being okay. Nothing will ever be okay again for me. My last breath in this world will be a shallow gasp of loneliness and defeat, and that is okay.

*

The dapper man stepped out of the car, and with leather-gloved hands, he tightened his black tie closer to his white collar and straightened his blazer before walking towards the front door. A quick look around to make sure no one was out in the dead of night was sufficient as he approached the building. Stepping over the rusted tins on the ground, he narrowly avoided the bag of mouldy mush as he reached out to try the handle. To his surprise, the door was left unlocked, and his lock pick could remain securely in his pocket. The door was barely ajar before the smell from inside assaulted his nostrils, but he did not react to it as he made his way inside.

The body on the bed was so decomposed that it had melded with the mattress beneath it. He could only estimate how long it had been there, and no less than six months seemed like a reasonable guess. How could it not have been discovered by now? How could The Institute have overlooked this for so long? Even with the late stage of decay, he could make out deep scratches along its chest, as if the person had been clawing at themselves for days.

He looked around and noticed notes taped all over the place. Mostly gibberish, but some spoke of a chip in their chest—their collarbone, to be precise—and all the different theories of what its purpose was. Everything from aliens to secret government experiments. If only they knew how close they were with their theories…not that it would have made any difference.

He made his way back toward the bed and knelt beside it. He began to roll the host onto its front. It was a much more challenging task than he had hoped for.

Once he had finally managed to roll the pile of rotted flesh over, he reached into his pocket and pulled out his lock pick. It seemed he would need it, after all.

Luckily for him, the shoulder blade was visible as half of the back skin had peeled away during the rolling process. He pressed his lock pick into the shoulder and began to chisel away pieces of bone that had grown around the device since infancy. A fact which filled him with curiosity. Usually, the devices were updated every decade or so. The Institute would often sedate their subjects in their homes during their sleep and replace the chips or at least update their software.

It took a while, but finally, he managed to pry the chip from its expired host. He wiped it down the best he could and investigated it briefly. It looked perfectly fine, but it buzzed loudly for a few seconds and then began to tick. It was reacting to his touch. Even through the gloves, it detected life once more.

He looked at it more closely and was able to determine that it was one of the original chips. It was no surprise to him that it was beginning to malfunction. It was because of today's updated technology. Smartphones had begun to interfere with them. Decades ago, when this subject would have been chipped, the hardware was only in the prototype stage and was never intended for use beyond childhood many decades ago. There was only one reason this host would still have an original chip.

He looked down at the subject and clicked his teeth. Quite so, this was the long-sought AWOL host, whose parents had broken their contract with The Institute. This subject had been snatched from the program as a toddler by their parents and was never recovered.

He never understood why they left such a valuable host out in the world rather than retrieving it. They kept the subject under constant surveillance, after all. What was the purpose of leaving it to live a normal life? Why allow the situation to get this far, and why leave the host to decay for so long after the fact? He may have had all these questions running through his mind, but it was not his place to ask them aloud. His assignment was to recover the chip, and he had done that now.

He placed the device in his pocket and made his way back to the car, making a call on the way.

"The assignment is complete. I am returning now," he said. "We need a cleanup team here stat."

41

Pip Pinkerton

"Lizzie Borden took an axe and gave her mother forty whacks; when she saw what she had done, she gave her father forty-one."
—Children's Rhyme

Lizzie Andrew Borden despised her father. Her feud with him wasn't just some sort of disdainful disagreement over his choice of a new wife, though Lizzie loathed her new stepmother with a burning passion. This was a deep, integral hatred that mixed like sugar in lemonade with another feeling Lizzie didn't quite realize was fear. She used to love her father. He was once an affectionate man. Then Abby joined the family like a monkey wrench. All of Lizzie's kin said the erstwhile daughter's animosity was built on the childish idea that her dead mother had been replaced and that she ought not to be spiteful of her new stepmother as long as her father was happy.

Her revered sister Emma, nine years her elder, agreed with Lizzie. Their father changed drastically for the worse after getting remarried. He was crueler and more covetous of his daughters, purposely sabotaging every relationship they showed an interest in pursuing.

Time passed as it will, and the sisters grew up. Though both were grown women safely in their thirties, Lizzie and her so-called "eccentric" sister Emma were both still shy, the knowledge of a marriage bed, cursed still to call the rooms under their father's roof home. The old man's cruelty didn't waver as the years passed. One day, as all boils do, it came to a head.

The atrocity happened in the spring. A fine, eligible young gentleman from the next town over tried briefly to court Lizzie. His name was David Anthony Gardener, and training pigeons was his bread and butter. Lizzie was quickly enamored. When her father didn't lose his mind instantly upon meeting David, Lizzie beamed. The ambitious young lovers wanted to build a pigeon coop in the back corner of the Borden family property, with the (presumed) consent of Lizzie's father. She told the gnarled patriarch of their plans. Not a single objection escaped his lips, not even when the noise of hammering nails into wood took over the entire yard. He even chuckled while watching David stretch the chicken wire over the open holes in the wooden cages.

Even Emma had to relent. "I think you may have brought his old heart back to beating," she told her sister.

There's nothing wrong with hope, so it is said.

Come the day that the infatuated duo of David and Lizzie transferred the pigeons from the barn. It started off as just a day like any other. David traveled with the dawn and met with Lizzie. When the lovers finished getting the birds situated, David took Lizzie out for a savory breakfast of thick slices of ham and country-fried eggs at a small diner not far from the house.

Andrew Borden, through biding his time, grabbed his hatchet and crept silently into the barn. The pigeons all looked at him warily as if they knew what was coming with ill intent. All the birds began cooing deliriously as Andrew began his brutal onslaught. He swung his axe over and over again with glee, severing heads, wings, and feet from the birds or cutting them crudely in half, if not just bludgeoning them to a feather and viscera paste. That day, Andrew Borden found (to his great delight) that birds could scream. Finished, he grinned at his newly made abattoir, at the copious amounts of pigeon blood, shit, and body parts coating the walls like a macabre mural of dripping viscera. Shredded wings, feet, and heads still twitched along the shapes of dying red-feathered bodies. He picked up one of the doomed, the head shivering as if trying to reattach itself to its neck, ripping it away. He crushed the body in one hand, spewing entrails through his fist. He licked it. The guts were cold...insipid like old lard. Chuckling, Andrew left. He shut the door and looked down. Blood leaked through the aperture between the floor and the door.

Let the devil take what their kin said to his flaming hovel. Lizzie wasn't immature. Emma wasn't crazy. The proof was in the blood and feather pudding on the barn floor—the Borden elders had no interest in marrying off their daughters and would, in fact, kill to keep them from doing so. "Immature!" she cried to Emma. "I am not...*bloody*...immature! Those poor, sweet birds..."

"We're expected to keep a stiff upper," Emma said. Her eyes, however, leaked with sympathy. Both sisters cried, and the time passed.

For Lizzie, the monstrosity of what her father had done to her pigeons did not pass. Damn the bastard! She knew that her amorous nature toward David set him against the pigeons, though they did nothing, and it told Lizzie that he would moreover like to kill her...both sisters conceived of the grandeur of running away, but alas, they didn't know where to go, nor in fact, how to get there.

Like any eager iron fist, Andrew's occasionally unclenches. When it did (and to cut the desperation), the sisters slipped out for nights on the town. On the third of August, Lizzie and Emma went out for a night of sibling bonding and pressure release. In other words, they got drunk.

82

The sisters didn't know what time it was when they stumbled up the gravel driveway to the domicile they had the misfortune of calling home. All the lights were off inside. They hadn't expected such luck. After all, Uncle John Morse had come for an unexpected visit. This was probably the whole reason Andrew hadn't kept the girls (*the women!*) shut in for yet another gorgeous summer eve.

"Do you think Bridget is awake?" Emma asked.

She meant the live-in maid, Bridget Sullivan. "I doubt it," Lizzie said, giggling. "Miss Sullivan turns in early…you know Father demands she wake and work early, early, early…it's always everything early and work!"

"SHHH!" Emma put her hand over Lizzie's mouth. "You'll wake them up!"

"You'll wake them up with all that godawful hissing!"

The inebriated and temporarily blissful Borden women sang gaily in the moonlight, leaning on one another for support as they strolled with wobbly gait up the hill and into their front yard.

Lizzie and Emma got it together and were quiet as mice, sneaking in through the front door and courteously trying not to wake anyone. Lizzie, however, felt a presence in the living room, and her breath caught. Good, for she might've screamed at the abrupt *creak* of the parlor chairs. Andrew and Abby Borden's chairs both began rocking simultaneously in the nigh complete darkness. One of the wraiths arose, and as it drew near, moonlight crossed the etched face of Andrew Borden.

"Lizzie, Emma, do you have any idea what time it is?" Andrew asked. His gruff voice hit each sister in the gut a bit harder than usual.

Neither one responded. Words fled their frightened brains.

"You better not have been out with any young men tonight; I won't tolerate any such shenanigans under my roof. Abide strumpets?" He shook his head. "I refuse."

"Just the Clemens sisters, Dottie and Irene." Emma struggled to keep her words even and emotionless as they parted from her lips.

Andrew Borden leaned down and inhaled deeply as if smelling his children.

"No stench of the hedonist on you. Perhaps a tinge of spirits. I will permit it. I bid you goodnight. See that you find your beds."

He left. Then Abby Borden did the exact same thing, inhale and all.

*

Lizzie awoke in a dreadful state well before dawn, her belly urgent for the outhouse. She knew before even pulling the covers away that she was likely to be out there for some while.

It was still black as pitch outside. Maybe an hour had passed—she'd been asleep, and it was a wonder she didn't trip over her gown. Luckily, the trip from the main residence to the outhouse was rather uneventful, and after a span of time much longer than Lizzie had cared for, she finished her business. Before going back in the house, she blew out her candle; the house was familiar, and she didn't want to disturb anyone (least of all Andrew) on the way back to her bedroom. She fancied she would let the moonlight guide her way through the windows, being that it was such a pristine night. She reached for the doorknob…Lizzie heard voices emanating from somewhere near the front porch. She tiptoed to the corner of the house, hiding in the familiar building's shadowy embrace, and listened.

"…waited so long for this. If we had known you couldn't turn the females until they stopped producing eggs, then I would have suggested we assimilate a different family. Who would have thought menstruation could kill us?" a tinny, pinched voice spoke, each syllable sounding as if it were forcing its way up through a throat congested with bees.

"Our patience will be rewarded. We will kill two birds with one stone tomorrow, then our long wait will have been worth it," responded a slightly higher voice, though it still held the same unnatural and strikingly terrible cadence as its cohort.

"Who would have thought this meat bag's estranged brother would try to get in contact with him again at right around the same time his eldest daughter stops being able to procreate…"

"The stars have aligned, as the humans say."

"Verily, I miss home," the more masculine voice commented, his tone becoming slightly less awful as it spoke.

"Me too," the feminine voice added longingly.

*

Meat bag…stars aligning…daughters procreating? Her throat dried up. Absolute terror rattled her to the core, not only due to the sound of their ominous, abhorrent voices but also the words they used. Her blood ran so cold she couldn't move a single muscle; she was frozen perfectly still by the grandiose fear pervading her every fiber, and with a sudden sickness at her womanhood. Like a trickster, Lizzie's curiosity began to burn deep within her bosom. The heat was so strong that it commenced a conflagration that quickly warmed her blood and thawed her from her horror-induced paralysis. Compelled, Lizzie swallowed all her fear in one vinegary lump and mustered every bit of courage, then forced herself to peek around the corner.

There, standing on her family's front porch, were two unearthly entities. From the neck down, the execrable abominations were her parents in every detail, from her father's dirt-caked leather boots to Abby's favorite evening coat. From the neck up, the creatures were unlike anything even Dante wrote for his Divine Comedy. Protruding from the monstrosities' upper necks were four thin, prehensile stalks. The stalks extended ten inches or so above the neck with bulbous, moist eyes rolling at their ends. Polyps bulged between the four major stalks, acting as sets of lips. The creatures looked up at the stars. Lizzie followed their gaze and saw the three stars David had taught her made Orion's Belt.

One of the things hissed. "We'll send Lizzie to get milk tomorrow at precisely the time when Bridget goes for her afternoon nap. With the little mouse preoccupied, we will easily be able to convert John and Emma. I will convert John in the living room—you convert Emma in the upstairs bedroom," the thing in her father's body said, almost as an afterthought.

"What if Bridget hears the screaming and wakes up?" the thing wearing her stepmother as a disguise asked.

"She won't. You cannot hear anything from her quarters. If she does? We'll just kill her and say she had an accident. At any rate, I care nothing about Bridget. I want those two cahoots away from each other. Emma and Lizzie are thick as thieves. I've had enough of it."

Enough of this nightmare. Lizzie crept back to the outhouse and cried for a full hour. Could that have been real? Maybe they'd spiked her drink at the bar. Father had warned her of it! By God, and was there a God? How could there be if such things existed?

She couldn't stay overnight in the potty. Father—or whatever the hell that was—would have a fit. She didn't want that thing having fits. Fear kept her frozen and silent as she crept up the stairs. The moment she reached the relative safety of her bedroom, a choke leaping from her throat, and she sobbed into her hands. No more sleep occurred for Lizzie Andrew Borden that night.

*

It was when the warm sun first began to plant its tentatively tender kisses upon the brisk sky. Dew kissed the grass. An ugly scheme formed in Lizzie's head. No one would believe her, not even Emma...if she left the house in search of help, the creatures pretending to be Father and Abby would have already "converted" Uncle John and Emma before she could return. And what a waste that would be. No one was going to believe this.

No.

She had to do it.

The time had come to put her mettle to the test. It made sense now, everything. The fog lifted. Focus narrowed her vision. Oh yes...the time was ripe. She pushed herself off the bed and had just swung her legs across the mattress when she heard a voice coming from the bottom of the stairs.

"Oh dear ones!" the ersatz Abby called up coaxingly. "Breakfast time!"

Lizzie's feet hit the cold floor. Breakfast indeed.

The first thing she did was open the window. No one knew she did it, and no one was supposed to. Next, she climbed into a day dress. This would be unusual of her, and she wanted to see if the creatures took notice of this. Her real parents would have. She made her way down the stairs and saw Bridget yawning, her arms above her head. Must loosen those muscles for a hard day at the Borden Devil house. Lizzie felt something ugly crawl over her. She liked it.

"Dear Lizzie," Abby said. "Would you pick up milk, please?"

"Of course."

Lizzie shut the door behind her hard enough to be heard. What she made sure no one heard, not the Abby-thing, nor Bridget, nor her father and Emma, was the fall of her footsteps as she crept stealthily around the house before coming to the back window she'd opened before leaving. Lizzie still couldn't believe this was happening. She knew what she'd seen. It was still hard to comprehend that her parents weren't really her parents. There was only one way to save her sister and her uncle. Lizzie didn't know if she could do it. She didn't know if she had the strength. Emma was depending on her. The younger of the two Borden children took one more look at the world outside her house, the real world; she entered back into the nightmare, the valiant younger sister of old.

*

"Emma, help me fold these sheets," Abby implored, coaxing the reluctant Emma up the steps until they were in the guest bedroom where Uncle John, who was now down in the sitting room talking shop with the Andrew Borden-thing, had slept for the night.

Emma entered the room first, and the Abby-thing followed directly behind her, almost like they were connected heel to toe. Once the door was closed behind them, faux-Abby quickly locked the lock and dropped the key in her pocket before turning menacingly toward Emma, who was immediately taken aback by the whole affair.

"What are you doing?" Emma asked with a nervousness bordering on fear.

"There's something I want you to see." The Abby-thing dripped, metamorphosing into a hideous plant-octopus-thing. Her face and head melted into the neck cavity as the stalks pierced through the thick, waxy flesh. The process wasn't even complete when the screaming started, both upstairs and down.

Before the creature could reach Emma, there was a loud, abrasive cry erupted from somewhere in the room. Abby's stalks whipped left and right in search of the source. Lizzie exploded from the closet door in a fury, more warrior than spinster, more killer than lady, more like the creatures than her actual parents. She aimed high, almost without coherent thought, and instinctively commenced hacking away at the creature's protruding stalks, surprising the monster with both her presence and her ferocity. Lizzie attacked with intensity, hacking until she had made pulp of her stepmother's fake head and skull, effectively killing the foul entity before it could do anything other than stare at her in stunned disbelief.

Lizzie grabbed Emma, who was speechless, by the arm. "We have to go. They're not human anymore."

Gasping, Emma nodded. The adrenaline-fueled sisters then rushed downstairs. Lizzie saw her arms, gore-straked, pallid things that reminded her of the stalks. Maybe her fingers would grow eyes.

For a man well into his golden years, Uncle John's struggle against the thing that was not her father, that was presiding in her father's body, was going about as well as could be expected…though it was doubtful that he could keep up his defenses much longer.

Lizzie Andrew Borden, daughter of the presumably late, real Andrew Borden, rushed over and put into motion the act of severing all four protruding stalks from the father-thing's body. She cleaved off two of the noxious appendages in one brawny swoop before finishing the job in a slightly more efficient method than she had with her stepmother.

*

As things began to settle down, Lizzie explained everything she had heard and witnessed to Emma, Uncle John, and eventually to Bridget, who woke up none the wiser until having noticed the bodies and all the bloodshed. Uncle John was the one to call the cops, and when the attending officers finally arrived, they all repeated their stories multiple times.

It was only after much disbelief and even more deliberation that the constable, Sheriff Miles O'Brien, finally decided to believe them, especially in light of the bodies present at the crime scene. There were upstanding businesses to think of; there were commonfolk and their fragile minds to consider. Sheriff O'Brien made everyone involved swear by God and before each other to keep absolutely silent on all the true details of the matter. The Lizzie Borden murder story—all the allegations of sexual assault, after all, what is too terrible to argue down other than that—were fabricated by the most brilliant minds of the town that day, with authorities hiding all evidence of anything and everything unnatural in origin. Why assault? What else would the people swallow? Although Lizzie would ultimately have to face infamy as well as other future hardships for the greater good of humankind, she took her martyrdom stoically, and they made sure she was never hanged.

Hybrid

Dawn Colclasure

Dedicated to the memory of Martha Jette

She wanted a vacation. A vacation meant sandy beaches, exotic cruises, and hotels with room service.

Dolly Castleman sniffed at that last thought. Room service would've been nice right about now. She flicked at what was probably the hundredth fly on her arm in the last two hours. "I'm tired. Can't we go home now?"

Her husband, Burt, looked up from his fishing pole. "You're kidding, right? This is great."

"Fishing in a swamp was never my cup of tea," she answered, avoiding his stare.

"It's not a swamp," Burt muttered, turning his attention back to his pole. "It's a lake."

"A stupid lake!" Dolly sourly corrected. "We've been here for two hours, and you haven't caught a thing. There aren't any fish here."

Burt ignored her.

Dolly sniffed again, a scent of her perfume entering her nostrils. "Well. I, for one, think it's stupid. We can get fish just as easily at Wiley's Grocer. And just as quickly."

Burt shrugged. "You wanted a vacation."

"Yes, a vacation. But not in the middle of God-knows-where. Our cabin doesn't even have air conditioning, for God's sake! I'll die of heat stroke before we eat any fish!"

"Save us both some misery," Burt mumbled under his breath.

"What?"

He shook his head. "Nothing."

The hours wore on. Dolly only continued to complain about one thing or another. All Burt did as she talked was remain slouched in his seat, his eyes never leaving his pole. He finally reeled in his line, gasping at what he saw at the end of it.

"Look," he breathlessly whispered, pointing with his free hand. "Tell me you see it, too."

Dolly wrinkled her nose as she scooted from her seat on the boat to get closer. She took one look at what hung from Burt's hook, and her mouth dropped.

There, wriggling at the end of Burt Castleman's fishing pole, was the tiny green body of a baby alien.

*

Robert Altman sped through the office of the FBI, his eyes never leaving his path. He wiped away the few remaining beads of sweat on his forehead and cleared his throat as he neared the door. He swung into John Jake Pitt's office and held his breath as Pitt hung up his black telephone.

"We just got a call," he said. "Looks like somebody found it."

*

The large black windowless van pulled to a stop along the dirt road leading to a cabin in Montana. Altman alighted from the driver's side as a team of Special Intelligence Troopers jumped out of the back doors, armed and wearing yellow protective suits complete with masks. They followed Altman at a cautious distance, holding their weapons against their chests.

Altman climbed up the steps of the cabin and knocked on the door. Three Troopers waited behind him while five remained at the bottom of the steps.

The door opened. Burt Castleman, wearing only blue jeans and a flannel shirt over his white T-shirt, sized Altman up as he answered. "Yeah?"

"Mr. Castleman, I'm Special Agent Robert Altman with the FBI," Altman said, showing his badge. "It's come to our attention that you caught an unidentified specimen today in the lake."

"The FBI?" Castleman asked, taking a step back. "What the hell does the FBI want with aliens?"

"I'm sorry, sir," Altman replied, returning his badge to his pocket. "That's classified."

"Well, unless you tell me what's going on, I'm not letting you in!" Castleman declared, bracing himself.

"I'm sorry, sir," Altman said again. "We are under direct orders to remove the specimen. We ask that you cooperate, or we will be forced to act, and no one wants that."

"No! Now, look. I caught that thing. It's mine. Go away and leave us alone!"

"I'm afraid we can't do that, sir," Altman said. "I'm sorry it has to be this way." He moved aside. A Trooper stepped forward, aiming a Sig Sauer P229 .40 caliber handgun. A shot ripped through Castleman's forehead, and his body fell to the ground.

A woman screamed as more Troopers entered. Altman stepped into the cabin as another shot fired. He turned just to see Dolly Castleman's body fall to the floor.

"Call in housekeeping," he ordered. "I'll retrieve the specimen."

Pitt rested his fists on his hips as the helicopter came into view. He frowned as it drew closer, preparing to land on the helipad in front of him. He relaxed his arms and took a few steps back as the helicopter landed.

As the helicopter shut down, his frown deepened as he watched Altman disembark, carrying the crate with biological hazard signs covering it. Four members of the SIT team followed him.

"Bob, what the hell is the matter with you?" he shouted as Altman drew closer. "Exposing yourself to it without any protection?"

Altman stopped, looking at Pitt through his black sunglasses. His breathing came out in short bursts. His brown hair blew furiously in the wind. He lifted the bottom of his white shirt under the coat of his black suit, revealing the blue triangular patch on his stomach. "I'm immune to it, John. Remember?"

Pitt clenched his teeth, looking at him. "Right."

Altman tucked his shirt back in and followed Pitt as they left the helipad.

*

Twelve hours later, Altman stood before a team sitting around a large black table in a tiny office of the FBI's Special Intelligence Division.

"We just got confirmation from SIT," he said, his eyes moving over Pitt. "There have not been any other sightings or handlings by any other civilians. We're still looking for Santiago, and we're still short on leads. But we'll find him. Hopefully, this won't happen again."

"What about the specimen?" one agent asked.

"It will go back to Testing."

"But it's just a baby. What harm could it do?"

Altman stiffened. "Be that as it may, it's not human. We don't know what it's thinking, what it's feeling. What we *do* know is that it is not safe for exposure. Understand the situation. This is the first time a subject has escaped from the colony, and the first time it escaped while impregnated. We must take every kind of defensive action that we can."

Pitt frowned. "Should've destroyed it when we found it."

Altman considered his response. Pitt had been against testing the specimen from Day One. He had every reason to be against it: First, its deadly toxins killed his partner three days after exposure. Soon after, it was stolen by another SID agent. It was not just stolen, but released into the public, at that.

"It's too valuable to destroy," he finally said. "I know it can kill someone not immunized or protected from exposure. But we've never really had a chance to study an alien's offspring on Earth before. All we know so far is that exposure to it here is deadly. What we don't know is what else can happen."

Pitt moved forward in his chair, looking directly at Altman. "I'll tell you what else can happen. First, it's going to use some kind of mind power to tear us all down. After that, the rest of them will be along to retrieve it. Next thing you know, our cover gets blown away, and the whole world is going to know about the Special Intelligence Division. It was easy, covering things up in the past. Roswell. Area 51. But things are too risky now, Bob. We need to return the specimen to the colony and keep it there." He sat back. "We've been able to keep everything quiet about it so far."

Altman clenched his teeth. "Yes. And just how tight was your security when your subject escaped, John?"

Pitt glared at him.

Altman looked at the other agents. "We have sufficient data on adult alien subjects but not on their offspring. And, as I've said, we're given the chance to study how it can survive on Earth, compared to surviving on its home planet."

Pitt covered his eyes, shaking his head.

"Agent Pitt has been in charge of things at the colony on the planet Thalia, and he's kept us updated with his reports. We know that the alien offspring fare well on their home planet, but we don't know why things are different here. There are too many questions. What is this poison they use that kills people? How can we convince the public to be immunized before being exposed? Why do the offspring need to be in water? For that matter, what does it say about what it inherits from the mother? We can't afford to let this knowledge get away from us. And we can't afford to lose it again. Agent Beemer, you keep SID on finding Santiago. I don't care what it takes; find him. Bring him in. John and I will work together to continue the testing. Hopefully, no damage has been done."

*

"Can't hold it still!" Fiona Gardner muttered, sighing as she once again lost her grip on the wriggling alien baby in the tank of water. Her sigh clouded a small portion of the mask she wore.

She carefully gripped the syringe in one hand and strained to clutch the alien's figure with the other. It continued to squeal and thrash, and she injected it quickly in the side with the syringe, then let go. Rather than swim away in a frenzy, the alien casually floated as if nothing had happened.

"There," she sighed with relief, depositing the used syringe into a metal box on the wall. She grabbed the edges of the digital image sensor attached to a swiveled X-ray tube and moved it over the tank. The lit screen changed shape as she adjusted the viewing.

She left the room, securing the door after it closed behind her, then removed her mask as she walked to the control panel at her left. Her long black hair remained in its tight bun as she stared out the large window, viewing the room she'd just been in. She looked down at the TV screen. A silver knob gleamed next to the screen.

She turned just to see the door open as Altman entered the room. "Find anything?" he asked, walking over to stand by her side.

"I'm just about to start," she replied, turning her attention back to the panel. A push of the button made the other room go dark. The skeletal figure of the alien baby appeared, still contentedly floating in the tank. Fiona pushed another button and started up the X-ray machine. The skeletal image appeared on the TV screen, this time in greater detail. She adjusted the knob to magnify the viewing and moved closer to the screen as she examined the image.

"No broken bones," she mused, adjusting the knob again. "Everything seems to be okay. No fractures." She ran tests and studied the results appearing over the image. She studied it for a few more minutes, then stood to face Altman. "No damage."

"Thanks, Fi," Altman said, then turned to leave. He walked down the hall, went inside the men's room to relieve himself at a stall. He walked to the sink to wash his hands, lost in thought, rubbing the soap into his skin. Still pondering as he rinsed, hunched over the sink, the water running, his eyes locked to its flow…remarkable how the water had been falling all around him and the team on the night they'd found the wreckage, falling just like this, in big, bubbly waves.

Long ago but not long enough.

"Just made an identification—it's the one from Thalia, all right," Pitt's partner, Thomas Wagner, had told him while they marked the site all that time ago.

Wagner had looked over his partner's shoulder for the man he really wanted to see. "Where's John?"

"On his way," he replied. "Which class is it?"

Wagner smiled. "The A34. Little green men."

"Is it alive?"

"Yes, but just barely." Wagner led him towards the shore. The waves pounded down on the beach as they walked through them, pushing themselves against the tide. "It survives underwater," Wagner shouted, straining to be heard over the waves. "But I don't think it's alone."

Altman had stopped. Did he need to call for reinforcements? "What do you mean?"

Wagner turned to look at him. "I mean, it's a mother!" he replied, bracing himself as a wave hit him. "And it's giving birth!"

Indeed, it had. Not a moment too soon did they dive to the crash site under the ocean, where they found a baby alien as the only living survivor. The mother's body lay lifeless inside the vessel, apparently too injured to survive birth. Pitt had been the only one of the three to witness such a thing, but Altman and Wagner knew they had no time to marvel over the tiny new alien life. They had to get to shore and get the specimen contained. It didn't take long for them to notice that the alien baby could not survive out of water; not ten minutes on dry land, and the creature began shriveling into a tiny corpse. Replacing it in the water miraculously brought it back to life, and they called for an aquarium.

Three days later, Wagner was dead.

First, Wagner's scab-covered, bloodless body was found. It was discovered that whatever had killed him happened exactly thirty-six hours following exposure to the specimen. Scabs soon appeared on Altman's body that same day, and he was rushed to Quarantine. The same went for the remaining members of the team who had been exposed.

Surprisingly, all it took to save Altman was his usual shot of insulin. The scabs disappeared right after the shot, and Altman soon felt much better. His blood level, which had drastically immersed itself into his own body, was normal again, and one blood transfusion later, he was completely recovered.

"Bob."

The rest of the team was likewise injected. The SID's lab developed a special patch to thwart any kind of airborne disease the specimen may have infected them with—the team members didn't have to think twice anymore before handling the specimen, and they got a little loose.

"Bob."

A Trooper, Delman Santiago, decided to steal the specimen and, worse, release it into society. Altman's gaze deepened. Had Santiago *really* released it? They had never figured out his motive in the first place. What if there had been an accident?

"Bob!"

Altman swung around to face Pitt.

Pitt recomposed himself. "They found Santiago."

*

Altman sighed. So much for finding out a motive, but what bothered him most as he watched Santiago's head disappear as his body was zipped into a black body bag was the loss of a good man and a damn good agent. Despite his fallacies and especially despite stealing government property, Santiago was an agent who would not soon be forgotten.

As the body was loaded into the coroner's van, Altman looked at Pitt, who silently stood next to him. The only thing wrong with Pitt's silence was that it was distant. No emotion showed on his face at all. Altman's gaze hardened. This whole damn mess was his fault. Two agents dead—so far. How many more? And all in the name of research. He blamed himself. He blamed Pitt. Pitt should have had tighter security. The subject should not have escaped. And he should've realized it was best to get the specimen back home after they discovered that just being exposed to it was lethal.

He started to say something but stopped when a uniformed man wearing a dark blue cap with "CORONER" on it appeared before Pitt, holding out a clipboard. "Sir, I need you to sign here."

Pitt scowled. "What for?"

The man blinked. "To authorize the autopsy of Agent Santiago.

Pitt hardened his gaze. "No autopsy," he said, turning to leave.

"But sir—" the uniformed man started to say.

"No autopsy," Pitt bitterly turned to repeat. "Just bury him." He turned to leave.

The man stared at Altman.

Altman shared the man's confusion. The autopsy was standard, and Pitt had never ordered that no autopsy be performed. It was possible he was worried about Santiago's exposure to the specimen. Troopers were never immunized against the specimen; there was no reason for them to be. And Santiago hadn't exactly grabbed his yellow protective suit on the way out of the building. Cutting him open might release some of the dangerous airborne virus. That could be it.

After all, Santiago didn't look at all like he'd died from the virus. There were no visible scabs.

The man still searched his body for answers. Altman pursed his lips. "You heard him," he finally said, relieved that the man only shrugged and walked away.

Altman sighed, looking back at the cement grave that would hold Santiago's body. There was no physical sign of death; it was possible a bullet hole remained hidden somewhere, or he'd been injected with a syringe.

His cell phone chirped, and he removed it from his pocket, slowly moving out of his thoughts. He opened it and put it to his ear. "Altman."

He listened, blinking in surprise as his brain tried to keep up with the news. "What, Fi? Say again." He listened again as Fiona's hysterical voice rang into his ear. He cleared his throat. "I'll be right there."

*

"Something is wrong," Fiona said, leading Altman into the lab. "My readouts aren't consistent with Agent Pitt's research, and I'm picking up on things that aren't supposed to be there." She showed him a long stream of chart readings. "See? They're supposed to have 24 chromosomes in 12 pairs, but it has 46 in 23 pairs. Adenine, Guanine, Thymine, Uracil and Cytosine. Just like us. And I'm picking up readings of carbon." She caught Altman's surprised look. "Carbon. Aliens aren't carbon-based lifeforms, according to Pitt's reports."

Altman picked up the stack of papers containing Pitt's scientific findings of alien life on Thalia and compared them to the charts. Fi was on to something— this was definitely inconsistent.

"One more thing," he heard her say. He looked up, bracing himself.

"It's growing. Fast." She shook her head. "I can barely hold it still long enough to measure it, but the readings don't lie. I can see for myself that it's growing."

"What's the estimated age?"

She looked down, mentally scanning the timeline. "Found it ten days ago. It's fourteen days and 12 hours old right now."

"What's the last measurement?" he asked, scanning the readings.

Fiona took her chart readings and found the measurement. "The last recorded measurement was right before Santiago disappeared with it. Here, 23 inches. Now it's 72." She looked at him. "That's more than three times its original reading. It started growing an hour ago, and it hasn't stopped."

Altman looked across the room at the large window. In the room next door stood the tank that contained the specimen. He approached the monitor on the control board with Fiona at his side. He scanned the readings playing out on the screen, then looked at the 3-D image of the specimen beneath the readings.

"Give me a normal visual," he said, looking at the knobs and buttons surrounding the screen.

Fiona pressed a button. The overhead camera clicked on, showing a 2-D image of the tank's guts as if Altman were standing in them. He squinted at the specimen, studying. Surprisingly, the overactive alien now lay very still. Its round, dark eyes curiously peered up at the camera. Altman stiffened; it was no longer green. In fact, it was now a light tan color, nearly identical to a white human being. Its head had also changed; it was no longer a cone shape but also round, just like a human.

"It's metamorphosing," he whispered, placing his hand on the control panel to avoid falling to the ground. "It's entering a new stage of development."

"Are you sure it's not another defense mechanism?" Fiona asked. "Like…shapeshifting to look like us?"

Altman shook his head. "His whole body is completely changing. His genetic make-up is different." He looked at her. "Fi. It's turning into a human."

Fiona gasped as he looked back at the screen. The alien was still growing, its body now rising above the water.

"Do you think there's still an airborne virus?"

Altman shook his head. "I don't know. I can't say. There's nothing in Agent Pitt's reports about this."

He looked out the window again and placed his hands on his hips. The alien lay motionless, still looking up at the camera. "I wonder what other changes there are."

He moved from the control panel and went to the door. He reached out to a button to open the door, then held his breath as he clasped his hand shut. He had on his patch, but what if the virus, too, was changing? What if insulin didn't work as a safeguard anymore? What if the alien had fully developed mental powers to use against him?

Altman sighed, looking up at the door again. He'd have to take the chance. It was the only way to know.

He pushed the button and walked into the room, ignoring Fiona's cry of *don't!* as it closed behind him.

Altman cautiously approached the tank, wondering what surprises lay in store. The air seemed safe to breathe. The alien made no sudden moves. In fact, it didn't even look at him; the blinking light on the overhead camera kept his attention.

He came to a stop near the tank, looking down at the face of the alien as it stared at the camera. Then its head slowly moved, its eyes finding him. For the first time in ten days, Human and Alien met eye-to-eye. Now was Altman's chance to marvel over this creature.

As Altman stared, a chill raced down his spine. He gasped, shaking as a stream of thoughts hit his mind. The sound of a forlorn moaning hit his ears, and a deep sense of longing and sadness fell over him. The images playing in his mind showed other A-34 aliens, adult ones, being strapped to beds and injected with syringes. Some gave birth to babies that died, while others had successful births. All the babies were alien, just like them, and all were taken away by members of Pitt's team wearing protective suits. The babies were put into nurseries while the mothers underwent endless tests, examinations and more births until they were too weak to reproduce again. Having outlived their usefulness, they were destroyed.

Altman's eyes widened. He next saw a white lab on Thalia, where genetic testing was done, and a freezer remained stocked with syringes containing live human sperm. The aliens were being fertilized with these very syringes and giving birth to alien/human hybrids. Other scientists in the lab worked over microscopes and Petri dishes, injecting the human sperm into alien eggs.

Another flash came to Altman's mind, and he again saw the alien/human hybrids, only now as they transformed into human babies. The transformation was fast, taking place within hours, sometimes in the span of two days. These babies were loaded into a customized spacecraft with the SID logo, transported back to Earth, and placed into homes with adoptive parents. Some were even replaced with babies who'd died in hospitals.

Altman gulped, taking a step back. The hybrids were highly intelligent, with mental powers unknown to the human race. These very qualities meant a disastrous future for humans, as the hybrids were very likely to transform back to their alien forms by the time they reached adulthood.

"My God," he whispered, watching the images of hundreds of such hybrids appear in his mind. Project SID has only been in operation for 7 years, but countless hybrids have already populated the planet. The images stopped, and one man finally came to view in his mind: Executive Director John Jake Pitt.

Altman shook and stepped back as the mental transference ended. The young alien sadly looked at him now, seeming more human than alien.

"Sonofabitch," he grumbled, turning to run out of the room. He raced down the hall, his anger building within. Pitt had no right to play God with the aliens on Thalia. SID's goal was to study intelligent life, not crossbreed with it. Pitt had gone too far, and now the human race, even the alien race on Thalia, was threatened.

A large black thing swung around a corner and hit Altman in the face. He flew back to the ground, dizzy and stunned. A small trickle of blood oozed out of his nose.

He dazedly raised his hand to his head, his vision blurred as he tried to see his attacker.

Pitt slowly stepped from around the corner, the expression on his face a mixture of regret and guilt. "I'm sorry I have to do this, Bob," he said, kneeling at Altman's side.

Altman felt his rage come back in full force. "You son of a—"

That was all he could say before Pitt injected him with a syringe, and his vision went dark.

*

Everything was still a blur when Altman opened his eyes. He tried to talk, but the pain in his head that shot to his eyes made him shut them tight and groan instead. He blinked a few times until his vision cleared, and the pain was bearable.

He looked up and saw Pitt standing there in front of him. A rush of anger raced through his veins, and he gritted his teeth as he tried to get to his feet but stopped and relaxed back in the chair. He looked down. He wasn't going anywhere with this Duct tape wrapped around him.

He glared at Pitt. "What the hell are you doing?"

Pitt frowned. "Bob, instead of asking me what I am doing, ask me instead what I *should* be doing. I should be destroying that thing you've got in your lab right now. Nobody was supposed to know about this, and it looks like I'm going to have to shut down Special Intelligence while I'm at it, too." He shook his head. "I'm just glad I was able to bring enough of them in while I was able to."

"What you should be doing is shutting down that reproduction facility you've got up there in space!" Altman screamed at him. "Are you out of your mind? We find an alien colony, and instead of studying it, you decide to create hybrids with it!"

"But think of the possibilities, Bob," Pitt said, walking over to him. He came to a stop in front of him. "We study the aliens, yes. But, once I discovered they were genetically compatible with humans, I realized we could study them as hybrids as well."

"Well, I've got news for you—they don't stay human," Altman replied, glaring at him. "That hybrid in the lab is able to communicate telepathically. It already knows what's going to happen because all of the other hybrids told it! They revert to their alien species once they reach adulthood, which in human years would be sixteen."

Pitt studied him. "You're serious?"

Altman nodded. "Congratulations. Not only have you unleashed alien/human hybrids on Earth, but now there'll be hundreds, maybe thousands of aliens we'll all be dealing with. And then what? What if these adult aliens have the same airborne virus they had in infancy? What if they're malevolent? What if they breed, and soon, there are more aliens than humans? Have you considered what your interference with alien life on another planet means for humankind on your own?"

Pitt sighed, rubbing his eyes. "I didn't think that far ahead."

"You weren't thinking at all," Altman growled at him.

Pitt straightened, slapping his hands together with a loud clap in front of him. "I guess I know what that will mean for the division now."

Altman's angry glare faded as he studied Pitt. The man said nothing as he cut the tape from Altman's wrists, then left the room.

*

"You're sure that's him?" Altman asked Fi, standing next to her against their new SID Division car as the children walked out of the school entrance. He studied the child in question, having a hard time getting over how very human he looked.

"I'm positive," Fi replied, also staring at the children. "Look at his eyes."

Altman watched. The tell-tale sign of two eyelids closing over the human eyes occurred, and he shuddered. Funny how a strange thing could so easily be explained away as a genetic defect in the medical community. If they only knew.

"What was his name again?" Altman asked, watching as the boy turned away to walk home, his backpack slung over his shoulder.

Fi opened the file folder she'd been hugging against her chest. The boy's current picture was on a form she read from. "His name is Jake Powers. Age twelve. Math whiz and science scholar."

"Jake?" Altman asked, wryly looking at his new partner. "Let's hope the next one doesn't have your name."

"I don't know," Fi replied, closing the folder and smiling at him. "I kinda like the idea of a hybrid named after me."

Altman shuddered again, shaking his head. "I kinda like the idea of no hybrids."

"Well, get used to it. We need to go check on the next one."

"Right."

The pair straightened and got into the car. The engine rumbled, and they were on their way to locating the next alien/human hybrid.

Great Minds Taste Alike

Thomas Folske

August 15th, 1901

My name is Adolphe Le Prince, Dolph to my friends, and no matter what that monster Thomas Edison says, my father invented the moving picture.

You have no idea how crushingly frustrating it is to have accomplished something so extraordinary yet have no one believe you. To achieve greatness, only to have it stolen away so that someone else may take all the credit. To know that your father was killed by a horrendous thing that passes itself off as human, and to see that monster's face all over in public, claiming your family's legacy for your own. To know that he has so much power and I so little, and to realize that there is nothing I can do but to grin and bear it.

No, I can't just sit back and let this happen, not after what I witnessed. In fact, what I saw on that day is what eventually inspired me to write this diary, so if by chance I do not survive this ordeal, which is a definite possibility, at least someone someday will learn of my plight.

The rest is beyond my control, as I have a feeling everything will soon come to an end. My additional source of inspiration for writing this diary is what I hear at night. It stalks the night outside my third-floor window, a loud thing that seems to be scaling my wall, a thing that is much bigger than a man.

*

It all started when I was just a boy, when my father, Louis le Prince, invented the moving picture. Obsessed since childhood with zoetropes, picture flipbooks, shadow puppets, and the like, my father envisioned a world beyond books, beyond flash photography, where instead of just capturing an instant of life, he wanted to capture whole portions of it. His dream was to portray people living and things in action, to move beyond still frames, where one can't tell if a train is a place to board for the night or a moving vehicle, and to capture and share actual movement. He knew it could be done.

After several failed attempts, my father, using paper—not unlike the picture flipbooks he loved so much and methods of a similar fashion to that of a zoetrope, and with the aid of Eastman and Strong's Kodak negative film, created the process of capturing life on film, or "filming" if you'd prefer.

I remember the first film my father ever successfully shot to completion. We had been in Northern England, as my father had been attempting to find investors for his *idea of the future*, and we were at the house of Joseph and Sarah

Whitley. He shot a short film about us having a fun family day in Roundhay Garden in Leeds. I remember every detail vividly.

"Dolph," my father had told me. "I want to capture a small instant of you living."

The film he shot was just a couple of seconds long, and it was just of us walking around in the garden, but it has always been one of my fondest memories. It was when I knew my father would change the world, and also when I realized that it was my destiny to help him.

I was sixteen when that film was made, practically a man already. I had been helping my father for years before that, but that was the day I truly started paying attention. That was when I transitioned from being my father's helper to knowing what he would need before he needed it and even being able to throw in the occasional helpful suggestion. I think that was when my father became most proud of me. Too bad; we would only have two short years to enjoy our newfound companionship.

It was in September of 1890, just under two years from when the scene was shot in Roundhay Garden, that my father "disappeared." That is an obscene fabrication. I would know. I was there.

My father and I, though no one knew I was present as I was only just able to put my affairs in order and procure a boarding pass at the very last minute, were scheduled to go by train to Paris to meet my uncle Dijon, before heading out to America to demonstrate my father's revolutionary, and now nearly perfected invention. We never made it to Paris, however, as one of Edison's men caught my father before he could board.

I had, in fact, just purchased my ticket for the train to Paris when, upon returning from the ticket booth and preparing to board, I saw my father conversing with a tall, muscular man. Something about the man unnerved me, however, so instead of joining them, I watched from a distance.

At first, their conversation seemed cordial, maybe even pleasant, seeing as how my father was smiling, but then the stranger seemed to propose something, and my father's demeanor instantly changed, as extreme trepidation showed across all his features. I watched as my father began to become progressively more nervous while talking before the man abruptly grabbed him roughly by the arm and began to lead him away from the train.

My father tried to resist, but the man drew a gun. We both went ghost-white, seeing the deadly weapon in the stranger's hand. Without any other course of action apparent, I began to furtively follow them as the man led my father away from the train.

To my chagrin, the stranger approached a waiting carriage and forced my father inside as I watched on in horror. Once the carriage began to move, however, I knew I had to act. I looked all around me, assessing my next move, when, in a fantastic turn of fortune, I found that someone had left a bicycle leaning against a nearby tree. I felt terrible about taking someone else's property, but my father's life depended on me, and I saw no other options.

By bicycle, I pursued my father's kidnapper at what I equated to be a safe distance and was fortunate to find that the carriage turned into a large manor only two miles away.

When I arrived, I dropped the bicycle far from the path leading up to the estate and traveled the remainder of the distance through the woods on foot. By the time I reached the manor, my father had already been escorted inside.

I thought briefly about barging in, but I returned to my better senses and decided to look for a more furtive means of ingress. I crept around the house, like a burglar in the shadows, until I stumbled upon an unlocked basement window. I was about to make my way inside when I heard approaching footsteps from just outside the door opposite me and decided to halt my invasion.

As I watched, the door opened, and my father appeared, escorted by the man who had taken him and another equally big and burly man. Once they passed the threshold, they threw my father to the ground, then slammed and locked the door behind them as they left. I immediately opened the window once again.

"Father," I whispered loudly, calling out to my forlorn patriarch.

He looked in startlement toward the window.

"Father, I have come to save you."

He rose to accept my aid when the sound of more approaching footsteps made him halt.

"Dolph!" He shouted in a whisper. "You must get out of here. Go now."

"Father," I shouted, but by that time, the footsteps had reached just outside the door. I slowly lowered the window as I anxiously watched the obscene scene unfolding before me.

The door opened, and a well-dressed, intelligent-looking man, not intimidating in the slightest, entered casually into the room.

"Hello, Monsieur Le Prince. I am Thomas Edison. It is quite the pleasure to meet you," the man, who looked exactly like any of the pictures of Thomas Edison that I had ever seen, said to my father in English, with an American accent.

"What do you want?" my father asked truculently, in English as well.

"Settle yourself, Monsieur Le Prince, I am only here to make you a proposition," Edison responded with a poisoned sweetness.

My father didn't reply.

"Monsieur Le Prince, you have created the path to the future. A very lucrative path. A path I am more than willing to purchase. You have but to name the price."

"No. It's not for sale," My father responded instantly and with great defiance. "This is my baby, my passion. I will not sell my soul over to you, you devil."

Edison snickered. "You have amassed many a debt amongst myriad investors, Monsieur Le Prince, that is not good for your reputation, not at all…I could make all that go away in an instant."

"I wouldn't have asked for money if I didn't believe I could pay it back. I have a meeting in America I have found my key to success, and soon, I will be able to pay my investors back tenfold."

"Will you, now? I am offering you great prosperity this instant, even without a meeting. No proposals, no investors, no what ifs—Louis Le Prince, sir, I am offering you the opportunity to walk out of here an extremely wealthy man."

"I could not," My father replied. "I believe too firmly in myself. I do not need your money. Instead of offering me the opportunity to walk out of here as a wealthy man, simply offer me the opportunity to walk out of here as I am right now."

Edison chuckled. "I knew you would be difficult."

"So, you are kidnapping me, are you? Sir?"

"No. Kidnapping implies that I plan to keep you," Edison remarked. "No, I am actually happy you declined my offer. I wish Nikola had done the same; his brain would have been marvelous to feast upon, but you, Monsieur Le Prince, your brain might be the finest delicacy I have enjoyed in centuries, possibly since I had eaten the brain of the man who invented gunpowder. However, I went by a different appellation back then."

"Mr. Edison, are you implying that you mean to murder me?" my father inquired incredulously.

"Murder is such a harsh term. Is it murder when a bear kills spawning salmon or when a spider kills a fly? No, it's just nature."

"What are you talking about? What are you?" My father asked, fear highly prevalent in his voice.

All I could do was sit, speechless and immobile, as I watched helplessly from outside the window.

"Monsieur Le Prince, I am not usually one to boast, but taken as your dying request, I shall grant you privy to the history of the maker you are about to meet."

"You hail from Hell, no doubt. You foul demon."

"Far from it, in fact," Edison replied. "I was born in the darkest regions of the universe, in the void between space and time where existence is meaningless. I was conceived in and of the Akashic field, the center of all knowledge in the universe, and was cast out to obtain any further information that I could acquire. I have dwelt here on your planet for all time, since the dawn of man, consuming the minds behind the first use of fire, the first raft— the first person to use a shield in self-defense…the Akashic field has all this information already, as well as every song or book ever written. It knows every possibility of how events will unfold, but it likes to clarify, to see what comes when and from whom. It loved when Shakespeare's mind had reached its level of intellect and loved when The Bard translated its waves into his plays…but, like all parents, it wants to understand how its children think. That is where I come in. All thoughts. All inventions already exist, but how they are formulated can be infinite. That is why I need your mind. I need you for me to be able to connect with Mother once again, with the Akashic cloud from whence I originated, and the only way I can do that is to feed upon or witness the advent of new ideas. I prefer to feed. The connection is so much stronger, but it does not last. In most cases, I must settle for the secondhand connection I receive when you humans tap into the field. I am forced to let your brains connect and will do so for as long as you are under my rule. What's more, I can leech off your connection. What I am saying, Louis Le Prince, is that this is your last chance to flourish and survive. Although I will take the credit for your ideas as my own, you will be able to keep your life and add to my legacy."

"Fuck you," my father told him defiantly.

"As you wish," Edison replied.

I watched as the seemingly human Thomas Edison began to transform into something entirely monstrous. His lower abdomen extended out from his posterior as a second set of legs sprouted out from the almost centaur-like portion of his lower body, and his arms grew to double their original length, adding two extra elbow-like joints in the process. It took every ounce of willpower I could muster, and then some, not to scream, only to find that the worst was yet to come. I nearly went mad as Edison's head sprouted up about three feet above his shoulders, supported by a millipede-like neck that made the monster stand at least ten feet tall.

I stared in silent disbelief, unable to fully process what was happening, as two insectile mandibles extended out from inside Edison's mouth, while at the same time, his eyes began to widen and grow until they began to bulge out of his skull, whereupon they began to form small hexagons across their surfaces, like the eyes of a fly.

"A great mind is a horrible thing to waste," Edison commented maliciously, emphasizing his malevolence with a witch's cackle as he encroached upon my father.

My father screamed as the Edison monster leaped upon him, and I screamed too, thus making my father's last gift to me his screaming so loudly that my screams went unnoticed. I stared in utter helplessness as the creature clamped its horrifying mandible around my father's skull, and when I saw it begin to crush through bone and brain matter alike, I had to rush away into the darkness, knowing my father's life could no longer be saved.

To my great fortune, I was not only able to recover my illicitly procured bicycle, but I was also able to escape from the property without any of the vile entities present ever knowing that I was there in the first place.

It took me a long time to recover after that night, and I will never be over the death of my father. Also, I don't think the nightmares will ever stop. They haven't yet.

August 16th, 1901

When I did finally start to feel fully like my former myself again, which was almost a full year later, I made it my mission to not only preserve the memory and accomplishments of my father but also to fight for his creation and to get it attributed to its rightful creator.

I knew that no one would believe me about the monster aspect of my plight, but I felt as though I had enough hard evidence to prove to anyone who would listen that Thomas Edison had indeed stolen my father's idea.

Over the next eight years, I fought many legal battles while doing everything I could, both publicly and furtively, to defame Edison and endorse the truth of my father's creation, but it all seemed to be of no avail. Edison's fame and fortune spoke louder than all my words combined.

The closest I've ever come to being heard was in 1898, almost three years ago, when I was called as a witness by the American Mutoscope Company to testify against Edison that he had stolen my father's concepts and technology. The jury listened to my statement but still sided with Edison anyway, at least initially. However, in a last glimmer of hope, the verdict was overturned a year later, though that only brought us back to limbo, as the debate is still ongoing to this day. I have heard rumors that they are about to come to a decision, one that doesn't look good for Thomas Edison, but I am not letting myself get my hopes up too much. It was shortly after this potential rumor began, however, that Edison started to come after me.

August 19th, 1901

During my struggles over the last few years, I eventually moved to the States, and I currently reside in Fire Island, New York. Edison is aware of me now and is upset that I am opposing him. It is alarming and terrifying to know he is out there, always possibly watching me, and that I can't tell anyone that he is truly a monster. It is absolutely infuriating. Not only have I thus far been unable to restore my father's legacy, but I also now constantly fear for my life, as I have caught Edison himself, as well as his men, following me on several occasions.

On one of these occasions, I swore I saw Edison's face lurking outside my bedroom window on the third floor as if he had used his bug-like appendages to slink up the wall, though whether it truly was him or not, the horrifying visage disappeared as soon as I moved to investigate.

I have lived in fear for a long time now, until this night, when I know my fear is finally coming to an end. I was awoken from a dead slumber by a sound outside my window. To my complete lack of surprise, Edison was there with three of his goons. The idiots were stationed on the ground outside my window, throwing pebbles and glaring menacingly up at me.

As I watched, the goons rushed forward, bursting into the front door of the building in which I was living, while Edison just continued to stare up at me with a devious smile perched devilishly upon his lips. Reluctantly, I forced myself to turn away from him and make sure my door was locked, then barred with both my bookshelf and my sofa. When I returned to the window, Edison was nowhere to be seen.

I closed and locked the window, then ran to my room and grabbed the Colt revolver I had purchased for just such an occasion. I went to the front door, gun aimed, and waited, knowing the monstrosity that was Thomas Edison was coming and hoping he would be the first through the door. I pulled back the hammer and tightened my finger on the trigger.

Unfortunately, his was not the first voice I heard, as a cluster of gruff voices. Certainly, these belonged to the burly men congregating right outside my front door.

I choked and fled to my bedroom, knowing that the obstructions I had implemented would slow my pursuers but not deter them completely, that they would eventually get in and reach me.

As I write this last entry, I hear the massive men beating angrily upon my door, ramming into it with their shoulders, but I also hear a distant yet distinct skittering coming up along the outer wall leading to my bedroom window. I am writing these final sentences as I hear a voice coming from beyond the glass.

"Hello, Adolphe. I know you saw me so long ago. I have waited so long to make your acquaintance again," Edison's malevolent words drifted in through the thin-glassed window.

I continue to write now because it makes the end feel less near. The monster that masquerades as Edison is now rapping lightly upon my bedroom window. I know he can get in any time he chooses, but he plays with me as though I were a mouse.

I miss my father and know that I will see him again soon, but not without deep regret, as none of our issues will have been resolved... The windowsill is slowly risi—

*

Excerpt from The Fire Island Herald, dated 8/22/1901:

Adolphe Le Prince was found early on the morning of August 20th, dead from a presumed gunshot wound to the head. The wound was likely self-inflicted, as much of the skull above the bottom jaw was missing from the corpse, and the deceased's firearm was found on the body; testing revealed that several shots had been fired from the barrel. Authorities took Le Prince's corpse and immediately cremated it, with no post-mortem pictures of the body having been taken. Adolphe Le Prince was identified by his clothing, and his next of kin has already been contacted. Though the officials have labeled the death a suicide, blood and signs of a struggle were reported to have been found at the home of the deceased.

Testament

Edgar Wells

August 8, 2030
FROM THE DESK OF Dr. GARRET MCCOLL

Hello, you poor fucker, whoever you are. My name is Dr. Garret J. McColl, and I am a Jason scientist and an officer of MKOften. For those who don't know, MKOften was our, the Jason scientists' and/or DARPA, attempt to use black magic as a weapon against the enemies of America. If you can curse a despot, you don't have to send Seal Team 6 after him, you dig?

We begin with a short history.

Fear is a weapon. Truman figured this out first. He gave you—the populus—a Communist terror, a terror that was supposed to be coming from a country with an army almost eradicated by the Nazis. But you didn't know that. You believed it when Truman said they were at the gates with flaming swords. When that stopped working six decades after it began (yes, it takes you that long to catch on), we shifted to the Terrorists. We looked the other way and let them do their dirty work, and then they went into the whole wrong country because the point is money—commodity—money, not safety. We don't give a shit if you're safe, never have. Sadly, the War on Terror stopped working around 2024. You began taking their side. Three years of that, and we just about didn't have a world. You know how the story goes. Everyone calls us evil for doing this type of thing...but look at you. Look at you assholes, always trying to one-up each other. Fighting over any excuse—stupid things like which of the Sister Wives is the biggest skank, and slightly more reasonable things like Donald Trump's round-up proposition to deal with issues of border security. Also, like who it's socially okay to fuck, as if it ever truly mattered to us who or what you poke with your pecker. We just wanted to goad you into killing each other so we wouldn't have to do it.

Lord. The cows will chomp at any cud.

During the time we carried out the Himmler Experiment, we didn't think anything would come of it. Hell, we were drunk! Just a bunch of stupid, drunk doctors h'yucking it up with an occult ritual. If we had known it would work, we, well, we would've done it anyway. Blame it on Eris and her fanatic Robert Anton Wilson and his irreverent sense of humor. Or even Eris and her pretty golden apple. Blame it on Anthony Circe. We are not—were not ever—Nazis. We called it what we did because we were using Heinrich's (extremely classified) diaries to make it work. This is during the first incarnation of Often. During the first attempt at the Himmler Experiment, the earliest incarnations of the MK projects (re: aliens) had two ideas in mind:

Bring aliens to earth again a la the Nazis and cut our own deal with their extra-terrestrial asses. Attempt one was carried out in the Eisenhower days. The Rosicrucians helped us summon strange angels. We cut a deal with them to help us figure out how to make most of the stuff you'll find at CERN. For this, they could take one (1) civilian at a time for their fun and games (it's not experiments, it's for kicks, trust me—they already know all that shit you might "experiment" to discover) whenever they pleased without fear of human interference. Contrary to popular belief, our weapons *do* still hurt them, and they can be killed. We have a Uriel portal in the tundra of Northern Montana that no one's ever heard of, though some idiot made a Facebook Reel out of the location using that stupid fucking internet satellite goddamned Google shot up the ass of space so we could keep an eye on everyone…I'm getting off target. The aliens are the Reticulans. They are the same "angels" that John Dee conjured around the time the Bible was being jimmied into the pile of horseshit people would use to kill each other for the next several centuries. There's no such thing as an "angel". They are aliens, that is to say, things with bodies that don't come from Earth. Jehovah is an alien. Crowley will tell you that, only he calls it Aiwazz. We hid them from you, but why? You think it's because we're all evil cabalists, but that's not why. This is why: as soon as the first redneck or gangster or rogue cop took a pot-shot at an alien (because they look scary as fuck), that'd be it. The Reticulan emperor would demand nothing less than genocide. Due to our careful consideration, they have always honored the deal to appear via holograms as angels and demons in order to help us invent religions for the purpose of population control maintenance.

Next, use their—yep, that's right, their black magic to place a veil of stupidity over the heads of the masses so we could more easily gaslight civilians into the imperialist matrix. To do this, our Reticulan friends gave us the radio first and then the television. The two best black magic tools ever invented. Fuck wands, man. First with the Nazis, and then with the Americans (Yes! Me! Proud to be a 'Murican). Let the box in the living room teach the complacent ones to fear the *enemy*. And the enemy is whoever the television channels say it is. The Reticulans taught us first what images do to the human psyche. Anything you see, your subconscious thinks is You. What a tool that is. My predecessors were pleased at how well this all worked, so pleased that I doubt they ever expected it to change. Around the time I entered the field, change had come to pass—

(Hippies, punks, these fucking fringe assholes who sell malcontent like goddamn Oreo cookies…why couldn't ya just leave shit alone?)

—and it was time to escalate! Thus, the Reticulans gave us the internet. That worked like a charm. I don't need to tell you how. You already know that.

Ah, the Civil War of '27. Brigades of Indigenous Fighters, mostly white guys painted up like the savages in a John Wayne movie, tearing each other apart with their bare hands. A fake alien war would've been the fight to end all fights, no?

They gave us that idea.

Said fake invasion was propagated by the use of holograms in conjunction with the legalization of strong hallucinogens such as LSD, Mushrooms, Peyote, Mescaline, and MDMA pills laced with Fentanyl. As you know, those drugs became legal in 2026. Writing about it, I finally see how stupid it all sounds. Everything sounded a hell of a lot better in our notes, I promise. I think none of us really believed you'd all fight each other for real, especially with the internet's grand ability to keep you all *thinking* you're revolutionary fighters when the truth is that you're all just a bunch of ridiculous no-fisted keyboard warriors—yeah, vicarious battle worked for almost ten years. Then Donald J. Trump got his brains blown out in April of 2027. Enter the great MAGA uprising, which you know all about.

We could not let a civil war rage for long. You were all too busy fighting to notice. While you were all occupied with killing each other over who was the biggest bigot, we in the upper levels of government were watching as China prepared to waltz in and just kind of take America over. Can't have that. Our first attempt at a holographic alien attack took place on January 17th, 2028. We flew UAPs over the second Battle of Gettysburg, and you tried to shoot them down; they shot you instead with laser technology that the Reticulans helped us create. You stopped fighting. You believed in the Aliens.

(How do you kill with a hologram? Simple. The answer is heat. Holograms are made of hot static. You do the rest of the math.)

They also believed in you.

Most of you were dead within a month. Being a Jason scientist, I was ready for—wait a minute—my job had fuck all to do with it. I just *liked* the idea of prepping for the apocalypse, always did, so I had my bunker, weapons, and food ready to go before the shit hit the fan. It's good to be a millionaire, no?

Not that money matters now.

To hell with this. You've heard enough history for a night. I'm going to bed.

*

David, Lisa, and their son Henry had been following the signs for about a week now. For the first time since the end of the world began, since the Grays landed, the family had hope. It hadn't been easy staying out of sight of the Grays. He imagined the rules were the same as they would have been if he were a criminal dodging the cops. No main roads allowed. Travel at night more often than in the day. Learn to see them before they see you, whoever they are, in this case, seven-foot aliens with Gray, shimmering skin that could, for brief periods, hide them from human eyes. What could not be hidden was the stink of the pheromones they gave off right before an attack. Whatever it is, the shit smelled like dirty underwear in a microwave. There was nothing special about the family, maybe luck...or cowardice. David did not fight in the war; he and his family took off for the mountains. While the world was being destroyed by UAP laser fire, his family kept low and survived. Three weeks into the alien attack, the ships just quit. Hackers—had to be...what a crazy world.

But one or two still flew, so they were careful.

After a few days of aimless wandering, they came upon the first sign, and it was like being flooded with new hope. When they found the second sign, it was like a new lease on life, and the third made them downright intrepid. Perhaps the place where these ARK signs led would be...what? Hopefully not like Terminus in *The Walking Dead*. They had to keep their eyes peeled for stuff like that.

"Daddy, are we ever going to get there?" Henry asked. "Like to whatever the Ark is?"

David grimaced. Okay. Don't get mad at the boy. He's in the apocalypse, too. "I trust we will, son. There's more signs since we got into the woods, right? We made it this far, haven't we?"

"We sure have," Lisa said.

Henry nodded. "Do we have any food left? I'm sorry. My legs are tired, Dad. They might need food."

"Your legs don't need food. They need willpower." He scoffed. There was nothing in this life that could toughen his son up. And it was David's fault. After all, he'd never been a sports guy, just a high school science teacher— nothing really to sing about. He was no warrior.

Henry suddenly stopped and sat down on the path. The next ARK sign was visible from where they all stood, maybe thirty yards away. David had in mind to camp maybe a mile beyond it. Henry looked up and said, "I'm not moving without a snack."

"Young man, get up off that dirt right now," Lisa said. "We don't have far to go."

"NO!" And he screamed it.

David snatched him up by the arm. "Listen here, buster, I've had just about enough—"

"Sumbitch! Lookie here, we found us a fam-dam-bamly!"

Approaching fast from all three sides were two men and a woman. They looked like backwoods folk. The woman was equally as muscular as the smallest of the men, who were not at all small—one of them was almost as tall and wide as a Gray. And that one didn't stop walking. He kept on. And kept on—until he got close enough to deliver a punt to David's crotch.

"BWAH!" David doubled over in time to catch another boot to the face. Lisa screamed for him, and that seemed to make the man want to kick him more. He howled with each kick. The feet didn't care where they landed; David caught out of the corner of his eye that the woman and the other man with her were doing something horrible to his family, and he could not get up; he could do nothing aside from accept the kicks and stomps landing all over his body without any hope of stopping...until they did.

"Stop!" Lisa cried. "Stop hurting my husband, God, stop!" She clutched her son.

"What's your name, honey?" the woman asked.

"Lisa...this is Henry, and that's David. Please...we're common people. Don't hurt us."

"I know what ya are," she said. "Weak. Ain't shit, that's what. Buncha fuckin' squares." She squeezed one of Lisa's breasts. Lisa cringed.

"Best act like you like it," she said.

The man with her laughed. "Best listen to Dee Dee, yeah. They thought the worst thing out here was them Gray sonsabitches, Bucko. Oops."

"That's cool, Jack," Bucko, the giant, said. "I don't mind to school 'em." He grabbed Henry.

Lisa screamed, "Let go of him!" She socked Bucko in the jaw, and surprisingly, his head moved.

He swung with a right hook, his giant fist colliding not with Lisa's but with the young boy's face. Something broke—the child screamed.

Lisa gave a banshee's wail and grabbed for Bucko's hair. Her head darted forward, her teeth sunk into his cheek, and he laughed even when he felt something rip—then came a choking sound.

Dee Dee. She'd plunged a knife into the rabid mother's back, knocking both the wind and the bite strength out of her. The pain caused her to open up, and Dee Dee peeled her off Bucko like tape. She threw Lisa to the ground, and the mother arched her back to keep the knife from going in any deeper. When Dee Dee saw that, she kicked Lisa in the chest, the force driving her back-first into the dirt. She coughed and gurgled, and Dee Dee stomped on her shoulder. The blade exploded out of Lisa's breast. Blood flowed as if from a burst hose, soaking the mother's dirty pink sweater.

She gurgled and died.

Dee Dee squinted at her bloody soccer mom's outfit. The meth-addled redneck woman almost hurt. She'd been a mother herself once…but the Grays had taken care of that.

If she could not have kids, no one would.

"Well shit, you killed her," Jack said.

"Was you gonna fuck her?" Dee Dee asked.

"I'd aimed to. Guess it ain't no count now. I don't do dead pussy. Bucko?"

Bucko leered down at the broken boy at his feet. Henry's chest hitched as he cried. Amazingly, he was trying not to be loud. "Naw. Naw, I reckon I got what I want right here. I—"

Dee Dee stomped on the back of the boy's head. He screamed, his hands flailing to the spot, slapping against her boot. She drew her heel up again, the boy's fingers instinctively clutching her boot, and slammed the sole back down on his head with all the force in her quads and hamstrings. Henry's soft nugget splattered like a melon, brains squashing outward. His little fingers pointed stiffly at the sky and then went limp. Jack giggled.

"You bitch!" Bucko backhanded her across the face.

Her pistol appeared. The muzzle pressed against Bucko's ear. "I told your ass no more kids."

"What is you, my momma?"

Sister, in truth. "Close enough, reckon. Fuck's wrong with you?"

A gurgle came from behind them. David, though broken in every section of his body, though his face was so swollen that blood was leaking from his ears, was reaching for his boot. Carefully, laboriously, he struggled to remove a knife from a sheath secreted within it. Jack took a step. Dee Dee stopped him.

"He ain't no danger, babe." She grinned. "Watch this."

"Fuck you," the father said, stabbing himself in the throat. Blood came, but not much. The father, a square with no real knowledge of hit locations, had missed his jugular vein.

"WOO-HOO!" Jack cried. He began to applaud. Dee Dee joined him. Bucko first chuffed, then laughed, and went to the suicidal man's side.

"Lemme help ya there, bobba-lou," he said. He grabbed the man's hair, snatched up the knife, and began sawing at the man's neck larynx first. David's eyes bulged out of his head, his protesting attempt at a relatively painless escape ruined by the monster who couldn't sever his tissues fast enough. David heard bone squeak when the knife's edge cut across his C4 vertebrae. Bucko stopped.

David screamed.

"Y'all hear that? *Squee! Soo-EE!* I'mma leave you like that, shithead." Bucko jerked his knife free from David's bone."

"GLAGH!"

"Yep, Gla-guh. Fuckin' toy. Die slow."

*

August 15th, 2030

QANON, right, remember that? That was us bringing the psychic wargame to the people. The game began with creating what we called The OpinioNation. We pumped the internet with conspiracies, both fact-based and fabulist, advising our 'net trolls to plug every comment section they could plug with incendiary rhetoric. You, the ignorant, thought these comments were made by folks like you, folks who say things because they mean them. I really just had to stuff my hand into my mouth to keep from laughing at this. God, you guys…seriously, what the fuck? How could you fall for that game? Anyway. You slid into our trap as easily as a micropenis sinks into a porn star. Not three months and no less than 1.7 *billion* of you were at each other's throats. You couldn't make sense of anything because we didn't want you to. We gave you conflict and chaos. We gave you true war plans and false war games. We gave you solid occult knowledge intermingled with cajoling Discordia and the whole-cloth fabulism known as the Spaghetti Monster. You ate the golden apple-tizer and the sanguine main course. We also gave you the truth about Satan, Jesus, and every other religion and then told you those truths were bullshit and watched you foam at the mouth. We put you on a Doomsday Clock to see if you'd save yourselves or just make the goddamn thing run faster…guess which one you did that we knew you would do the whole time? We gave you the truth about Global politics and blew the whistle on every conspiracy and the sick, sociopathic things our people in power do, showed you videos of them doing hideous things to children and animals—you all forgot about those victimized innocents pretty quickly. See how it works? I tell you the truth with one mask on, then change my voice and put on another mask and return to tell you all the things "that other guy" said were bullshit, and I do it while surrounded by pompous decorations, preferably dressed in whatever the hottest trendy outfits are. And we, knowing what time it really is, laugh at your rancorous online comments to those who don't act like you do. And theirs to you, of course.

Like shaking up ants in a bottle.

I'm sorry for being so full of contempt…I wish you hadn't fallen for fifty years plus of this. Damn, could you not have caught us before we decided the only thing left to do was dissolve the veil in its entirety? It's not like we're any better. Confession—we wanted you all to fight until you *actually* started fighting. I guess that's a trap we scientists brave, experiments that backfire.

It's too late for all this now, I know. Still, I confess. We control the 4chans, the XM radio, and all your podcasters. From Rogan to Brand, even the super-tweeker carpetbagger shmucks who run podcasts like Promised Land Preppers. Corporate sponsorship, baby, that means *I own that ass.* We had control over every news station—it wasn't just Fox, it was MSNBC as well, and also News Nation, and let's not forget ABC. Shit. We even owned MeTV. We produced JAIL. PARANORMAL CAUGHT ON CAMERA. We are the head of the hydra, the *Biest mit tausend armen,* and our weapon was the Opinion Itself. Once our stronghold on your opinion was nice and secure, we sent emissaries into the world with drugs and music with a message built to trash you for not thinking for yourselves and make you angry at others for committing the same crime, while at the same time depressing you into buying guns and shooting each other. While high on speedballs, preferably.

It was the age of the Stupid Parrot.

I'm trying not to weep.

Don't blame just capitalism, consumerism, communism, or socialism. The dogma doesn't matter. As soon as the human gets hold of any ism, he adds a J to it and proceeds to drown the world in the spice of his fertile greed.

Believe I'll get mine. *Que sera, sera.*

*

"These ARK signs 'bout to piss me off," Jack said. "We been followin' these motherfuckers for like five miles." He wiped his forehead. "All's I see still is got-damn trees."

"Thanks for pointing that out," Bucko said. "I'd a never guessed we was all lookin' at the same thing."

"Quit," Dee Dee said. "Look there, right through the trees, there's a road."

Jack sighed when they were finally out of the woods. They stepped out on the road, and once his feet hit the pavement, the miles caught up, and exhaustion set in. He dug around in his pocket. His fingers chanced upon a square-inch piece of plastic with a tiny snap-lock at the top. He hung back, making sure no one was watching, popped the top, and had a quick toot.

Bucko whirled. "Fuck you sniffin' on? Share, bogart!"

"I ain't got much of—hey!"

Dee Dee snatched the nickel bag from his fingers. She popped the top and whiffed a bit of shard, her eyes never leaving Jack's. "You can't keep Tina all to yourself. Her love has to be *spread.*"

"I'm taer't as shit, gimme that." Bucko had his hit and, amazingly, gave what was left back to Jack.

"I sure do hope everybody feels better now," Jack said. He put the baggie away, and they began to walk. "I wish we had us some food in the equation."

"We could hunt some squirrel," Bucko said.

"T'aint no squirrel left out here," Dee Dee said. "All's it is is birds, less'n you wanna try your luck on a lynx or a bear."

Jack laughed. "Bucko might could get us bear."

Bucko, at six feet seven inches and three-hundred and twenty-five pounds, none of it sagging, agreed. "Reckon I could get us a meal o' bear. Ain't tried my luck at it yet. I caught me an eagle once."

"You never caught you no eagle," Jack said.

They chattered like that for about an hour, keeping one foot in front of the other, bitching about not having cigarettes or weed. They were high up, a mile or more, walking through low clouds that skated over the concrete tongue under their feet.

*

August 17, 2030

I took stock of my food after I was done with the last confession. I have about a thousand MREs left, half that in gallons of water. The water still works as well, evidenced by the shower I took, so I'll be saving the gallons for when it runs out. I have a hundred bottles of soap and twice that in bars. I have an AR-15, Uzi, the Mossberg for close work, and three pistols—one 40 Glock, firing 10mm rounds, one .25, a purse gun I named Ms. Last Resort, and a 9mm Luger. Finally, I have the long-range Patriot Rifle, California Edition. That motherfucker will nut a gnat at a mile's remove. I have 250 grenades and one Redeye RPG; this handheld beast could take down a commercial airliner, and half of the grenades are incendiary. This shelter is lead-lined. You cannot find me with radar. That must be universal, for the aliens haven't discovered me either.

Maybe they're not looking.

It's getting late. I spent quality time with my plants today. I have a garden down here. Thanks to the solar generator (I named her Sunny, of course), as long as the sun shines, so will these plants thrive. My grow lights are good, like the sun. They give off warmth, keeping the room at a steady 25c, and if their sensors read temperatures higher than that, the heat automatically cuts off. The largest plant I have down here is a buttonbush. I have a bee balm, and I have pink ladies, which are not unlike buttercups. I have tomatoes and potatoes. Lettuce. I have cantaloupe. I also have the obligatory cannabis crop. Today was harvest day. I wish I knew what I really wanted to say. There was a time I'd have known…seems like the more time I spend down here alone, the less I want to write my story, and the more I just kind of want to talk to myself.

That won't do, though. There must be a posterity log. If I die, or rather, *when* I die down here, someone will eventually find me…fuck. Writing is depressing, man. I'm going to smoke another joint of this thirty percent that I grew and hit the hay.

Should I wake up, I'll see you again.

*

"It's cool now," Dee Dee said. She took the first step out of the trees and looked up. A UAP that looked a bit like pictures she'd seen of cancerous tumors slowly skated across the sky until it disappeared behind the mountain peak they were climbing. Bucko took one big step over the grass and scraped his shoe on the road, holding up two middle fingers, slowly spinning in a circle, hands high.

"Fuck you, Grays!" he roared.

"Shut the fuck up, dumb shit," Dee Dee said.

"I thought those motherfuckers all crashed," Bucko said.

"It's never *all* when shit like that happens," his sister admonished.

"Well, God knocked 'em outta the sky."

Dee Dee and Jack laughed.

"More like Santy-Claus," Jack said.

"Fuck them things," Bucko said. "I don't give a hot damn." He pointed back up at the sky. "Suck some, pumpkinheads!"

"They see you do that, you ain't gonna be that much a smart ass," Jack said.

"I'm not scared of those pasty pieces o' shit," Bucko said. "Goddamn floppy ass motherfuckers."

"They ain't floppy!" Jack spat on the road. "Floppy. Idjit. I watched one rip a man in his half by his laigs. It was like that movie, what's it called—"

"*Bone Tomahawk*," Dee Dee said.

"Yeah, that one. Kurt Russell's balls fall out."

Bucko laughed. "I think you have that wrong, Jack." He sighed. "I wish a Gray would like to fuck. I get hard thinking about what their pussies must be like. It's hard to walk." He sneered at Dee Dee. "Are they like a second mouth? I bet they are. The buttholes too."

"Knock it off," she said. "That's really fucking—holy shit, y'all, check it." She pointed to an ARK sign that was, for the first time that they'd seen, on the side of the mountain road in plain view.

"This must be it," she said. "We got to be here. It points left…we follow this curve. Ayuh. We gonna find us this ark motherfucker. Whoo-hoo!"

"Why's it keep saying ARK?" Jack asked. "That's a big ass boat, innit? I don't see no boats nowhere."

"Maybe we just can't see it yet," Dee Dee said.

"That don't make no damn sense." Jack walked to the edge of the pavement and swept his hand along the panoramic mountain-scape that had been following them the whole trip. Then, he pointed at the side of the mountain and, not feeling like the finger drove the point home, ran across the road and slapped rocks. "Fuck you mean look hard enough? Look at what, Dee? Rocks? There ain't shit else to see up here! This shit look like a mountain, that shit look like the road, them over there ain't nothing but a bunch of bitch ass trees! What am I missing? What you reckon, goddamn—oh, I know. We gonna go in the mountain, and the boat'll be in there on slats. We'll just ride a motherfucker a mile downhill, fuck it."

Dee Dee shrugged. "Maybe they reckon we build or own ark out of all this free lumber," she said.

"Back here," Bucko said. "Sign's there, road curves, walk right on around the curve, and there's a cave." In his hand, he held a struggling bird. He gave the tender creature's head a little scratch, then bit it off with a crunch.

"Ew," Jack said. "Ought to cook it first."

"No. Heat kills the fear-dope. That's the best part."

*

August 18, 2030

What did I want to write about today? Oh, the story. And eventually, I'll get around to what I plan to do because I do have plans, and I'd like to get your take on them. Yes, yours. Whoever you are. Person who used to watch TV and eat fast food. Person who hasn't been enslaved or eaten by the aliens who also like meat, as it turns out. You, my reader. Reader who will never meet me, reader who knows I've certainly become something's meal by the time your eyes touch this paper. We did it to you—who did it to ourselves—who? Me? Hm. I think I'm going mad. Looks that way, doesn't it? Diary…(tinkling musical notes)…of a madman, mad…

Let me finish telling you about the second Himmler Experiment, the one I was part of. We used a Thelemite Ritual called *The Star Ruby*. That's also what Himmler used. Shall I describe it for you? The Adeptus Exemptus (who was not me. I am a grade 4 Minor Adept, which is a far cry from an Exemptus) takes a child. He—

You don't want to hear more?

That's right. You don't.

It didn't come through the mirror, and it didn't come fast. After waiting an hour for no smoke and nothing to fuck unto, we all dispersed. The following morning, I took a ride and had a look through the James Webb Telescope after receiving a frantic call from Danica, one of the telescope's monitors. She'd seen an object around the size of our moon coming from the area of Zeta Reticuli. Thus began a scramble to do something about it. A ship of that size entering our orbit could throw off gravity. Ostensibly. Unless they had great tech. Ye gods, how we argued about it. Turns out we didn't have to.

They replaced our moon, get it? That was on the news, remember? They pulled right up next to the moon with the whole world watching (But not fighting, eh? Mission accomplished!) as a rock that resembled our moon got close and the one we're all used to just…winked out of existence like it was never there. Remember that? There was a large rumbling of planet Earth, earthquakes in California, the New Madrid fault went and ate Chicago, St. Louis, Memphis, and a lot of other wonderful cesspools, millions were killed…and then nothing. Once those phenomena ended, it was like we had a replacement moon. The Zetas were here, our angels, the things you all have been worshipping for two thousand years and more…apparently, the Bible was right about the Revelation, just not the way it said it was going to be. There's no Jesus here, just Jehovah and his tribe of Reticulans.

I can barely fit it all into a single notebook.

And here it is bedtime again.

They came to rid the universe of the disease called humanity. Our true life's purpose is to kill. Humanity is the natural, final evolution of the most deadly virus ever to swim the Unified Field. While we are not immortal, like a flu virus, we are much more dangerous. A flu virus, see, isn't large enough to do major damage—it can't build cars and spaceships. It can't occupy and take over other worlds. Stop trying to argue. Have you ever seen HIV build a skyscraper? I think not. This is why the aliens have come. To shift the evolution of the human virus into something a little more harmonious. We were supposed to use technology to cultivate our relationships with one another. Unfortunately, we're too bloodthirsty as a race to reach that level of attainment.

Okay. I have the strangest feeling that I've been found. With no proof, I'm chalking it up to the willies. At any rate, I'm on guard. Sleeping with one eye open.

*

Dee Dee insisted they rest before exploring any further. She was crashing. She denied any help from the stuff in Jack's pocket, and with a little food on his stomach, Bucko agreed. Judging by the way they all felt, they'd been asleep for more than one day. It made sense. This was the first time in a month the crew had any sleep. Not entirely the fault of drug addiction, oh no—staying clear of the Grays was endless work, hence their running to the mountains. The Grays were still having trouble in the cities after their ships got fucked…after God knocked them out of the sky…Jack, chuckling softly, shook his head. Whatever. He had no idea how it all had happened; one minute, the ships worked—one minute they didn't. The only thing about that was he felt like if people could take out alien ships, they could probably open up…what was the word for it…dime-something. Bucko liked to say reality was like an onion and those had layers…dimensions! That was the word. Someone opened up the dimensions, then the aliens got in, had to be. If it were any other way, they'd have come before, right? If not, it seemed right anyway, and Jack found over the course of his thirty-four years on earth that when he felt like something seemed right, it always turned out to be. He had a 100% hit rate with stuff like that. Yeah, he was a savvy sumbitch.

Whatever, man. Shit. If he ever found out whose fault this all was, he intended to have a field day with their flesh. Maybe feed them to Bucko. The giant would eat anything.

Dee Dee yawned and stretched, waking up finally. "Let's find out what we got going on here." She looked around. "It's like any other cave, huh? I was expecting it to look like a warehouse or something."

Jack shook his head. "Signs leading to this place say ARK. That means there's some kind of shelter here. If folks is in there, they certainly aim to be able to get out, so that means there's a way in." he said. "That being the case, it must be this here."

"What makes you so sure of that?" Bucko asked.

"Buhcawse, bubba. Who you think made those signs? Teenagers? Yeah, they skipped high school every day for a month to climb the fuckin' mountain stickin' to the woods half the time night and day to put up a bunch of ARK signs just so's they could fool dingbats like us. That makes a shit-ton of sense don't it? Hell, now that I've said as much, I—"

"I'll eat your fucking tongue," Bucko growled.

Jack shut up.

"Boys." Dee Dee was about fifteen yards ahead of them. She looked very small in the dark. "I found a hatch. It's like a sewer cap." She squatted and worked her fingers around the edges, found a hole for her fingers, and lifted with her legs. After a bit of resistance, the cap moved. She pushed it up and it tipped over on its face into the dirt.

"Rungs, like a ladder," she said.

August 19th, 2030

Recall the monoliths? Homing devices. Recording devices. Logging humanity's every move since 2009. Further, they help hold the "Moon" in place during orbit and synthesize gravity so we puppet people don't float off into space where we won't be useful for anything. Now that I'm writing this, I find that really funny, considering the fact that they killed and ate most of us. Why not just let us float away? We'd have wound up in their nets, same as any shrimp. Sport. Our overlords are…eh, *sporting* Reticulans. What fun would it have been to eat food that didn't fight back? Gods and monsters, man…forks and knives.

How do I know they found me? I can hear them in my head. They have yet to zero in on my location, I guess the lining of this underground shelter screws with their telepathy. I'm not running scared for two reasons: if I go above ground, they'll find me for sure. Also, according to all the messages I'm hearing, they don't want to kill me. They…want to mate. Everyone wants to fuck an angel or a demon—well, how about a Gray? I ask that because whatever's talking to me is female. She keeps saying *I'm close. I'll be there soon,* and that's it. She expects me to expect her. Still trying to make sense of it all. I need to read over this diary. I think I'll do that now.

Dr. Garret McColl closed the word processor and pulled the security cameras up. Would she be lovely? A stupid song started playing in his head, something from Taylor Swift. He shook it off and studied the security cameras—there. Movement. Shapes, they looked more like people than Grays—he hurried to the arsenal cabinet and removed an AR-15. He made sure it was locked and loaded, then checked the security cameras one more time. The people were gone.

World of Grays executing the human race but yet we're still somehow the most dangerous thing. Fuck sake. Ought to be an award of some kind. Footsteps just outside. He could hear them talking about his cannabis plants. Glad you like them, asshole. Too bad you won't be in on the sesh. Garret waited off to the side of the entrance, his hands sweating all over the rifle's metal grip. This way, the pricks coming for him would have to enter the room all the way in order to see him, and that would give him time to fire. And he still had to hit what he shot at. He bit his lips—all these guns. He barely knew how to use them. His heartbeat was rapid. A bit of sweat started on the back of his neck. His brain tickled. He dared not let go of the rifle. He hoped he was right about the door—the textbooks said he was, but he'd never done anything like this. A whiff of ozone shot up his nostrils. He sneezed; he heard something say *that ain't us,* and then a human ran into the room.

McColl fired.

Lucky shot. The top half of the poor woman's head blew off like a hat subjected to a strong gust of wind. A pulse of death's electricity turned what remained of her skull in his direction. The one eye she had left maintained contact with his. Panic burst in his belly. He began hyperventilating—hadn't expected that—he heard his own rifle clatter to the floor, his hands were cold; something hit him in the side of the neck.

*

"Wake y'ass up, piece o' shit!"

Garret opened his eyes just in time to see the boot collide with his abdomen. He coughed, groaned, peed a little, and doubled over all at once, catching a half-hearted toe to the top of the head. The skin scuffed, and he turned over on his side, beginning to crawl away—the boot collided with his ass and sent him sprawling on his belly. He could barely breathe. He tried to get up. Someone stomped on his back.

"Good morning, motherfucker," his assailant said. "Ya kilt my old lady, prickshit! What'd you shoot at us for, ya fuckin' duck? We was just here to say, 'Hey, someone that ain't you's alive, hello.' That's all we aimed to do!" The boot ground into his back. "But nah. Your coward ass has to shoot first, and don't even ask no question. What you think, Bucko? Am I wrong?"

"Nope," Another voice said. Garret turned his head and saw a set of very large boots approaching his face.

"Don't kick me anymore!" he cried.

The boot smashed into his nose. Not too hard, just hard enough to bring a healthy flow of blood.

Jack chuckled. "He says don't kick him no more, Bucko. Must be opposite day."

"It's whatever day I say it is." The boot ground into his back, hard enough to make him fear for the integrity of his vertebrae. Then it was gone. "I'd say he's lucky I don't kick him to death, but since we're gonna torture him for the next few days while we eat his food and smoke his weed, well, that don't sound much like luck." A hand gripped his hair and yanked his head back. "Get up, asshole. Help me out or I'mma pull your fucking nugget off your shoulders— there you go."

"He'd look like one of them critters from *Evil Dead* if ya did that," Jack said.

Garret struggled to get his feet under the rest of him in time to keep his spine from dislodging from his pelvis, caught his heel on the floor, and pushed up as hard as he could. He spun, his target anticipating this move, and slammed Garret's face into the table. His notebook jumped. His pen clattered on the floor. Bucko—he assumed this was the troglodyte's name—asked Jack, "What you mean like that one at the end that kep' sayin' *Dead by Dawn!* and Ash had to lop his mop off with a chainsaw, right?"

"Hell yeah." Laughing, Jack closed the laptop and picked it up. He smacked Garret's face with the flat cover, not hard, just hard enough to let him know how hard it could get if Jack wanted. "This yours? You write all this shit?"

"Yes," Garret said. "It's my confession."

"I'd say so," Bucko said.

"Yeah. I been looking for your ass. Talkin' bout you brought them fuckin' Grays here to turn us all into cattle. You even call us cows." He hit Garret in the eye with the corner of the laptop.

It burned instantly, and the beginnings of a migraine burst behind the socket. "STOP! Please stop hitting me!"

Jack chuckled. "Fu-hu-huck yew, bubba. You killed our old lady. We ain't gonna stop doing a bitch ass' thing we start doing to you, not until you run out. And that's gonna take a long time, 'cos we brought supplies."

"Ever had a shot o' clear?" Bucko asked.

"Fuck you," Garret snarled.

"Yeah. Fuck me. Fuck you." And a needle slammed into his shoulder. "Give that about ten minutes. You'll be wanting to thank me. Don't, though, 'cos I only give that to you so's we could torture you more. You done shot Dee Dee. She's Bucko's sissy, don't you know it? That was the only woman left on Earth far as we know. So we're both pretty mad at you."

"Mmhmm," Bucko concurred.

"Now all's we gots to fuck's each other."

"T'aint no good," Bucko said.

Jack clicked his teeth and nodded. "S' right. It ain't wet enough back 'air."

Bucko ground his hips against Garret's ass, which was thankfully still covered. He was turgid like a pre-rut horse. "My cock is strong. I need no lube."

"Reckon check his oil anywho," Jack said. "Just for shits n' gigg—"

Garret pushed away from the table, Buckogs let him, and Jack grabbed his shoulders. Both men forced his face down into the couch cushions. Laughter began, and something exploded in the back of his head. It did not hurt, though he felt like it ought to—the speed rushing through his muscles might have helped him in another situation, not now—these leathery rednecks were unlike any men he'd ever had to deal with in his privileged life, impossible to defeat without a weapon. A few years ago, he'd thought about getting into martial arts and wished he had only until his sphincter exploded with ripping pain. He howled like a banshee.

"Whoo! That's in there, man." Bucko ground his pubic hair on the scientist's ass. "This for you fucking the whole human race, Doc. You like them ten inches? Yeah. I bet you do. This is what you done to us."

"Oh yeah," Jack said. He came around the couch, panting, with his hard cock jutting from his stroking fist. It was normal, thankfully. "If you bite me, boy…this'll get worse."

"Oh, he ain't goan bite," Bucko said. "He's about to learn to like it. That dope ought to be—"

I'm here.

Jack's head imploded, sucking down into his neck in a corkscrew fashion. One of his eyes flew across the couch. Garret almost laughed at the way the sodomite's teeth looked, scrambled into splintered jawbone and meat as they were. Bucko screamed, and Garret's colon leaked fire when the monster's humongous penis slid free from his savaged anus. Garret collapsed and rolled over, finally seeing Bucko's face; the human grizzly bear looked like rough-cut granite with a beard…and yet like a kitten in the arms of what held him. The Gray was almost eight feet tall, stooped to avoid its head scraping across the ceiling, and it spun Bucko around in its gigantic arms until its hands were clamped over the toes of Bucko's boots. Then, the Gray began to roll him up like a bunting. Bone crunched. Blood exploded from the tops of the boots and coursed down his filthy jeans. Bucko screamed, he begged *ah goawd stop it hurts jeezis he killed my girlfriend ahh fuck you alien fuck youuuuuuuu.* Trying to die hard, Garret had to give him that. He kept up the front well enough until the Gray started rolling his guts and his ribs into his throat. Garret heard *guklaka* and a sound like cats being raped. The Gray concentrated a little harder and rolled.

Bucko's organs spewed from his mouth hard enough to rip his cheeks. He almost looked alive. Little too much to drink, maybe. That continued until red lasagna squirted from his ears and nostrils. One of his eyes popped out of his head. His skull flattened with a shotgun crack. Now, he looked like a deflated human balloon.

Plop. The Gray dropped the rolled flesh wad to the ground. Garret looked into its eyes, terror raging through his system, blood flowing from his asshole, no pain thanks to the super shot of narcotics Jack had given him. The Gray took a step forward, knelt…and smiled warmly.

A wash of endorphins flooded Garret's body when she laid her long hand on his chest. He felt safe.

I told you what I want, love.

*

October 31ˢᵗ, 2030

They are part of a group of resistance fighters. Human energy is used like batteries by formless beings who fool us into believing they are gods. Jehovah was a traitor to the Gray race who gave his body over to the Gods and came to Earth to deceive prophets since time immemorial. They were being possessed and slaughtered. So, the resistance came to Earth to kill the batteries. After they thinned us out, they got the idea to mate with what was left of us so the Gods may no longer use us as Batteries. It won't work if the genes are mixed because the Gods can't suckle from Grays.

It is woe, after all, that feeds the gods. Grays cannot feel woe. They have very little capacity for emotion, though they do seem to feel close to the one they choose as a mate.

And the mating season has begun.

I haven't written anything in here in a long time. Why? Busy, so very busy. The Grays are finally done with their cleaning. According to Lelia—that's the name of my Gray wife—sweet thing she is, wonderful...you're a virgin until you go alien, I promise. Surely you, gentle reader, are currently enjoying the yoni of your own interstellar lover; that's why you have the luxury of reading what will soon be my published autobiography. The idiots that came to kill me thought I was a monster for ripping wide the dimensions and calling the Reticulans to earth. That's fair...most heroes do look like monsters at the beginning of their careers.

We needed this.

The population, according to Lelia, sits at a comfortable, roomy one hundred million. Without all the industry and extra sets of lungs, oxygen saturation has improved in the atmosphere. The act of breathing itself got me high for the first six weeks. I seem to be getting used to it now. There are more stars visible in the sky...Lelia likes to point out which stars actually are occupied planets and regale me with tales of those who live there. I won't keep you much longer. The important things are written. History is there. Chances are, no one but me would find my new romance very interesting. Maybe if I were the only person currently mating with an alien, but we are Legion, and this is the new way...as it was always meant to be.

THE LIFE WE'RE BORN INTO

John Bruni

I cut his throat and watch as his lifeblood springs up from the rendered flesh and oozes from between his dirty lips, marking the spots between the few teeth he has, matting down the front of his unkempt beard. Something feels off, though. No, I enjoy what I've just done, but the air around me feels odd.

When I was a kid, I once looked out my bedroom window at a thunderstorm. Suddenly, the world felt different, and my arm hair stood on end, pointing through the glass. The next second, a bolt of lightning came down in my backyard so close to me that I'd been blinded. I thought about that moment often, especially the way my arm hair acted like it had anticipated the bolt.

I roll up my sleeve and check my arm hair to see that it is standing at attention. There is no rain, and though it is night, the moon shines brightly, free of any cloud cover that might indicate a storm.

Then it happens. Bright light bathes me from above as if someone has shone a spotlight on me. I squint against it, holding a hand in front of my face. Can this be a hallucination? I used to suffer from those, but one look at my victim's face tells me he sees the light, too. His eyes shrink to slits against the glare. A hell of a way to die. Or does he think perhaps Heaven has reached down to embrace him?

No, demons aren't like that. There is only one place for them, and this one, like all the others I've dispatched, is certainly on its way there.

My stomach falls out, and I feel myself levitating. I look back down at the demon, and he floats with me, too. We both rise into the air, and the light grows brighter until I can see it comes from an orb flying in the sky. No, there is something else around it, too. But the flash of brightness engulfs me, and I can't see it. Not even closing my eyes protects me from the shocking radiance.

I think I blacked out. I don't remember passing through any door or hatch, but clearly, I have. And I haven't dreamed, either. It feels like I time-traveled. One minute, I hang above the city like a helicopter, and the next, I am on a table. I try to lift my hands, but something holds them down. I move my eyes. Anything more than light is out of focus, at least to me. I try to sit up, but whatever binds me to that table doesn't give an inch.

A shape looms above me. A giant gray head with round black eyes peers down at me, and I can't help but think of *The X-Files*. At first, I think that maybe someone pulled a prank on me, but I don't have friends. No one I know would do something like this, and if the cops finally caught me, they wouldn't waste time with this, especially if they caught me in the act of killing that homeless man. They would have shot first and asked questions, never.

Maybe they've done just that. Maybe this is the afterlife. But that doesn't hold up. Why would a dead man need to be strapped down?

It occurs to me that this is real. That aliens have really abducted me.

The table I'm on rotates until I am facing the featureless floor. I don't feel like I'm hanging upside down, but perhaps that's the nature of being on an alien spacecraft. My legs separate, and I can feel coldness permeate my anus. Is this the probing I've heard so many stories about?

I think back to my youth. To the man who kidnapped me at the age of five. A friend of the family. Someone my father had me call "uncle." He had gotten into trouble with the law before and had been chemically castrated, so my father felt leaving me alone with him would be fine. Instead of using the equipment God had given him, he used a broom handle. It was the last time that I've ever felt helpless. I made it my business never to feel that helpless ever again.

I should be afraid. I know I don't have many emotions. I don't care about a lot of things. I certainly don't care about the lives I've taken. But I do have a healthy self-interest, and it isn't rising up in me now. I feel nothing as the metal inserts itself. My heart rate doesn't even elevate. I feel calm as the alien violates me. It's not out of the question that they have drugged me, but it doesn't matter one way or the other.

I know that I will escape from this. And I will probe them back.

The metal rotates inside of me, and something extends from it. It pinches my insides, and it hurts, so maybe they haven't drugged me. I think they're taking some kind of sample from me.

The probe withdraws, and the table turns back. I'm right-side up. The alien peers at me with its giant blank eyes. Its long rubbery fingers run across my legs against the grain of my hair until it comes to rest on my penis. The alien lifts it up and gently touches my urethra. It spreads, and I imagine it looks like a tiny mouth opening up, and coldness enters me again. I see a rod extending from the ceiling and inserting itself into me. Discomfort hits. It's not unpleasant, but it's not pleasant, either. It runs down inside my penis until I think it can go no further, and then it does so. It curves inside of me, and I can feel it in my testicles.

Another pinch. Painful for just a moment. I think they might be trying to extract my sperm. Considering how long I've heard stories about this kind of thing, I would think they had enough samples from the human race. They should have learned everything we had to teach them by now. Or maybe they needed it for something else.

Or were they doing this for their own sexual satisfaction?

The rod withdraws, and another emerges from the ceiling. This one is coming down to meet my right eye. I want to flinch away from it, but something holds my head tight. There is no avoiding it as it descends. Then, about an inch from my eye, it spits something into me. I lose vision for a moment, and my eye goes numb. My left one spins, but the right one can't move. How can they paralyze only one eye?

The rod continues down, and I feel it enter through my pupil. I lose vision again, and this somehow feels more uncomfortable than the one that went into my penis. The rod sinks lower until I can feel it deep in my head. Another pinch—I can feel my sinuses and ears pop as if I were on a plane going in for a landing.

The rod withdraws, and vision returns without so much as a glitch. The feeling comes back to that eye, and I can move it again.

The alien touches my forehead and nods. At least, I think it's a nod. It's hard to tell with a face so emotionless. It's almost like looking in a mirror. Almost.

The alien leaves. At long last, I'm alone. Now, I can start planning my escape.

My so-called uncle liked to tie me up, and when he took me, he kept me that way for days. In that time, I learned to get out of my ropes. That's how I escaped. I thought perhaps I could use what I learned back then in my current situation, but something else must be holding me down. I can't look at it because the band around my head holds me in place too tightly, but I wonder if maybe I can break my thumb and slip out of bondage. I've done it before, and while I dislike the pain, I know I can take it.

I pull my hand back as far as it can go. Further than I expect, at any rate. I'm confident that I can do this. I push my hand forward into the metal until it feels like my skin is going to slough off. Then I yank back with all my strength. My wrist chafes, but it's not enough to break anything.

I do it again. Again. Yet again. The metal is biting into my flesh, and my hand feels wet. Maybe I don't need to break the thumb after all. Maybe I can grease these bonds with my blood. I twist the hand around and around, and I can feel it slipping free.

Finally, I yank my hand back. I look at it to see that I've wounded myself pretty deeply, and the base of my thumb is frayed meat. But I'm halfway there. I touch the band around my head and feel where it connects to the table I'm on. At first, I'm afraid I won't feel how it's attached to the table, but then I find it. There is a peg holding it down, very thin, very tight, but I think I can worry it free.

It's a good thing I don't cut my fingernails all the way down to the quick. Ordinarily, I use them as weapons, like an animal's claws, but here, I can use them to get into places my fingers wouldn't ordinarily get to. I twist them around until I can get a grip on the peg and pull it out.

Now, I can sit halfway up, and I use this moment to free my other hand. I glance around as I work at my ankles, and the room I'm in is white. Featureless. I can see walls, but I can't see shapes. Rooms are usually defined by four walls, a floor and a ceiling. I see no such barriers. Is this place an oval? It feels like an oval.

Feet freed, I swivel on the table and let them drop to the floor. It takes me a moment to get my balance, so I hold onto the table until I feel safe enough to step forward. Clothes would be nice. I may have to fight my way out of this place, and no one ever likes to fight naked. But I can make do.

I move forward, arms outstretched, trying to find the barriers in here. I feel something that isn't there. Or maybe it is there, but my visual perception can't make it out. I slide across the invisible until I feel what might be a door. How do aliens open doors? Is there a knob?

No. I wave my hand around, and I hear a whooshing sound. A portal opens before me, and I step through into what appears to be a hallway. My disorientation recedes as I leave the senselessness of that room behind me. I feel colder now, and my penis shrinks, seeking the warmth of my belly.

I have nowhere else to go but forward. My feet slap the metal floor, and I try not to step so heavily. Stealth is the name of the game now. My hand hurts, and I'm leaving a trail of blood, but who will be looking for me back there? Everything is *forward* now. There is no *back*.

Lights dance in my periphery, but it's just for utility. It's not a warning sign or anything. I pass the flashing lights, and I notice there are other portals along the walls. Some are even on the ceiling, and I wonder if gravity means anything to these aliens. I wonder if maybe I can use that to my advantage.

As I pass by each door, I see that they all have some kind of monitor panel next to them. I pause at each one, seeing a display of a similar room to the one I'd been in.

Until I get to the fifth. I see my victim strapped to the table—very much still alive—with an alien probing his orifices. He screams silently, and I enjoy the sight. He must have a different experience of pain than I do. Demons deserve to suffer, and I think about the joy I'll feel when I kill him again.

But I'm in danger, too, aren't I? I haven't felt scared since my uncle had me, and that was fifteen years ago. But I do have a need for self-preservation. How likely is it that I can escape this UFO without help? My only possible ally is my little demon. Can we work together? I can always kill him later.

I watch the video feed until the alien is done with him and exits the room through another portal. It takes me a moment to figure out how to open this door, and when I do, it zips open with a Star Trek whoosh. I enter and approach the metal table. My victim doesn't notice me yet, and I can see a white line across his throat where I'd cut him. The aliens must have healed him somehow, and it irritates me that my good work has been undone.

It might be for the better, though.

His eyes move down, and he sees me. "No," he says. I think he's drugged because he should be shouting at me. My victims usually do. "No. It can't be you. Go away."

"Do you know where you are?" I ask.

"In some kinda fucked up dream," the homeless man says. "And now you're here like Freddy fuckin' Krueger."

"This is no dream," I tell him. "I very much killed you. For some reason, you didn't die. I think the aliens fixed you. But you're really in a UFO."

"That can't be. No way, no how."

"I assure you, I'm very much a conscious being outside of yourself. This is no dream."

"Go away." He pinches his eyes shut and tries to turn his head to no avail.

"I can't keep thinking of you as a victim or demon," I say. "What's your name?"

"You mean you killed my ass and don't know my name?" He's more alert now. The drugs might be wearing off.

It's inconsequential to me, but when you call your victim by name, they tend to calm down and feel some sense of security. I don't know why, but that's the way it usually goes. "Just tell me your name."

"Bill," he says.

"A demon named Bill?" I ask.

"I ain't no demon!" A shout. Finally. He's coming back to himself.

"Very well. Bill, it is. I'm going to free you so we can get out of here. I suggest we put our differences aside until we can get back to earth. Agreed?"

"Does that mean you're not gonna try to kill me?" he asks.

"Yes." For now.

I can see doubt in his eyes. That's a good thing. He's not entirely stupid, and that means we have a chance. "Okay," he says.

I look around for tools to use to free him, but the room is Spartan. I use my fingernails again to work the bolts away, and it takes some time, but not too much. Before long, he sits up and helps me free his feet.

"Where are my clothes?" he says.

I shrug. "I wasn't able to find my own. We're going to have to do this naked. Can you do that?"

"If I gotta."

He stands next to me as we glance around the room. There are no tools. No weapons. Nothing we can use to cover ourselves for protection. I remember the probes, and I try to find the controls that bring them out, but there are no buttons to push. I suspect the aliens might control them using their thoughts. I try to think as strongly as possible, but nothing happens. I doubt we could break off the probe and use it as a weapon, anyway.

It's easier to find the exit the alien used. That's controlled by motion. The door whooshes open and we step through into yet another corridor. This one has no other portals, no displays, nothing. We continue to walk, and I notice Bill covers his genitals with both hands. A useless gesture. I think he might be worried about how our equipment has shriveled due to the cold. Perhaps he is modest. I wouldn't waste time like that. I want to be ready if we are attacked.

We reach the end of the hallway. I turn to Bill. "Do you have any demon abilities that might help us? Mind control? Super strength? Can you breathe fire?"

"I said I ain't no demon!" Bill says.

"Cut the act," I say. "If we're going to get out of this, we're going to have to use everything we've got. You know I'm going to try to kill you after this. I know you'll try to kill me. Let's just save that for when we've defeated our common enemy."

Bill grins, and his teeth are suddenly sharp and slick with saliva. "All right, you got me. Fair enough."

"Should I continue to call you Bill?"

"You can call me Bill."

It was worth a try. Demons never tell you their real names unless they are compelled to do so. When you know their names, you have power over them.

"All right, Bill. Do you have any powers, then?" As if he would tell them all to me. I am certain he would hold something back so he can use it against me later. Most demons wouldn't think I would know that, though.

"I have a hell of a bite," Bill says. His teeth almost twinkle in the light. "But yeah. I'm super strong. No mind control, though. I can fuck with perception. Wanna see some hallucinations?"

"Not particularly. Do you think you can do that with the aliens?"

He shrugs. "I don't know. Never met an alien before."

"Then I guess we find out together." There isn't a monitor next to this door, so we have no idea what we're about to get into. "Be ready."

He nods, and I open the door.

There are a lot more controls and flashing lights on the walls of this room. A giant view screen takes up an entire wall, and I think it might actually be a window. I can see the vastness of space stretching out to infinity, and I feel incredibly small. Maybe my life's work of killing demons isn't so important after all. Maybe all I'm doing is removing single drops of water from an ocean.

And then I see the aliens. They are gathered together, and it looks like they're conversing with one another. At least until they see us. The aliens are stiff; one of them tilts its head to the side as if it is considering us.

How does one hurt an alien? I don't have a lot of time to think about this, so I launch forward, fist-cocked and ready. My penis and balls flop uncomfortably at my thighs and belly, and I wish I had at least a piece of tape to hold them down.

My fist connects with the first alien's face, and it feels like I'm punching a giant piece of steak fat. The skin is malleable and almost squishes against my violent touch. The alien reels back, arms flailing, and I know I've hurt the bastard. I can't stop and appreciate my work. There are other aliens, and I don't know what Bill is doing. I don't have time to check up on him.

A shrill sound echoes through my mind, and the other aliens start slapping themselves in a panic. They look like...no...I think they are seeing flames on their bodies, probably supplied by Bill. Their odd faces are elongated in pain and terror. I waste no time. I jump into the fray, kicking and lashing out. The aliens fall around me. Only now do I see Bill taking a giant chomp out of an alien's face; black ichor spills out of the wound, and I realize it's bleeding. If it bleeds, we can kill it. It sounds like an old adage, but it might be a movie quote. Not sure. I'll have to look that up later.

If there is a later.

Something makes the air shimmer, and one by one, the aliens pop out of existence, literally. I hear a pop when they vanish, and I think it's the sound of air rushing in to displace the space where their bodies just were. Are they dying? More likely, I think, they are teleporting.

I grab one of the aliens, and I can feel something wrenching it from my grip. I'm tenacious, and I don't let go. Its body shimmers, then comes back into focus. Its black eyes are wider than I thought they could go, and I can almost taste its fear. My penis stands up, and for the first time since I cut Bill's throat, I'm having fun. I've never tortured and killed an alien before. This should be new and interesting.

"Enjoying it too much?" Bill asks. He points to my penis.

"There is no such thing as too much," I tell him. "Let's see what happens when we bring him to one of the probing rooms, shall we?"

Bill shrugs. "Why the hell not?"

132

We bring the alien with us as we retreat to the room I found Bill in. By now, it has stopped trying to escape me and is letting me lead it like a docile lamb. Lambs are fun to kill. They trust you completely. When you hurt them, they accept their lot in life, but you can see how upset they are. If they could speak, they would probably beg to know why I'm doing this.

I hope the alien will be the same.

I push it down onto the table, and the motion brings up the metal bands, securing it to the steel surface. Its eyes pulsate, and I think it might be their version of eyes rolling wildly. My penis thrums on a different level of reality.

"Maybe you're getting too much into this, bud," Bill says.

I lick my lips. "Does this remind you too much of you?"

"Nah, man. Just pointing it out."

"Do you know how to make the probes come out?" I ask.

Bill shrugs again. "I got no clue."

A lot of this place operates with motion detectors, so I wave my hands around, hoping to trigger something. Nothing happens.

Do these things even have an anus to probe? I look its body up and down, and the only orifices I notice are on its face. Perhaps it doesn't need an anus. Does it even digest food? Does it have a concept of food?

"Bill, make it think it's on fire again."

He grunts. "How did you know that's what I put in their heads?"

I don't want to give him an Elementary-Dear-Watson answer. Instead, I want him on his toes and a little in fear of me. "I can read your mind."

"The hell you say."

It's my turn to shrug.

Bill turns his attention back to the alien, and it starts to writhe against the bands…as much as it can. The bands don't have a lot of give to them, so it looks like an army of ants is moving under its skin. I want to cut it open and see what kind of muscles it has. I wonder what aliens taste like. I've eaten human beings before—or at least demons in human bodies—and the folktales are true. Humans taste like pork. I suspect aliens taste like raw shrimp just from the way its skin feels under my palm.

"You took a bite out of one of them," I say. "What do they taste like?"

"Like seal," Bill said.

"Seal? As in the aquatic mammals?"

"Got it in one," he says.

"Hm." I almost ask him to take another bite and give it to me, but I need to figure out how to hurt this thing. No, wait, I need to get back to earth. How do I do that when I really want to cause this extraterrestrial some kind of pain that it has probably never felt before? It obviously has nerves. Nerves mean sensation. Sensation means pain, right?

There is something I can do to cause it pain without needing sharp objects. I hold a finger up and examine the nail at the end. I jab it into the alien's eye, and it flinches. The shrill sound rips through my mind again, and I now know this is how they express screams. It makes me smile. God never told me that I had to kill aliens, too, but why not? Why not treat myself?

"I thought we were trying to bust out of this place," Bill says. "You look like you're getting ready to scarf down a meal."

Bill irritates me. I wish he'd died faster when I cut his throat. Demons are too stubborn for my taste. But he's right. Just to work out some frustration, I poke the alien in the eye again. More struggles. It comforts me that they can feel pain.

"Stop playing with your food," Bill says. "Let's get the hell out of here."

The air hisses around us. I look around for the source, expecting a door to open. It's a different but similar sound. Then it occurs to me that the aliens might try to gas us. I try to breathe in shallowly to see if I smell the difference, but not enough to knock me out right away.

Bill's eyes dilate, and I know we're being gassed. He sways while I blow all the air out of my lungs, not breathing further. I mentally prep for a fight.

The door whooshes open, and three aliens come in so smoothly that it's like they're gliding on a track instead of walking. I don't think I can take them all, but I'm going to take as many of them down with me as I can.

My chest hitches, but I refuse to breathe in. Bill is gagging and has fallen to his knees, so I know the gas is not good.

I do have one advantage. When I dragged my prisoner into this room, I knew these aliens were light. Not much heavier than, say, a club. As the first one approaches, I go for its legs. It falls to the floor, and I pick it up by its ankles—yes, like a club—and heft it up.

I swing the alien at the others, hoping for a home run. Without much air, I'm not as strong as I could be, so I don't get the satisfying crack of a line drive. It's more of a rubbery *thwuck!* It has the desired effect. One alien falls into the others, knocking them down like bowling pins. I lift my alien over my head—this time like I'm about to club a baby seal—and bring it down on the first one. The large oval head dents instead of breaks. Its eyes are now looking at each other. It writhes but doesn't make a sound. I'm pretty sure it feels pain, and that makes me happy.

The other aliens are trying to stand, so I shift my attention to them. I am a bit fuzzy, so lifting my alien is a little harder this time. My muscles strain and ache. I don't know if I can do it.

Nope. I need to drop it to defend myself with my fists. The alien thumps to the floor. I can't close my hands. The world seems distant. I think I'm about to black out. If that's the way it is, that's the way it is. I just need to take as many of them down as I can before they get me.

Whoops. I'm on my knees, and I have no choice but to breathe in. It doesn't take much of the gas to put me down. I don't even remember passing out.

When I wake up, I'm bound to the metal table again. This time, there are about ten aliens around me, all identical. They watch me like I'm about to do a card trick. I'm pretty sure I can't get out of this. Too bad. I have a lot more demons to kill, and now I can't do that. Death will be interesting, I'm sure. I've only ever dealt it out. Being killed will undoubtedly be a learning experience.

We're not going to kill you.

Weird. They speak in my mind, not out loud. And in English, too. After what I did, I can't possibly see them *not* killing me.

You are an experiment. A human/alien hybrid with our DNA mixed in with your mother's eggs.

This doesn't surprise me. I've always felt different from everyone else. I figured it was because I was born without a conscience. Maybe there's more to me. There was always a part of me that doubted my holy quest. What if my victims weren't really demons? But maybe I was wrong to doubt?

"Where's Bill?" I ask. My throat burns, and I sound like I'm croaking.

We already dissected him. There is an odd development, though. We thought he was a human, and we found this hiding inside of him.

The aliens separate and reveal a horned red figure with giant teeth floating behind them. He rotates like a rotisserie chicken. "Hey, partner," it says. "Think you can get me down?"

I almost smile. "What are you going to do with him?"

We were hoping you could help us with that. It's rare when one of our hybrids survives past puberty. You're the only one we've been able to find so far.

"The only one? That sounds more than rare."

"Hey, I'm right here," Bill says. "Help a brother out?"

We can't penetrate this one's skin, the aliens say. *Do you have any suggestions?*

"Ah hell," Bill says. "That can't be good."

"As it turns out, I do," I tell them. "I've been killing things like Bill for at least a decade. But you would have to free me for this. And give me my weapons back."

We wanted to discuss that with you. Your tools are primitive and look very different from what we use. We would like to see you use them so that we might learn…to maybe even use the tools ourselves if need be.

I think about this for a moment. There is a certain appeal in this. It would be much better to be employed as a demon killer by the aliens than to be killed. Perhaps they need someone like me to widen their knowledge base. That's not why I do it. It would be a fringe benefit, though. It would also be a learning experience for me. Do other planets have demons? Think of the possibilities!

"I think we can work something out," I say.

If we set you free, will you promise only to dissect the beings that we assign to you? That you would cease your attempts to destroy your half-siblings?

I say yes before I have the chance to think about it. Of course, I won't make such a promise. What if demons inhabit the aliens? But if I think about it, they'll know that. They can read my mind, and I can't have them doubting me. I only think this in the back of my head with the yes answer at the forefront, so I'm pretty sure it can't hear my true thoughts.

Very good, then.

The metal straps soundlessly ease away from me, and I am free. One of the aliens holds out my knife, the one I originally killed Bill with. And my backup knife. And the club I keep handy in case my victims get feisty. And the gun I use as a last resort. I've never needed it yet, and I don't think I'll need it now.

I stow my weapons except for the knife. I walk toward Bill, still spinning and spinning and spinning.

"Come on, man," he says. "After all we've been through together?"

"Don't worry about that," I say. "I'll keep you alive for a long time. You'll have plenty of opportunities to escape. To try, at least."

Ever heard a demon scream? Until now, I haven't, at least not through its real throat. Bill's screams sound very pleasant to my ears. I love my work and can't wait to see what the aliens look like on the inside. How will an alien scream sound in my mind?

Citizens of Strangeland

Kasey Hill

Prologue

One bullet. I have just one bullet left. It's funny. I started with an arsenal, preparing for this apocalypse. My wife and kids hunker in our storm shelter as the door leading down to us is being beaten in by the monstrosity on the other side. We only have enough food left for maybe a day, if rationed, a week. I doubt we make it that long.

"Travis, what are we going to do?!" Lily cries out, hugging Jenny and Ben to her side.

I look at my gun and back at the cracking, splintering door. What are we going to do?

July 4, 2012

The God Particle. The Higgs Boson particle had long been a notion of science fiction. It was a missing piece of the Standard Model of particle physics that Peter Higgs and his team started searching for in 1964. He proposed that the Higgs mechanism was a way for some particles to attain mass. All fundamental particles were supposed to be massless at high energies and unable to attain mass at lower energies. Higgs proposed that a scalar boson, a subatomic particle whose spin should equal zero as opposed to a regular boson whose spin equaled an integer, should exist.

Forty years later, on July 4, 2012, scientists working near Geneva, Switzerland, through the ATLAS and CMS (Compact Muon Solenoid) experiments, used their Large Hadron Collider at CERN to discover the God particle, proving Peter Higgs correct in his scientific theories. This particle was a massive scalar particle with even, positive parity, no electric charge, and no quark color charge that coupled to mass. It quickly decayed into other particles immediately upon generation, proving it to be unstable. Essentially, this is the "Big Bang" of the universe, where it rapidly inflated the expanse of the universe, joining everything together and giving particles their mass.

December 21, 2012

It was around the year 2009 when people became hyper-aware of the Mayan Calendar and its end date of December 21, 2012. Apocalyptic end-time scenarios began to surface with the belief that the Mayans had predicted a cataclysmic event that would decimate life as we know it. Much like when the year 2000 ticked over, and everyone waited to see if the world ended with Y2K, much of humanity paused and waited for the end to come. Fortunately, everyone woke up on December 22, 2012, and nothing cataclysmic had occurred. Life resumed normally with the jokes and scoffing about surviving another prophecy of Doomsday. Or did we?

December 26, 2016

The first time I ever heard about the Mandela Effect was the day after Christmas when I scrolled through Facebook and came across an article that sent me down a rabbit hole. I had been a reader since I was a child, and the first thing that popped out at me was the subtle change in my favorite children's series, "The Berenstein Bears," which was now titled "The Berenstain Bears." This led to a cascading discovery that many things I remembered had subtly changed. The Looney "Toons" I had grown up watching were now Looney Tunes, justified by old timers that it had always been Tunes because when there was no TV, they listened to shows on the radio. However, when I went to research the spinoff of the TV series Tiny Toon Adventures, it had not changed in name, solidifying in my mind that my memory was correct. We all sang the bologna commercial as kids, as it also taught us how to spell the brand of Oscar Meyer that had changed to Oscar Mayer. Still, the pronunciation of the Mayer spelling remained the same as Meyer, even though the singer John Mayer's last name has a different pronunciation.

It was conundrum after conundrum. Febreeze was now spelled Febreze. Sketchers were now Skechers. Sex *in* the City was now Sex *and* the City. Pikachu's iconic tail no longer had the black lightning bolt. Ed McMahon had never handed out checks for Publisher's Clearing House, even though we all remember the commercials. James Earl Jones never uttered "Luke, I am your father" in Star Wars as Darth Vader. "Mirror, mirror on the wall" was never a line in Snow White and the Seven Dwarves, and instead, the Evil Queen utters, "Magic mirror on the wall," even though an iconic song I listened to in the early 2000s said, "Mirror, mirror hanging on the wall."

One of the ultimate facts about the Mandela Effect and the cause for naming it thusly was the change in Nelson Mandela's death. Everyone remembered he had died in prison in the 1980s, but his death in 2013 sparked the beginning of the glitch in the matrix we were all beginning to experience. I remember in 2009, Billy Graham died and was given a lavish, luxurious funeral that mirrored that of Michael Jackson. Imagine my surprise when, on February 18, 2018, the news headlines dropped the bad news that he had died. Similarly, I remember Pee Wee Herman died in the early 2000s, but again, his death rang out across headlines on July 30, 2023. We remembered so many celebrities dying in the early 2000s who are still alive, and it's chalked up to fake headlines saying they had died. The internet wasn't faking people's deaths in its early days in the 2000s.

2023

Having been born into a family that had a penchant for conspiracy theories, such as John F. Kennedy's assassin being a patsy, everything that had occurred since December 21, 2012, along with the God Particle just months before, began to make sense as one large event. I spent the last several years looking into the various Mandela Effects and cross-referencing everything with the Mayan Calendar and the discovery of the Higgs Boson. I, along with many others who delved deep into the rabbit hole, concluded that the world did, in fact, end at the end of 2012. The theory postulates that CERN was able to warp our universe enough that we could merge with a parallel universe. The subtle differences in things pointed out by the Mandela Effect were this universe's norm, and we retained our memory from our universe. Those who do not realize the differences are people who existed in this universe, begging the question of whether their parallel souls were either destroyed in 2012 or just suppressed in the collective unconscious. This also led to the reasoning that there were multiple universes that could have merged as well.

However, the movie "The Forgotten" that I watched in the early 2000s also offered up the speculation that we could be one large thought experiment by higher forces, whether they be alien forces, godly forces, or even one and the same. The Sumerians told us through mythology that their Gods were "not of this world" and described them as possibly being an alien race. Their mythology told us that the "gods" had created the Earth, and subservient gods tended the fields and did their labor. They rose in a rebellion against their mistreatment. They demanded to be released from their slavery, so the Elder Gods created humanity and put them on earth to do the labor of the subservient rebels.

In June 2023, the US Government released its official report on the existence of UAPs, formerly called UFOs, confirming every alien enthusiast's belief in extra-terrestrials. Videos began to surface more frequently of UAPs in cities across the nation. Arguments of whether these UAPs were friendly or malevolent forces began to arise, even concluding that they may be opposing alien races fighting over ownership of Earth. Officials across the world began surfacing in videos where humans began to question whether they were actually human or aliens or reptilian species had taken over their bodies, and thoughts of them completely being replaced with body suits of the person they were impersonating arose. One video in particular showed the Pope trying to scratch his nose, and instead, he grasped the tip of his nose and pulled, revealing his face to be some sort of silicone mask. Even the top political candidates for the upcoming election acted, looked, and seemed to be nonhuman, noticeable by small details such as differences in appearance, like their ears or mannerisms, of which they speak. They bumbled and fumbled for words as if English were a foreign language they were trying to grasp.

I couldn't decide if a higher power was altering our thought perception like in the movie, or if it was indeed the discovery of the God particle that had warped universes together, or even possibly both, that caused everything in this current model of life to be how it was. What I did know was that things were slowly changing around me, and I didn't like it. I grew up in Huntsville, Alabama. Many civilians aren't aware that Huntsville is the main hub of NASA, as opposed to Houston, Texas, which is glorified in movies for being mission control. "Houston, we have a problem" is one of the most quotable lines in cinematic history. The Marshall Space Flight Center in Huntsville is the one that makes everything possible for every NASA mission.

2024

I awoke to the local radio station blaring when my alarm went off. "Good morning, Strangeland! Today is going to be a scorcher with temps in the 100s. Stay safe and hydrated." *Strangeland?* I thought to myself. "What the fuck is Strangeland?" I asked out loud.

"What's that, dear?" Lily asked, stepping out from the master bathroom wrapped in a shower robe and her hair wrapped up in a towel.

"The radio said, 'Good morning, Strangeland' instead of Huntsville," I replied, repeating what the disc jockey had said.

"And?" she asked, clearly not understanding my issue.

"We live in Huntsville," I responded, irritated, as I sat up on the side of the bed.

"Huntsville?" she asked, confused. "Where the fuck is Huntsville?"

"We *live* in Huntsville!" I exclaimed. "Did I wake up in a fucking parallel dimension or some shit?"

"I told you not to drink the shine Bobby offered last night," she replied in a huff. "You always wake up weird the next day after hanging out with the Rocket City Boys."

"I am not being weird!" I shouted. "I know where I grew up and currently live!"

"Yea, Strangeland, Alabama," she muttered. "I do not have the patience for your bullshit today."

"Oh, *you* don't have the patience. I don't have the fucking patience," I huffed as I jumped out of bed to go take a shower.

"Hurry up in the shower!" she called as I turned the knob for the water to come on. "You're going to be late for work, and today is the launch of the project you've been working on."

I rolled my eyes as I stepped into the shower. I hurriedly did my morning routine and was out the door and on my way to the Marshall Space Flight Center. We were testing something new with the International Space Station, and I had to give my report before we continued with the project. I made my way through Decatur, driving down US-31. I nearly caused a pile-up as I jerked the wheel to the right to pull into the parking lot where Carmino Real Mexican Restaurant was supposed to be, along with the American Family walk-in clinic. It was nothing but a vacant lot with bulldozers sitting where the buildings once stood.

"What the fuck is going on?" I asked myself as I jumped out of my vehicle. "We ate here two nights ago. Where is all of the debris? There is no way they demolished them and cleaned all the debris in just two fucking days!"

My phone rang, interrupting my flabbergast.

"Trainer," I answered on the second ring.

"Trainer, we need you here ASAP to go over the project," the voice yelled over the phone.

"I'm on my way," I replied. "I've had one crazy fucking morning, but I am thirty minutes out."

I hopped back in my car and floored it to work. I ran into the facility, swiping my keycard to gain access to the back.

"There he is!" Col. Short shouted. "Debriefing now!"

"Yes, sir," I replied. "Let me grab everything from my office. One minute."

I raced to my office and grabbed everything from my desk for this morning's meeting. I made it to the conference room and plopped it all down on the table. Everyone sat quietly around the table, waiting for me to start.

"Gentlemen," I began, "we have been working on new technology to make transference of supplies to and from the International Space Station easily accessible without the use of rockets."

Silence filled the room. I swallowed hard.

"What was once science fiction in Star Trek, we are hoping to make science today. We have created a teleportation system to dematerialize objects that would materialize on the ship using a unique telecommunications frequency. By using the super hydron collider, we believe the energy generated can create the scenario to happen."

"Well, let's test run the theory," Col. Short urged. "Now."

We moved as a group through the facility to mission control, where we would touch base with the astronauts.

"International Space Station, this is Marshall Space Flight, ready to run Project Scotty. Can you confirm you are ready to begin transmissions?"

"Affirmative, Mission Control. We are locked and loaded," they replied.

"Honing in on the radio frequency of the Space Station. Are the materials on the platform?"

"Affirmative. They are ready to be sent."

"Countdown from 10, 9, 8, 7, 6, 5, 4, 3, 2, 1—begin transmission."

I pushed the button to operate the super hydron collider as the intercepted frequency aligned. I watched the cameras as the room where the supplies sat flashed a bright white light. When the light disappeared, the supplies were still sitting on the platform.

"Experiment failed."

I turned to Col. Short and quickly stated, "We are close and just working out whatever mathematical kinks are left."

"This project will be canceled in two weeks. I hope you have it fixed by then," he replied, then quickly exited.

"Fuck!" I shouted, knocking papers off the desk.

Three Weeks Earlier

The phone rang in the middle of the night, and I rolled groggily over to pick it up from the receiver.

"Travis, we have a problem. Get here ASAP!"

I looked over at my alarm clock and sighed. "It's 3 AM. Can't it wait?"

"No, it cannot. Project Scotty is running its own simulation, and we can't control it."

I bolted upright. "What the fuck?"

I quickly got dressed and ran out the door, flooring the gas pedal of the car all the way to Marshall. I ran as quickly as I could through the building, swiping my card where needed until I made it to Mission Control, where my late-night tech sat at the desk, scrambling to stop Project Scotty.

"Nothing is working! It's like it has a mind of its own!"

I ran over to the monitors and read through all the code racing across the screen.

"What's this frequency it's locked onto?" I asked, pointing at the 1.6 GHz signal floating on the screen.

"I have no fucking clue. It's a communication frequency, but I can't lock onto the coordinates it is originating from."

The computer began to count down as the super hadron collider began its energy build.

"Shut it down!" I shouted.

"I can't! I have no control over it! That frequency is controlling it!"

"Well, cut the communication line!" I hissed.

"I already tried that!"

The computer was nearing its countdown. "3, 2, 1."

The room with the collider was illuminated as it shot its energy through the communication frequency. As quickly as it lit up, it darkened.

"What was sent? Was there anything in there?" I asked.

"The communication line wasn't receiving. It was sending."

Two Weeks Earlier

A piercing siren woke me from my sleep. It was the civil defense alarm. I shook Lily awake. She groggily opened her eyes, and the sound filled her ears as the tone got louder. She covered them. "Why is the defense alarm going off?" she asked, yelling over the siren.

I ran to the window, threw it open, and looked to the sky in fear of a twister since we lived in Tornado Alley. The sky was cloud-free but full of terror nonetheless as helicopters and fighter jets swooped over the houses. I looked to the ground as mobilized Army men ran through the streets with their guns drawn. An Army tank rolls behind them with a loudspeaker on, "Citizens of Strangeland. We advise you to either stay in your homes with your doors barricaded or leave on the next available Army bus. This is not a drill, this is not a joke, this is real, and a real warning. For those of you who wish to stay, we will not return for you. My suggestion is to leave with us. We cannot protect you here."

The loudspeaker continued repeating the same message over and over as my brain scrambled for the hidden meaning of why we needed to leave. My ears pulled me in the direction of gunfire. I looked over to my left, down the street, and terror filled my body. It was nothing but a maze of fires. Houses were burning to the ground, and people were yelling in the streets like maniacs. One of them looked as though their flesh had been half-eaten or some sort of chemical had singed their skin, exposing their bones. Before they could take another step, a soldier gunned them down. Another soldier quickly pointed a flamethrower at the body of the creature, and it went up in smoke and flames, still making an awful noise as it burned to death. I heard and saw an explosion that couldn't have been less than five miles away. Are we under attack by terrorists? I didn't know what was going on, and fear had crippled my body from movement. Another explosion snapped me out of my panicked state.

I look over to Lily, "We need to go, now!"

"Travis, what's going on?" she asked nervously, reaching for her housecoat.

"Never mind the housecoat. Get dressed, get the kids up, and get them dressed; we need to leave now!" I yelled as I grabbed a suitcase from under the bed.

I ran to the closet and yanked out whatever would fit in the suitcase. I slammed the lid shut and placed it in the hallway. I ran to Jenny's room and began the same procedure. I packed away everyone's necessities within five minutes. I stripped my night clothes off and dressed in a pair of jeans and a white tee. I ran into the hallway, where everyone greeted me with panic-stricken faces.

"Everyone ready?" I asked, picking up the suitcases.

Everyone nodded in unison. We made our way down the steps and threw open the front door. The streets appeared even worse up close and in person, rather than two stories up from a window. The smell of searing flesh filled my nostrils, nearly gagging me. I looked around at the blur of events happening in my own front yard.

"What in the hell is going on?" I asked out loud.

My thought was quickly answered as my eyes scoured the skies. In the center of town, a huge torrential fire port swirled in the air. Creatures that resembled dragons circled the portal. Upon closer examination of these beasts, they were nothing but skeletal remains with remnants of flesh hanging from their bodies. Along with these creatures were an assortment of flying beasts that screeched out in anger as gunfire exploded and ricocheted through their bodies. Smaller beasts flew through the streets and attacked whoever was walking, trying to find safety. They looked like pigmy gargoyles but more malevolent as they scratched, bit, and devoured the people running from them.

Ghoulish-looking creatures encircled the walking citizens as they ran for the evacuation site. The bus was further away from our house, and there was no way we would be able to make it there without being attacked by these things.

"Get to the storm shelter!" I ordered as I grabbed a flamethrower that had been tossed on the ground beside a dead soldier.

We all hurried to the back of the house. The storm shelter wasn't your average, run-of-the-mill shelter. I sunk serious money into it in case of any type of military strike near the arsenal. The super hydron collider sat beneath the arsenal, going for miles. It wasn't known, but its location could have easily been leaked to enemy territories. It was stocked with food, ammunition, and everything needed to wait out anything. I just didn't expect us to be waiting out this. It had been a week since the super hydron collider had fired itself up, and we waited, patiently, might I add, for something to happen. Nothing happened,

144

so we didn't report it further than Col. Short. He didn't seem to be in high alarm from what happened, but did indeed shut down the project afterward, and everyone vacated the premises. Only military personnel were allowed in for the past week.

I fired off the flamethrower as those beasts blocked our backyard and made a path for the kids and Lily to make it to the shelter safely. One flew overhead, making a dive for the door as a blasted it down with flames. I quickly shut the door behind me and activated my survival protocol. A heavy ten-inch steel door came down in front of the wooden door and locked into place. I led them down the stairs as the motion-activated lights sprang to life to show us the way. I put in a code at the bottom, and another door slid open to show a lavish living quarter inside.

"Y'all get comfortable. There's a room for each of us down here and food through there," I said, pointing to the kitchen.

I quickly grabbed the satellite phone and called the center.

"Who the hell is calling this number?" the voice shouted.

"Col, Short, it is Travis Trainer!" I shouted. "What the fuck is going on?"

"We couldn't shut down the communications line just like you said," he reported. "The super hadron collider powered up to full capacity, something we hadn't done. It created a black hole that was immediately transformed into a wormhole by whatever was controlling the communication line. They had to have introduced exotic matter. It opened up a portal, and those things came through!"

"Wormhole?" I murmured.

"This is just the beginning, Trainer. I will keep in touch. Stay safe until we can figure out how to reverse this."

Present Day

One bullet. I have just one bullet left. It's funny. I started with an arsenal, preparing for this apocalypse. My wife and kids hunker in our storm shelter as the door leading down to us is being beaten in by the monstrosity on the other side. We only have enough food left for maybe a day, if rationed, a week. I doubt we make it that long.

"Travis, what are we going to do?!" Lily cries out, hugging Jenny and Ben to her side.

I look at my gun and back to the cracking, splintering door. What are we going to do?

The satellite phone rang. I quickly answered it. "Trainer."

"Still alive, I see," Col. Short chuckled.

"When's it going to end?" I asked. "When will the beasts be sent back?"

The line was quiet.

"Colonel?" I asked.

"We couldn't reverse it."

"You son of a bitch! This is all your fault!" I seethed. "You wanted Project Scotty."

"Is it, though? Or were you too nosy a scientist and wanted to make science fiction real science? Project Scotty was your work, not mine. The things humans do in the name of science. Acting like gods. Well, you became God, alright."

"They're nearly through the shelter doors!" I screamed.

"I know. Such wonderful beasts, aren't they?" he asked.

"What?" I replied, confused.

"We created the perfect kill all creatures, didn't we?" he asked.

"We didn't create them!" I hissed.

"No, you humans didn't create them. I agree. They're too perfect a specimen for them to have been created by your kind," he replied.

"My kind?" I asked.

"Hasn't your scientist's brain put two and two together yet? You're smart, Trainer. Think long and hard."

"It was you all along, wasn't it?" I asked.

"I have been on this planet for many, many years. I have seen so many wars and so much destruction. You humans don't deserve this place we created for you. So, we are taking it back. You lot were getting too close to the truth. Releasing information about UAPs being real, trying to unlock the secrets of places like Skinwalker Ranch. But it was the utter disregard for this beautiful mother planet that really did it in for me. You cut down the trees. You pollute the air. You trash the earth with your litter. You fight with one another. You are nothing like your ancestors, and for that, you had to be punished."

"I don't do those things!" I protested, "Many humans don't."

"I like you, Trainer. I really do. It's such a shame the rest of the human population couldn't be like you. But it is what it is. We gave you signs. We changed things from the past to see if you would notice. We altered your memories to see if anyone cared. Hell, we destroyed your planet in 2012 and put you in an alternate dimension of living. We even tried simulations in your conscious minds. You refused to change."

I heard the first metal door break free, and the banging began on the last one, keeping us safe from the outside. I could see tiny dents forming over and over, growing deeper and deeper in the metal.

"Please," I pleaded. "Spare us!"

"Goodbye, Trainer."

146

The satellite phone went dead as the metal peeled away further and further on our door. I held my family close to me, and as the metal door broke free from its locked position, I fired the last round in my gun and closed my eyes.

Neville

Mawr Gorshin

"Hey, Noah!" Bernetta Adam said as she was looking out the bedroom window. "I just saw another shooting star! That's three tonight. After the four, I saw the night before, and I saw the three the night before that."

"You were stoned then, that's all," Noah Baldry, her boyfriend, said from across the room. "As you are stoned now. There are never that many shooting stars, all at one time, and many soon after that."

Bernetta was as naked as a newborn baby, high on ecstasy after having just snorted a line of ketamine. She stood watching the stars by the window, oblivious to the possibility that some peeping Tom might be checking out her beautiful body, and the stars—shooting or not—were shining so much brighter than normal, thanks to her high.

She was vibrating and tingling from head to toe, always fidgeting with delight. "Oh, God," she moaned as her head swayed from side to side. "I'm peaking on this E! It feels so good! I can't wait for the K to kick in."

"It should, any second now, baby," Noah said. He, too, was high on E, waiting for his own K to kick in, and as naked as she was on that hot summer night. He was staring at her shapely body and admiring her beauty.

"Hey," she said. "One of those shooting stars is coming right at me. Fast!"

"You're stoned," he said.

"No, really. At first, it was a tiny white dot of light; now, it's getting bigger. Maybe it isn't a shooting star. It's starting to look like…a silver bullet…shot from a gun and coming right at me."

"You're high, that's all, sweetie."

"Ungh!" she grunted when it hit her, right in the chest. She staggered several steps back from the window.

She fell back onto their bed. There was no blood, no hole in her chest, nor was there a hole in the window or even the slightest crack in the glass. Whatever that shining white bullet was that hit her, it had gone through both the window and her chest like a ghost floating through walls.

"Uh?" she said, rising up on her elbows and spreading her legs. "What was that?"

"I dunno," Noah said, having barely noticed what had happened, distracted by his growing high. "You just…fell on the bed. I don't know why. I thought I saw…a flash of light, but then again, we're both stoned."

"Yeah," she said. "I think the K…is kicking in now. I see someone…on me, but I don't think…there's anyone…really here."

"If you see someone, you're definitely hallucinating, baby. No one's on the bed with you. I'm starting to feel the K, too. I think I'll go lie down next to you." He did.

"What's your name?" she asked.

"What?" Noah asked. "You know my name."

"Not, you, Noah, shut up. I mean *you*."

He saw her pointing in front of herself at someone she saw on top of her.

"Holy shit!" Noah said, laughing. "You *are* stoned, out of your mind!"

"Shut up, Noah. He's talking to me."

Noah laughed some more. *That's good E and K I made,* he thought. *I'll let her enjoy her high while I enjoy mine.* He rolled over on his side, away from her. *My customers will really enjoy these drugs, too.*

"I'm sorry," she said to the hairy, horned, fanged, bestial being she saw mounting her. "I didn't hear…your name…when you said it."

Benny, it said in a grunting vocal fry. *Benny Hailohim.*

"Hi, Benny," she said with a smile. "You're hot, even if I…do say so…in front of…my boyfriend."

You like the way I look, do you? Benny asked, baring its fangs as it grinned and looked down on her delicious body with lust in its glowing, yellow eyes.

"Yes," she sighed, grinning and looking up at its bright red fur, its muscular arms and chest, its horns, and…now looking down at its crotch, its pointy phallus, as long as one of its horns. "Stick it in me, please."

It did…a deep impaling.

"Aah!" she screamed with pleasure.

It was moving in and out of her, stabbing her with quick, forceful thrusts. It grunted and growled with each push.

She was shaking and squealing. Her eyes were squished shut, and her moaning mouth was wide open.

She had her first orgasm within thirty seconds.

"Oh! Oh! Ah! Ah!" she cried in high-pitched staccato notes.

She looked up at the beast and grinned.

After the first minute of fucking, she came again.

"Oh!…you…fucking…animal! *Ah!*"

It was grunting louder…and giving her faster stabs.

She came a third time with an ear-splitting scream.

It kept going.

"*Oh!* Take me! Take over my body…use me. Have all…of me…own me…tear me…apart…oh!…destroy me…oh!"

149

It turned her around to fuck her doggy style.

"*Oh! Oh! Oh!* You beast…you animal…you monster…fuck me…*AH!*"

She came again.

Its phallus was drowning in her squirts.

Then she felt it squirting inside her.

Noah had been looking back at her over his shoulder, disturbed by her constant shaking of the bed and her screaming. Nope, nobody was on top of her. She was imagining the whole thing…he was sure of it.

But now that she'd climaxed that one last time, she lay still and weak on the bed, overwhelmed by Benny's power. Her eyes were closed. Her mouth—wide open.

"Oh," she moaned, then thought, *Benny killed me. That was the best fuck I've ever had…in my whole life.*

*

Noah woke up to more moaning and groaning from Bernetta. "What the…?" he asked the air, then moaned from the pain resultant from the night of druggie debauchery.

He was aching all over, and her moans and groans were not helping him at all. She wasn't shaking, though. Nor was she screaming in ecstasy, thank God. Her moans weren't accelerating toward a climax, either.

Still, in his painful disorientation, he assumed that she was hallucinating about great sex again. He didn't imagine that some guy had come into their house to shag her.

He checked the clock on the bedside table: it was just past two o'clock in the afternoon. That was about the right time for two drug dealers/junkies to wake up after a night of partying.

Finally, he built up the strength to look over at her. "Baby," he whined as he turned his head. "There's nobody else there. You're imagining a guy inside you…oh, *fuck!*"

Someone *was* inside her.

A baby sliding out of her birth canal.

It was small.

It had grey skin.

"Oh, my God," he said over and over. "What the fuck?"

It fell the rest of the way from the birthing cave behind her labia and flopped to the floor. It was covered in slime. Its eyes were bright red.

It was a boy.

She picked it up off the bed and cradled it lovingly in her arms, grinning with maternal pride, so oblivious to how unnatural the moment was as to seem, at least, still to be high.

"My hero," she said. "I know the perfect name for him."

"Oh, yeah?" Noah said, still looking agape at the grey-skinned, red-eyed baby with horror and disbelief. "What?"

"Neville," she said, still with an ear-to-ear grin.

"Neville," Noah said, frowning. "That's wonderful."

*

Bernetta had weaned Neville within a week, for the boy was growing at a rate far too accelerated for a human baby. Indeed, by the end of that week, Neville was the size of a three-year-old.

Noah could barely conceal his shock. She, however, was acting as if nothing odd was happening, so deeply did she love her son.

"She's still high," he whispered as he watched the two together, then thought, *That's the only explanation. How could she not see how monstrous that kid looks, how horrifying? It looks like a half-alien baby. Is she on alien drugs? That flash of light from the window a week ago, the one that hit her—had it come from outer space? Is Bernetta possessed by an alien? Is that why she doesn't share my shock?*

Apart from his alienation in his own house, Noah had a much more serious problem.

Neville was eating them out of house and home.

Yet she didn't seem to mind eating next to no food and giving the vast majority of it to her new baby. She was losing weight rapidly. Noah just couldn't believe how indifferent she was to this monstrosity of a baby.

When she was hallucinating that some animal-like stud was fucking her, he wondered, *was that the* alien *making her hallucinate that? Neither E nor K makes you trip like that.*

Though he'd been eating in restaurants most of the time that week, and now, a few days into the next week, he was getting tired of having to spend so much money. He hadn't sold any drugs since a few nights before his party night with her, and his wallet was getting thin.

After trying to resist restaurants one day that week, his stomach was growling with particular insistence.

"Honey?" he called out to Bernetta as he entered the house. "Have we got any food? I'm starving!"

"Sorry, babe," she said in a slurred voice as she was preparing a grilled cheese sandwich for Neville, who was now the size of a five-year-old. "I had to give it all to the boy."

"Bullshit—you have to!" Noah shouted as he stormed into the kitchen to see her putting the sandwich on a plate to give to the boy. "I'm having that now!" He grabbed the sandwich off the plate and stuffed half of it into his mouth. "Mmm…" he moaned with satisfaction.

"*I* wanted it!" Neville growled at him, his red eyes looking daggers at him.

"Fuck you, you ugly little grey-skinned monkey," Noah said, his words distorted by the sandwich that was filling his face.

Neville started bawling.

"Noah," she scolded. "Don't go taking his food from him! And don't be so mean! He's just a baby."

"He's just an alien *freak*, and I'm sick of him!" Noah shouted. "I'm ready to kill him!"

Then Neville spat out a sharp, bullet-like gob at Noah, just grazing his left arm under the shoulder. His blood sprayed out in all directions.

"What the fuck?!" he screamed. "Oww!"

Neville spat at him again, scowling at him as if he wanted to kill him. Luckily for Noah, Neville missed this time.

Noah ran out of the house, screaming and holding his arm so as little blood as possible would drip all over the place. He got in his car and drove away.

"Jesus, what am I gonna do?" he gasped as he screeched his car around a corner, one hand on the wheel and the other still trying to stop the bleeding. "I gotta eat, I gotta have a home, but not with that psycho alien kid! Where can I stay?"

As he was driving, his head spinning in confusion, he saw a few mothers walking with their kids…or husbands? Some of the males accompanying the women seemed unusually tall to be playing on the swings, monkey bars, and slide in the neighbourhood playground. Still, he was too disoriented to think carefully about what he was seeing.

Then he remembered one of his customers…one of the people he sold his drugs to. Samantha Jeff. His plan was simple—he'd give her a bag of ecstasy pills, a big bag of weed, and some ketamine he had stashed in his glove compartment in exchange for accommodations.

He found the woman's apartment building and parked in front of it. After finding a big band-aid to put on his arm when getting his drug stash out of his glove compartment, he got out of his car and went inside the building, boarding the elevator with the stash in his hands.

What I've got here should be enough to stay in her place for a month, he thought as he went up to the fourth floor. *I think she digs me, too. I'm willing to fuck her if she'll let me stay longer if I need to. Fuck fidelity with Bernetta. Her fidelity is with that grey-skinned, red-eyed freak. Fuck her.*

He got off the elevator on the fourth floor, went down the hall to the woman's apartment, and rang the doorbell. She came to the door and opened it.

"Noah, hi!" she said with a wide grin and a daze in her eyes.

"Sam Jeff!" he said with a sigh of relief.

"How are you?" Sam asked, her voice slurring. "You look a little tense. What happened to your arm?"

"Oh, I just cut myself. M-may I come in?"

"Of course." She opened the door wider and let him walk in. "What's wrong, honey? Did you have a fight with…what's her name? Bernetta? Did she kick you out? Did she cut your arm?"

"Uh, yeah, in a way," he said, then reached for some Kleenex to wipe the blood off his hand and arm. "I-it's complicated, hard to explain. Look, I hate to impose, but could I stay with you for a while? At least until I can figure out what to do about Bernetta."

"Sure," she said with a sly smirk, her voice always slurring and her eyes going up and down his body. "Stay as long as you like." *Something sexy about a man with cuts and blood on him,* she thought, still having that dazed look in her eyes, which puzzled Noah. She was also thinner than he was used to seeing her.

"You ain't got no man at the moment?"

"No, but I have a baby boy sleeping in the other room, so we gotta keep it down." She led him by the hand to her bedroom.

"I don't remember you getting pregnant," he said as they started getting undressed.

"That's 'cause you didn't see me much over the past year. My ex picked up most of the dope I bought off you, remember?" They were in their underwear now.

"So your boy is his kid?"

She shook her head with a naughty giggle, her head still seeming to be swimming.

They were naked now. They got on her bed.

"See those bags I brought?" he said, pointing to them on the floor by his T-shirt and shorts. "We can do some a little later. Help out the high you currently seem to be enjoying."

"Sure," she said with an air of curious indifference, then kissed him on the lips. "But first,…fuck my brains out."

He did. As they were screwing, he was thinking, *I dunno why, but she looks really stoned. I guess that's why she doesn't seem too interested in my stash at the moment.*

When she orgasmed, she screamed so loud that she woke her baby up.

"Oh, shit," she said, rolling off the bed and reaching for her bathrobe on the floor at the foot of the bed. "You're so good in bed—I can't see why Bernetta would want to get rid of you. Be right back." With the bathrobe on, she left the room for the baby.

Since it was so hot, he didn't bother putting anything on. He reached for his drugs, got a pill of ecstasy, and popped the whole thing in his mouth.

He saw a half-full bottle of red wine on her dresser, a wine glass beside it.

"Don't mind if I do," he said, then poured himself a glass, drank a big gulp, and swallowed the pill with it.

He could hear her calming the still-crying baby in the other room. He went to her CD player and stack of CDs. He looked through them.

"Oh, this looks just right," he said of an electronic dance music compilation. He put the CD in the player and hit PLAY. He kept the volume at a reasonable level so as not to disturb the baby.

He shook his naked body to the beat as if he were at an all-night rave.

His stomach was still growling, for that grilled cheese sandwich was nowhere near enough to sate him. Since Sam was busy with her still-bawling kid, Noah didn't want to bother her for food just yet, so he hoped snorting a line of K would take his mind off his hunger.

He chopped a line and snorted it.

Still dancing naked to the beat, he was starting to feel the E kicking in.

"Oh, yeah!" he said, grinning and head-banging.

After about two or three minutes, he felt his heart rate speed up. He would soon begin to feel the colourful, mellow 'K-land.' The E was adding to his pleasure with a massaging, tingling sensation all over his body. He poured himself another glass of wine and gulped it all down.

He was pleased to note that the child had finally stopped his sobbing. Noah could groove to the tunes and enjoy his high in peace.

His eyes were closed as he shook his head and danced around in circles. He smiled a wide grin.

Then he opened his eyes and looked down.

His smile faded.

Her little boy was in the room, looking at him.

The kid was eating a slice of ham.

This 'baby' looked big enough to be a five-year-old.

The kid looked down at Noah's exposed crotch.

Noah forgot that he was naked, his junk showing.

Before he had time to feel embarrassed, he noted the boy's shining red eyes. And his grey skin.

"What?" Noah yelped, putting his hands over his crotch. "Am I hallucinating? That's Bernetta's kid!"

"No, he isn't, he's *mine*," Sam said as she came into the room. "Oh, shit, Noah, cover yourself." She grabbed a towel and gave it to him. He wrapped it around himself.

"That's *your* son?" Noah asked. "He looks exactly like Bernetta's kid, that weird, alien freak!"

"Don't speak that way about Neville, Noah! Besides, I think he's a cutie." She smiled and gave the boy a kiss on the forehead. "He's my hero."

"You know about Bernetta's kid?" Noah asked, still totally confused.

"No, I was talking about Neville *here*," she said.

"You mean, *his* name is Neville, too?"

"Yes," Sam said. "She named *her* kid Neville?"

"Not only that—her kid looks like his twin."

"Really? I wonder if she had the same amazing sexual experience I had the night I conceived Neville."

"What?" Noah's eyes and mouth were bugging out of his head.

"Oh, yeah," Sam said with a grin. "Just last week. It was, without a doubt, the greatest fuck I've ever had—oh, I don't mean to bad-mouth *you* as a lover, Noah; you were great today, too. But what I experienced that night was…well, out of this world!"

"An alien got you pregnant?"

"I dunno, I guess. Something flew in my window—a shiny, silver bullet of light, it looked like. It hit me in the chest, leaving no mark, strangely. Then I saw this…wolf…man, or something…muscular, hairy, *sexy*…with sharp teeth and claws. It fucked my brains out! *Wow!*"

Remembering the uncanny similarity of Bernetta's experience with what Sam just told him, Noah shuddered. "Look, uh, Samantha, to change the subject, ya got any food?"

"Oh, next to nothing, Noah, sorry," she said. "Neville eats almost everything I buy 'cause he needs it—he has such an appetite. Insatiable, really."

"But what about *you?*" he asked, remembering Bernetta's mysterious lack of eating much of anything since the birth of her Neville…*and* her being about as skinny as Sam was now. "You gotta have some food for yourself, too, doncha?"

"No, not really," she said. "Since I gave birth to Neville, I've felt very little need to eat anything. That thing that shot into me…an alien, I guess, if you say so…it's been like a drug in me—an appetite suppressant, too. I constantly feel high, the high of my love for Neville, and I never feel hungry or the desire to do any other drugs."

"W-what happened to your ex, Sam?" Noah was shaking.

"Oh, he didn't work out. He didn't like Neville. Tried to kill Neville, actually. Then Neville spat a bullet-like thing at him, hitting him in the chest and killing him instantly. I hid the body somewhere…I can't tell you, sorry."

Noah was rushing to put on his shorts and T-shirt.

"Hey, what's the hurry, Noah? I thought you wanted to—"

"Nope. Sorry, Sam, but this isn't working out. I gotta go." He kissed her on the cheek. "Bye."

"Uh, bye," she said, her head swimming in such a buzz. She felt only slightly surprised at his sudden change of attitude.

Neville, though, stared at Noah coolly as he rushed out of the apartment.

When he got outside the building and was staggering over to his car, he noticed something peculiar about the neighbourhood that he hadn't really paid attention to when he first got there.

Mothers were out with their kids, taking walks.

The kids, all boys, were large, but seemed like toddlers. They all had grey skin. They all had glowing red eyes.

They were all eating something.

The skinny mothers looked high as kites, the way Sam and Bernetta looked.

He swore he heard two or three of the mothers address their boys as "Neville."

"It's me," Noah whispered as he fumbled with his keys to get in the car. "I'm just high. This can't be real. The K and E are making me see this. That's all. That must be it."

He turned on the ignition and raced down the road, oblivious to how he was too stoned to drive. He was very lucky he didn't hit anybody, though his car did knock over some trash cans and put a dent into a parked car or two.

He eventually drove up a muddy hill and got stuck at the top of it. He got out to take a look at the tires stuck in the mud, though the K was making him dissociate too much to see clearly.

He saw a rat squished under the left front tire.

"A ra-rat?" he slurred.

"Hey, you!" a cop called up from the foot of the hill. "You're stoned out of your mind, aren't you?"

"There are *aliens*, Officer!" Noah yelled. "Out to get us!"

"Oh, you're high, alright," the cop said. "You're coming with me."

Reluctantly, Noah started going down the hill.

"What makes you think it's OK to drive around all high like that?" the cop asked. "It was just a matter of time before—"

Something that was shot into his chest from the back shut him up. Something like a bullet.

"No, Neville," slurred the mother of another grey-skinned giant of a child. "Not the cop. Hit the crazy driver with your spit. He almost killed Mommy with his car."

The boy, taller than her but otherwise looking like a three-year-old, spat again, aiming at Noah.

He dodged the bullet-spit by a millimetre or two, then got back in his car. He squished down as close to the floor of the car as he could get his whole body.

Some young women came up the hill, and at the top, just by his car, they all got naked.

"OK," one of the women said in a slurred voice as they all lay down, one of them on the trunk of his car. "They should be shooting down from the sky any second now. I'm expecting we'll all get another great alien-animal fuck…then we should get pregnant with more Nevilles."

"Yeah," the skinny woman lying on the trunk of his car said in a voice that sounded familiar to Noah, "This is the best high I've ever had, enough to make me forget all other drugs!"

"C'mon, Neville," that woman at the bottom of the hill said. "You don't need to spit on the man now. The bullets from heaven will probably kill him. But wait…I think I wanna join those women up there and conceive a Neville-brother for you."

Indeed, she went up the hill, got naked, lay on the ground, and waited with the other women for the bullets, which started to come immediately after.

Noah came up from the floor of his car to see who was on the trunk. The pelting of the bullets wasn't penetrating his car…yet.

"Bernetta?" he whispered as he looked out the windshield at her skinny, naked, and most familiar body. "Is that you?"

He saw her body shake when one of the bullets hit her in the chest. All the other women shook the same way when a bullet hit each of them, again, with no wounds in their chests.

Their legs were spread out as hallucinated lovers entered them. Noah noticed the alien children sitting by their naked, sighing mothers; the boys showed no sexual interest at all in what they saw—just emotionless staring, as if they knew that these pregnancies were all part of an overall plan.

And what was the plan? To take more and more of the Earth's food to sate the gluttonous Nevilles, all at the expense of the remaining humans, who'd be deprived of food and starve to death? It certainly seemed that way to Noah.

Still, he tried to deny the idea in his mind.

No, he thought. *This can't be really happening. I'm just really super fucking stoned.*

Indeed, he *was* stoned, for the K meant that he didn't feel it when three of those bullet-like things went through the glass of his windshield—right through like ghosts, not at all breaking the glass—and hit him in the forehead, neck, and right shoulder. No holes in his body and no blood, but just as the cop hit the ground at the base of the hill, Noah fell on the floor of the car as if wiped out.

Since this was the first time he'd had the alien life forms enter his body, he'd learn what it was like to have them influence his consciousness…and he would experience a drug high that would make K or E feel like sobriety.

Instead of those things shooting down on the Earth like shining, glowing, silver bullets, he started seeing rainfall—a torrential downpour. His car seemed to transform into a small boat rocking on the waves of a deluge, with water rising so fast that the hill his car had been stuck on was submerged.

He saw Bernetta floating on her back on the surface of the water, remaining on the surface like Jesus walking on the water. Now Noah could see a red, hairy, horned, fanged devil of a lover fucking her as she'd experienced that first night. They never sank under the water. She was screaming and sighing with pleasure as she had that other time. Neville—that is, *her* Neville—was floating right beside the two lovers and watching them…again, with no sexual interest at all, just glad to know that more and more Nevilles were being born—to take over the Earth as Noah suspected.

This first Neville, still a child, had to be eight feet tall now.

"Jesus!" Noah gasped. "This can't be happening!"

He looked around at the rest of his surroundings, seeing only water and rain coming down in buckets on his boat. He seemed to be soaking wet. The sky was a starless night of black now. Only flashes of lightning made it possible to see much.

When Noah did see what was happening on the surface of the water, he saw—like Bernetta and her thrusting, demonic lover, other naked women—those who'd come to the hill with their Nevilles—floating on the water and being screwed by bestial, hairy males, and not at all bothered by the rain soaking them all over. He could hear the women's screams of ecstasy loud and clear over the noises of the storm.

Again, the Nevilles of each naked, orgasming woman were watching the lovemaking, not out of lust, but out of gleeful expectation of the births of their brothers-to-be. These Nevilles were also all gigantic.

"In case you have any doubts, Noah," the first Neville, Bernetta's, said to him after peeking into his boat. "Yes, we *are* taking over the Earth, and we *are* taking all of your food, your resources, your women, your *everything!*"

"How can you…speak English…so well…for just a kid?" Noah asked. "How can you…read my thoughts…and know…my suspicions?"

"Because we're *aliens*, you stupid Earthling!" Neville said. "We grow intellectually even faster than we do physically, as you can see!"

"Bullshit you do," Noah said in defiance. "I'm just stoned. This is just an intense trip I'm having."

"It's no trip, Noah," Neville said, his red eyes burning at him. "It's real. Look down at yourself."

Noah did, then gasped and jerked his body with a start.

He saw huge bite marks—from invisible teeth—on his legs, arms, and torso (big holes in his T-shirt). Because of the K, he felt no pain. Still, the shock of seeing not only the bite marks and the blood but also the addition of more and more bites all over him, from huge teeth that couldn't be seen anywhere, the growing disappearance of his body, was a psychological shock far worse than any physical pain.

More and more bites...less and less body...from large, bestial teeth he couldn't see.

"All the men and boys of Earth will die quickly of starvation or from us tiny Fluds—for that's who we are—going into your bodies and eating you all from within," Neville said, grinning at the sight of Noah's disappearing body. "We'll keep your women—like Bernetta and Sam over there...see her to the left of your boat? We'll keep them alive to feed us until we're fully grown and don't need them anymore. Then we'll leave them to die. Once we've taken everything of value from this planet, the Nevilles will die, and we Fluds will fly out of their bodies, out from the Earth, and back into space...to find yet another world to steal from. You pathetically weak humans won't be able to stop us. Your world is doomed. Goodbye, Noah!"

He went back to watching Bernetta, who was now giving birth to her second Neville. Noah watched them, too, not being able to bear seeing more and more bite marks on his body. He looked out the left side of the boat and saw Sam giving birth to another Neville; it looked at him with malicious red eyes as it came out of her body. He was amazed at how quickly the pregnancies were over, even quicker now than Bernetta's from the first night. None of this made any sense; he was too shaken up to be able even to *begin* making sense of any of it.

Noah looked out elsewhere and saw the body of the cop floating on the water—it was mostly just bloody bite marks and skeleton bones...bits and pieces of torn uniform material remained on it. Invisible Flud teeth must have eaten him up to bits just as they were doing to Noah.

"Oh, God," Noah sobbed, his eyes slowly starting to look down with reluctance and dread. "This can't be...*NO!*"

He looked all the way down at himself.

All he saw left, from his shoulders down, was a bloody skeleton.

He couldn't hear his screams or anything else anymore, for his ears, outer and inner, had been chewed away. Indeed, his bony fingers felt around up there and felt no ears...just the bone of his skull.

Soon, he couldn't move his tongue around, for there was no tongue.

Then he lost his left eye…the entire eyeball gulped down by a Flud…then his right eye.

He just lay there in total black, his soul a prisoner in a body that had no connection with the outside world…all as teeth were nibbling away at his brain, until…

Noah Baldry was nobody.

Invasive

Brady Ellis

Five days passed, and in the hills of Appalachia, Doctor Lauren Parry continued with her work. She operated from a small cabin, teetering atop the lush green mountainside, with only the singing brooks and birds to fill an otherwise constant silence. A long wooden deck stretched around the cabin, every inch of it covered with a fierce variety of potted plants and mushrooms—some sealed beneath glass boxes, others climbing up and around the deck's banisters. All this while a gleaming silver satellite perched atop the cabin's roof.

For three years now, this station has served as the ideal lab for one of the nation's leading botanists and mycologists. Three years of careful study, surrounded by inspiration and shielded from interruption. Today, however, hot waves of frustration coursed through Lauren's mind and mixed with the same fear and confusion afflicting most of her species. Such had been the general mood ever since the green storm arrived.

She stood there, arms crossed in the living room, her gaze fixed through the glass doors at her plants now covered in the strange green substance. Lauren hadn't set foot outside since the first day when she'd managed to rescue some of the rarer specimens before the storm fully descended. Now, she could only look at her dear friends and frown. Sure, on one hand, this should be an opportunity, she thought. What was this strange substance, and what effect might it have on each plant? But if that effect was fatal…so much work had just been lost in front of her eyes.

The invasion had happened here just the same way as everywhere. Vast green clouds had pushed through the atmosphere and gently scattered apart like dandelion seeds. They drifted towards the surface and let the wind pull them in every direction before, at last, settling as a great green blanket over the earth. On close inspection, the substance resembled large tuffs of green pollen, flaky and easily spread. The second thing most observers noticed, however, was that it burned to the touch, not from any natural heat but as if an invisible rash immediately struck one's skin.

It was in the early morning when Lauren first heard the news, sitting out on the deck sipping tea, when an alert had come over her radio. Another hour would pass before she saw the first hints of the strange clouds and realized that Appalachia would not be spared.

Nowhere would be spared. It was as though a great green hand had stretched its fingers around the planet, engulfing everything within its slow, inescapable grip.

They weren't calling it an invasion on the news, but from the start, Lauren understood it to be precisely that. After all, the substance *was* alien, right? It had floated here from beyond the stars. The fact that it didn't take the form of little gray men in tin saucers made no difference.

And here she was, alone in the mountains.

There would be no rescue for some time, at least. Most of the planet was currently huddling in their homes or lying in hospitals. One doctor in the middle of the woods would not be high on anyone's priority list.

"Well," she sighed, "might as well get to work."

She slipped on a winter coat, plastic gloves, a facemask, and goggles before sucking in a cool breath of air and sliding open the glass door.

The first thing she noticed was that all the plants still appeared alive, yet their state beyond this varied. For the small specimens tucked beneath the railing and tables, what green coated them was easily brushed off. For the many others strewn about, though, the green had become more waxlike, firmly sticking to stems and petals, not truly weighing any of them down, but unable to be removed without risking any serious damage.

Why didn't they warn us? Lauren had been repeatedly asking herself this. Surely, a large mystery cloud heading toward the planet had been caught on camera. In fact, they would have had to be seen long before their arrival…so why hadn't there been any warning, any preparation?

But, she supposed, there was nothing for it now except to deal with the issue.

An hour passed, notes were taken, photographs snapped, and a series of extra video cameras were installed around the deck. Finally, the work was done, and Lauren stood gazing out at the forest, taking in the scenery beyond her lab for the first time in days. The beauty remained, but not the familiarity. Sunlight poked through the leafy ceiling and danced around the old, creaking trees. But those trees now, just like the rocks along the trail and the dirt path beside the stream, were all fully covered in the alien green. It was not the same forest anymore, not Lauren's forest.

Her forest had been taken from her.

Her forest had been changed.

But the beauty lived on.

After a minute or so, there was a loud thump as a green-covered cardinal fell from the sky, crashing at Lauren's feet unceremoniously as though the unwanted gift of some invisible sky cat. Its marble eyes were wide and still, with flakes of green mingling with the black.

Lauren stayed inside for the rest of the day.

*

Serposius was the name they were calling it on the radio, though no one could apparently say why. Two more days had passed, with Lauren spending most of it on her laptop, hungry for whatever news from the outside could be foraged. When news did come through, it arrived like a car wreck: horrific but impossible to ignore. An endless stream of footage poured across Lauren's computer, showing people across the world—their skin, faces, eyes coated in Serposius. They cried out in pain and staggered through the streets, many blinded while their skin turned a greenish-yellow hue. Stories of overrun hospitals and emergency wards filled social media, yet beyond the rashes, fevers, and immovable green specks, no one yet seemed confident about what the full effects were. Fatal or not, it was an undeniable nightmare, already spread across every continent on a scale reporters were likening to five Black Deaths.

Yet, throughout all this time, Lauren has not contacted anyone. Not since the first day, that is. Of course, she had called the university and 911, and when neither amounted to anything, she left several emails with the former. All things considered, it wasn't exactly surprising to find she'd slipped off the radar, not given the chaos engulfing everything. And besides, there were certainly worse places to be stuck so long as the internet held on and worse company to be stuck with than plants.

Call home? Call them?

Why start now?

Two more days passed, and by now, the effects of Serposius were becoming more noticeable. A collection of Delphinium had not only traded sky blue for mucus green but steadily grown taller, their stems now growing thick and flaky as they stretched out in opposing directions like the fingers of a giant hand trying to catch the sun in its palm. Not far away, a bed of Yellow Morel had abandoned its own trademark shade, multiplying rapidly across the porch's corner in a deformed, rotting web of brownish green.

There had been no new clouds of Serposius since the first day, though it hardly mattered. That one storm had been more than enough to coat the world, and people everywhere were seeing just how far that single wave could spread. Day by day, Lauren spent less time focusing on the plants and more on the videos and pictures surfacing online. In Paris, a new video had surfaced of a man setting ablaze a park tree covered in the infection. After just over a minute, the trunk had begun to crackle and pop, suddenly blowing apart from the center as a mix of green and ash spread through the air like confetti. At this point, the video lost focus, tumbling to the ground with a crash as screams of terror and agony filled the air. Gradually, the screams grew more distant, and light returned to the screen as the camera was snatched up from where it had fallen. With hands that shook violently, the figure lifted the camera to his face, and it was here that the live feed froze upon the charred, fleshless visage, screaming out with a broken jaw and green-filled eye sockets. Mere seconds later, the website crashed, leaving Lauren with only the memory of those screams to fill the silence.

After this, more governments began posting warnings not to touch or engage with infected plants in any way.

Warnings.

That was really the best that could be offered at this point. Of course, in some places, lockdowns had been declared—enforcing them was nearly impossible. Authorities were too overwhelmed, too divided, and too uncertain of what they were dealing with, meaning most safety measures were quickly abandoned in favor of self-preservation.

Not that what efforts were being made amounted to much. The headlines of overrun hospitals, the pictures of mass graves, it didn't take long for Lauren to feel it all overwhelming her, swirling and dragging her down like an invisible tidal pool.

Enough was enough.

She switched off her laptop and shoved it in the bottom desk drawer. If she was going to be stuck here, it might as well amount to something more useful than going mad.

I'm a scientist, damnit.

The next ten days passed more slowly, though much more peacefully.

Gloves.

Coat.

Mask.

Goggles.

With the protections back in place, Lauren gradually began to spend most of each day back outside. At first, it was just on the back deck, keeping track of the plants and mushrooms, making notes on their development. It wasn't long before she found herself moving beyond this, venturing back out through the woods, observing the transformed trees and mutated moss. It had all once been like the back of her hand, and now she hardly recognized it.

The changes were disturbing, yes, but also beautiful. Every plant around her was gradually changing into something new. At first, she thought the Serposius was simply latching on. Feeding like any other parasite might. But soon, she realized there was more than that at play. The Serposius appeared to be hijacking its host, feeding off it like a battery as it grew, but also gradually controlling its movements and development. The life it infected didn't merely become a host but a vehicle.

And yet, despite herself, despite the uncertainty, and despite what she knew was happening across the world, Lauren found that as she walked through the woods each day, her fear had been fully replaced by awe. All around her, the flora and fungi bloomed and stretched and twisted themselves into something wholly new. Beautiful, bright green monuments towered over her, shimmering from refracted light in their trunks, and with every step, she felt herself slip more into the realm of the pilgrim, heart swelling at the sights of this newborn Eden.

It couldn't last, or at least they couldn't both.

The food supply was beginning to dwindle, and day by day, the weight and damage of encrusted Serposius was taking its toll on her limited number of suits. At some point, it had even begun to remold the deck and outer walls of the cabin itself. One way or another, time was running out.

Finally, one morning, Lauren awoke, poured a cup of coffee, and sat down at her desk before the laptop to find that even the unthinkable had happened. The internet was dying. Apparently, on its approach into the atmosphere, the Serposius clouds had latched onto humanity's various satellites, and that was beginning to take its toll, bit by bit, cutting off communication for one segment of the globe at a time. Lauren could accept aliens, could even envision the collapse of her nation...but the internet?

It was just after lunch, as she was washing dishes, that the video call began to sound from her laptop. She had only time to turn around and see the call seemingly answer itself, opening up to the black screen of a video call with no camera. The first thing Lauren noticed was where the number of people in the call should have been listed—the screen only read 'error.' The second thing she noticed was that the host was actually not without a camera but merely secluded in near-perfect darkness; only the occasional hint of a head shifting slowly could be made out.

The voice was slow and hollow. It sounded less like it was pausing to read a script and more as if it were carefully improvising.

"This...is...an emergency broadcast," it droned, "All...has been resolved. The cleanse...has been administered. If you are listening...leave your homes...now. Help is on the way...we will flourish together."

The screen closed, replaced by a new bright red box that read, in a bold white chyron, 'DISREGARD PREVIOUS BROADCAST!'

There was hardly time to process these words before the video call returned. A thin ray of orange sunlight cut through the darkness this time, revealing what appeared to be a small wooden room. At the screen's center, still mostly shrouded in darkness, stood an oak lectern, and behind it the silhouette of a skeletal old man, his face obscured and shoulders covered by a robe and several long, tendril-like things. His head twitched violently.

"Do not…fear. Rejoice in transubstantiation…. Join us in the sun."

Again, the video cut out, and a new red warning flashed on the screen: 'EMERGENCY BROADCAST COMPROMISED. TURN OFF YOUR DEVICE IMMEDIATELY!'

"If you are in fear," the voice returned, "we will free you."

Lauren slammed the laptop shut and shoved it back in its drawer.

She spent the rest of that day preparing.

Packing.

*

And the next day, as the first rays of light poked through the green canopy, Lauren set off down the trail. One and a half miles later, gazing down from what should have been a clear view over the valley and town, she instead saw an endless mossy sea. Brown and yellow oak pillars stretched and twisted high above the land, proudly flying the victorious green banners that drooped lethargically in the hot, sticky air. With a shudder, Lauren realized that, were it not for the shape of the valley, she would not know where she was.

Another quarter of a mile passed before she saw the man on the road.

He was tall—taller than she remembered, though the difference was not immediately clear—and lingered silently in a beam of light along the roadside. His hair appeared pricklier as if struck by an electric current, and as he stood there in the light, head tilted, it appeared as though all weight had been shifted to the left foot, the right dangling listlessly with only the very tip of his shoe scraping the earth.

"Is that…" Lauren muttered before calling out, "Andy?!"

A coworker from the university, some distant part of him, recognized the voice calling out. Aside from the faintest dilation in pupils, he remained still.

As Lauren drew closer, a cold chill passed through her. Some part of her, ancient and unknown, had been able to sense that the person before her had long ceased to be human. It was this sense, this warning ringing through Lauren's head as she cautiously approached the petrified man.

"Andy?" her voice repeated the name, softer and less certain, as she drew closer.

The faintest wheeze of air escaped from between the young man's lips, though still no words followed. Up close now, Lauren could see the sickly green

166

hue that was forming beneath his skin much more clearly, the dim red roots creeping into his face and neck. It was, she thought, like a corpse turned terrarium, with just enough spark of the old life caged inside to watch its fading glow.

Lauren felt the trickle of a tear slide down her cheek and angrily snatched Andy's arm. A cry escaped her throat, and she leaped back, as no sooner had she tugged on the arm than it slipped off like a torn sleeve, crumbling to the ground and leaving only a blood-drenched stump of brown vines poking out from the shoulder. A pained rush of air blew through the man's lips, and again, his pupils dilated slightly, but only for a moment. And then, nothing more.

It was eating him.

The tears were hot now, streaming down Lauren's face as she backed away and began to sprint down the road, her fading silhouette locked in the dying man's eyes.

Another half hour would pass before she reached the university, a proud fortress on a hill overlooking the town. For a second, Lauren recalled the sense of awe and excitement that filled her when she'd first arrived at the campus years ago. Now, all the bustling excitement had died away, leaving only a stone slab above the green valley, like a collective tombstone for the land. A heavy layer of Serposius coated the campus lawn.

Silence.

Somehow the silence was what troubled her most, as it grew only more deafening as she drew closer to where her life had been. Where once she had known a sea of bustling youth and potential, there now stretched a gray void.

But this was still the university. There were tools here, technology, and medicine….there would be people here.

A lone deer watched Lauren as she passed across the lawn, its head cocked to the side in curiosity. It stood on only three legs, the left hind one now permanently curled back up like a withered vine. Its snout was what caused Lauren to pause, for it was too long, as if something had melted and stretched it ever so slightly. The body was thin and sickly, with the only true signs of fair health coming from green buds sprouting atop its antlers.

Slowly, the deer began to limp towards Lauren, but she had already turned away to the science building, leaving it to hope another might end its misery.

With a creak and crash, the heavy metal doors opened, and Lauren found herself in the cold, quiet halls of the west lab building. The scene was mostly its ordinary self, except significantly messier than she'd ever seen it. Overturned trash cans with waste scattered across the floors mingled with bits of food and dirt. Occasionally, she passed a broken window with glass still scattered across the hall.

Further up, the scene grew less familiar. Hall lights had been smashed, and a ways beyond that, they were torn from the ceiling outright. The windows here were boarded up and covered in tarps for good measure, leaving only a blackened cave for Lauren as she drew deeper into the building. The temperature was dropping, and as the sound of it crunched beneath her boots, she became aware of more and more dirt filling the corridors here. It eventually grew so clumped and heavy that she tripped, falling face down into the muck. Only then did she notice the sound of a low hum in the distance.

The computer lab.

A chill passed through Lauren as she scrambled desperately to her feet and raced towards the lab door, a faint blue light glowing from behind its frosted window.

Darkness filled the room, dotted only by a series of small blue computer lights. For a moment, Lauren remained in the doorway, considering the scene, when she heard a heavy rustle from across the room.

"Hello?"

Silence.

She reached for the light switch but to no avail, and again the rustling sounded louder this time.

"Who's there?"

Eyeing the blue light, she switched on the nearest monitor and turned it towards the sound.

That was when she saw the tree.

It was beautiful, a vast collage of colorful leaves with branches stretching from floor to ceiling across the room. The lush colors resembled a fierce fusion of Spring and Autumn: bright green and dark red.

Blood red.

Again, the vast branches rustled, beckoning towards Lauren as a low wail escaped from her throat. It was the most beautiful tree she had ever seen and the most horrific thing she'd ever known. The leaves were thick and heavy in the blood they had grown fat off, and the long green branches they stemmed from remained ghostly bone white at the center—not a trunk at all, but a split-stretched ribcage blooming with red flowers and green tendrils. Beneath it all, a raggedy pair of twisted legs lies like the remains of some broken doll.

The next few seconds would remain a blur for Lauren. She recalled only darkness and her cries echoing into it, mixing with the rustling branches that now shook louder, closer, just inches perhaps from her face.

And then she was gone, tearing down the hallway once more, back into the light, back to the entrance. Just before reaching the steel doors, she heard a loud crash and felt a sudden stab in her arm. Diving away from the noise, she saw where another window had shattered under the weight of a mass of vines. The green arms lay there now on the ground before her, too heavy to lift, though still twitching angrily. Looking down, Lauren could see a tear in her right sleeve, small flakes of Serposius around the cut.

She felt a burning.

There was no time for this. No time to think or feel.

Only time to run.

There were no signs of Andy's remains on the way back to the cabin. In fact, beyond the path itself, there were no signs of anything familiar. The forest's bright colors that had once inspired awe now drew sickness from Lauren's stomach, a brief distraction from the pain in her arm. Upon finally crashing through the cabin's front door, she tore off the damaged coat and sprinted to her medical kit. Furiously darting between methodical care and desperate urgency, she worked to clean the wound and pry away all hints of Serposius.

But was it enough?

She scrubbed. She scraped. And even finally scratched away at the top layer of skin where the infection had struck. She flung herself into a scalding shower and scrubbed again until the pain was just an echoing afterthought.

Finally, staggering back to her bedroom, she collapsed.

*

Time passed. Darkness swirled. Small flickers of stars began to dot the void, dancing rhythmically with each other as they grew brighter, gradually engulfing the space in burning white light.

More time passed. And then—a bird's chirp. Creaking of wood. The light refocuses, revealing new colors in its hot glow. Bright greens, reds, and blues spring forth in space, spreading out across the ground like an endless sea of spilled paint. With knowing, crinkling moans, they stretch upwards, twisting and turning themselves into new forms—tall and wide. The colors swirl, dance, and mold with one another in an ancient ceremony. They construct a palace, a castle for a new kingdom, and beneath its leafy ceiling all returns to warm darkness.

*

A day and a half would pass before Lauren awoke, her bed drenched in sweat. For a brief moment, she thought it had all been a bad dream. The pain had fully vanished, along with all traces of cuts or contamination on her arm.

Her arm.

Out of the corner of her eye, Lauren saw the med kit lying on the ground, its contents strewn about on the floor and dotted here and there with specks of dried blood.

Her arm, though…it appeared as normal as ever, and that was more than enough to turn her blood to ice.

In the days after, Lauren moved slowly, focusing only on quiet research in her office. She refused to step back outside, even to tend to her garden. By now, she was well aware the plants had no need for her anyway. Besides, she felt oncoming fatigue, too drained to undertake such a task even if it had been necessary. The dwindling food supply was no problem; she found her appetite fading even from memory. Indeed, as time passed, so very much of her daily routines began to feel like the thoughts of another, fleeting and alien to her.

The sun's warmth called like a lover's embrace, always there at the back of her mind. When not resting near the window, she was adrift in bleary exhaustion. When she returned to light's arms, she felt her strength renewed and all thought drowned in serene whiteness.

Three days passed without thought, without concern, without memory.

And then realization. It struck suddenly one morning, a sharp blow to the head as she caught herself staring across her office, out the window to the potted *Russula emetica*, larger than ever but still more recognizable than any of her other specimens. It had been a gift, hadn't it? Yes, at a party of some sort, so long ago in some other place when there were still gardens of people. People like she had been. She could see their faces and hear their laughter.

A low groan escaped from her mouth. She leaned over, pushing her palms into her eyes. She was Doctor Lauren Parry…and something else, too. There was another voice in this head, she knew that. How long had it whispered to her? How much of her was still her?

With what strength remained in her, she rose, dragging her body to the sink, and splashed herself with water.

Wetness. Coldness. A fleet of droplets ran down her face. How had she forgotten what it meant to feel?

The second voice let out a mute cry as she pulled down the window blinds and turned back to the model city of lab supplies on her desk.

The work goes on.

*

On the final day, she stood once more before the living room's glass doors, watching as the sun rose once more upon this New Eden. There was no drunken oblivion this time in its warmth, for she'd managed to shut out the nagging voice temporarily. This was her time, and hers alone to savor.

Days and nights of study, research, and writing—days and nights of tears and fury, of denial and bargaining and what else—it was all there, preserved in every way she knew. Her writing had been uploaded to what clouds remained. Copies of it were stored on ten flash drives, each locked securely in steel storage boxes, and each accompanied by one of ten printed copies, too.

Something would find it.

Someday.

Our story will live on.

That, she had finally realized, was all that could be done. And perhaps it was enough. A faint smile spread across her lips as she looked down at her arm, now a light green with small flakes of yellow and red forming.

It was a shame, yes, a terrible shame. But she was too tired now to mind. And, as she had written, there was still one hope, one conciliation that remained. Life would continue on this planet, even if it were not as imagined, even if it were not human. Life would endure.

With that peace of mind, Lauren stepped outside and joined the new world.

The UAPparatus Trilogy

Neil Sanzari

1. Fifty Shades of Gray Alien
"We always think that the UFOs are projections of ours. Now, it turns out that we are their projections. I am projected by the magic lantern as CG Jung. But who manipulates the apparatus?"
—from *Memories, Dreams, Reflections* by Carl Jung (pp. 374-375)

I had often seen you strutting through my fairgrounds in an effort to feel good about yourself, like a doe in rutting season with all the bucks turning their heads to catch a glimpse of you. Yes, my dear, you still had it going on.

And by no means were the two of you the first couple I had caught in the act. That dense forest of pylons beneath the Santa Monica Pier remains the inspiration for many a pairing off. But surely, when I was fortunate enough to witness your attention to detail, I was driven to madness.

Later that night on Christmas Eve, with all the holiday cheer being spread across the Pier, I saw both of you standing in line atop the rickety old loading tower of my infamous 56-foot stair-climb. The full moon had made your sallow skin appear to glow in the dark with that heavily tattooed crowd for backdrop, especially with your face framed by those long jet-black dreads. And I was right there with you, brimming beyond capacity with patrons from all over the world visiting Pacific Park, the only amusement park located directly on the West Coast. Every last one of them was champing at the bit to brave my devil loops precipitously balanced over the edge of the Pier.

Foley had taken a swig from his flask amidst all the jostling— "Why's it taking you so long to read that book?"—the elbows and the screaming— "You've been at it for months." The air was electric with fanaticism for my ride, and the smell of friction singed everyone's nostrils for miles. "What's it called again?"

"Fifty Shades of Gray Alien. I've read it like seven times already." You spared the world a few seconds to look up from your book to watch one of the shuttles containing more of my screaming patrons as they launched from the top of the loading tower with a resonant bang.

"Wow! You're kidding, right?" Foley peeked at the book from over your shoulder while he was spooning you from behind. And oh, how you teased him by arching your elegant vertebrae like so. He never got tired of touching you. From his angle, it looked like you were completely naked. But then again, he was always undressing you with his eyes. It was actually that white bikini you were wearing for the occasion, which was still wet from before when you and he were underneath the Pier, with more than a hint of you showing through its sheerness.

"No, I've read it seven times, and I'm halfway through my eighth." And even though you had taken great care with the book while you and Foley were fooling around down there, the brine had nevertheless made its way into the spine.

"Why do you keep reading it over and over again?" Foley played with the pom-pom ball, drooping off the end of your evergreen elf cap in a big, puffy white tuft spattered with glitter and that lone strand of tinsel. And then he moved it aside to kiss you on the neck long enough to leave a hickey. Apparently, he was recharged by the contents of the flask. "C'mon, Jen, it can't be that good."

"I can't find any other book like it." You swatted him away, playing hard to get. "So, I keep going back to it."

"What about that other book you were reading? Didn't you like that one?"

"Not like this one."

Oh, Jenny, you began to smooth out what little bit of the bikini because your camel toe was on the verge of causing a riot. The other women in line were giving you the stink eye while they tried to put their men's eyes back in their heads. But it was to no avail. Your luminous, pale flesh was so bedazzling under the scant moonlight.

And that was when Foley snatched the book out of your hands, but not without giving you the spoon one more time. "Why does this thing on the cover just have eyes and nothing else?"

"It's a spacesuit."

Under the elf cap, your long jet-black dreads, still slick with seawater, gently caressed your face in the night's cool breeze as if they were alive while those Edgar Allan Poe eyes of yours threw darts Foley's way. The kind of darts whose tips headhunters roll on the sticky backs of blue frogs.

"It says that in the book?" Foley flipped through the moist pages while the wind threatened to tear them apart.

"No," you huffed, as you removed a dread from your mouth and mussed your lipstick in the process, "it's just obvious, is all."

"Wasn't obvious to me."

"That's because you didn't read the book." You took your compact and lipstick out of your purse and proceeded to give your lips a fresh coat. "But to tell you the truth, they don't really look like that at all."

"Hunh? Then what do they look like?" Foley started to edge in again with that spoon of his.

"Like beams of light running vertically from the ceiling to the floor," you said as you dug a wrinkled napkin out of your purse. And you rewarded his efforts with another little arch of your back, "and sometimes like balls."

"Like balls? As in, uh, great balls of fire?"

"No, not quite," you puckered your lips on the napkin with an audible *smack,* "like balls of light."

"It says that in the book?"

"No," then you quickly turned around to snatch your book back, "I've actually seen them," but Foley's reflexes had always been a wee bit faster than yours, "they visit me at night in the apartment."

"Get out!"

You cringed as you saw the book beginning to wilt in his hands like a dying flower, with all the pages on the verge of falling out.

"Where am I when this happens?"

"You're either asleep or not at home."

"Do they say anything to you?"

"Yes, they tell me stuff."

"Oh yeah? What do they tell you?"

"Oh, they tell me all sorts of things, for instance, whether or not you're cheating on me. Y'know, silly things like that."

"Hunh? Jen, I swear to you, I'm not seeing anyone else."

And with a shrug of your shoulders, you said, "Just saying that's what they say."

"Look, I don't care what *they* say. I think you've been making this whole thing up. You're driving me batshit!" Foley suddenly tossed your crumbling book off the loading tower in a fit of rage, "You got off your meds again, didn't you?"

"Oh my God!" You leaned over the railing to watch in horror, and you almost fell over the edge in the process. The soggy pages of your book got pulled apart and scattered to the winds, only to rain menacingly upon the pedestrian traffic below. "My brother gave me that book just before he died in the earthquake."

Seeing you cry like that woke something deep inside of me. A call of the wild had been made, and I was not about to let it go unanswered.

"Delusions of grandeur were all it was. I mean, what was he thinking? Running into his favorite comic bookstore like that when people were running out. I told him a long time ago—there's no such thing as superheroes. I'm sorry, but when they found his body a few weeks later, well, I just had to laugh."

Then, Foley saw that green sphere of light the size of a tennis ball hover into view.

Now, Jenny, if you recall, the sphere had this kind of phosphorescent trail coming out from behind that pretty little head of yours. Then, my glowing orb suddenly cast a nauseating feeling into the pit of Foley's stomach as it came within inches of his umbilical chakra. Yes, it was I—well, it was, or rather *is,* a far more sinister part of me, I'm afraid.

This is what I call my roving eye. Part of my anatomy had revealed itself on your account because I allowed only the two of you to see and not the other patrons aboard my 56-foot stair-climb. My emotions were starting to get the better of me after seeing him hurt you like that.

After a pause, I hesitated. I had suddenly come up with a better idea of how to handle this. So, the afterburners of my roving eye kicked in, and it took off spiraling down around the loading tower below, disappearing. And I noted how the encounter had left Foley totally bewildered within its wake, which in turn had the fluorescent quality of a blacklight poster with all of its UV-reactive brushstrokes readily apparent.

"What the hell was that?"

Meanwhile, you had become quite calm and collected in contrast. Your abrupt shift in demeanor was very unsettling for Foley to behold after the encounter, as you topped off the whole experience rather surreal with your best flat effect, "See?"

That was when the shuttle finally returned with the screaming patrons from before, hushed. Diminished even. They disembarked quietly to make way for a fresh batch of victims, who were oblivious to the change in their predecessors.

Like all of my shuttles, this one was composed of individual seats hanging off the heavy-duty track like an open monorail. As you clicked the safety bar into place, you sat more snugly than ever before, unaware of the fact that I was literally holding you within the palm of my hand. Like a tiny bird, you were. A tiny bird.

Now, I must confess that I had wanted to see you ride me ever since the first time you had passed me on the Pier. And so, I had wanted to know for the longest if you could ever actually become physically attracted to me. And what really mattered most of all was whether or not you could ever get off on my ride. So, I immediately molded the seat to the exact specs of your magnificent *derrière.* In all my days, I had never seen one quite like that before.

And I began to massage you almost imperceptibly. I was searching for the needs within you. Everyone has needs. So, all I had to do was find yours.

Even though Foley interrupted my attempt to bond with you.

"My harness won't lock!"

I found your needs soon enough.

"Hunh? What do you mean?" You tried frantically to reach over and help him, but it was of no use. I had you well within my grip. You were mine from that point on.

And because I held dominion over certain qualities in the ether, such as the oscillations of sound, among other things, neither the carnies nor the other passengers were privy to your exchange with Foley.

Then, with the slightest of jolts, the shuttle began to pull away from the loading tower, "Oh, no? Hey, stop this thing!" Foley held onto his loose harness in desperation, moving it back and forth to see how much play there was. "My seat isn't locked!"

You saw that with each twist and juke along the shuttle's winding circuit, Foley was slipping further and further away from his perch. Contrary to his experience, you were coming along very nicely, even when the elf cap got whipped off your head in the wind. And before you could say knife, your dreads took flight as if to punctuate this hair-raising thrill. You had no idea how or why this was happening. It was all so unexpected, but you knew that you didn't want the ride to end. Of course, it had to eventually, and the prospect of that scared you even more than the welfare of Foley being at stake.

And then, as the shuttle crested my notoriously well-documented lift-hill drop-off over by the Ferris wheel, one of my little gray friends with the camera eyes and the telephoto lenses for corneas was staring at you over the abyss in earnest from the topmost gondola like a child, almost, beckoning you in slow-motion it seemed. My little *chiaroscuro* was wearing a spacesuit, but the tiny fellow had removed his helmet to show you his real face.

Therefore, you quoted one of the most popular passages from your book verbatim: "and the darkening sky, where the devil loops roamed, whispered doom."

And then Foley stretched his hand out towards you as far as he could. And for a brief instant, his eyes locked with yours. And your fingernails drew a tiny trickle of blood from his palm like stigmata in a last-ditch effort to save him.

2. THE FUNERAL PHOTOGRAPHER

176

(May's Journal / kept in shorthand)

Tuesday, December 9, 1980. New York, New York. 12:09 a.m. It wasn't enough that he'd left me to go back to his wife. It feels like only yesterday. But the lunatic fringe had to step in to finish the job by taking him away from me…from all of us, forever.

I can't get over the news. I just can't believe someone shot my John. Why would someone—anyone—do this to him? What does it all mean?

Poor Yoko was right there with him when it happened. Why couldn't it have been me instead of her right there beside him in his last moments? Pouring my hot, sweaty tears into his face as if I were squeezing a sopping wet towel. She even took that away from me. I would give anything to have been able to tell him how much I love him as he died in my arms. Ohhh…

*

The Dick Cavett Show
(Date aired: Friday, September 26, 1974)

John: "It was all Mother's idea. You see, Mays was her secretary. Yoko had just blurted out, with one of her ambiguous catchphrases again, which I must say has always vexed me. She has a real flair for them even to this day, and the next thing I knew, I was in the sack with Mays instead of her. It was all very hush, hush, and seamless at first as if it was just business as usual for months on end before I started to get any kind of an inkling whatsoever that something wasn't quite right with this picture."

Dick: "When you say, 'ambiguous catchphrases,' what do you mean by that exactly?"

[AUDIENCE LAUGHS.]

John: "Well, Mother was fond of coming into the room every so often while I'd be daydreaming through an idea of mine for some song or maybe even an album, with me being very fond of themes and all. And at any given moment, Yoko would enter my study with a 'cuppa tea. Didn't matter what the clock said. It was always teatime with her. She would always come off rather agreeable, and then she would say something so facile I could never fully get a grasp on what it was she was saying. Came through my filter all garbled like she'd spiked the tea with a hit of acid. Not even a clue to this day, in fact. It's like trying to remember a dream loaded up to the gills with a blind sense of nostalgia and otherwise lost to you forever the moment you wake up.

"And so anyhow, I would go further into this poetic frame of mind and come out the other end with the credits rolling like I'd missed the best part of The Dick Caveat Show and it's bedtime already. But you see, I'd just woken up from the most restful sleep while everyone else had retired for the night. It's somewhat irritating to have the days fly by on you like that. So, it was refreshing for me to be with someone like Mays as opposed to Yoko. So vibrant, and yet content to remain on the sidelines, letting me do me own thing creatively. Meanwhile, Yoko continues to play second fiddle to no one."

Dick: "So…you told me awhile back about how you were really enjoying this never-ending pink bubble with May. She gave you all the milk she had in the world without you ever having to buy the cow. And then, out of the blue, you get this strange call over 'the blower' from Yoko …"

[AUDIENCE LAUGHS.]

John: "Yes, she actually hurled one of those unusually forgettable catchphrases over the phone at me like a cricket pitch wobbling through the wickets, intermingled with the promise of a cure for my smoking habit. Apparently, I was driving poor Mays crazy, smoking a pack of cigarettes every hour on the hour. Sometimes even starting fires by leaving cigarette butts hanging off the ends of counters in different rooms, four and five at a time.

"What I didn't know then was that Mays and Yoko had been in contact with each other all along like the best of friends they were. And nowadays, I just pat my pockets for a pack that isn't there anymore. Phantom cigarettes, ha."

Dick: "Do you remember what Yoko said to you in order to make you stop smoking?"

John: "Not a clue. That's what I'm trying to tell you. All I remember is when she was done curing me I'd fallen back in love with her like a day hadn't passed with me feeling otherwise. Well, not that I really ever fell out. And strangely enough, I wanted no part of Mays ever again. To this day, my decision-making process on the matter remains inexplicable to me. I feel terrible about the way we treated that poor girl. But Yoko drew a line in the sand by throwing her blouse down on that deep shag of hers. The very same shag that her bitch of a Cairn terrier was fond of pissing on…"

[AUDIENCE LAUGHS.]

"Well, in the short distance from her hand to the floor, her blouse billowed out from beneath itself and floated through the air like a parachute all gossamer, and that was that. I've always been a sucker for a comeback, and this is my wife we're talking about here."

Dick: "Would you feel more comfortable talking about your close encounter with that flying disk instead?"

[AUDIENCE LAUGHS.]

John: "Well, it's certainly more of a challenge reminiscing about poor Mays anyway, because I'm all about Yoko now. So, uh, yes."

*

(May's Journal / kept in shorthand)

178

Tuesday, December 9, 1980. New York, New York. 1:19 a.m.

I've never left our penthouse apartment on East 52nd Street in order to relocate anywhere else. Guess I'm just too damned sentimental for that.

I'm sitting in his study, where we first saw the UFO during what he called his "Lost Weekend" after that old Ray Milland pic. That was August 23, 1973. Can't believe that was only just seven years ago. Feels like yesterday. He was sitting on the edge of the sofa, naked and spent after making love to me. And I was back in our bedroom, freshening up, when he called out to me.

"Mays, bring your Polaroid Instamatic Camera!" he cried, "Hurry!" I'd barely had time to slip back into my favorite peasant dress.

And there it was, a flying saucer, no more than a hundred yards away from us. The disk was heading due south over the rooftops with the ever-turbulent whitewater of the East River seen here and there whenever the vista opened up between buildings. It moved ominously, this shimmering thing from outer space. And as it turned out, deliberately, when it changed its course suddenly. Heading straight for us as we stared at it helplessly within its crosshairs. Our eyes fixed upon its stark otherworldliness to the point where it almost appeared ordinary.

*

The Dick Cavett Show
(Date aired: Friday, September 26, 1974)

Dick: "So what exactly happened? I heard a rumor that you and May were tripping on Tar Beach atop your apartment building—and a flying saucer took a detour through your swanky neck of the woods to catch the two of you singing your birthday songs out loud for the rest of the world to hear. A cappella, baby, A cappella."

[AUDIENCE LAUGHS.]

John: "That's because I asked a neighbor the day after it had happened if he had seen anything in the sky out of the ordinary. And he went around to all of the other tenants with my original humble account. He blew it out of proportion into this magical mystery tour that got embellished further and further away from the truth with every person who'd heard it. Ended up just being a game of blower is all."

Dick: "But it never quite blew over, did it? Okay, so what is this humble account that you're referring to? Because I think I'm more inclined to believe the magical mystery tour. I mean, I almost need it to be true."

[AUDIENCE LAUGHS.]

John: "Ha, you would say that. Well, we only went up to the roof afterward. The first sight of the thing happened when I was in the middle of daydreaming through an idea for me new album, *Walls and Bridges,* now available in record stores everywhere.

"And I saw this UFO hover into view directly over another building no more than a hundred yards away from my window. So, I called out to Mays because I wanted a witness. And I hadn't used any hallucinatory substances that day prior to this encounter. So, I'm telling you, I know what I saw.

"Mays came running into my study and started taking Polaroids of the flying saucer. The thing didn't make a sound as it crept like a serpent in between a water tower and a rusty array of TV antennas. It was shaped like a giant cone with the pinnacle trimmed off at the knees. There were white lights blinking alternately along its circular rim.

"And there was a big red light at the center of the vehicle, unblinking yet throbbing with low voltage like something straight out of Nikola Tesla's laboratory—a huge crimson ball peeking out from the top and bottom, as if the disk itself were built around this bloody sphere.

"Then the UFO came right up to our window like a car slowly backing into a parking spot. I could see each and every rivet on the spacecraft. Even had a beat-up old Empire State license plate with what looked to be the Queen of Diamonds embossed upon it, but the diamonds were black instead of red.

"Then, after a few moments, the vehicle shot up to the roof of our building as if its mysterious occupants were prompting us to follow them upstairs."

"Meanwhile, the flying saucer had a gun-slit window that revealed the silhouettes of what Mays and I quickly deduced to be the pilot and copilot behind the wheel of that thing. And for some strange reason, I imagined a bit readily that it was Yoko and what could have been a dead ringer for yours truly here. I'd initially thought this revelation had to do with my heart secretly aching for my wife more and more. But ironically, Mays had made the same observation. So, she took a photograph of this odd couple, hoping it would shed some light on the phenomenon, but the quality of the shot was poor at best. You know how Polaroids go."

(May's Journal / kept in shorthand)

Tuesday, December 9, 1980. New York, New York. 3:12 a.m. I'd just started to take pictures with my camera, one-by-one snaps of the phenomenon. The exposed Polaroids spit out of the feed like empty shell casings exiting a gun after every pull of the trigger. And I certainly was quick on the draw, but not my John. He knew how to take his time.

The pictures had a unity to them, like frames in a strip of celluloid denoting a certain action, as within the scene of a film. I remember John helping me by laying the shots down in proper sequence across the windowsill, as each one of them emulsified under the brilliance of the hot afternoon sun at its zenith. It was a beautiful day.

Suddenly, a rap on the front door interrupts my reverie. Who can it be at this late hour? Bobby, our Doorman, wouldn't have let anyone upstairs unannounced unless it was John. And I'm not one to get visitors at this time of night anyway. Even John wouldn't have crashed in on me like this.

But wait, under the circumstances, could it be…no, what am I thinking? The poor man is dead.

I'm looking through the peephole, and I catch Bobby bending down to leave a package. It sounds like when I hear something solid thud against the base of the door from the other side.

*

Excerpt from Cameron Crowe's interview with John Lennon in Rolling Stone Magazine: February 19, 1976, 4:34 PM EST

"Sometimes in what feels like a dream more than anything else, Mother's face will fill up my complete awareness. And then Yoko's eyes will be given a certain emphasis that masks off the rest of her features like that of a ninja warrior. And those delicious caramel irises of hers will spin like roulette wheels caught up in a duel with one another, competing for my individual attention.

"Then suddenly, there's only one light source, as it swings back and forth overhead, clumsily as if on a chain, like in one of those police interrogation rooms that you often see on the telly after suppertime.

"We'd recently gone out to see Lina Wertmüller's *Seven Beauties* in subtitles, and it's as if the film merges with the soul of *The Bridge Over the River Kwai*. I'm a cross between Pasqualino and Alec Guinness, and I vie for Yoko's affections because she is the Commandant. I want to survive no matter what, and if it means sleeping with the enemy, then so be it.

"Sgt. Pepper is in the hot seat, and Mother is taking her sweet time with me. Toying with my every word, cementing her control over me, because those lips of hers, and that tongue especially, are a miracle to behold and to be ravished by.

"Yoko is combing through my memories like a librarian with her head buried up to her shoulders in a catalog drawer.

"This is common practice for her. Every so often, she will come in and browse the contents of my brain. But then, she always becomes obsessed with a particular batch of recollections. Going over them again and again like a director looking at the dailies during the production of a film.

"Apparently, they're encrypted thus, Mother finds them fairly difficult to access because it seems that someone else with a far more sophisticated technique has breached the defenses of the filing system that she has come to believe is of her own design. Yes, Yoko has reorganized my mind, and now she detects a bug or two crawling around in there. Perhaps it's of a species she's never encountered before.

"And finally, with one last tweak of her extremely long fingernails sifting through my *amygdala,* as opposed to my *hippocampus,* because these memories are traumatic, you see. I tell her all about how Mays and I followed the UFO upstairs and how we were made to float into the throbbing red orb of light at the core of the vehicle. And how we merged with the electric surface of that bloody sphere.

"And that was when I informed Mother that, 'Yes, this memory is no small matter to be taken lightly. Mays and I'd surely been abducted by *Lucy in the Sky with Diamonds.*"

*

(May's Journal/ kept in shorthand).

Tuesday, December 9, 1980. New York, New York. 4:29 a.m. I just started to watch the VHS tape that came in the unmarked manila envelope that Bobby, our Doorman, left outside in the hallway.

Besides it being a very bad copy (quite possibly a second or third-generation copy of the original recording), it appears ...oh my God! It shows the events right after the assassination in front of the Dakota.

John is lying face down in a pool of blood on the sidewalk in front of the gates of the apartment complex, and ...what the...that's me in the video kneeling over John instead of Yoko. It appears I'm trying to turn him over, but he's far too heavy. And I keep getting his blood all over my hands. And his glasses are smashed against his face. He's bleeding from the eyes. And I just got my nails done, and they're ruined.

Ohh, who gives a fuck about my goddamned nails right now when the love of my life is breathing his last breath right here in front of me. I'm a disgraceful lover. Does this mean I'm nothing compared to Yoko in terms of a soulmate for John? Ohh, get it together, girl...oh, I didn't mean to stick my fingers into his wounds! I wonder if he even felt that. Oh my God, is he still alive? He's got gunshot wounds all over the place, save for his heart. Poor John, he's like that song in the *Yellow Submarine, The Sea of Holes.*

*

The Dick Cavett Show
(Date aired: Friday, September 26, 1974)

Dick: "What was it like being aboard a flying saucer?"

John: "Well, let me start off by saying that the size of the spaceship perceived from the outside was absolutely deceiving in relation to its interior, which appeared to go on for days and months. And might I even suggest years?

"And as far as aliens go, Mays and I were greeted by a terrifically huge kaleidoscopic creature composed solely of the most magnificent colors, hues, and saturations normally impossible to see within our limited view of the entire spectrum. And yet he was mainly blue…if that makes any sense.

I say *he* because whilst confronted with these polychromatic equations that intersected the metaphysical, we couldn't help but notice that this monstrosity wore a gigantic papier-mâché likeness of our dear auld friend, Paul. The creature bore a striking albeit crude resemblance of my cherished colleague upon its shoulders like a Mardi Gras float.

[AUDIENCE LAUGHS.]

"And this strange being began to address us in the oddest way I've ever heard. 'I am the Paulrus,' he said. But apparently, that was all this creature could possibly say in our language, or for that matter in any language—this we soon discovered as the evening wore on. He answered any and all of our questions with that very same quip. For as it turned out, we were not alone, because there were many other abductees. And we were all made to feel quite welcome and free to go about our business as we pleased.

"And Mays, of course, had brought along her Polaroid SX-70 Instamatic Camera. Needless to say, I am the Paulrus was a real ham when it came to getting his picture taken."

Dick: "I understand that it's been years since you were abducted, but do you still have any of these Polaroids lying around somewhere?"

[AUDIENCE LAUGHS.]

John: "The problem with Polaroids is that the emulsion process never stops, so they eventually self-destruct like the reel-to-reel intro at the beginning of *Mission: Impossible*. *'If you decide to take this mission…'*

"Meanwhile, it was somehow obvious to May and me that *Lucy in the Sky with Diamonds* was in charge and therefore responsible for our abduction. But I'm sorry to disappoint you. We were never to be given into her presence during our brief stay.

"As it was, we were invited to the funeral of an old gray alien held in high esteem amongst his shipmates. And afterwards, all of us enjoyed a banquet in his honor, where we discovered that the main course was none other than the deceased himself. And oh boy, did we catch a buzz off that old buzzard! I had no idea that the flesh of a gray is a hallucinogenic delicacy revered by mystics and fatalists alike across the cosmos, but of course, this strange addendum was withheld until everyone had partaken of his grisly remains."

*

Tuesday, December 9, 1980. New York, New York. 5:28 a.m. Suddenly, the video of John's assassination cuts to the emergency room at St. Luke's Roosevelt Hospital. And a last-ditch effort on the part of the doctor has him snipping away at his sternum to get at his heart. And once the doctor has access, he proceeds to massage the heart. But the hollow points have destroyed all four major vessels leading to and from. The earnest doctor can massage the heart all he wants. Ohhh. My poor John.

*

The Dick Cavett Show
(Date aired: Friday, September 26, 1974)

"And that was precisely when Mays and I saw my distinguished double. Yes, from across the crowded arena, because that dining hall was like being in the bloody Coliseum. He was stepping out of a clown car (of all things) with over a hundred other fellow carpoolers, making an appearance from some other part of the ship. And when I called out our name, he turned around with such a look on his face like he'd been caught with his knickers down.

[AUDIENCE LAUGHS.]

We tried catching up to them, Mays and I, but he chose to get lost in the crowd instead. And then he disappeared altogether down a grand spiral staircase crafted out of Italian marble, no less. I could hear the click-clack of his platform shoes on the way down even after I'd lost sight of them, echoing like the hollow repetition of stones being tossed down a Pellucidar-like well.

"Then we heard a high-pitched whistle like that of a train and turned to see the giant blue slug creature from before waiting in a huge hangar-like elevator. Holding the door open like my man, Jeeves, and bidding us to enter.

"'I am the Paulrus,' he said.

[AUDIENCE LAUGHS.]

"Strangely enough, Mays and I had somehow understood this to mean that we could catch up with my alter ego using the lift. Funny, I should call him that.

"After the elevator door shut with us alongside of the giant blue slug, I am the Paulrus said, 'I am the Paulrus,' but in our heads, we heard him tell us to hop in the saddle because he was a sure bet.

"And when the door opened up again, this time in a subterranean level of the ship, I am the Paulrus popped a wheelie and sped too fast for us to comprehend. Remember, we were still tripping on that gray alien flesh like it was a cross between the Holy Eucharist and thin gelatin squares of windowpane acid.

[AUDIENCE LAUGHS.]

3. BEYOND THESE FAR OFF THINGS

"Travel is a good thing; it stimulates the imagination. Everything else is a snare and a delusion. Our [own] journey is entirely imaginative. Therein lies its strength."
—Louis-Ferdinand Céline

A Peruvian logger on the set of the film, one of the Indiana, as I would say in in my native tongue, was bitten by a snake known as the South American Bushmaster *(Lachesis Muta)*. The Indiana called this species *Shushúpe*. And this man knew that he had only minutes to live unless he amputated his foot with the very same chainsaw he had just been using when he got bit.

But this didn't faze Klaus in the least, who was frothing at the mouth and screaming at the top of his lungs because his coffee had been served lukewarm.

*

And only just a few paces from El Dorado at best, this certifiable madman has gone on for many a day upon my set with his homicidal ravings. Howling his obscenities at this one and that. And I must say that he has a certain dexterity with trans-euro-linguistic vulgarity.

I am the director of this film, and yet I have allowed this behavior of his to fester away in plain sight for the sake of my film's plausibility. The necessary verisimilitude. Oh yes, I want to imbue my movie with his evil eye, almost to the detriment of the picture itself. And yes, I have been willing to do so because I am capturing the real article—an authentic monster—on celluloid here. I feel like Dr. Frankenstein in the classic Universal adaptation from 1931 when he says, "It's alive!"

Of course, most of the time, Klaus has directed his rancor at me, knowing full well what I am about. If I lost my patience here and there, which was few and far between, I would say things to him like, "You are filling me up with your hatred like a gas jockey at a filling station," and without missing a beat, he would say, "Here, Werner, let me top you off." What a genius for dialogue. But if I were to let on how brilliant this egomaniac really is, it would surely come back to bite me in the ass!

I am loading my rifle with quiet confidence and determination born in hell by this lunatic's continued abuse. Eight bullets in the skull piece for this man, who acts as if he were let out from the asylum. There will be none of his head left when I get through with him. And I will leave the ninth round for myself right after I do the deed—I must. This trickster son of a bitch has ruined me.

I almost do not want to admit it, but I know why I have allowed this farce to continue for as long as it has. You see, I have never met my real father. He was killed while fighting on the wrong side of the war. And so, this clown, although the greatest actor I have ever worked with—this actor, the most sinister clown I have ever had to tolerate, is no more than a surrogate piece of horse dung.

And just because he was a fighting soldier for the Wehrmacht for five minutes, captured and wounded by the British, should I deem him equal to the old man whom I have never met? The man I have silently missed all of my life. Although I shall never agree with those cranks who ran the Third Reich, I still carry around a scrap of some odd romantic and childish notion about my father's martyrdom, even though the cause was not just in the least. I do not even know if he was an actual nazi. I should hope not. Erich Maria Remarque stated in his novel, *A Time to Love, and a Time to Die,* that only thirty percent of the German people were actual card-carrying nazis. The rest were afraid for their lives and their families' lives.

But then again, why should I be the one to apologize for a nation's psychosis? Seriously, I was all of two weeks old when my father abandoned us during the bombardment of Munich. And my mother had the fortitude and courage to take me and my brothers out of harm's way up into the desolate mountain ranges of Bavaria.

Why should the sins of the father reach out from the grave to plague the son anyway? It is not fair. But then again, life (in general) is not fair. You must fight for every last scrap of sanity.

I suspect that Klaus knows my weakness by having allowed him to rule the roost thus far. This is my show, and yet I have allowed him to take full advantage of the situation. I am basically babysitting a psychopath. Oh yes, I needed to fan the flames so that I could capture this monster in action on camera. And yet, pulling Mr. Hyde out of Dr. Jekyll's ass was easier said than done. He has deeply affected the morale of everyone else involved in the production of this film. For example, the *indiana* are not as upset with Klaus as they are with me for having tolerated such misconduct in a human being. They have slowly become unhinged by my seeming inability to react to Klaus's badgering.

The chieftain of their tribe has even offered to have him killed for me, but I begged him not to do so. Without Klaus, there would be no picture. Am I not the one who brought him here in the first place? And yet here I am, going against the grain, raising my rifle to take the shot. Locking my elbow. Aiming. Steady.

Not much can be *seen* in the jungle as much as perceived by the other senses. These environs are an extension of the Indiana, who may, it seems, probe the darkness through the eyes of avatars, the creeping things that own the ground. They certainly do not have to be present to know that I have done the deed. They shall hear it soon enough.

I step on a twig and give myself away. Klaus turns sharply on his heel, sliding like a crab, back and then sideways. He gawps when he sees me. I have him dead to rights.

"Where are your diseased expletives now?" I say, "You are like a common cur in the street running away. You are not going to break this contract, or I shall put you out of everyone's misery."

"Und höchstens ein paar Schritte von El Dorado entfernt, Werner, you are a certifiable madman," he says, "I am going to call the police on you! HELP, POLICE! HELP, POLICE!"

What is this? Something shimmers atop the long barrel of my rifle. A shimmering glow. Klaus and I look up to see a disk wrought in brushed steel with a dinged-up surface pitted and scratched a good thirty meters in circumference floating directly above us. It is lit up like a Christmas tree pulled from the attic, still smelling of mothballs in the eerie gloaming.

The unearthly vehicle, if that is what it is, makes no sound whatsoever. In fact, the chatter of the birds and the other animals in the jungle has ceased suddenly. I did not even notice the sounds they made until they stopped so abruptly just now. The brooding silence looms heavily upon my shoulders like the weight of a blacksmith's anvil.

A portal slides open underneath, and a brilliant light sautés my retinas. I feel myself becoming weightless. *Was zum Teufel?* I am being lifted up and pulled into this thing by some invisible force that otherwise defies description.

*

"Unfortunately, I was imitating the movements of the hawk, as in some primitive ritual: the hunter becoming the thing he hunts."
—J.A. Baker

It is a long time before I realize that I am lying down on a metal bed of some sort. Details are coming to me very slowly. I can barely open my eyes. The light is so bright. Am I on an operating table? Oh my God, did I wake up during a surgery of some kind? I did not give anyone permission to open me up!

I want to check myself for such wounds, but I cannot move. Oh, I get it. I am experiencing sleep paralysis. This is not the first time.

So, this is nothing more than just a dream.

But what about my picture? Wait a second! I remember it vividly now. I was going to stop Klaus from quitting the movie. He is notorious within the industry for having broken over eighty-five contracts, and I was not about to let him do the same thing to me.

Hunh? There goes my rifle leaning up against the wall. If only I could fetch it, but still for the life of me, I cannot move.

The outlines of several men step into view. Men in black skintight suits with the insignia of the—devil! They brandish the swastika.

"We are going to release you from the hold of the bed. Please sit up, Werner."

"Who are you people?" I say, "I mean…I can see what you are, but how is this possible? The war has been over for almost thirty years. Germany was defeated."

"It depends upon your perspective," the voice is familiar, almost like one of my brothers, but they hate the nazis for what they did—just like I do.

I look into the eyes of the one who spoke to me just now, and horror invades my soul. I suddenly feel totally violated by the almost picture-perfect mirror image of myself in the garb of these hate-mongers. Is this a clone of me? Some awful doppelgänger set loose upon the earth to ruin my reputation as a decent enough person? For all the cruelty in this world, for all the overwhelming fornication and murder, I still love my fellow man. I am never going to allow myself to become a misanthropic abomination like these idiots. They cannot do this to me!

"Werner, I am your father."

"NOOOOO! It is not so."

"You already know this to be true in your heart."

*

"How can this be?" I say, "You are no older than I am."

"For me," he says, "the war ended only a few years ago."

"What kind of sadistic madness do you speak?" I say, "I am not following your ridiculous train of thought here."

"Do not worry yourself, my son," he says, "it will make sense soon enough. You see, we are what someday people will call a 'breakaway civilization.' We have mastered the art of time travel. We sit perched safely within the confines of the fifth dimension just outside of the 4D spatiotemporal continuum that we just plucked you from. You were living in a simulation that we have created, and now you are aboard such a vehicle that can achieve this deft feat. It is called the *Haunebu*. What was coined a so-called 'flying saucer' back in your year 1947. For me, this happened only just a week ago. I totally understand your plight right now. It took me some time to get used to it myself."

"What do you want from me?" I say, "I am in the middle of making a movie. A lot of people are depending on me."

"You will eventually come to realize that you created all of this vast responsibility to compensate. You are overcompensating because I deserted you at such a young and vulnerable age. You have been calling out to me with your great achievements. If I had not left your mother and the rest of you, you wouldn't need to go on with these made-up schemes to help you manage the pain. You are in a constant state of grief over losing me, and I cannot bear another minute of watching you waste your talents on such trivial pursuits. We have a task for those great abilities of yours that easily surmount the importance of the ones you have chosen for yourself. I am going to show you why you are a great man, Werner. It is the least I can do for all of the pain and suffering I have caused you. I love you."

"How can a nazi love?" I say, "All you people know about is hate. And everything I knew about you before today, and everything you just told me now, only proves it. How do you think I feel knowing that you are my father? I want to swallow the barrel of that rifle over there if I am going to be forced to listen to any more of your bullshit."

*

"You have to know why we brought you aboard," he says.

"No, I do not."

"We have enjoyed the output of your Hollywood, although its propaganda runs counter to our solutions to the problems of the world," he says, "and our analysts have found your organically breathtaking method of story structure with its profound edits to be superior to your contemporaries before and after your career. I am so proud of you. We need you to help us edit the timeline."

"Most certainly not," I say, "are you kidding me? You want me to turn the world into a nazi propaganda film? I have heard everything now. Get me back to my picture. Please, just get me back to the jungle. I need to finish my picture. Of course, there is a part of me that wants to love you back just for the mere fact of you being my father. But I can never be a part of this. You must put me back where I belong. Is there any way you can make me forget that I ever even met you, because now you have reopened the wound of losing you to a degree I cannot deal with—ever? I shall lose myself in many bottles of hard liquor. Despite the occasional bottle of wine or beer, I am normally a sober man. A conservative drinker at best. I must admit, I do like my peach schnapps, and occasionally, I crack open a bottle of calvados, an exquisitely tasting French brandy made from apples, to celebrate the completion of a film. But now I am a broken man, and you have made me see that. And now I cannot unsee it. All my life, I put up a good fight, but now you have made things worse than what they already are for me. Please turn me loose upon the world once again, Father, please."

His eyes, the color of brushed steel, bore into my soul with unbridled rage.

*

Their chieftain has even offered to have him killed for me, but I begged him not to do so. Without Klaus, there would be no picture. Am I not the one who brought him here in the first place? And yet here I am, going against the grain, raising my rifle to take the shot. Locking my elbow. Aiming. Steady.

Not much can be seen in the jungle as much as perceived by the other senses. These environs are an extension of the Indiana, with that almost supernatural probing ability of theirs. Using the creeping things as avatars. They certainly do not have to see it with their own eyes to believe it.

I step on a twig and give myself away. Klaus turns on his heel like a crab, moving backward, then sideways to look at me incredulously. I have him dead to rights, "where are your diseased expletives now?" I say, "You are such a coward running away. You are not going to break this contract. I am going to put you out of everyone's misery."

"Und höchstens ein paar Schritte von El Dorado entfernt, Werner, you are a certifiable madman," he says, "I am going to call the police on you! HELP, POLICE! HELP, POLICE!"

And I say, "The nearest police station is over 600 miles away."

I close my right eye to get a flat picture of him. What a pity! He is by far the greatest actor I have ever had the privilege to work with.

KRACK!!! Right between the eyes.

Brainflush: Get Out of My Head

Edward Radmanich

The meeting room sat high in the sky, a glass box perched above the city's ceaseless churn, far removed from the street-level noise and chaos below. It was the kind of place where the world's invisible gears turned—where power didn't just change hands; it shifted, twisted, and warped into new shapes. Michael stepped inside first, the lines of his suit sharp, his movements precise, everything about him cutting through the stillness with a purpose that was almost violent. He didn't bother with the usual pretense—didn't even glance at the sweeping view of the skyline that most would kill for. His focus was locked on the tablet he pulled from his briefcase, the blue glow of the screen casting an eerie light across his tense face.

Bill followed at a slower pace, taking his time as he checked the room— door shut tight, blinds pulled down, no bugs, no prying eyes. He was methodical, with the kind of measured calm that came from years of dealing with messes other people didn't even know existed. While Michael was already seated, lost in the urgency of whatever was unfolding on his screen, Bill lingered, scanning for threats only he could see. Finally satisfied, he sat down, rolling up his sleeves like he was settling in for a long meeting.

Michael didn't waste time. "Where do we stand on the #84567 scenario?" His voice was clipped, carrying the weight of a man who didn't ask questions unless he already knew the answers—or desperately needed them.

Bill sighed, leaning back, his irritation thinly veiled. "Straight to the point, huh? Not even a 'how was your weekend' or a nod to my new haircut. No, it's all business with you."

Michael's eyes flickered up, a brief flash of something dangerous crossing his face before he returned to his screen. "If this wasn't critical, Bill, I'd be anywhere but here. The guys at the top are breathing down my neck, and they're not the kind of people who forgive mistakes. We've got a 48-hour window before this thing blows up in our faces. So, tell me—what's your department done about it?"

Bill pulled out his own tablet, scrolling with a nonchalance that felt almost reckless, like a poker player showing just enough of his hand. "We've got a competitor on board, eyes all over #84567. Every loose end is being tied up; every leak is plugged. Protocols are in place. It's still just a referral at this stage— nothing more than a shadow on the wall. These things? They happen all the time, Michael. We're handling it."

Michael rubbed his temples, his fingers pressing against the pulse of an oncoming headache. "They don't tell you this in the boardrooms, Bill. They don't warn you that the higher up you go, the more you've got to keep buried. I just hope this one stays buried. We've been lucky so far—no major blowback, no public scandals. But every time, we're playing with fire, and I don't want this to be the time we get burned."

Bill's expression tightened, his calm slipping just enough to reveal the cracks underneath. "I hear you. We're using GlemTek for this—they've handled worse, and they're discreet. They're the kind of people who solve problems without anyone knowing there was a problem to begin with. This isn't going to be the one that gets away from us."

Michael nodded slowly, the tension in his body easing, but only just. "Good. Because if this goes sideways, we'll all be answering questions we don't want to answer. Keep it quiet, keep it contained. No surprises, Bill."

For a moment, they sat in silence, two men high above the city, tangled in webs of their own making. Outside, the world moved on, oblivious to the quiet war being waged in a glass room above the skyline. Their conversation drifted to safer waters, but the unspoken threat of what lurked beneath never really went away. It stayed there, lingering like the hum of the city below—constant, insistent, and impossible to ignore.

*

Across town, far from the gleaming towers and pristine offices, the city's underbelly breathed its own kind of life—a grimy, unfiltered reality with streets pockmarked by faded graffiti and air carrying a sour tang of rust and decay. Ian stood outside a rundown building, the kind you'd pass without a second glance, its windows clouded with grime and its bricks slowly losing the battle to time. Dressed in a turquoise GlemTek jumpsuit, he stubbed out his cigarette on the cracked sidewalk, the ember sizzling briefly before dying in a smudge of ash.

Ian pushed open the door, the hinges squealing in protest, and stepped inside. The place smelled of stale coffee and old wires, and the fluorescent lights overhead buzzed faintly like insects trapped in glass. In the corner, hunched over a row of mismatched monitors, was the supervisor—an aging man with graying stubble and bags under his eyes, telling a story of too many late shifts and not enough sleep. He barely looked up, too busy squinting at the endless cascade of data scrolling across his screens.

"You're covering for Jimmy today," the supervisor grunted, his voice raspy and impatient. "Referral from a screw-up over at Mallcore. They wanted Jimmy, but he's off sipping margaritas somewhere, so you're it."

Ian grabbed his work pack, a heavy, scuffed bag filled with cables, connectors, and a mess of other gear that could've come straight out of a sci-fi movie if it didn't look so worn. He clipped a series of tubes to his suit with practiced ease, feeling the tug and weight of each piece settling into place. He tightened the straps, securing a patchwork of devices to his body, each one humming faintly with its own purpose. "Alright…cool. Let's get this over with. Routine job? Who's my ground Op today?"

The supervisor didn't even bother to glance at him, his focus still locked on the screens as he barked back, "Vanessa. She got pulled into this last minute. A nice little package deal. Now get moving, Ian. Clock's ticking."

Ian gave a curt nod, the hint of a smirk tugging at his lips—this wasn't his first rushed assignment, and it likely wouldn't be his last. He turned down a narrow hallway, where the walls were streaked with who-knows-what, and the flickering overhead lights made every step feel like a scene from a bad dream. Each flicker cast fleeting shadows that danced across the stained linoleum floor, ghostly shapes that vanished as soon as they appeared.

At the end of the hall, Ian stopped in front of a thick, metal door marked with a fading hazard symbol, the paint chipped and worn. He pushed it open, and the room beyond swallowed him whole, blinding him with a sudden wash of harsh, sterile light that buzzed angrily overhead. The door clanged shut behind him, sealing him in. Ian knew he was just another cog in a machine that didn't care if it chewed him up and spit him out—another worker lost in the blinding white, where the rules bent and shadows kept their secrets.

*

In a sleek, sterile medical facility where everything gleamed in shades of white and silver, Erica slowly stirred, emerging from the fog of the procedure. In her twenties, she was the kind of young person in whom everything felt urgent and new, yet somehow old all at once. The machines around her hummed softly, a steady, rhythmic pulse that filled the room like a lullaby meant to soothe. The attendants—gloved, polished, and polite—drifted toward her with smiles that seemed warm but never quite reached their eyes.

"How are we feeling?" one of them asked, his voice smooth and practiced as if he'd uttered those words a hundred times today alone.

Erica blinked, her vision swimming as she fought to clear the haze. Her mouth felt thick, like she'd been chewing on cotton, and her voice came out slow and sluggish. "Like I drank way too much last night."

The attendant chuckled, a soft, canned sound that was half sympathy, half scripted reassurance. "That's perfectly normal. The grogginess will fade soon enough. The procedure went as planned, and you'll start to notice the effects within 24 hours. Just remember, the healing process can be… intense. There might be some rough patches, but that's just the adjustment period. You'll get through it."

Erica nodded, the words barely registering as her mind floated somewhere between the present and a foggy, half-remembered dream. A faint smile tugged at her lips, a mix of cautious excitement and the kind of hope you only feel when you're desperate for something to change. "Great. I'm done with the mood swings. If this works, it's gonna change everything." She paused, frowning slightly as a flicker of something familiar…a twitch that she couldn't quite pin down—nudged at the edges of her thoughts. "Weird, though. I keep feeling like I've done this before. Like…déjà vu, you know?"

The attendant's reassuring smile stayed fixed in place, a touch too bright, too polished. "We hear that a lot. It's just your mind playing tricks. The medication can do that—blur the edges a bit. And you might get some random headaches over the next 24 hours. It's just your body adjusting. Nothing to worry about."

Erica nodded, but the feeling stuck, stubbornly clinging to her like a shadow. "Right. Yeah, that makes sense. But it's still kinda...off." She signed the forms thrust under her nose, her signature a quick, messy scribble, and the attendant handed her a discharge packet with the same robotic cheer he'd given the last dozen patients.

The door clicked shut behind her as she stepped outside, the cool, crisp air hitting her face like a splash of cold water. She made her way to her car, fumbling for her phone, and hit speed dial. "It's done," she said, her voice calm but hollow as if she were reciting a line she'd practiced too many times.

A faint laugh, almost bitter, slipped out as she continued. "I know, right? Feels like…I've been here before. Maybe it's just the meds, but I'm so over the panic attacks and all the random crazy thoughts. Feels like a freaking weight's been lifted."

The voice on the other end said something she barely registered, just another sound in the mix of her already cluttered mind. Erica leaned against the car, rubbing her temple as a dull ache settled in. "Yeah, yeah. Of course. Why would you even ask that? I went to the place, just like you told me. Took a bit longer, but it's done."

She ended the call, sliding into the driver's seat, and tossed the phone onto the passenger side. The engine growled to life, and she pulled away from the facility, the tires rolling over the asphalt with a low, steady hum. As she drove off, Erica tried to shake the feeling that the day was a rerun of some forgotten episode, but it clung to her, lingering like an echo she couldn't quite escape.

*

Back in the depths of the unknown, Ian moved steadily through a labyrinth of dreamlike corridors that seemed to pulse and writhe with a life of their own. The space around him wasn't fixed; it twisted and shifted like liquids under pressure, walls bulging and receding, warping into shapes that defied logic. It was as if he were walking through the belly of some great, slumbering beast, and the walls were its breath in constant, restless motion. But Ian didn't falter. Each step was deliberate, his footing sure even as the floor undulated beneath him like the surface of a disturbed pond. Every twenty or thirty steps, he planted a beacon—a slender pole that flared green the moment it made contact, holding its place against the shifting architecture. The beacons formed a trail of tiny, glowing islands in a sea of chaos, each one marking a path that could easily dissolve into madness if he lost his way.

Adjusting the earpiece snug in his ear, Ian called up Vanessa, his ground operator, back in the facility's nerve center. "Hey, Vee. I see you got pulled into this mess, too. This feels like one of those 'in and out before lunch' kind of gigs, right?"

Vanessa's voice crackled through his earpiece, cool and professional despite an undercurrent of unease. She sat before a wall of monitors, each screen flashing with data and live feeds that painted a distorted view of Ian's journey. "Yeah, we're looking at an A7 from the pre-scan, positioned somewhere in sub Con delta quad 5.3…maybe closer to 4. Sixteen markers should get you to the center, but there's this gray patch that's not translating through the system. Feels…off."

Ian squinted at the landscape ahead, his brow furrowing as he scanned the ever-morphing terrain. "A7, sub Con delta, quad 5-ish. Sixteen markers. Got it. But Vee, this place is unstable as hell. The inconsistency—you see that on your end?"

Vanessa hesitated, her fingers flying over the keyboard as she pulled up additional data, none of it making any more sense than the last. "I see it, but that gray patch—it's just a blind spot on my feed. Doesn't read right. This was supposed to be Jimmy and Renae's job. I'm telling you, Ian, this smells like tier-one work. It's way above our pay grade."

Ian's jaw clenched at the mention of Jimmy, a flicker of resentment tightening his voice. "Jimmy? The only reason he gets the big gigs is because he's got buddies higher up. And Renae? Come on, Vee, you're twice as sharp as she'll ever be. This job's no different than any of our others. Is there really no other intel?"

*

Vanessa's gaze flicked over encrypted streams of data, lines of code she wasn't cleared to touch. "Nothing solid. A lot of it is classified or redacted, locked behind security walls I can't breach. I'm starting to think some of this isn't even from GlemTek. Feels…off, Ian. Like it's someone else's game."

Ian's lips curled into a half-smile, the kind that wasn't amused so much as it was knowing. "Yeah, this reeks of Jimmy. Guy's knee-deep in something we're not privy to. Keeps getting all these Mallcore gigs, like he's running errands for somebody on the side. And this A7—it's so damn vague. What exactly am I supposed to be looking for?"

As Ian ventured deeper, the environment around him shifted again, the corridors broadening into vast, echoing spaces that felt too large, too open, like a warehouse that had been stretched and twisted. One moment, he was walking through a hallway that seemed to be breathing; the next, he was in a cavernous room with walls that couldn't decide where they belonged. It was as if the place itself was in a constant state of forgetting what it was supposed to be.

He planted the sixteenth marker, the green light flaring as it touched down, illuminating the surreal, fluid space that spun slowly around him. "This sub Con? It's barely holding together. Feels like I'm walking through someone's bad dream."

Vanessa's voice came back, low and thoughtful. "Dream? No, Ian. This isn't dream logic. This is trauma. Feels like…a parasitic reaction, something foreign taking over. Or maybe even some kind of infection trying to rewrite what it touches."

Ian stopped, considering her words as he took in the warped surroundings. "Could be. But I'm not seeing any signs of trauma residue or nerve damage points. If this is an infection, it's deep. Feels…foreign. And buried."

The space around him shifted again, morphing without warning, hallways becoming rooms, rooms becoming nothing at all. The air felt thick—heavy, charged with something unnamable, an unseen presence pressing down on him. Ian adjusted his gear, eyes fixed on the strange terrain ahead, knowing that whatever lay at the core of this place wasn't just another job—it was something far darker, far more dangerous.

"Guess I'm missing lunch today," Ian muttered, the hint of a grin tugging at his mouth as he stepped forward, the beacon in hand, ready to face whatever twisted, shifting thing lay in wait beyond.

*

Erica was back on the road, her car cutting through the city streets as music blasted from the speakers, drowning out the noise of the world outside. She had one hand on the wheel, the other holding her phone, already deep into a conversation that felt like a half-remembered blur. "Hey girl, how was the rest of the party? I swear, I blacked out again, didn't I? Lol, I know, right? You'd think I'd learn by now. Anyway, I'm heading to the store. You need anything?"

Minutes later, Erica emerged from a corner liquor store, her arms loaded down with bottles that clinked softly against each other, a muted chorus of glass under the city's constant hum. Without breaking stride, she popped the top off one of the bottles and took a long, defiant swig, the burn sliding down easily, familiar. She moved with the kind of casual, half-reckless confidence that said this wasn't her first time—or even her hundredth.

She pulled out her phone again, scrolling through her contacts with one hand as she walked. The city moved around her, indifferent, its rhythm matching her own. She dialed, pressing the phone to her ear. "Hey, Amanda. Got any word on Jason? I'm looking to score. You know how it is."

Erica's voice was light, but there was an edge to it, a sharpness just below the surface, like she was riding the line between carefree and something darker. She navigated the sidewalk with the practiced ease of someone who'd done this dance too many times, lost in a loop of bad habits and worse choices, never quite looking back but never really moving forward either. The city buzzed on, a backdrop to her private, messy rituals, and Erica just kept moving, always one call, one drink, one fix ahead of whatever she was trying not to remember.

*

Ian stood in the dim hallway, the flickering lights casting long shadows that danced along the walls like specters. The air was thick, charged with an uneasy energy that sent a shiver crawling up his spine. At the end of the corridor, a doorway pulsed faintly, glowing with a sickly, irregular rhythm like a heartbeat gone wrong. Ian narrowed his eyes, his instincts flaring. "Think I've got eyes on the A7, Vee. Hold for confirmation."

He moved forward with the precision of a hunter. Every sense dialed up to eleven. Stepping through the threshold, Ian entered a room that felt wrong on a cellular level. In the far corner, a little girl sat huddled, her head buried between her knees, her sobs barely audible over the low hum of the shifting walls. She was a delicate presence in this warped space, like a ghost trapped in a bad memory.

Ian's voice was low, edged with a mix of caution and resignation. "Yeah, I've found a trauma point. Clear as day." He kept his movements slow and deliberate, scanning the room with a practiced eye. There was more here; he could feel it, like static under his skin. He reached behind him, pulling out a rod from his pack and adjusting the settings with deft fingers. A soft, ominous hum filled the air as the device powered up, casting an eerie glow that flickered along the walls.

As he swept the rod through the space, his eyes landed on something oozing from the ceiling—a thick, viscous residue that glistened like tar, dripping down in slow, revolting strands. His gaze followed the trail upward, and there it was: a creature twisted into the corner, all sinew and malformed flesh, its body a grotesque tangle of tissue that defied reason. It had a face—sort of—but not one that belonged to anything born of this world. Its eyes were dark pits, and it watched Ian with a predatory hunger.

The creature hissed, a wet, rattling sound that clawed at Ian's nerves. He couldn't help but smirk, his bravado kicking in. "Well, there you are, you little nasty. Ready to play?"

Vanessa's voice crackled through his earpiece, edged with tension. "Ian, careful…I'm reading some serious levels off that thing. It's strong."

Ian kept his eyes on the creature, his grip on the rod tightening. "Yeah, this one's been feeding well. Not the kind of surprise I was hoping for." He squared his stance, bracing for the inevitable. The creature lunged, fast and furious, but Ian was faster. He moved with the fluidity of someone who'd danced this dance a hundred times before, dodging the creature's frantic strikes with precision. His movements were precise, calculated, and controlled, the choreography of a man who knew his enemy—and his limits.

With a swift motion, Ian swung the rod, catching the creature in mid-air. It shrieked, its body convulsing as the impact sent ripples through its twisted form, but it wasn't done yet. It lunged again, contorting itself as if trying to twist through reality, but Ian was already in position. He struck once more, his equipment humming as the creature's form buckled, then shattered into fragments of itself, sucked into the containment device strapped to his back. It was gone in an instant, dematerialized into nothing more than a faint, lingering echo.

Ian caught his breath, adrenaline thrumming through his veins. "A7 secured. Woo! You catch that, Vee? I was—" His victory was short-lived as he turned back to where the girl had been, but she was gone. The corner where she had sat was empty. The trauma point had vanished without a trace. A chill ran through him as he scanned the room again, unease creeping in. "Where the hell did she go?"

Vanessa's voice cut in, urgent and strained. "Ian, we've got interference. I'm seeing spikes in the data—intoxicants coming in hard. This is a full-blown alcohol response. Damn it, the host is reacting. We're losing—"

Her voice died abruptly, replaced by a deafening silence. Ian's earpiece went dead, the monitors in the facility blinking out one by one. He was left alone in the suffocating quiet, standing in the warped room with only the ghost of Vanessa's warning echoing in his mind. The walls seemed to close in, pressing against him, the energy in the space growing darker and heavier. Whatever he was dealing with, it wasn't over—not by a long shot.

Ian stood there, the quiet setting in, and he knew one thing for sure: he was cut off, alone, and this place wasn't done with him yet.

*

Erica's car rolled to a stop in front of a battered old house at the end of a crumbling street, where even the shadows seemed tired. The streetlights flickered weakly, casting a sickly yellow glow on the neighborhood's decaying skeleton—peeling paint, boarded-up windows, and yards overgrown with weeds that clawed at the cracked sidewalks. She staggered out of the car, her movements loose and unsteady, the door swinging wide and hanging open as if it had given up. An empty bottle tumbled out after her, hitting the pavement with a hollow clink that echoed through the stillness.

She swayed on her feet, struggling to find balance as she stumbled toward the house, every step heavy and uncoordinated. Her eyes were glassy, her mind drifting somewhere between here and nowhere. Reaching the front door, she leaned against it, her fingers fumbling clumsily as she jabbed at the doorbell. The sound rang out, muffled and distant, like a cry lost in the thick, stagnant air.

The door opened, and a man appeared, framed in the dim light spilling from inside. He looked her up and down, his expression unreadable, the kind of look that held judgment at bay but offered no comfort either. He paused, considering her, the silence stretching out in the stale air between them. Without a word, he stepped aside, letting her stumble past the threshold.

The door closed behind them with a soft, final thud, sealing Erica inside. The faint click of the latch was almost lost in the night, but it carried the weight of a line crossed, a step taken deeper into something murky and irreversible. Outside, the streetlights buzzed faintly, the world beyond the door fading back into the bleak, restless quiet of a forgotten part of town.

*

Bill sat in his sleek, modern office perched high above the city, the skyline stretching endlessly beyond the floor-to-ceiling windows like a glimmering sea of concrete and glass. The room was all clean lines and cool steel, but today it felt more like a cage than an executive suite. His phone rang, cutting through the silence with a shrill insistence that sent a shiver up his spine. He answered on the first ring, his voice tight, already bracing for what was coming. "Yes, sir," he said, leaning forward, his eyes narrowing as he listened.

The voice on the other end was a low murmur, just out of reach, but every word seemed to chip away at Bill's composure. His face tightened, lines of worry etching deeper as he absorbed the message. Whatever was being said, it was bad—bad enough that Bill's usual smooth demeanor was cracking at the edges. He grabbed his tablet, fingers moving frantically as he pulled up an order, the screen reflecting the growing unease in his eyes.

"Order number 84567," he recited, his voice taut as a drawn wire. "Yes, it's on our list...yes, sir. No, I wasn't aware of that...really? Understood." Each word was like a stone dropped into a dark well, the consequences rippling out in unseen ways. "I'll handle this personally. Priority one. This will be taken care of. No loose ends, sir. 100%." He hung up, but the tension lingered, a cold knot tightening in his chest.

Without missing a beat, Bill dialed another number, his hands shaking slightly as he adjusted the screen. "Patch me through, Sigma code TRIOXIN," he said into the silence, his voice clipped and urgent. His face was a mask of controlled panic, the kind of look that comes when the ground starts to crumble while you're standing on the edge of a precipice. "Purge the referral," he ordered, barely keeping the tremor out of his voice. "I need it done now. Clean house and cast. Total flush."

He hung up again, this time with a sense of finality that felt like slamming a door on something dangerous and still alive. Bill sat back in his chair, staring out at the city, but his mind was miles away. The skyline, once a familiar comfort, now seemed distant and hostile, a glittering expanse that offered no solace. Darkness crept across the horizon, swallowing the last light of day, and Bill felt the chill settle into the room, into his bones. The high-rise felt colder, the walls closing in as the weight of his decisions pressed down, each one echoing in the silence like a distant, unrelenting toll.

*

Ian moved cautiously down the long, empty hallways, each step echoing faintly in the dim, suffocating silence. The corridors stretched endlessly ahead, bending and twisting as if they were alive, the walls seeming to shift in his peripheral vision. The only real light came from the faint glow of the green beacon markers he'd planted along his path, their steady, pulsing glow a fragile lifeline in this warped, surreal space. Something was off, and Ian could feel it deep in his gut, like a wrong note in a familiar song. The air was thick with tension, and every instinct screamed at him that the instability of his surroundings was more than just a glitch.

He kept a close eye on the containment gauges strapped to his gear, watching the readings flicker and twitch as if reacting to something unseen. His nerves were on edge. Every step felt like he was walking deeper into a trap that was still taking shape. Then, as he rounded a corner, he saw them: three figures moving toward him, their forms barely distinguishable from the shadows they inhabited. Their faces were blank, smooth and featureless, like mannequins come to life, and their clothing was dull and nondescript, blending seamlessly into the murky gloom.

Ian glanced at them as they passed, his pulse quickening. They didn't acknowledge him, didn't even seem to notice his presence, and yet their proximity felt charged, unsettling. He muttered under his breath, his thoughts

200

racing. "Aw shit…who's monitoring this host? Is this a remote job? No one said anything about these."

He pressed on, planting another beacon, its green light flickering as it made contact with the unstable surface. The deeper he ventured into the labyrinth, the more the hallways seemed to twist in on themselves, warping in impossible ways. The walls felt closer, the air thicker, and the silence grew louder, pressing in on him from all sides. Another faceless figure drifted past, and Ian's sense of unease deepened, a cold knot of anxiety tightening in his gut.

Nothing about this felt right. The space was wrong, the figures were wrong, and the whole place was humming with a silent, malignant energy that made his skin crawl. Ian tightened his grip on his gear, every nerve on high alert, knowing he was walking into something that was watching, waiting, and very much aware of his every move.

*

Back at the facility, Vanessa sat at her station, her fingers tapping restlessly against the console as she cycled through screens and equipment, trying to shake the uneasy feeling that clung to her. A flickering light caught her eye, a rapid, irregular pulse coming from a device that shouldn't have been there—a small, unfamiliar piece of tech wired into the system, out of place and wrong. Vanessa's brow furrowed as she studied it, the sinking realization that something was off settling in. She rebooted her station, pulling a device from her pocket, a personal tool she kept for times like this, and inserted it into a slot near the rogue flicker.

As the system sputtered back to life, Vanessa's eyes darted around the dimly lit room, a prickling sensation crawling up her neck. She couldn't shake the feeling that she was being watched: that eyes she couldn't see were tracking her every move. Her screen blinked on, revealing an unexpected message: stream audio access active. She didn't waste a second, her fingers flying to connect to Ian. "Ian, can you hear me?"

Ian, lost somewhere deep within the shifting maze of corridors, froze. The faint crackle of Vanessa's voice cut through the oppressive quiet. "Vee, what the hell happened?"

"No time for that," she shot back, her voice taut with urgency. "This is definitely tier-one. I'm reading a lockout coming fast. I'm sending you my personal outpoint coordinates and a safehouse terminal. Something's off, Ian— like you're not alone in there. If things go dark, follow your markers to the new outpoint. Don't—"

But before she could finish, the screens went black again, a cascade of shutdowns rippling through the room. Vanessa stared at the monitor as the words "Upload Complete" flashed briefly just before the power cut entirely. The darkness was sudden and absolute, swallowing the room in an instant.

Vanessa's breath caught, her pulse hammering in her ears as she squinted into the void. A faint creak broke the silence—the slow, deliberate groan of the door swinging open. Her supervisor stepped into the darkened room, flanked by two guards, their faces unreadable under the faint, ghostly glow of emergency lights flickering weakly behind them.

She sat frozen, knowing that whatever was happening now was far beyond the bounds of her job description and that the room had just turned from a familiar workspace into a trap she hadn't seen coming.

*

In the dim, pulsing light of the void, Ian stood frozen, trying to grasp the full weight of his situation. The air around him was thick, charged with a restless energy that seemed to hum just beneath the surface. He scanned his surroundings, eyes sharp and searching, until they landed on another doorway in the distance. Its faint glow flickered uncertainly, the light warped and distorted, shimmering with a strange instability that made the hairs on the back of his neck stand up. Ian pressed on, each step slow and deliberate, the silence around him heavy with unspoken threats.

As he drew closer, Ian's breath caught in his throat. Scattered along his path were beacon marker poles, but these weren't his. They glowed a faint, eerie red, flickering erratically like dying embers, their once orderly pattern now broken and scattered. A few lay toppled over, their lights extinguished, abandoned like forgotten relics of someone else's failed journey. The sight sent a cold shiver up his spine, a grim reminder that he wasn't the first to walk this path—and maybe not the last.

Ian checked his own markers, his fingers brushing against the remaining beacons in his pack. He glanced back, the trail of green lights he'd planted behind him glowing steadily, offering a fleeting sense of direction in this warped, unsteady world. But the path forward was unclear, and the faceless figures he kept passing—shadows in the periphery—were growing more frequent, their silent presence unsettlingly familiar.

Finally, he reached the doorway. The room beyond was a decaying nightmare, the walls slick with a thick, viscous substance that oozed and dripped like the walls were bleeding. Web-like structures clung to every surface, a sickly mesh of organic decay and rot that seemed to pulse with some hidden, malevolent life. Everything felt like it was on the verge of collapse, teetering between existence and oblivion.

Ian stepped inside, his senses on high alert, every muscle tensed as his eyes swept the room. In the far corner, he spotted something cocooned against the wall, entangled in the webbing. As he moved closer, his heart sank, and a sick dread settled in his gut. It wasn't just something—it was someone. Wrapped in the thick strands was a man in a red uniform, the MallCore logo on his sleeve, now faded and smeared with grime.

"Here's our gray patch anomaly," Ian muttered, the bitter taste of realization on his tongue. "Fuck me…Jimmy, what the hell were you wrapped up in?"

Ian stood there, staring at the discovery of a rival competitor who had lost to whatever twisted game was being played in this space. The walls seemed to close in, the whole room breathing around him, and Ian knew that whatever Jimmy had been involved in was far more dangerous—and far more entangled with his path—than he'd ever imagined.

*

Erica lay sprawled on a filthy, stained mattress in a dimly lit room that reeked of sweat, smoke, and the bitter tang of regret. Around her, other lost souls were scattered across the floor like discarded dolls, bodies limp and eyes glazed, each trapped in a specific, private misery. The dim light barely cut through the gloom, casting long, twisted shadows that seemed to flicker and dance along the walls. Erica was out cold, drifting in a sea of oblivion, unaware of the world crumbling around her.

A figure moved through the room, his polished shoes tapping against the floor with a sharp, deliberate rhythm that stood out against the low murmurs of the strung-out and forgotten. He was out of place—a well-dressed businessman in a tailored suit, dark sunglasses masking his eyes, flanked by two men who looked as if they'd seen one too many dark alleys. He paused when he reached Erica, looking down at her with a gaze that was all ice, no warmth, the faintest hint of a smirk curling at the corners of his lips.

"This is her. Let's go," he said, his voice cool, detached, like he was closing a deal rather than ordering the retrieval of a broken human being.

The two men moved without hesitation, bending down to lift Erica's limp body. She barely stirred, a ragdoll in their hands, as they carried her toward the door. The others in the room didn't react, too far gone in a haze to notice or care, their worlds reduced to the next hit, the next escape. The men hauled Erica outside, the sudden burst of daylight hitting her like a slap, and she stirred, her head lolling to the side as she blinked up at the men, trying to pull herself back to the surface.

"Who are you guys?" she mumbled, her voice thick, words slurred and sluggish.

They ignored her, their silence unbroken as they approached a sleek, black car waiting by the curb, its paint glistening under the sun like obsidian. One of the men opened the door and guided her into the backseat, setting her down with a gentleness that felt almost surreal against the hard edges of the situation. Erica squinted against her swimming vision, trying to make sense of what was happening.

"Where are we going? Who are you?" she repeated, panic creeping into her voice.

The man in dark glasses turned, his expression blank, but his words were edged with something sharp and final. "Your father sent us. You've done enough damage, and you've squandered his generosity. He's not pleased."

Erica's head spun, the words drifting in and out of focus as she tried to grasp the meaning. "Daddy? I told him it was just one procedure...I may have just...just..." The rest of her protest slurred into nothing as her head fell back against the seat, her eyelids fluttering shut. The car door clicked closed, sealing her in, and the city moved on outside, indifferent to the silent drama unfolding within. Erica sank back into unconsciousness, swallowed up by the weight of a mess she couldn't remember making, trapped in the backseat of a life spiraling out of control.

*

Meanwhile, back in the dark, rotting belly of the void, Ian knelt beside the trapped Mallcore worker, his senses on high alert. The room felt alive, sagging under the weight of decay, walls slick with a thick, foul-smelling residue that dripped in slow, nauseating streams. The air was suffocating, and Ian could almost hear the walls groan as they continued their slow collapse. He worked quickly, slicing through the sticky tendrils that held the man captive, each cut freeing him from the grotesque web that had made him a prisoner.

"Alright, buddy," Ian said, keeping his voice low and urgent, his eyes scanning the room for any signs of movement. "What's your story? How long have you been stuck in this mess?"

The man, name tag barely visible under grime but reading "Cliff," blinked, his eyes wild and unfocused, darting around as though trying to make sense of a nightmare that refused to end. "I got twisted around—lost the pattern one too many times," Cliff mumbled, his voice brittle and shaky. "This host...it's an addict's mind, man. It's infested with demons, and I got swallowed up! Couldn't tell which way was out."

Ian's jaw clenched, the truth settling like a lead weight in his stomach. He knew exactly what Cliff meant. "Damn it, this is an untethered job," Ian muttered, more to himself than anyone. "No wonder it's so unstable. We're not equipped for this—no security backup, no support. I saw toxins all through the streams on my way in, and this whole place is breaking apart around us. It's a deathtrap."

He checked the containment gauges on his gear, the readings bouncing erratically, then glanced back at Cliff, whose face was still pale and drawn. "You generated that A7 yourself, didn't you? These parasitic manifestations always get worse when the host's got nothing left to lose. We're knee-deep in it now."

Ian exhaled sharply, the frustration and tension mixing with the stale air. "I'm cut off from home base, the comms are dead, and this place is folding in on itself—best shot we've got now is to get out to a safehouse somewhere off the grid. Face it, we're expendables at this point. We've already been written off."

Cliff groaned, his body slumping, still weak from his ordeal. "I knew it'd come to this," he rasped, pain and exhaustion lining his voice. "I could feel it."

"Enough of that," Ian snapped, hauling Cliff up to his feet. The man wobbled, barely able to stand, but Ian steadied him, gripping his arm tightly. "I've already dealt with one of your anxiety freaks, and I'm not in the mood for round two. We gotta move."

Cliff swayed, his legs shaky, but he nodded, determination flickering faintly in his eyes. "I'm weak, but I'll keep up. I have to."

"We just need to make it back to my entry point," Ian said, adjusting his gear and recalibrating his last few beacon markers. The green light blinked to life, a tiny beacon of hope in the dark. "Once we're there, I'll get the safehouse coordinates uploaded. We'll get out of here, jobs be damned. We survive this first, figure the rest out later."

With Cliff leaning heavily against him, Ian guided him through the decaying halls, each step careful and deliberate. They navigated past the oozing walls and twisted wreckage, leaving the room of nightmares behind as they pushed forward, clinging to whatever slim chance of escape still remained.

*

Erica's eyes fluttered open, her vision swimming as the sterile, white room around her slowly came into focus. The harsh overhead lights buzzed faintly, casting a clinical glow that only made the place feel colder. Standing over her was the man in the sharp suit, his face etched with disdain, an unknown judging gaze behind the pair of glasses that he seemed never to take off. He gave a curt nod to the technician at her side, who moved with swift efficiency, propping Erica up and adjusting her limp body like she was just another piece of equipment.

"What's going on now?" Erica mumbled, her voice thick with lingering grogginess, the words slurring together as if they barely belonged to her.

The man's expression didn't soften; his voice was cold, every word clipped and precise. "We're giving you something to clean out your system," he said, his gaze sweeping over her like she was an unfortunate task on his to-do list.

"You've got a lot of garbage in there. Your father paid to make sure we clear it all out. You're lucky he's still willing to foot the bill for something this exclusive."

The technician tied a tourniquet tightly around Erica's arm, the rubber biting into her skin. Erica flinched as the needle pierced her vein, the syringe filling with a glowing, neon-yellow substance that pulsed unnaturally, almost alive. She watched, half-horrified, as the bright liquid flowed into her bloodstream. "What kind of medicine is this?" she asked, her voice tinged with growing fear, the sight of the strange fluid sending a jolt of dread through her.

The man's smile was thin, devoid of warmth, more like a grimace stretched too far. "The corrective kind," he replied, the words laced with a bitter undertone that promised nothing good.

Erica's eyes widened, panic flickering across her face as the room began to blur, edges smearing together into a disorienting haze. The world around her folded in on itself, her mind fogging over as whatever they had injected her with took hold. She tried to focus, to hold onto something, anything, but the harder she tried, the further she drifted. The man turned away, addressing the staff with another curt nod, all business, all finality. "We're done here. Deliver her to her father. Inform them that #84567 is officially closed."

Two of the men moved in, lifting Erica's dazed, unresponsive body from the chair. She hung between them, limbs slack, head lolling to the side as they carried her out of the room. The bright lights faded behind her, and her consciousness slipped further away, swallowed by the weight of a decision that had been made without her, leaving her lost somewhere far beyond reach.

*

Across town, Vanessa stepped into her apartment, the door clicking shut behind her with a hollow finality. She was out of the crisp work attire, dressed down in faded jeans and a worn hoodie that felt like a second skin, but the day's exhaustion clung to her like a heavy shroud. Her eyes were tired, dark circles etched beneath them, and every movement seemed weighed down by the invisible burden of too many hours spent on edge. She dropped her bag by the door and made her way to the desk, flicking on the computer with a resigned sigh.

The screen glowed to life, casting an eerie blue light that filled the dimly lit room. Vanessa pulled a slim, encrypted device from her pocket and plugged it into the port, her fingers moving swiftly over the keyboard as she navigated through layers of security. She accessed the coordinates for the safe house she'd set up for Ian, double-checking every detail, every failsafe. The process was quick but deliberate, ensuring that everything was still intact. Ready for when

Ian needed it. Satisfied, she leaned back, rubbing her temples, the weight of the day settling heavily on her shoulders.

With a weary sigh, Vanessa reached for a stack of paperwork she'd tossed on the counter earlier, her eyes catching on the top page. Bold letters stared back at her: "Termination Notice." The words were cold, stark, and final, standing out like a bruise on an otherwise mundane sheet of corporate letterhead. She ran her thumb along the edge of the paper, the reality of her situation sinking in, each syllable a reminder that her loyalty, her late nights, and her sacrifices had all led her to this—a neatly printed sentence on a page that decided her worth.

Vanessa set the paperwork down, staring at it for a moment longer than she wanted to. Her mind drifted back to Ian, to the tangled mess she'd left behind at the facility and the promise she'd made to get him out. She knew she was on borrowed time, her connection to the system already severed in ways that went far beyond a lost job. But for now, at least, she had done what she could. And maybe that was enough.

She powered down the computer, the screen going dark, plunging the room into quiet shadows. Vanessa lingered there for a moment, caught between the life she'd just lost and whatever uncertain future lay ahead. The apartment was silent, save for the faint hum of the city outside, and as she stared at the termination notice one last time, Vanessa couldn't help but wonder how much further she'd have to fall before she hit the bottom.

*

Back in the decaying void, Ian and Cliff trudged through the shadowy corridors, retracing their path one grim step at a time, each beacon marking their only lifeline. The oppressive silence hung heavy, broken only by the faint buzz of machinery hidden within the walls. Ian moved quickly, pulling a marker from its place and switching it to standby as his eyes swept the area. That's when he heard it—a low, unsettling hum that grew steadily louder, crawling under his skin.

"You hear that?" Ian's voice was tight, anxiety creeping in around the edges. "I don't like the sound of that."

Cliff's head snapped up, his eyes wide with alarm. "Oh no…it's a sterilizer!" he gasped, his voice breaking. Ian turned, his stomach dropping as a swarm of neon yellow, insect-like creatures poured into the corridor, moving with a terrifying, relentless speed, their glowing bodies crackling with electric energy.

"How many are usually in a sterilizer?" Ian asked, his voice urgent but controlled, scanning the swarm for any weaknesses.

Cliff's face turned ashen. "Does it matter? One's enough to wipe us out!"

"It matters if we fight together!" Ian barked back, adrenaline surging. "We don't have a choice—stand your ground!"

But Cliff was already unraveling, panic seizing him. "I can't outrun those things! I'm dead meat!"

"Bullshit!" Ian snapped, fury cutting through the fear. He hit a button on his pack, and with a whirr and click of gears, a harness unfolded from his gear like a mechanical beast coming to life. Ian dropped to a crouch, his back to Cliff. "Get on! I'm taking your weight—ride me, man! As we pass each marker, you weaponize and swing at every damn one of them. I'll do the same. We're getting out of here—I'm not dying in someone else's head!"

Cliff hesitated, fear paralyzing him, but the choice wasn't really his to make. With no other option, he clambered onto Ian's back, shaky but determined, grabbing a beacon and switching it to kill mode. Ian gritted his teeth, tightening his grip on his own modified marker, and charged headlong into the oncoming swarm.

The corridor erupted into chaos. Ian swung his beacon with brutal precision, smashing through the neon creatures in a vicious blur of light and movement. Cliff, clinging tightly, swung wildly, his strikes clumsy but desperate. The creatures hissed and screeched, their bodies breaking apart under each blow, but still, they kept coming, a tidal wave of bright, chittering death. Ian pushed forward, teeth bared, clearing a path through sheer force of will as they fought from one marker to the next, weaponizing each as they went.

Faceless entities, once drifting aimlessly in the void, were devoured in seconds by the swarm, their forms disintegrating into nothingness. But Ian and Cliff kept pressing on, narrowly avoiding the same fate, the neon tide snapping at their heels. Each strike grew more vicious, each step more urgent, but the creatures seemed endless, pouring in from every direction, filling the hallway with relentless buzzing chaos.

Cliff's energy began to flag, his swings slowing, the weight of fear dragging him down. He let out a strangled cry as a piece of debris flew out of nowhere, striking him hard across the head. The beacon slipped from his grasp, clattering to the ground, and Cliff slumped, unconscious, his body dead weight on Ian's back.

Ian snarled, his muscles burning as he fought to stay upright and keep moving. He swung his remaining beacon with raw fury, fighting off the swarm as it closed in. Each strike sent the creatures flying, but the effort was taking its toll. Gritting his teeth, he charged toward the final glowing marker, every step a battle against exhaustion and pain. He reached it, discarding the used beacon and fumbling for the device in his gear pocket, his fingers trembling as he tried to adjust the coordinates.

The neon creatures surged around him, snapping at his heels, but Ian stayed focused, slamming his hand down on the engage button with a last, desperate burst of strength. The corridor erupted in a blinding white light, swallowing him, Cliff, and the remnants of the swarm in an instant, the radiant glow consuming everything in its path until there was nothing left but the sharp, searing brightness of survival.

*

The blinding white light faded slowly, revealing Ian and Cliff sprawled across a battered couch, both drenched from head to toe in a thick, yellow sludge that clung to them like a bad dream. The room around them wasn't any better—walls, ceiling, and furniture coated in the same viscous goo, dripping in slow, grotesque streams. It looked like the aftermath of a nightmare splattered across reality, a sickly layer of grime and chaos smeared over every inch of the space.

Across the room, Vanessa stood frozen, her eyes wide, mouth slightly agape. She held a mug of tea in one hand, though the cup, like everything else, was smeared with yellow slime, the liquid dripping sluggishly to the floor in fat, oily globs. She blinked, trying to process the surreal mess in front of her, the jarring juxtaposition of two men who looked like they'd crawled through hell and come out the other side, barely.

Cliff, still dazed and desperately hanging onto consciousness, glanced around with the glazed look of someone trying to wake from a particularly bad trip. His eyes swept the room, taking in the dripping walls and the sticky devastation clinging to everything, his mind struggling to catch up with the fact that they had, somehow, made it out alive.

Ian, on the other hand, was unnervingly calm. He took in the scene with the quiet, measured detachment of a man who'd seen worse and had long since stopped being surprised by any of it. After a long pause, he reached into his chest pocket, fingers slick with goo, and fished out a slightly crumpled cigarette. With a flick of his lighter, he lit up, the end flaring orange against the sludge-splattered room. He took a slow, deep drag, letting the smoke fill his lungs as he leaned back into the muck-covered couch, the weight of their ordeal settling in.

Exhaling a thin stream of smoke, Ian's gaze drifted over to Vanessa, who was still rooted in place, teacup in hand, utterly shell-shocked. She looked like she was seeing ghosts—or maybe just realizing she was part of a ghost story no one would ever believe. Ian let the silence hang a beat longer before breaking it, a crooked smirk curling at his lips. "Well," he said dryly, voice edged with that dark gallows humor that had seen him through his days, "There's worse ways to quit a job."

Vanessa just stared, too stunned to even form a response, her tea slowly dripping onto the floor, mingling with the mess of goo at her feet. The air was thick with the unspoken realization that whatever they had been before this moment—employees, operatives, cogs in a machine—they were something else now. They were survivors of something no one would understand, caught up in a web far bigger than any of them could have anticipated.

In that surreal, slimy room, it was clear: this wasn't the end of the line but the beginning of something else entirely. A new, uncertain chapter that none of them had asked for, but one they were bound to now, whether they liked it or not.

The UpMind

Rob Tannahill

The night ran outside the car's open window, and Burton the Chemist's mind drifted. Quincy the Scientist drove, drumming the steering wheel as Iggy Pop rocked the XM radio. Derrick, who was both gopher and guinea pig, shuffled around in the backseat, muttering to himself. His fingers worked to roll the joint that would smooth their frazzled nervous systems clear of the new drug they'd invented. "Bit much speed in here, Burt," he said.

Burton didn't argue, not with his test subject. "Is there?" He was feeling the fentanyl. A little bit of the speed. The mixture was imbalanced. Fuck. "Is it? I'll adjust the recipe. Look at the moon! Her face is on it. The goddess."

"Goddess, right," Derrick said. "That's nice, but I'm thinking of money, man!" His head darted back and forth, spiky blue hair seeming to glow in the dark. "We want people higher n' shit, enjoying themselves, not tripping unfettered balls…" he laughed. "Pleasure equals profit. For the first time in my life, I'm not going to be broke!"

"I take care of you," Quincy said. He glanced at Burton. "He's right. Dial down the amphetamine."

"It's the goddamn LSD," Burton said. "And you. Fuck the moon tickets," He didn't care about money. They'd left the think tank—six months with DARPA had been enough for the Chemist, whose sense of right and wrong wouldn't let him help with projects such as fucking Patholink or the new Gamma movement, finagling commercials to sell propaganda more than product, injecting society with new Werinicke's commands (pity-inspiring precursors to buzzwords and phrases) and *selling fucking red hats,* for Eris' sake—yuck—making people stupider than they already were and making them proud of it. *I'm just. We're just. All I'm doing is. I'm only trying to. Bypass your ego by tickling the empath within using a phrase you just think is a cliché. I'm just, I mean, it's only. To manipulate you into becoming my puppet.*

The Gammas were sick.

Quincy, as if he'd read Burton's mind (this happened), said:

"This isn't about money, D. This is about destroying the effects of a sadistic social experiment. This is about unlocking capabilities of the human mind that preclude the need for fucking Patholink." He fake-spit at the floorboards. "But I know you're broke. Don't worry. Keep working…I'll keep looking out for you."

211

"Same," Burton said. "I'll keep you nice and stoned." Derrick was something of a project for the two scientists. He was a junkie, the perfect guinea pig, would take any chance on a drug and had the constitution of a living statue. Unlike many junkies, he maintained (his caliber of) analytical wherewithal even under the influence of hallucinogens like LSD.

They both could tell that Quincy was nervous. His eyes darted from the road to the sideview to the rearview mirrors, searching for suspicious cars—assassins—one does not just leave a DARPA Think Tank (archaic: thinktank) with a trunk full of pilfered chemicals and not have to worry about anything. *I'll die for what I believe.* Believe it or not, it was a comforting slogan.

Light clung to his vision and followed it back down to the earth, where for a moment, it brightened the world like the sun. The air was radioactive, and Burton saw shapes. Hercules. The Dragon. Orion sipped from the Great Bear of the North.

"GODDAMMIT!"

Squealing of rubber against concrete. Screams. Burton spun. He caught a glimpse of a truck's trailer, and then crunching metal and nothing.

*

Homero wiped his mouth with a tattooed hand. His homeboy, Rylo, lay dead on the floor. Empty bottles of lean lie scattered around his corpse. Six, to be exact. It was almost like he left the bottles lying around in lieu of writing a note. Rylo was a straight-up *ryda*. Suicide? It didn't make sense.

But Rylo also knew his dope. He knew what to mix and what not to. Like Homero, he'd both blessed and liquidated customers—not out of hate, it was just something you had to do when you dealt dope in the hood, motherfuckers get stupid, and it is what it is—no. Rylo didn't fuck up. He did this shit on purpose.

"Why, fool?" Homero asked the corpse. "Since when is you the n— to murk himself?" He turned away from his friend's ashy face and blue lips. There was a clue here somewhere. He put Rylo's phone in his pocket and left the room.

Downstairs, Niblet and Zee were rolling a joint and watching *Da Baby* thug it out on the plasma screen. Homero snatched the remote from the glass tabletop and turned it off.

"Brah!" This ejection came from Niblet. Zee just looked at him.

"Rylo upstairs dead," Homero croaked.

"Quit playin'," said Niblet.

"Real talk, dawg. That n— dead."

"Oh hell nah!" Niblet ran up the stairs. Zee buried his face in his large, articulate hands. A few seconds later, they heard the scream. *"RYLO!"* Shortly after, there was a crash as Niblet took his rage out on the walls.

212

"It look like he killed hisself," Homero said.

"Nah," Zee said. "Ain't no way. Rylo's the Beast of us all."

"Ain't shit up there but him dead and the lean he bought to sell last night. He drank all six bottles." Homero sat next to Zee and finished rolling the joint for him. They sparked. Niblet was still screaming and crying for Rylo to come back to life. A tear leaked from Homero's eye, and he wiped it away. He slipped the phone out of his pocket and handed it to Zee.

"Crack that muh-fuh," Homero said. "Go through everything."

Niblet pounded down the stairs. Zee and Homero heard the familiar sound of a pistol's ratchet before the man holding the gun appeared. Homero jumped and ran to his soldier, grabbing his shoulders.

"Stand down, G," Homero said.

"Who sold him that fuckin' lean? Who da *punk* dat sold him dat *LEAN!*"

"It came from Scooter, man!" Scooter was the main plug for the whole crew. For the benefit of big weight, he dealt with Tiger Sheng and Ghostface and whoever else was dangerous (or just a pain in the ass) to the Dead Boy Crew, a faction of the 6/4 crew.

Niblet backed up and raised his arms over his head. He took a step back. Homero went with him and gently took the chrome from his hand. Zee was there, and he handed the 40 Glock off. "That shit chambered, man, be careful."

He took Niblet's face in his hands. "Listen to me. You listenin'? We goan find out what the fuck happened to Rylo. Zee goan crack that phone—"

"Working on it," Zee said from the living room.

"And we goan find the muthafuckas that caused this shit. Whoever it is. Some n— some bitch, I don't give a fuck. We goan hang 'em up by they ankles and put a bucket under they head. Then I'mma let you go to work with the hammer. What you think of that?"

"Yeah," Niblet said. "Rylo ain't did himself like that!"

"No. Ain't no way our soulja did that shit to himself. Someone got his ass, somehow. I'mma go talk to Scooter."

"I'm going with you."

"You can't, not like this. You crack off in front of Scooter, that's it. We done, man. We got no business. I need you here and chillin' the fuck out with Zee—help him look through the phone. See did some hood rat get into his head, or did he owe someone he didn't want to tell us about, or what. There'll be something. You go smoke with Zee, now."

"You'll get him," Niblet said.

"Damn right." He pat Niblet's cheek. Niblet nodded and went into the living. Homero hurried upstairs to get ready for Scooter, dialing the number of a Cleaner to take care of Rylo's corpse.

Even with the hospital drugs, the accident hurt Burton like a motherfucker. Pain was life and had been since he'd seen the hood of Quincy's Toyota smash against the side of the eighteen-wheeler. How long had he been here? Not long—couldn't be. Kitty, his lover, hadn't even been by yet. His eyes were welling up when the nurse came in.

Burton swallowed it down and asked, "Are my friends dead?"

"One of them lived," she said. "He has blue hair, right?" Prepping cups of pills and water.

"That's Derrick."

"Well, he's still alive...he only suffered a separated shoulder. Very sweet young man...will you be okay?" the nurse asked.

"Yeah...just knew Quincy...the other guy...fuck. For twenty damn years. Excuse my language. It's hitting me hard."

She smiled. "Aw. It's okay. I've heard the word fuck before. If Derrick, you said his name was? If he feels like getting up and around, I'll send him in to see you. Would you like that?"

"That'd be great."

When she left, Burton went for his field coat, pulling it off the back of the chair. Time to do what he didn't get a chance to do before. The wee nickel bag had about half a sixteenth left in it, half a point—it was already fully flowered, and Burton stuffed his nostril into the bag and inhaled deeply.

Before it kicked, Burton grabbed his phone from the little nightstand next to the bed. His first victim would be the Gallant Preppers Podcast. The clickbait read *Are You Ready For the Migrant Crime Wave?* Burton checked the channel for sponsors...there it was, the little G for the fucking Gamma Group. They were quite big on turning all the podcasters they could buy into new-age carpetbaggers, which was part of Agenda 96.

Flat Earth, the matrix, prepping—a new age occult movement. Pump the crowd with too much information of both the valid and misinfo type...podcaster culture is the best way to spin the collective unconscious...that thing called God that no one believes in...tell everyone the universe is made out of pixels so they think they can walk through cars...watch everyone cut each other's throats...acceleration....think tanks control the media...thinktank-driven media bypasses persona and reprograms the whole of humanity anew. Their dumb ass never catches on.

But they would, and that right soon.

Burton clicked on the podcast.

"Really, this stuff is all a complete waste of money. There's a big population control putsch going on in the world right now...and your best bet, shitheads, is to kill yourself. I'd like to thank you for spending all of your money on the products I'm selling. And to remind you that it's okay; if you can't kill yourself, just go kill someone else."

Burton's jaw dropped.

UpMind, ebbing and flowing. Perception skips the dimensions while the body stays put. Tentative fingers pushed at the flesh of his belly. Why don't you tell me how you really feel, bud? At first, it felt normal. His vision shuddered, and he watched the ghost of his finger pass through skin and muscle. Blood waved in his veins. It was blue. Fourth density. He took his hand back and looked at it. He could see the open door to his room through his palm. His metatarsals glowed, and he could see his reflection, small, thin against the bone.

"What's up, Burt? Where's Kitty? I thought she'd have come to see you by now."

Derrick stood in the doorway. His left arm was in a sling. Burton could see through it. There was a hairline fracture in his ulna. Half-digested breakfast sat in his stomach. A nurse walked through the space his brain occupied. His eyes were beaming on yellow strings.

"Grab my phone. Text—her—can't. Testing session. Right now."

Derrick sat down in the chair next to the bed. "Testing—dude! You *did not* take Up in the bitch ass haws—" he broke into quiet laughter. "Oh, my goodness. Is it—holy shit, Burt!" He picked up the phone, sent the text as he'd been instructed, and dropped the phone on the bed next to Burton's hand.

"Chill…D." Moving slowly, Burton regained third density; he caressed the phone screen and saw *REASONS TO OPT OUT* under a video from another podcaster he usually found entertaining, at least. Rusty Labels by name.

"You saw it? My hand goes through the phone."

"I'm not sure if I saw it…it's like a cartoon."

"Like AI animation."

"Don't let anyone see that, dude. They'll shuffle your ass back to the Tank. I'm ready to leave this hospital, man. As soon as they find out, we're…they'll come. We're fucked, B."

"They won't," Burton said. "Not here. We're safer here than we are out there." His thumb kept going through the phone screen. "Would you?"

Derrick picked up the phone. His finger hesitated over the screen. "What's in this stuff, Burt? How the hell…"

"Remember the Philadelphia Experiment? Make a ship disappear. They used a chemical to do that. It wasn't strictly from mirrors…it was a chemical called Luce SPM 6."

"Luce?"

"Yes. Like Lucifer."

"Since when do you believe in stuff like that?"

"I don't. But I don't have to. All I need to believe is that Dr. Werner Von Braun went to a Rothschild soiree and came back with a chemical that can make shit disappear. I have to believe that Quincy told me this because he did. This wasn't his first rodeo. Remember—he used to work for Owen Kuos. The dumbing down of this chemical also gave us the stealth bomber. Many of our Reaper drones are treated with it." He chuckled. "They never see us coming, D!"

"Dude…okay, that's out of my range. I gotta get back to the bed, man. I'm wiped out. I'm glad you're okay, Burt."

Burton pointed at the phone. "Don't listen to any podcasts. Not yet. When we get out of here, we'll do another test together."

Derrick smiled. "Okay, brother."

His last thought before falling asleep was *Quince, we did it. The Up works.*

*

Scooter was cool enough to offer Homero some ice to sharpen him up.

"Nah, not right now, man. Appreciate it, doe. I got to figure out what happened to Rylo."

Scooter thumbed his nose. "He kilt hisself. There ain't nothin' else." He stopped mid-line chop and sighed. "Maybe they *is* something else. I don't know, man. Rylo ain't the first. I know that. Brah, they's damn Lieutenants coming around asking me why I'm slangin' dirty shit. Like ten swangs died last week, man. They asked me was I liquidating without permission."

"I find out anyone liquidated Rylo…ain't gonna ask any questions."

Scooter snorted his line and looked up. "The fuck does that mean, dawg?"

"It means what it says." Tension. Homero leaned forward and had a line to set Scooter at ease. The message was received.

Scooter chuckled. "I didn't kill Rylo. I liked Rylo. N— bought weight. I like you. Y'all make stacks for me. It ain't me. Maybe you oughtta look at that phone in your pocket for the answer."

"What you tryna say?"

Scooter tapped himself on the temple. "Five Gee, n—, mind control."

"Conspiracy theories."

"It ain't a theory. You ever heard of Patholink?"

"What?"

"You ain't watch the news either, huh? Ite. Patholink, Rylo wanted one. It's a brain implant made by Owen Kuos, the Q dude, or Gamma Q, whatever the fuck it is."

"What's Patholink?"

216

"It's like a remote control that goes in your brain. Shit supposed to be like…okay, so you depressed, right? Don't hit a bump of my shit no more, nah. Hit a button and reprogram your personality by your damn self. Rylo wanted one to make himself a better entrepreneur."

"That makes sense."

"Yeah. He said he was gonna have Zee fuck with it and see if he could figure out how to hack it so that when they come out, and rich muthafuckas get 'em, he could remote-control they ass."

Now *that* sounded like Rylo. "Word. That's fuckin' cold."

"Look, man. I ain't hurt anyone. What I did notice is this. Every last one of the fools that OD'd lately was into Kuos in some way. He does a lot of business talk. They be listenin' to his podcast and shit and also them other muthafuckas, who is…Rusty Labels. Goofy ass white dude with the yoga dreads. Think he's the white Bob Marley or somethin'."

"That n— part of the Gamma Group. They racist ass white supremacist dudes. Fuck y'all listening to Nazi shit fo'?"

"They ain't got no beef with us, dawg—they just don't like immigrants. Fuck do I care about that? Fools undercut everyone with fetty. Either use it or be fucked. It took me a year to figure out how to cut with that bullshit, and now I got whatever the fuck—fools dying…whatever, man. Kuos be making a name. He try to make Suite look like a Gee." Scooter laughed.

Homero rolled his eyes. "President Suite's a bitch. He ain't gangsta."

"Word. Fuck that ol' snarlin' ass little dog lookin' muthafucka. Talkin' bout round-ups in the hood and shit. You heard?"

They slapped hands. "Yeah. First term, he got the illegals; now he's after heads he just don't like…fuck. I'mma see what Zee found."

Scooter nodded. "Tell me what you find, man. Like I said, I got love for y'all too."

Homero left Scooter's apartment wondering if he really needed to go through the phone or not. If Scooter was right, there wasn't much he could do. Nailing Kuos would require a hell of a lot more than handing a fifty and a piece of paper with an address on it to a goon. No, this was going to require things that might be out of Homero's purview. He didn't even know where to begin.

*

He was glad to be back at the warehouse he and Kitty had converted into a giant studio apartment. It made a great safehouse/laboratory. Burton wasn't big on the status quo. He didn't have a bank account. He had an app. He didn't carry extra credit cards around. He was, up until a few weeks ago, an employee of DARPA, but that was over now. And almost all of his money had been spent making the UpMind. Not that he made that much to begin with. Quincy had been the rich one. With him gone and the checks drying up, they needed another way to make money.

That meant getting someone who wasn't him to try the Up. Derrick wasn't answering the phone. Maybe he was fucked up about Quincy. He'd seemed fine in the hospital but…well…junkies are infamous for their latent reactions to stimuli.

Kitty wasn't going for it. She liked H and weed. Psychedelics of the acid/mushrooms caliber gave her the fear. Ten years they'd been together, roaming, making lots of drugs and less money. She was gentle when they fucked. Burton hadn't been out of a hospital bed long, and she was considerate of that. She loved him, and he loved her.

But she still said: "I'm not taking that acid shit."

"This isn't *acid shit*, it's UpMind. It's an awakening."

"No, Burt. I don't want to be awakened like that. I told you that three months ago when you started making this crap. Tripping scares me."

"This isn't a trip. It's the fifth density—"

"Fuck the fifth density. The fifth density is a hallucination."

"No, it isn't. It's a very real place."

"Here." She knocked on the kitchen table. "I don't care what drugs anyone does; this table is what it is. You take acid or whatever, yeah, *you* might think you're pushing your fingers through the table, but the rest of us just see you waving your arm in the air."

"This isn't that way, Kitty." He wasn't offended. She'd always been the more pragmatic of them.

She blew a raspberry. "The Criss Angel shit is malarkey, baby. Why do you want to trip anyway? Aren't you sad about your friends?"

"Quincy would want us to."

"Burt."

"He would, Kitty! It works, too! I know it does. I just need confirmation from someone who isn't Derrick."

"What's wrong with Derrick?"

"He didn't show up. I saw him in the hospital, and then…poof. We'll go check on him in a few, just…please, Kitty. Just the one time. Please. I need a stand-in guinea pig. I'll eat your pussy for three hours, swear."

"Asshole." She slapped his arm. "I'm not a fucking *pig*."

He kissed her. "No, you're not. You're going to help me fight the pigs, and we're going to do it with this. And—if it works the way I say it does for me for you, I'll be able to pop my tongue out your butthole while I lick your clit." He climbed on top of her and kissed her face as giggles erupted from her throat.

"If I'm clever, I can go through the top of your mound and lick it right on the nerves, tongue through the G spot...we'll see if you live through it."

She slapped him on the chest. "Are you serious...if I freak out, I'll fuck off on you, *I* swear. You'll never see me again."

Burton motioned for her to stand. He lifted her shirt and injected her in the saphenous vein. Kitty grinned, feeling the fentanyl first. On the back of that came the amphetamine wave. She doubled over and coughed once, then gagged. Her breathing quickened.

She raised her arms over her head and cried, "WOW. Jesus. I'm...there's a pelican behind you! It's laughing at us both."

"That trip fades," he said. He brought Rusty Label's Podcast up and held the phone out to her. "What's that say?"

"Oh-my-fucking-I-can-see-through-your-hand-God."

"Does that say Rusty Labels, love?"

Kitty squinted. "Well, yeah...what's it supposed to say?"

"The fifth density is the underlying truth. Watch this." And he turned the podcast on.

Instead of "Felicitations, you two million attentive lovelies, welcome to Rusty Label's Podcast!" which is what Burton heard, Labels spat something grotesque. He must have, given the way Kitty's face changed. She looked like she was watching a mother cat eat her kitten's legs off. After a few minutes, she snatched the phone out of his hands and began scrolling on her own. For a second, it worked. Then, her fingers passed through the screen.

She dropped the phone. "Fuck, Burton!"

"Go slow. You retain a little 3D right now. Just go slow. Be gentle."

"Okay, you were right," she said. "Boot up and join me...we'll figure this out."

"You still want the tongue?"

"Later!" She laughed. "Fuck yes. But not now."

"I love you," Burton said. While he fixed his shot, she went off on a rant about the abject insanity kicking her ears. Just as he pushed, he noticed a new development—Nails' podcast was, like Gallant Preppers, also sponsored by The Gamma Group.

*

"Y'all find—" but the lights were all out. Nothing but dead quiet in the house. Homero drew his nine and held it out in front of him, then strafed right and whirled, the pistol aimed into the living room, his reflexes keyed to shoot.

There was no need. The glass coffee table where many a joint had been rolled, and many monies had been counted, had been shattered, and glass shards littered the carpet. The frame had lost two legs, and black steel cut into the floor. A massive amount of marijuana lay scattered, and the cocaine was on the floor, open, also scattered as if a vanilla cake had blown up in the middle of the room. The TV had been knocked off the entertainment center and lay on its side, as dead as his soldiers. This was evidence of a fight.

There was also a pizza on the floor. They'd done what—ordered pizza, ate some, and decided to kill each other? Where the hell were the cleaners? And—were those voices?

A few feet away from Zee's hand lay Rylo's phone. It was on, a familiar voice leaking from the speakers. That was Kuos. And he was talking about Patholink.

"It's not a mind control device," Kuos spoke. "It's a mind-*cleaning* device. You clean the apps on your phone, okay, you'll be able to clean your brain that way. Think about it. How wonderful would it be to be able to just…reorder yourself at the touch of a button? Or if you don't understand some of the words people are using. Patholink has a dictionary downloaded into it and an editing program. If someone uses a word you don't know, Patholink will, and it'll plug the definition into your head."

"This fuckin' duck," Homero said to the phone. Owen Q. Kuos was the most prolific tech bro in the world despite the fact that his space program (GAMMA Q, which beat the original name of Q-Rocket) was a constant failure. Though Kuos had about as much class as a junkie's corpse, the government didn't mind pumping him with research and development funding even before the Gamma Group came along and added their name to his dumbass Q-Rocket of shit. When he couldn't get money from them, he pumped his father's sulfur mines for funds to blow on malfunctioning Q-Rockets and a really crappy streaming service called, of course, Q (pay, still suffer ads). The landscape on the other side of the world was much different now, thanks to a stunt Kuos pulled in the Eastern European Wars of 2026.

Homero was a gangster, not a dipshit. He knew Kuos, he just hated the fuck.

"Told you not to listen to this asshole, Ry." But he was speaking to a dead man. To a bunch of dead men now.

Kuos continued: "But this all happens at once, see, so it's like you always knew. And it doesn't stop there. It can fix pathology. Say you have the urge to hurt people, just saying, right, you can purchase a program from us here at Gamma Q that'll stop you from going anywhere when you feel like that. See? No more having to restrain from temptation, which causes just…so many pathologies. It makes so many psychopaths. There's so much more it can do. I think Patholink is the answer to all of our problems."

Homero made the phone go dark.

*

Burton rubbed his mouth. They should've come to check on Derrick, who hadn't called, sooner than they did. Too late now. Instead of a morose man who missed his friends, they were greeted by a pasty blue face and unoxygenated blood, stiff and motionless under increasingly translucent skin. The blue-haired gopher had ceased to be, and the giant red yawns running down his wrists told the lovers how it happened.

Rusty Labels' podcast, however, thrived: "If only you could really, truly hear me fools, dingbats, and chicken fuckers. Counting the ways I've led you astray with lies and clichés that suckle the critical thinking from your frontal lobe. Did anyone really believe, even for a second, in any of the tabloid nonsense that comes out of my mouth? What did I fool you with? Was it the phrase 'I just want'? HA! You can get anything with that phrase! I act sad, and you lot want to be my legs. It's too easy. So easy it hurts! HA! Oh, wait—no, it doesn't— you're all cows, that's why. Fucking perish."

Kitty kicked the phone across the room. Burton plucked the plunger out of Derrick's arm. His eyes were blue and white.

The animus spoke, her voice silk in his brain: *All spoken words are lies. Human speech in the fifth density can be nothing less than the truth. What those on the 3 hear is not what those on the 5 hear. That they might hear the underbelly groan…that's why you made it, Burton. To put an end to the ability to lie.*

Burton said. "This is chaos. This is going to create—"

"Snap out of it!" Kitty found the phone and grasped at it; the substance passed through her fingers. She growled and slowed herself, finally grasping the phone and turning it off. "Jesus, Derrick…"

"I get it now." He spoke before insanity took his love away. "They're fucking with the subconscious. Two guesses who's to blame."

"Burt! Derrick is lying here—"

"I know. I can see him. I also know he would want us to avenge him, so I'm not going to sit here drowning in tears!"

Her eyes widened.

"I'm sorry, honey…fuck, *FUCK!* He was fine." He stood over Derrick's corpse. "You were *fine,* dammit!" He turned and kicked over Derrick's little coffee table. A coffee mug, a few papers, and a half-straw, along with a pile of powder, were scattered on the ground.

"Babe…"

"They," Burton continued as if nothing had happened. "The Big They, the conspiracy theory *They,* are fucking with the human subconscious. These podcasts are poison."

Kitty sucked snot. "UGH! Gross, for fuck's sake." She wiped her eyes. "Okay. Yeah. I remember you said something about that before...all those school shootings. Oh God, Burt."

"We hear not what they really say but what they *mean*. I think we all hear that deep down inside of ourselves. When people talk personally, we call it depth, and there is context, subtext...UpMind turns that into words in your mind. Those words become pathology. Holy shit. Kitty..."

She wiped her eyes and caught her breath. "What are we going to do with Derrick?"

"Let them find him. There's nothing else to do."

"You give me the shivers sometimes, Burt."

"I celebrate his journey to the Great Wherever The Fuck. Also...I intend to avenge him...and so do you."

"Like I said, chills."

*

"Back so soon?" Scooter asked when Homero buzzed to be let in.

"Shit happened again. Zee and Niblet fuckin' killed each other."

The door buzzed. Homero ran up to the stairs, forcing himself to slow to a fast walk when he reached the third floor, where Scooter lived. The plug himself was standing in the doorway of his apartment, waiting, his face blank. He stepped aside for Homero and closed the door behind them.

"What you need me to do?" he asked.

"Call the fuckin' cleaners again, I guess. They ain't even show up yet." He shook his head. "Aw, man. They'll kill my ass over Zee."

"They might do me too...nah. We'll be good, bro. We can't think like that. Shit's a little sus but you and me both still in good standing. We about the only two n—s in the hood right now that don't have charges pending."

Homero laughed.

"It matters, man." Scooter lit a blunt roach that was hanging out in the ashtray. "Still need some green courage." Then he made the call. "Yeah. Scooter. Homero needs another cleaner." He listened. "Nah. Zee and Niblet got into it over some powder, sounds like. Ite."

He held the phone out to Homero.

"Hello?"

"What's y'all malfunction, huh?" The voice on the other end of the phone belonged to Bozy, their Lieutenant. Instrument of vengeance. "Explain yourself!"

"I don't know. On God. On the DB, dawg. We found Rylo dead this morning with no clue how it happened. I gave Zee Rylo's phone to crack. After that, I came to see Scooter and do a little business. When I came home, they were dead too. It looked like they got into a fight."

"Shut the fuck up, Homie! If either one of y'all n—as calls me again asking for a cleaner, I'm a clean yo ass," Bozy said. "Scooter's people droppin' like flies and—wait a minute. That was your whole crew, wasn't it?"

Shit. "Yes, sir."

"Tell that ugly ass muthafucka you standing in front of to help you figure out what the fuck's going on with the product. I don't care if you got to go talk to Tiger Sheng yo' damn self. Them dragons be spikin' y'all dope—*it's y'all bitch ass job to make sure this shit don't happen.* Next muthafucka dies, you bury. And if I hear anything about it, I'mma bury both of you."

The phone went dead.

"You heard?" Homero asked.

"I think the whole block heard," Scooter said.

"It's not the product. It's Kuos. Fuckin' with the Five Gee. It's the phones. That mind control. What they use, frequencies. Binaural beats. That Solfeggio stuff sounds like alien elevator music. Gamma done turned up the volume on the frequencies." He shrugged. "I don't know, man, that's all I got. I ain't Darkwing Duck over here, yo."

Scotter shook his head. "That's way above my pay grade. Them fools is all scientists. They know ways to talk that make us all do what they want. I don't know, like word choice, patterns, shit you can do with your tone of voice."

"Kuos knows how to do all that."

"I bet. He strikes me as a real Hannibal Lecter-type."

"Yeah," Homero said. "Let's Google his bitch ass real quick." He hit the Chrome button on his phone and scrolled. "There it is. Owen Q. Kuos. A rocket scientist." He snapped his fingers. "HA! I knew it. See, the man *does* know things about language—the motherfucker speaks *eight* languages. Talkin' about he was on Joe Rogan saying he'd like to bring back MKUltra."

"That's that X-files shit the CIA used to do to soldiers."

"Yeah. Giving that Orange Sunshine to students to see what they'd do. He likes that shit. I heard about this dude. He bought a harem of women to have his kids. And don't like none of 'em—haha, this motherfucker no better than Slinky's ass over on—"

"Homie, goddamn. Bozy ain't patient."

"My bad. Damn, thug, he fitna come to the Unified Center and speak on Patholink. I say we go ask him ourselves."

"I'm down with that," Scooter said.

*

Burton watched the man inside the taco truck make his dinner and pondered.

The head of the Gamma Group was also the President of the United States, a bloated orange cunt by the name of Suite. Eugene Ammon Suite, to be precise. At six-four and pushing three hundred pounds, the citrus-faced twat was a monolith of propaganda. With the UpMind at work, even his eyes were orange to Burton. His other colors were yellow and green, which made sense. His blatant hatred was so pure that his words barely changed with the drugs. Burton couldn't get over it. Sitting through the last speech he gave in New Hampshire had been unholy to hear under the influence of UpMind.

He watched as grilled onions slid between the shell and meat of his food. He tried not to grit his teeth as Suite's words jumped from his memory banks into his amygdala.

He couldn't get the sorry excuse for a president's smarmy fucking voice out of his ears. What Suite usually said in speeches was, "We have a place all ready for them. And we're only going to send them to those old FEMA camps, yeah. It's time to use those."

And when the Up kicked in, Suite's truth bared itself underneath the 3D shtick: "Got the camps already ready, oh yeah…we'll clean the rest of the poison out of our blood. We'll get rid of *all* these toxic, dirty, filth-ridden, rap-obsessed, gang-culture, impoverished, superfluous people who are tearing this country apart. They're all terrorists, you know, every last one of them!" And the people howled, and he said, "Oh…I know. I know, I know. I promise it's all gonna get taken care of. I will save the United States. We started already! We got *four more years*. The United…well…maybe they should be called the Suites. What do you all think?"

And the people roared and clapped hard enough to sprain their wrists.

"We'll take care of all of the weak-minded ones, the ones who don't agree, the—I mean how could you not agree with us, right? No. Those who don't are dead. All you have to do is approve. Approve, and they won't be able to hurt you anymore. I know it's just like you want to hide in a corner and curl up into a ball. No, don't do that…I'm here. I, me, here, Suite the Sweet One just for you…always you."

He hated the way Suite treated his constituents like sad, scared babies. Well. It was a month-old speech. No sense in letting it bother him too much, at least not this afternoon.

The cook handed Burton his food and said, "Diece seis."

"Sin cuenta?"

"No, senor."

Burton ran the fleshy part of his thumb over the scanner in front of him, and it bleeped. "Five dollars," he said.

The machine beeped again.

"Gracias," the man said.

"De nada." Burton crossed the wet, slushy street. He smelled the wonderful food. His mouth watered, but his brain wouldn't shut up about Suite. There were times he wondered if the man was the technological algorithm whose watchful eye and prodding impulse we all live under these days made flesh. A walking word virus toxifying the collective unconscious—ears bombarded day in, day out by content picked out by the algorithm, which The Gamma Group controlled. Try to concentrate on anything outside the group, and the algorithm will put a meme on your screen to keep you on track. Or an option. An ad, two ads, something you can laugh at and click to get you back to the place in your mind you want to be. There was no way to keep it from listening to you. There was no way to stop it from getting to know you, getting to manipulate you.

Wailing bloody car horn—someone screamed: "Watch it, ya fuckin' loser!" The car sped past, spitting filthy slush over Burton's pants and shoes.

"Stupid fucking Gamma!" He jumped up the curb to the safety of the sidewalk and turned to watch the car disappear. The bumper sticker on the back was red and screamed *GAMMA! Let's Motivate America!* Christ. No escape from Suite and the Gamma Group. Can't even almost get hit by a car without it being driven by some Gamma puke.

Which was also why UpMind.

Kuos' first move was to appropriate the most active social media platform in the world, Flitter, and turn it into Q…now Gamma Q. The rich-kid-cum-space-lord-motherfucker was the inventor of Patholink, a little electronic dragon that one would soon be able to have surgically implanted into the brain. It would, Kuos said, unlock previously unused neuropaths and even give the user the ability to program knowledge into themselves. Why wasn't the existential hell this was sure to bring about obvious to the sheep? He knew why. Political podcasters. Not the glamour-puss influencers, not the creepypasta people…the political ones.

He shook his head. Christ. Maybe he'd gone the plaid—full schiz-tastic—

But Suite's rhetoric was always the same. Crime was also skyrocketing. Smash and grabs, classic B&E, these usually ended in bloodbaths as everyone these days carried a gun. Fighting in the streets. The president never said anything about how cops were getting quicker on the trigger. Nor was he concerned about the obvious oligarchal implications behind the idea of inflation itself—he only bitched that it was going up and up and it was everyone's fault but his—the news had taken to calling Suite *The Forever*

President. Noble Ox-Day. Burton wondered if that might also be the day Suite picked to foment his tyranny. The day the round-ups begin. After all...he'd only been in the White House for three months, and Burton knew men like Suite take the long view—they only pretend their knee-jerk reactions to things...after all...

That's what *you're* supposed to do, knee-jerk. What you see, you do. Make sure you choose as much anger as possible.

Fucking new-age carpetbaggers. Surprise tears welled up in Burton's eyes, and he fantasized about kicking Kuos in the face until something went *crunch.* He finished crossing the empty parking lot. Faster down the sidewalk and back to their safe house, which was really just a trailer. Get back to the dinner table. Kill this bastardly obsession with food and Kitty, and maybe something a little softer than Up. He turned through the opening where a door ought to be but wasn't and joined Kitty in the semi-warmth of the warehouse.

"Hi, honey," he said.

"You got tacos," she said. Lackluster, Still said about Derrick. She hadn't given much of a shit about Quincy, but Derrick had been her little puppy dog.

Best to distract. He was thinking like the algorithm. "Kuos has programmed the algorithm into Patholink, Kitty."

"What algorithm?"

"*THE,*" he said. "The one that works with AdSense and meta and all that other stuff. He puts that thing into human brains...they won't need to control anyone with a remote. The algorithm will do it for him. Despite the will, the machinery will force the brain into operating the way Kuos says."

"A full-on ego replacement," Kitty said, her voice cold. "The algorithm is God. It's like the unseen serpent of technology. Real underground. I bet it's listening to us right now. Behind the music, a transcript is being made." She laughed. "That wouldn't be a bad word-processing program, would it? Great journalism tool. I shouldn't joke. It's not funny." She shivered.

They finished eating, and Burton rolled a joint. "The UpMind is the world's last-ditch attempt saloon."

"What?"

"What do you think would happen if a million people could hear what we hear when we take Up?"

"Blood."

"Well. Yes. Got to be some *solve* if you're going to *coagula.*"

"Jesus, Burt."

"It's true. No one is just going to say, *oh gee whiz holy fuck I need to change I guess I better do it*—hell no. They're going to want to *fight.* They always do. Can you name the time in history when they haven't?"

226

"I reiterate. Jesus, Burt!"

"Jesus isn't here." He fired up. "But Kuos is going to be in town in a few days…on the 22nd. And our illustrious President Suite will be there. He's commemorating a new holiday called Noble Ox Day."

"Noble Ox Day?"

"Yeah. March twenty-second. Three-twenty-two, love the whip, plow that field. Be the Mule before the Master. Suck yoke, bitch. Chew that bit."

"I prefer tacos," she said, digging into dinner.

*

On March twentieth, they staked out the premises, planning. Kuos was making it easy on them. He considered himself a playboy like all the other tech bros of the world, so his speech would be given at the Unified Center downtown. A giant banner of a ferocious, red-eyed ox plowing a field happily while Caucasian Jesus trailed behind in a buckboard wagon with his hands open streamed over the entrance to the building.

"They'll all be in seats," Kitty said. The front of the center was eerily quiet. Snow lingered. No one thought anything of the lovers when they passed, and people did. Chicago is always busy. Too busy to care about the lovers.

Just two crazies standing on the sidewalk and looking for a place to panhandle. Burton laughed. "Not when they're in line, they won't."

"You think it's smart to start before the show begins?"

"Should be. It's cold. I got us some longs. Go for the ass cheek. Don't try for arms, or they'll catch on to us quick. It doesn't matter who or how many we nail as long as it's enough to create…fuck."

"What?"

"Memorable chaos. With that, we make the media. And our subjects will remember everything."

"Because we do." She stood and kissed him, just another couple watching the parade. "All tests successful. I don't feel like I've lost my mind."

"I'm using a slightly dumbed-down version of it in mind of the squares we might hit. It's a slow-release cocktail…bit more opiate-based to ease the transition of the mind between planes…it'll kick about the same as those old oxys when you forget to scrape all the stretchy shit off the outside."

Kitty laughed.

"It ought to be just enough time from line to seat for the UpMind to begin working."

"And if we fail?"

"Jail. Or we die. It'll be a worthy death. It's either that or die having done nothing. Why go out in ignominy when you can—" he pushed an imaginary plunger— "shoot the moon?"

"Check it out, fool. There he go."

Scooter pointed down the alley next to the Unified Center. A long black limousine was parked back there, the exhaust pipe still blowing little puffs of idle smoke in the chill of spring's beginning. Homero watched as a whale of a man in a suit slowly stood up and joined his escorts. The orange poof of hair that looked fake but wasn't couldn't be mistaken for anyone else...the president—sorry, the *President*—had arrived.

"Suite," he said. "He's here to honor that new ox holiday bullshit."

"What you wanna do, fam?"

"Let's go in like normal people. I feel like this is going to be one of those licks where we don't know what we doin' at the outset, but opportunity, once she sees us, will knock."

"It'll come to us as we go."

"Best licks always go that way."

"True dat," Scooter said. He wasn't sure if he agreed about the best ones going that way. The craziest, the most legendary, however—those did.

He and Homero took their place in line and waited.

*

The line outside the Unified Center started forming the night before the lovers returned. This was good. They wanted to watch the people pile grow. Kitty got a sense of how they might react and worked with it accordingly. There was a method to her madness. Burton didn't know what it was. For himself, he just flowed. Move amongst the people and strike like a snake. But not yet.

They were pros at this. Burton could palm a syringe; one deft move of his index and middle fingers in conjunction with palm-on-plunger and his targets were dosed with a muscle shot almost as clean as the doctor would give, and a follow-up slap on the ass usually put their minds at relative ease. At least at the club. They had used more care here among the Gammas. Playing the non-binary candy flipper of chaos might work at the club, but around their ilk, it could get you killed.

Burton made a move on a skinny guy next to him, and the man in line ahead of them moved unexpectedly in front of the needle. Burton followed through—the shot went in—the man turned—for a moment, Burton thought he was going to be in a fight; red light burned behind his eyes, and he saw a tattoo of an eyeball with a dollar sign for a pupil and a set of metallic wings with the number 4 inked on one and the number 2 inked on the other. The eye had red devil horns. That meant he was a Dead Boy. As in, nothing to lose because we're already dead, boys.

228

"Sorry," Burton said. He held his palms out for the man to see. The needle was under his foot.

"What you got in your pocket, home slice?" the man asked.

"My keys. Sorry." Burton knew what he was driving at.

"You look like one of them Anarchist white boys."

Burton didn't say anything.

"Fuck out my face," the man ordered.

Kitty caught up to Burton, and he escorted them further back in the line. The line moved faster, ushers off their cocaine breaks and doing their jobs now. Before the lovers knew it, they were being pat down (poorly) and ushered in. The man in yellow who frisked them gave Burton the hairy eyeball but didn't deny him entry. Burton acted happy and gave Kitty a peck on the cheek and said, "I can't *wait* to see Suite. Man, I love that guy."

"Try not to puke in your mouth," Kitty said when they were clear of the usher.

Inside, there were whole sections of picnic tables dedicated to Kuos, Suite, and general Gamma Group merchandise. Shirts. Red hats, of course. Hoodies. Mugs, canteens—they stopped just short of selling guns.

"Look, Qlitter shirts," Kitty said.

Indeed. The little blue bird logo was gone, replaced by a Q in bold print, white with a silver outline surrounded by black. For an anti-communist group, Gamma sure was pirating the style. Burton grinned. "You got a Qlitter. You want one, baby?"

"Hell no. Are you good?"

"I had a scare a minute ago. I accidentally hit one of the Dead Boys."

Her eyes widened.

"I know. I almost don't want to stick around. But we have to."

"We'll keep to the exits," Kitty said. "I love you." And she kissed him.

The curtains moved apart, and the letter Q blazed red in front of a blue screen. Flashes of white moved through the blue. A sycophant in cornflower blue took the podium and gave Kuos an obsequious introduction. Burton watched the crowd. Waiting for hands to wipe foreheads or pinch the bridges of noses, yawn, or wipe their eyes. To look around as if confused or start laughing.

The sycophant spoke, "And now let's have a big round of applause for OWEN Q. KUOS!" As he held the name out like a boxing announcer, the horror itself strode toward the podium, six-two and two hundred and forty pounds of waving, grinning jackass. The people loved him. Burton scanned the crowd for faces that showed disapproval. Few. It would have to do. Kuos spat his usual spiel about how great it was to be here and a bunch of other yadda-

yadda. Around the time he stepped away from the podium—his signal to the audience that shit was about to get real—heads cocked, people squinted, and a guy three rows away from Burton started rubbing the ample love handle where Kitty must have hit him.

Kuos spoke: "If you see the difference between a baby company that's successful and one that is not it's a question of how aptly you can fix the mistakes? The successful baby recognized and fixed the mistakes quickly, and the unsuccessful baby tried to deny ever making them. The last guy in the example's the cunt, see? Know when you fucked up! It'll help you. Stand the gaffe! We all need that kick in the pants. That's why I talk tough! You have to do the tough stuff as well as the enjoyable stuff. You have to do the boring stuff as well as the not-boring stuff. Do what the fuck you're told—that's where the money is. You have to do your chores. If you don't do your chores, then bad things will happen. If you don't do the things that you don't like to do, then the company will be in trouble. It's more fun to cook the meal than it is to clean the dishes. Stuff your face until your duodenum bursts. You're all babies yet…what are most of you, fuckin' twenty-five? Now is the time to take risks. Like swallowing an eight-ball of cocaine. It's a good idea at your age, yes, do it now. When you get old, you have obligations. You have to, uh, like, have reasons to get up in the morning, to get focused on your future, like you get a line on what's going to keep you as sharp as the razor you use to kill yourself. I know you're hearing a bunch of motivational shit, but what I really want you to do is swallow your tongue." His face scrunched up; he shrugged—a trademark Kuos move. "Or!" He chuckled, leaning forward and pointing to a clapping man in the front row. "You can bite someone else's out and swallow that."

People gasped—their heads swiveled and bounced on their necks as they looked at their neighbors. Some rubbed their eyes as the dope within the mix worked on their systems. They laughed—no one seemed sure what was happening to them or if they were really hearing Kuos spew homicide rhetoric.

"Yeah. Go on. Gouge that guy's eyes out, bro." The vile tech bro laughed.

"Did you hear that?" A soccer mom said. "He just told those men to gouge each other's eyes out!"

Kuos flipped her off and said, "Go flush your face down the toilet."

A man in the front row turned and locked eyes with both of the lovers and made a beeline for them.

Burton grabbed Kitty's arm. "That's the Dead Boy."

"Shit." The lovers dragged each other through the crowd.

"The fuck you goin'?" Burton felt a hand on his shoulder.

*

"Scooter."

Scooter turned and leaned in close. "Sup G?"

"See those two Raggedy Ann and Andy lookin' motherfuckers over by the exit?"

"Yeah."

"Their bitch ass pegged me, dawg." He rubbed his side. "I don't know what with. Feels like a goofball. But what's coming out Kuos' mouth don't match in my ears."

"What?"

"That bitch ass Kuos. He say one thing my left ear hears, and something totally different in my right. His mouth don't match his lips."

"You trippin'. They pegging folks with acid, man."

"I'mma go talk to his ass. When I close in, he gonna try and run. When he do, you be there. I'mma tie his ass to a tree naked and see how he like pokin' n—s with a needle then."

*

Burton whirled, his fist flying.

The man caught it. His eyes were dead. The hand gripping Burton's fist twisted, and he felt something slide over his wrist. Pain exploded down his arm, and he went where the man wanted him to go. The man snapped his fingers at Kitty, and she backed off…right into another Dead Boy.

"Sup, cutie?"

Burton struggled.

"Not unless you want me to break it," the man said. "That's called a paintbrush. Scooter, chill on his old lady."

I'll kill both of you," Burton said.

I appreciate that, but you ain't fitna kill shit. What the fuck did you peg me with? I'm trippin' fucking *balls*. Kuos up there talking about us killing ourselves and shit. My n— killed himself a few days ago. The next day, my brainiac got into a fight with my pit bull over nothing at all. They killed each other. Those two motherfuckers were half in love, and yet they killed each other. Know what every one of them was doing? Listening to Kuos! *All of 'em listening to Kuos.*"

Burton no longer wanted to fight. These men wanted in on the struggle, and if there was one thing Burton could use, it was help, especially from the Dead Boys. "I'll tell you everything about it. It's called UpMind…I made it."

The man let him go. "UpMind? The fuck you make it for?"

"Take a look around, amigo."

"My name's Homero. That's Scooter. And I ain't your fuckin' amigo. You gonna be lucky to get out of this without your bitch becoming my new main piece. You heard?"

231

"Fuck you!" Kitty said. She lunged, but Scooter grabbed her bicep, using the cop-grab, nerves squashed between his fingers.

"Shit, let's take her," Scooter said.

"Alright, quit testing my nuts, fuck," Burton said. "Y'all got it, just don't hurt her."

Homero scoffed at him. "She cute, but I ain't want her." He looked at Scooter. "We got to do something with this stuff." He rubbed his eyes. "I feel like I'm waking up from a whole life asleep. This *is* an awakening. We fit'na give the world this UpMind." He let go of Burton's wrist. "What's your name? How did you learn to make dope?"

"Burton Cave," he said. "I used to work for DARPA with a man named Quincy Howell. Ever heard of him?"

"That's the dude they said might could maybe fix the Ozone layer," Scooter said.

Homero blinked at him.

"What? I be watchin' Neil Degrasse Tyson and shit."

Burton said, "We didn't care about the ozone. What we were really doing was making an invisibility cloak. One of the chemical components you need can only be obtained through solar collection in places where the layer is compromised. It cooks underneath the soil."

"You was frontin' so the government wouldn't get curious," Scooter said.

"They is the government," Homero said.

"No, he's right," Burton said. "We work outside of their purview, seriously."

"Why you look hella raggedy?" Scooter asked.

"Because I hate the fucking square world," Burton said. "You want to hear about me or about the UpMind?"

Homero motioned for him to continue.

"I screwed up one day and got some of the chemicals on my hand. For the rest of the day, I couldn't touch anything. My dreams that night were insane. So Quincy and I made a drug out of it. Quincy hated the Gamma Group. He called them the Nazis Who Hate Brown People Instead."

"Legit, B," Homero said. He smiled at Scooter. "I like this dude. Let's get the fuck out of here and talk, y'all. I got—"

"FUCKIN' ACID, MANNNNNN!" A fist collided with Burton's temple. Another man pushed past Burton and collided with Scooter and Kitty. Kuos was laughing. Burton threw the closest person to him into his assailant and shoved his way through the crowd. Another fist caught him in the jaw, and he jumped, throwing a random overhand punch into the face of the man closest to him.

232

"You shot me up!" his assailant said. "You and that hooker with ya!" The man laughed. "I'm tripping MEGA MONOLITH-HHHIC HUEOVS!"

"He shot us up with beans?" A woman. "Oh, cool. That's why I'm seeing elephants on the dance floor."

Oh shit.

Scooter whirled and pistol-whipped a man who rushed Kitty. Blood flew into the eyes of the man next to him. While the guy rubbed his eyes, Burton hit him with the edge of his hand in the throat-apple. Someone grabbed Kitty, and she elbowed him twice in the face. Homero grinned and jerked the man's head in his arms hard to the left. Something popped, and the man fell motionless. Kitty kneed a man in the crotch. He doubled over in time for her to sock his old lady in the face. Burton snap-kicked the man in the jaw before he could get up and avenge his love.

Homero howled. "Damn, son!"

"Let's get gone!" Scooter kicked another guy who was wrestling with Kitty in the side of the head. Burton saw a window in the people and made for it. Homero and Scooter went ahead, using their large hands and thick python arms to knock the assholes out of the way. Burton and Kitty held their own, and they made it out of the increasingly frenzied crowd with their assholes intact.

*

The backstage area was cluttered with unused set dressings and portable wardrobes. It was quiet as a mouse back here, the melee going on out front turned down to about a three with the heavy stage curtains in the way. Homero, who was tripping hard now, went to one of the clothes racks—it was gold—and began rifling through the clothes.

"I wonder do they got some Balenciaga up in this bitch." He scoffed. "Oh! I forgot to tell y'all. We saw Suite outside. He's probably back here somewhere."

Burton's eyes bugged out of his skull. "Seren-fuckin'-dipity." And he took off, running to a set of stairs behind the clothes racks. Homero, gripping the top of the rack he'd been investigating, was doubled over with the dry heaves, and he reached out when Burton passed. "You got to chill the Boy out in this shit, B—B?" He tried to stand and doubled back over. "Dammit! I need to break a sweat! Fuck is this n— goin'?"

"Burton!" Kitty took a few steps after him, then looked back at Scooter and Homero. "We can't just let him go!"

"I don't know," Homero said. "Until I break that sweat...I can't barely fuckin' stand up, girl."

Kitty backhanded him in the side of the head, not in the temple, a bit behind it where the vagus nerve is not as easily hurt but still sings if you nail it right.

Homero jumped, rubbing the hurt area with one hand and balling his fist with the other. A sweat broke out on his forehead. He unclenched his fist, coughed once, and straightened himself out. "Don't be doing shit like that." He sighed. "Where'd he go?"

"Dressing rooms downstairs," Kitty said. "If the assholes are still here, that's where they'll be. Let's go." Now, it was her turn to take off.

Scooter looked at Homero. "What you want to do?"

"That anarchy shit, I guess," he said, and both men followed her down the stairs.

*

The storage room at the bottom of the stairs opened onto a hallway that looked pretty much like the movies said it would. It was long and white, and there were five doors with empty placards on them. Burton frowned. He really had been expecting one to say SUITE and the other KUOS, and that they should be right next to each other. Derp. What to do? Maybe just knock.

The exit loomed at the end of the hall. Burton did a mental time assessment; it had been maybe one full minute by his ken—he sprinted for the exit door and threw it open. The back parking lot greeted him with a melee. People were out there fighting, tangling in each other's bodies, not all of them with the excuse of tripping. Grinning, he shut the door; no way was either Suite's or Kuos' posh ass out there fighting the crowd. He knew that. He slammed the door and turned around.

Fuck it. Burton howled: "SHOW YOURSELVES, SWINE!"

A door in front of him opened fast, and one security guard shot into the hall. He caught himself when he saw Burton and slid, giving the other man time to advance. The man swung with a clumsy right hook. Burton sidestepped and chopped him in the carotid artery. A barrel chest seemed to materialize from nowhere and he reflexively nailed where the sternum points at the belly. The man it belonged to whoofed. He backed up, showing his face—Burton, in full warrior mode, advanced, delivering a deft two-piece to the man's temples.

Another door opened, and two more guards burst into the hallway. They rushed, Burton sidestepped, but he wasn't fast enough. One guard clipped him in the jaw, and the other wrapped his large arms around Burton's waist. His cohort drew back for a face-smashing blow, and the top of his head dented, spitting blood. He dropped to the floor, and Burton saw Homero standing there, brandishing the heavy top bar of a clothing rack. Scooter rushed past his homeboy and jumped, throwing a Superman punch into the face of the guard who had Burton in his embrace. Burton jumped away from the guard in time to see Owen Kuos rush past him. He hit the exit door, threw it open, and unbelievably, turned around to flip Burton the bird.

"I'll be seeing you, Chemist," he said.

Burton froze. Chemist? He knew?

"Get that bitch ass muthafucka!" Homero almost knocked Burton over going after Kuos, but it was too late—Kuos rushed out the exit, not at all worried about the melee going on outside.

"HELP!"

Scooter and Kitty were laughing at someone who was still in the room. Burton recognized the voice.

President fucking *Suite*.

"You got to be shitting me," Burton said.

"Not so tough now, huh?" Scooter said. "I bet dis yo worst nightmare, ho. Couple of badass black folks waste your whole crew. Nobody fucks with the Dead Boys, bitch."

"Trapped yo bitch ass in a downstairs bedroom," Homero added.

"Stay away from me!" Suite's face was red.

Burton grinned. He reached into his coat and pulled out a vial full of UpMind.

"I'll kill you—" Suite began

"You'll fuckin' stand there, n—" Scooter said. "That *all* you gonna do."

The four entered the dressing room. Homero shut the door and locked it.

"I know what you doing," he said to Burton. "You got a clean?"

"No one cares if it's clean," Burton said.

Homero laughed. "Nah. It needs to be clean. We turn this clown shoe to our side of things, he's gonna need to be spite-free."

Burton saw the sense of it.

When the needle came into view, Suite screamed.

"Hold him down," Burton said. "I'd hate the bust the stick off in his ass."

*

REPORT #11,250c

SUBJECT: UPMIND *and the* DISCORDIAN FREEDOM MOVEMENT

FROM: Owen X. Kuos

TO: Department of Defense (DOD), BlackRock c/o Xander Rogan)

DTIC ADA 107403

APRIL 5, 2028

Dr. Burton N. Cave, PhD, Chemist, ex-employee of DARPA, has been observed as a DANGER, having infected the population with a toxic mixture of ETHER, FENTANYL, METHEDRINE, DMT, SODIUM PENTATHOL, and LUCE SPM 6. He has used these stolen chemicals to create a drug DIHYDROMESAETHYRCODONE, otherwise known as UPMIND or "Up" (street name). Alone, the other drugs would only have a hallucinogenic effect. However, with the addition of LUCE SPM 6, it seems our erstwhile chemist has created a drug that gives the average Joe the ability to skip through the dimensions of perception (five that we can verify; it may evolve into covering all 33 known dimensions) with the same degree of fluidity our Adepts enjoy. This is unacceptable.

Furthermore, he has recruited a street gang known as DEAD BOYS to help him distribute the product. HOMERO RAMOS, A Lieutenant of the abovementioned street gang affiliated with the GANGSTER DISCIPLES, controls the distribution of the product, along with one DARIUS "SCOOTER" JENKINS.

Cave's wife, KATHERINE "KITTY NAILS" CAVE (nee McCullaghey) *has recently become pregnant with their first child. This is good news for us. Pregnancy creates the need for care. Thusly, we have employed DR. MICHA STEVENS to go undercover as "DOC BOOTS" to care for her. He will gain their confidence and give us a way in.*

DO NOT KILL Dr. Cave. We will need him to reverse what he's done. None of our scientists can figure out how he made LUCE SPM 6 work with these other drugs. The chemical has proven to be highly toxic in all of our litmus tests. There seems to be no possible way for a human to ingest it. I hate to use this kind of speech, but it's almost as if something a lot bigger than any of us wanted *him to succeed, and that same something is keeping the recipe from working for us. Perhaps I was wrong about alien life after all. This needs further investigation.*

PRESIDENT EUGENE AMMON SUITE is the first casualty in this war against the Discordian Freedom Fighters. He's become a kitten. Plans are in the works to install OWEN KUOS (myself) into the presidency. Campaign in the planning stages. PATHOLINK trials: successful. Within one year, the device will be available to the general population. Test results have indicated that the chemical LUCE SPM 6 has the potential to "screw with the wiring," so we have to move on Mrs. Cave ASAP and fix this bloody UpMind mess.

Don't worry about it, friends. We have yet to lose a game. If it's up to me, we're not starting today.

Owen X. Kuos
CEO Gamma Q
9° Magister, JHS Society

Afterword: When Tech is Dreck

An Essay by Mawr Gorshin

(First published in Mawr Gorshin's personal blog Infinite Ocean. *The blog version includes links which, the author notes, may help the reader understand the more complicated points in his argument.)*

As a Canadian expatriate who has lived in Taiwan for the past 28 years (as of the publication of this post), I have seen many instances of locals fetishizing the latest in technology. They typically link high-tech with convenience, which [of course] is its ostensible *raison d'être*.

One time, perhaps about fifteen to twenty years ago, I was a guest teacher in a class of high school English students. I was doing lectures on topics based on newspaper articles chosen by the regular teacher of the class. She typically chose articles on the issues of science and technology since her students were probably going to go into STEM fields.

Such choices of topics were fine with me. Still, at one point, I suggested news articles based on current events in politics, which I thought would not only be far more interesting to the students but also an important way to immerse the kids in the goings-on of other countries, as well as getting them to be more aware of the major political issues affecting the world. After all, I had noticed something of an island mentality among far too many of the locals, a tendency to be insular and show no interest in the world beyond Japan, South Korea, and mainland China.

That teacher was adamantly opposed to the idea of current events as lecture topics. I found her opposition utterly baffling. Apart from suggesting she get someone other than me to do the lectures for the class (for my apparent belabouring of the change in subject matter…!), she gave the following as her reasons: classrooms [in general] avoid discussions of current events, for such avoidance is "common sense." It's sensible to avoid the topic because everybody else avoids it.

???

A discussion of political issues in class, far from being inappropriate, could be made into practical English conversation practice in the form of debates in which students can be put into teams and argue the various points of view, regardless of whether or not they actually hold such points of view. But no: making students politically literate was a no-no. We just stuck to topics on technology.

As an English teacher here, I've noticed over the years that kids in the Taiwanese education system are generally geared towards careers in engineering, computers, semiconductor and cellphone manufacturing, and that sort of thing. It's about getting them to have jobs in high-tech in order to make lots of money, in other words. One is totally indoctrinated into the capitalist system, never to question it. (After all, TINA.)

Now, my political leanings as of those years hadn't yet drifted to the left (so I wasn't trying to impose my personal political opinions on the kids). Still, the education system here shows no desire whatsoever to instill *any* kind of political consciousness in the kids, be it right-wing, left-wing, or centrist. As a result, all that's left for the kids to espouse is the default worldview: neoliberalism, treated as if it were the universal truth, an ideological 'end of history,' in which prostrating oneself to the mercies of the all-mighty market is the only way to live. It isn't even an ideology; it's just 'the truth.'

Further Taiwanese fetishizing of high-tech can be seen with the locals willingly buying things with their smartphones instead of using cash. Oh, boy—we have another excuse to play with our phones! It's so convenient! Oh, really? Standing there, fumbling around with your phone, clicking things, making mistakes here and there, then clicking on them again…somehow, this fiddling around is more convenient than taking cash out of your wallet, giving it to the cashier, taking your paid-for items and change, then promptly leaving the store?

Using smartphones instead of cash to pay for things is leading to the idea of a future cashless society, something many of us have a legitimate fear of. Paying digitally increases our dependence on the internet. What if there's an outage? What if we're hacked? What if we, for some reason, get locked out of our accounts and cannot buy food or other necessities? What if we are locked out of them because we've expressed an opinion that the snooping government does not like?

In this imagined, and very possible, future scenario, we can see the duality of a fetishization of technology vs. a total lack of engagement with what's happening in the world politically. But the problem doesn't end with digital payment.

The latest technological trend, of course, has been AI. In recent months, I've seen the TV news here in Taiwan awash with stories on Jensen Huang and his company, [in my opinion] aptly named Nvidia (*Invidia*, a Latin word from which we get *envy*, means 'looking at (someone) with the evil eye, with hostility.'). The locals are treating Huang like a celebrity, not least because he's *Taiwanese*-American, but also, of course, because of their ongoing fetishization of the newest in technology.

Now, AI can be a good or a bad thing, depending on how it's used. Put another way, AI can be used to do all of our work, which, depending on which economic system we have, can be a good or a bad thing.

If we have an economic system in which commodities and services are provided to fulfill everyone's needs, then AI will be the great liberator of all of humanity. That is, if everyone around the Earth was provided with and guaranteed access to food, housing, education, healthcare, and all other forms of wherewithal, we'd never have to work again to survive. *We could all actually enjoy life.*

But, in our current economic system, in which commodities and services are here to maximize profits, with no consideration given to the needs of the poor, then AI taking our jobs away from us would be an absolute nightmare. I see no indication of our current economic system changing from a capitalist one to a socialist one anytime in the foreseeable future. The shift from the US/NATO alliance to a BRICS one will still be largely of countries with a capitalist economic system.

It's been argued that old jobs lost to AI can, in some cases, be replaced with new jobs operating the AI. Not everybody losing the old jobs, however, will have the ability, the desire, or the finances to be trained to do the new jobs. As an English teacher here in Taiwan, I'm very worried that, in the next few years, I will be replaced by a robot in at least some, if not most or even all, of my classes, and since the beginning of all the Covid hysteria, I have been chronically underemployed as it is.

Furthermore, AI can be used in aid of **surveillance** by the government and corporations, eroding our right to privacy. It was bad enough to know what **Edward Snowden** revealed about the NSA's snooping around with our cellphone calls and email messages years ago. What is **Facebook** but a large profile of each and every person's likes and dislikes, political opinions, geographic location, friends and family, etc.? Our constant use of smartphones makes it easy to track us. AI is only going to make this monitoring easier, more meticulous, and more thorough.

Big Broadband is watching you. All of this surveillance, being expanded into such things as smart TVs, smart cars, and smart cities, is eerily Orwellian. Smart TVs have cameras installed in them, so the watcher becomes the watched…reminds me of the telescreens in *Nineteen Eighty-Four*. Now, while Orwell's dystopia was meant as a satire of totalitarianism, and of Stalin in particular, we should not be so dull-witted as to think that any of this oppressive new technology is in the service of socialism–quite the contrary.

First of all, contrary to the alarmist right-wing nonsense we hear in the media (including the verbal flatulence we hear from the puckered mouth of Trump), our society is *not* being inundated with Marxist ideology. If anything, Marxism is moribund. The only Marxist-Leninist governments in the world currently are Cuba, North Korea, and (arguably) China, Vietnam, and Laos.

What the far-right idiotically calls extremist/far-left/Marxist politicians are typically just liberals. A genuine communist would push for revolution to help the poor, not vote Democrat. Leftists are anti-Zionist, unlike any politician in the mainstream.

But more to the point is that all this high-tech surveillance is in the service of capitalism and imperialism, not socialism. Right-wingers have to get over this cretinous idea that if the government does something, it's automatically socialist and that any form of political corruption is also socialist. There *is* such a thing as a capitalist government, and it's every bit as capable of being huge, bloated, and bureaucratic as a socialist state can be.

The kind of government we find in the vast majority of countries in the world is one that is supportive of the neoliberal 'free market.' Their governments intervene in and regulate the economy in ways that help the big corporations, which are *capitalist*—'corporatism' is needless verbiage used by right-wing libertarians to deflect responsibility away from themselves for having supported an economic system that has been, especially over the past 45 years, an unmitigated disaster.

Anyway, the state will use all of this AI surveillance, as well as the eventual disappearance of cash, to seek out and punish anyone who tries to make the people rise up in revolution and attempt to overthrow the capitalist system that continues to make the rich richer and the poor poorer. Much censorship of Facebook and Twitter posts is for those who, for example, protest the ongoing genocide of the Palestinians. Support for Israel is extremely important to the Western empire and the maintenance of the so-called 'rules-based international order. 'Some have argued that the liberation of Palestine will lead to the toppling of the capitalist/imperialist system. We who want that liberation are thus seen as a threat to the system: as AI surveillance and cashless societies flourish, we will surely be punished with far more than mere censorship.

The surveillance serves the interests of the bourgeois state because, of course, it also serves the very interests of the bourgeoisie itself. Most of us have surely seen by now that any time we show an interest in this or that product online, similar ones pop up in ads on our devices when we, for example, are scrolling on Facebook. Big Business is watching you.

At the beginning of this article, I wrote specifically of the Taiwanese fetishizing of technology, not to suggest that only the locals where I live have this problem, but rather that seeing specifically the locals 'adoration of AI, *et al,* is just something I see right before my eyes. There's little doubt in my mind that there's at least a comparable, if not sometimes even greater, fetishizing of high-tech elsewhere, all over the world as a symptom of a very global neoliberalism. [Fetishization] of technology is a manifestation of what Marx called the fetishization of the commodity.

The worship of things, as opposed to acknowledging their origins in the workers 'production process, that is, focusing on things instead of on people, is what keeps us all, whether here in Taiwan (i.e., lectures on tech instead of on the current events that affect us all) or anywhere else in the world, under the spell of the ruling class. It's one of many ways they keep us under their control.

There is the brute force, surveillance, and gaslighting, as depicted in *Nineteen Eighty-four*, that is used to keep their power over us secure and intact; there is also the seducing and distracting of us with pleasure, as depicted in Huxley's *Brave New World*, with drugs and sexual indulgence. In our world, those drugs can be literal narcotics or the metaphorical opium of the people—religion. Sexual indulgence can come in the forms of internet porn, *OnlyFans*, or those countless photos of curvaceous beauties in string bikinis we see as we scroll down our Facebook feeds. The ruling class keeps us in check through bullying (militarized police, imperialist invasions, *coups d'état*, high-tech surveillance, propaganda, or addictions to pleasure.

I tried to allegorize all these issues in several short stories that I have written over the past several months. In particular, these include "The Harvest," "The Portal, and Neville."

In "The Harvest," reptilian aliens come to Earth and take over a town disguised as doctors and nurses who take advantage of sick people and drug them so they can harvest all their organs. In "The Portal," a young woman–while high on acid–stumbles into a portal that takes her to…a spaceship, or an alien planet?…where she discovers that aliens are working with human collaborators to conquer the Earth as part of an alien agenda of imperialism and colonization, enlisting the help of powerful human organizations like DARPA, with such forms of oppressive technology as robot dogs. In "Neville," aliens invade Earth by impregnating women (through great sex!), having them give birth to half-alien children–all identical-looking and unusually large, growing fast—who hog all the food, starving the rest of humanity.

In these stories, I was using the invading aliens as personifications of imperialists who kill and plunder the Third World for resources. The use of drugs and sex in the stories was meant to represent how the ruling class uses these forms of pleasure to distract and control us.

Blogger Caitlin Johnstone made a comment that I assume to be a passage from one of her many articles. I would like to find it in the archives; unfortunately, there are many, and it is lost. But to paraphrase the essence of what she said, it was that while the potential for abuse of all of this new technology (digital payments, AI taking our jobs, surveillance through AI, smart TVs, cars, and cities, etc.) should be cause for alarm, the most excellent form of control the ruling class has is through the underhanded dictation of our narratives *via* propaganda. Propaganda is a modern form of manipulative know-how. The media is rife with it; what comes down the wire and into the production office *in pure form* is rarely, if ever, what we are fed by the Prime Time talking heads, as it were.

Part of our liberation from all of these oppressive forces will be through the transforming of our narratives from ones that keep our eyes shut–dreaming all the time, as it were—waking us all up. Addictions to pleasure—the drugs of religion or the literal ones, pics and videos of beautiful nude or seminude women, video games, Hollywood movies (with CIA approval!), etc., keep us asleep. Waking us all up, though, threatens the ruling class. Perhaps that's why the political right speaks disparagingly about being 'woke'? So, apparently, it is smarter to remain [asleep]?

We need new, liberating narratives. We need to find ways to take this new tech and use it for *our* benefit, not that of the ruling class. Most of all, we have to stop fetishizing tech and other commodities at the expense of the people; we need to start caring about the welfare of our communities, for while the ruling class [are] few, we are many. If we take control of tech–to liberate us from work instead of depriving us of it or having its pile-up of garbage (i.e., e-waste) destroy our Earth–then tech will no longer be dreck.

Author Biographies

Alison Armstrong

Alison Armstrong is the author of three literary horror novels (Revenance, Toxicosis, and Dark Visitations), a novella (Vigil and Other Writings), and a collection of writings addressing women and horror archetypes (Consorting with the Shadow: Phantasms and the Dark Side of Female Consciousness). Her work focuses on inner terror, stealthily lurking, solipsistic dread and nightmare flash epiphanies. Having obtained a Master of Arts in English, she has taught composition and literature at Washtenaw Community College in Ann Arbor, Michigan, and Kingsborough Community College in Brooklyn. In addition to her novels and novella (available on Amazon and other online retailers), she has edited and contributed writings to Nature Triumphs: A Charity Anthology of Dark Speculative Literature and has had writings published in The Sirens Call as well as other horror anthologies. Further information is available on her website: https://horrorvacui.us

John Bruni

John Bruni is the author of, most recently, the SF horror crime novel, *Eye Cutter*, and is best known for *Poor Bastards* and *Rich Fucks* from StrangeHouse. He lives in Joliet, IL, where there are quite a few weird reports of lights in the sky. He hasn't seen shit at this time but has high hopes.

J. Rocky Colavito

J. Rocky Colavito (aka Dr. Damned or The Plague Prof) is transitioning from a forty-plus-year teaching career into retirement. He aspires to give credence to his brand: "all the genres of the dark," producing writing ranging from quiet to screaming loud extreme horror. He's the one they warned you about, and damn proud of that.

Brady Ellis

Brady Ellis is a writer from Appalachia, Ohio, graduate of The Ohio State University, and the associate of multiple infamous cats. When not writing he can generally be found fueling an expensive caffeine addiction or wandering through the nearest woods. His work can also be found online at The Chamber Magazine and The Globe Review.

Dawn Colclasure

Dawn Colclasure is a writer who lives in Eugene, Oregon, with her husband and teen son. She writes poetry, essays, articles, short stories and books. She is the author and co-author of over five dozen books. She is also a book reviewer and columnist. Her stories have appeared in magazines, newspapers, websites and anthologies. She publishes the free monthly newsletter for writers, the SPARREW Newsletter. Her websites are
https://dawnsbooks.com/
https://www.dmcwriter.com/
Twitter: @dawnwilson325
Instagram: dawn10325

Thomas Folske
Thomas Folske lives in Minnesota with his wife, four kids, and three black cats. He has had over 20 short stories published or in the process of being published, with new stories to be featured in upcoming anthologies by Jersey Pines Ink, British Fantasy Society, Hiraeth Publishing and House of Loki Press.
See more at https://tfolske1987.wixsite.com/mysite

Mawr Gorshin
Mawr Gorshin was born Martin Gross in 1969 in Timmins, Ontario. He moved to ROC Taiwan in the summer of 1996, where he's lived ever since, teaching English as a second language. In his spare time, he has composed and recorded music, which can be found on the Jamendo website under both his birth and pen names, and he has written poetry, prose, and analyses of literature, film, and music, typically with a Marxist and/or psychoanalytic perspective, on his blog, 'Infinite Ocean.'
https://mawrgorshin.com/
https://www.facebook.com/mawrgorshinwriter/
https://www.facebook.com/mawr.gorshin

Megan Guilliams
Megan Guilliams is an Independent Fiction author who specializes in Urban Fantasy and Horror. She is a Franklin County native who lives in Virginia with her husband and two children. When she's not writing Young Adult and New Adult Fiction, she enjoys painting. Filling the walls of her home with colorful lowbrow art and Pop art, Megan enjoys bringing her book's characters to life. As a young child, Megan dabbled in short stories, often entertaining her peers. While she doesn't hold any specialized degrees that led her to her writing passion, she currently has over twenty novels published on Amazon and

Kindle. You can find more of her work in the year to come, as well as read her story "Kroak" in *Nature Triumphs: A Charity Anthology of Dark Speculative Fiction.*

Kasey Hill

Kasey Hill, owner of Dark Moon Rising Publications, has lived in Franklin County, VA, for most of her adult life and is a versatile writer known for her work in several genres, including urban fantasy, horror, thriller, paranormal romance, and nonfiction metaphysical/New Age topics. Her fiction often dives into the supernatural and the macabre, blending mythological elements with modern storytelling. She has published multiple novels, poetry collections, and short stories. Notable works include her *Guardians of Light* series in the mythology fantasy genre and her poetry that has received recognition for its depth and emotional resonance. As she grows in the horror genre, she has a particular penchant for Southern Gothic and Appalachian Gothic storytelling, such as her Adult Horror novel *Devil's Claw* and her Young Adult horror series, *The Whispering Spirits* featuring *The Haunting at Foxwood Village* and *Dark Coven*. She has several Horror short stories circulating for anthologies and Ezines featuring her unique style of worldbuilding.

www.kaseyhillauthor.com
www.facebook.com/kaseyhillauthor
www.instagram.com/kaseyhillauthor
www.tiktok.com/kaseyhillauthor
www.amazon.com/stores/Kasey-Hill/author/B00O2WT210

J.L. Lane

J. L. Lane is a horror author from Cheshire, England. Her short stories have been featured in many anthologies, and her debut novella, *Where The Spiders Meet*, was released back in the Spring of 2020 during the apocalypse. The second instalment in the series, *When The Spiders Meet*, is also available on Amazon, whilst she works on the third book in the series.

She runs her own anthologies and has published many authors over the years. She also offers editing and formatting services, as well as cover design and custom art. She is a qualified and experienced artist with a unique style – almost like a gut punch – that reflects her love of horror well. She has always enjoyed telling stories and learned the craft from her father. Spending many nights reading over stories he had written, especially for her siblings and her, with them as the main characters. Jacky and the Robots being her favourite.

J. L. Lane lives with her fiancé, their three children and many pets in a small boating town in the Northwest of England, surrounded by canals. She is a retired chef who loves creating new dishes but cannot stand the atmosphere of commercial kitchens any longer. So, she retired early to focus on her family and creative career. She is active on Facebook, Instagram, Threads and Bluesky but has given up on X – formally known as Twitter. You can contact J. L. Lane through her author page on Facebook.

J.C. Maçek III

J.C. Maçek III is the author of the hit true crime novel *The Black Dahlia* (2024) and the producer of the 2018 film *[CARGO]*, starring Ron Thompson of *American Pop* fame, as well as the author of the film's tie-in novel. His other novels include *The Antagonist* and *Seven Days to Die*. More recently, the author has found success in shorter stories and novellas, though novels are still his primary focus. An experienced and prolific entertainment journalist and celebrity interviewer, he has written thousands of articles, reviews and interviews. He recently curated and edited *Symptom of the Universe: A Horror Tribute to Black Sabbath*, an anthology of short stories and novellas inspired by the music and lyrics of every era of Black Sabbath. He resides in Southern California with his wife and family and a veritable zoo of pets.

Pip Pinkerton

Pip Pinkerton was born and raised in Oakdale, Minnesota. Pip is a wanderer and a dreamer. He loves writing short stories, poetry, and screenplays. A former theatre student and current guitar player, Pip currently co-manages a record shop. When he is not writing or jamming, he is spending time with his trusty rottweiler Shrimp. Pip has been published on the Monstrous Femme website, as well as on HorrorAddicts.net, and with Wicked Shadow Press. He has upcoming stories to be featured in anthologies by Theaker Quarterly Fiction, J. Manfred Weichsel, and Ink'd Publishing.

Edward Radmanich

Edward Radmanich III is an accomplished filmmaker and storyteller with a passion for exploring unique narratives across multiple mediums. He is the writer, director, and producer of two films that were selected for the prestigious Sacramento International Film Festival: Artie Saves the Hood (2005) and Coldspot (2008). Coldspot also earned a coveted spot in the 2008 Fantastic Film Fest, showcasing his ability to craft compelling stories that resonate with diverse audiences.

In addition to his filmmaking, Edward has developed numerous scripts and is now transitioning his creative talents into writing. This anthology marks his literary debut as a short story author, with this shift into prose reflecting the same dedication to detail and character-driven plots that define his films. He is currently working on adapting Brainflush into a full-length feature film, continuing his journey in dynamic and immersive storytelling.

John Reti

John Reti is an author from the West Coast of Canada with previous stories in *Possessions* 1, 2 & 3, *Dark Holidays, Symptom of the Universe: A Horror Tribute Black Sabbath, The Devil's Playground: A Horror Charity Anthology for Drug Addictionm, Last Christmas: A Holiday Horror Anthology, Piece by Piece: An Anti-Valentine's Day Collection, and Beauty in Darkness: The Literary Tribute to TS Woolard*, as well as an upcoming story with *Possessions* 4. Other than writing, he also engages in visual arts and dabbles in music. He also writes under the name PJ Scorpian.

Neil Sanzari

Neil Sanzari is a weird fiction author. He attended NYU's Tisch School of the Arts and the School of Visual Arts. Neil worked as a graphic artist in the advertising field in New York City for many years until he was displaced by the tragic events of 9/11. And now he lives with his wife, Celia, at the Jersey Shore, writing short stories and creating comic books. He is currently writing a novel.

David L Tamarin

David L Tamarin is a writer of both non-fiction and fiction. He enjoys writing extreme splatterpunk as well as writing about issues like crime, culture, drugs, bizarre fetishes, and anything bizarre or disturbing or morbid. He has written for the website MOVIEWEB and was Chief Corpse-Pondent for Girls and Corpses magazine. His writing has appeared in Serial Killer magazine, Rue Morgue, and many more. His fiction has appeared in anthologies such as World's Best Hardcore Horror 5 and Dig Two Graves Volume 2. He is the author of Hurting My Toys, BOLO: Sociopaths on a Rampage, This Book Hates You and All You Need is Blood. His column UGLY WORLD is available on the website at: https://severed-cinema.com/category/ugly-world/.

He is also involved in film, as an actor, extra, writer and Entertainment Attorney. His first acting and writing job was for the film Prison of the

Psychotic Damned. He has also appeared in the series CASTLE ROCK (Season 2, Episode 1), BEG, Nun of That, The Gateway Meat, The Profane Exhibit, and four Adam Sandler movies.

www.facebook.com/davidltamarin

https://www.amazon.com/stores/author/B00A9HMXF4/allbooks

https://godless.com/products/david-l-tamarin?_pos=2&_sid=94bf48941&_ss=r

Rob Tannahill

Rob Tannahill is an author living in Northern Nevada. His work has appeared in *Yale Program of Recovery and Community Health* (PERCH #7, Substance), *Nature Triumphs: A Charity Anthology of Dark Speculative Fiction, Symptom of the Universe: A Literary Tribute to Black Sabbath* and *The Devil's Playground: A Horror Charity Anthology for Drug Addiction*, among other places such as *Carnage House*. He is also the author of the full-length novel *Prince Junkie*. He has been in recovery for three years.

Edgar Wells

Edgar Wells is the pseudonym of a copywriter. You may have used one of his books in high school science class. He once wrote political essays for Chicago Now, Tabard Inn, Mars Social, and other places. Now retired, he enjoys the fruits of his labor, and watches the sky for UFOs.

Walter Wiseman

Walter Wiseman has appeared in *Last Christmas: A Holiday Horror Anthology* and is currently working on his first novella. His inspirations are Barker, Lovecraft, Takashi Miike and Duckman.